# *Passing Strangers*

*New York Times* Best-selling Author

# Angela Hunt

# Passing Strangers

# *Prologue*

**Tuesday, November 6**

In the ticket line at a Little Rock train depot, a pair of young lovers, blue-jeaned and rumpled, wore battered backpacks and carried Starbucks cups. Behind them, a silver-haired grandmother clung to a toddler's hand and stood, eyes straight ahead and lips sealed, as rowdy teenagers swayed and shouted behind her, fouling the air with words that would have drawn numerous public rebukes thirty years before. On a bench in the waiting area, an aged black man lowered his newspaper and watched the teenagers, one brow lifting in what might have been curiosity . . . or disbelief.

Into this swirling amalgamation of humanity walked Janette Turlington, a woman on the far side of forty and the back end of a hard week. After moving through the depot's double doors, she strode toward the ticket counter without looking around. She carried two suitcases, a small bag piggybacking atop a larger one, and wore a long wool coat in eye-catching red. The coat and its wearer looked as though they had seen better days — the garment was ten years out of style and a purpling bruise marred the woman's eye socket.

When at last she reached the ticket window, Janette shielded her face with a trembling hand and leaned on the metal counter. "One adult ticket, please." Her voice was far unsteadier than she would have liked. "Coach."

The bored-looking cashier narrowed her eyes. "Where to?"

Janette took a step back and looked around, her gaze sweeping over posters taped to the window and tacked to a bulletin board. All of them featured blue and silver Amtrak trains set against dazzling scenery, but one headline caught her eye: Ten-day Southern Heritage Tour. She could not care less about southern heritage, hers or anyone else's, but ten days away from home sounded like the perfect escape.

She propped an elbow on the counter. "I'll take the ten-day tour."

"Excuse me?"

Janette pointed to the poster. "That one—ten days in the south."

The round-faced girl lifted both brows, leading Janette to assume that this station didn't sell many package deals, but the cashier's elongated nails rattled against her keyboard. "When did you want to leave?"

Janette glanced back at the double doors. "As soon as possible."

"That tour departs out of Union Station in D.C. You want to go to Washington from here?"

Janette nodded.

"You'll be traveling over thirty hours to get there. So do you want a sleeper car or a roomette?"

"How much are they?"

The girl clicked at the keyboard again, then shook her head. "The roomettes are sold out. But I can get you a bedroom for an additional two hundred dollars."

Janette swallowed hard, knowing she would have to be careful with her cash. "I'll pass. I can sleep in my seat."

"Most people do. They're actually pretty comfortable."

The girl typed again, then reached toward a shelf divided into cubbies, each compartment filled with a stack of brochures. She plucked a flyer from a cubicle, then stepped over to a noisy printer and ripped a length of perforated cards from the tray.

"You'll be takin' the 22 Texas Eagle, departing at 11:39 p.m." She folded the cards into an accordion pleat as she returned to her stool. "Be sure to sign each of these tickets. You'll arrive at Union Station in two days, then you'll go to your first hotel — the voucher printed with your tickets. Throughout the tour, you'll disembark at stations marked on the schedule, spend two days in each city, then get back on the train to your next destination. Hotels and onboard meals are included in the package. Details are spelled out in the brochure." She stuffed the tickets and brochure into a paper jacket, then slid it through the opening beneath her window.

Janette gulped when she saw the total. She had thought a train tour would be cheaper than a nervous breakdown, but now she wasn't so sure . . .

Too late to change her mind. She pulled her wallet from her purse and slid several smooth, crisp fifty-dollar bills and some change through the well at the bottom of the window. "I think that's the right amount."

The girl smiled as she handled the crisp currency. "Straight from the bank?"

"Straight from the drawer where I keep our emergency fund."

"Better than under the mattress, I guess." The girl tucked the bills into her cash drawer and smiled at Janette. "Thanks."

"Is that all?"

"Got any bags to check?"

Janette considered her hurriedly packed bags. She could check both bags, but if she was going to spend more than thirty hours in the same set of clothes, she'd better keep her deodorant and toothbrush nearby. "Just one."

"Take it over to baggage drop. And have a nice trip."

Janette unhooked the smaller bag from the large wheeled suitcase, then rolled the bigger bag to the window where a uniformed man leaned against the counter. He smiled and hefted her bag onto a scale, then touched two fingers to his forehead in a jaunty salute. "That'll do it, ma'am."

No claim check, no baggage fee, no body scan? "That's all you need from me?"

"Yes, ma'am. We like to keep things simple 'round here."

She thanked him and grabbed the handle of her small suitcase, then took her first look around the crowded waiting area. If the train to Washington ran on time, she'd have to wait here more than three hours—long enough for her husband to realize that she'd done more than make an emergency grocery run.

As the kitchen filled with neighbors who'd signed up for the annual progressive dinner, Harry would assume Janette had run out for some missing ingredient. Finding himself responsible to entertain guests and serve the soup, he'd call to make sure she was on her way home.

She wouldn't—couldn't—answer. He would hang up and talk with their friends, allowing one of the other ladies to serve the simmering soup. He'd joke that Janette was so directionally impaired that she couldn't find her way out of a paper bag and he'd apologize profusely for his missing hostess.

He wouldn't have to apologize for long. The guests would drain their bowls and move on to the salad house, but Harry wouldn't go with them. With growing alarm he would call her again, but she wouldn't answer this time, either. He would worry that she'd been in an accident, so he would get in his car and drive to the grocery, looking for disabled vehicles by the side of the road.

When he didn't find her car, Harry would phone her friends to ask if anyone had seen her. By ten he'd call the local hospitals in a full-fledged panic, and by eleven he'd be fretting by the phone and wondering if he should call the police. Janette didn't think they'd do anything, though, because cops on TV never became really concerned until a person had been missing over twenty-four hours.

And by that time, Janette planned to be smack dab in the middle of someplace miles away. Maybe she'd call Harry at midnight, leave a message to say she'd be back in a week or two, after she'd had some time to think. She'd also mention that he needed to call the thrift store and say she'd be away for a few days.

She didn't want her husband to worry, but neither did she want to give him an opportunity to talk her into coming home. As the night deepened, and he began to panic, he might go out again, broadening his search until it included the airport and the bus depot.

Which is why she'd left her car in front of a friend's house and taken a cab to the train depot. It was the last place on earth her husband would expect her to be.

### Reston, Virginia

A thousand miles away from Janette Turlington, Matthew Scofield walked through his front door and heard a babysitter's ultimatum: "I'm sorry, but this is too much, Mr. Scofield. I'm not ever coming back."

Matthew blinked and dropped his laptop case onto the foyer table. "Hang on, Brittany, let's back up a minute. Did the kids give you a hard time?"

"I'm not upset with your kids." Her voice trembled as she met his gaze. "Your kids are great; but you're never home when you're supposed to be. I had a date tonight, but I had to cancel because seven o'clock came and went and I couldn't reach you."

"I gave you my cell number."

"And it went straight to voice mail every time I tried to call. Or maybe you were ignoring the phone, but it doesn't matter. I'm done, so please don't call me again."

He drew a deep breath and searched for some sign of weakening in the teenager's face, but the girl's eyes were as hard as diamonds. Since when had eighteen-year-old girls become so determined?

He glanced past her and saw his children leaning against the wall, their faces downcast. They liked Brittany, and apparently they were old enough to realize that they kept losing babysitters because their father worked too much.

"I'm sorry." He reached for his wallet, pulled out two fifties, and offered them to the girl. "Here—take this."

She glanced at the bills. "If that's a bribe, it won't work. I'm not coming back."

"It's not a bribe; consider it payment for damages. I made you miss your date, so ask the guy for a rain check. Tell him dinner's on me."

A corner of the girl's mouth twitched in annoyance, but she took the money and picked up the oversized purse she'd dropped in the foyer. "Thanks."

"Before you go, do you know anyone else who might be interested in this job? I'm going to need someone the rest of the week."

"None of my friends want full-time jobs," Brittany said, moving toward the door. "I'm supposed to be earning money for college, but I'm not going to sacrifice my social life to do it. Not even for kids as cute as yours."

She turned and gave his children a sympathetic smile. "Bye Roman, 'bye Emilia. Hope I see you around sometime."

Matt closed and locked the door behind her, then rubbed the back of his neck. How was he supposed to explain this to his kids?

"Daddy?" Roman's voice broke the silence. "Are we bad kids?"

Something in the boy's voice tugged at Matt's heart. "Bad?" He forced a smile. "No way. You're the best kids in the universe."

"Then why doesn't anybody want to stay with us?"

Matt rarely found himself at a loss for words, but how could he explain that lawyers worked long hours and most babysitters didn't want to stick around that long?

He pasted on another smile and knelt to his kids' level. "Everybody loves you guys, but they have other things they have to do, that's all. So hey—how's about we order pasta for dinner? I think the Italian place will deliver if we say pretty-please."

Roman thrust his hands into his pockets. "We're not hungry," he said, his tone unusually formal for a nine-year-old. "We ate mac-and-cheese with Brittany."

"It was good," Emilia echoed. "And Brittany was nice. Are we going to have a new babysitter tomorrow?"

Matt leaned against one of the foyer pillars and sighed in exhaustion. His life had never been easy, but his wife's death and his nanny's retirement had made his situation unbearably difficult. With a job that demanded an eighty-hour workweek, how was he supposed to be mother and father to two vulnerable kids?

"I don't know what we'll do tomorrow," he finally said, standing. "But everything's going to be fine. Since you've already eaten, I'll eat in the kitchen, unless one of you wants to join me. If so, I could order a little extra—"

Roman tilted his head. "Are you working after dinner?"

Matt glanced at his laptop bag, bulging with a case file. If he didn't start on it right away, he'd be reading all night. "Yes." Reluctantly, he met his son's gaze. "Sorry bout that, buddy."

"Then no thanks." Roman turned and moved toward the hallway that led to his bedroom. "I got stuff to do."

"Me, too," Emilia said, following her brother. "Lots of stuff."

Matt bit the inside of his lip and watched them go. His bravado hadn't fooled them. If he couldn't find a sitter in the next few hours, tomorrow he'd have to ask his secretary to pick them up from school, bring them home, and watch them at the house. And while Mrs. Wilson never balked when it came to typing briefs or digging through ponderous files, he had a feeling she wouldn't want to spend her afternoon driving through the carpool lane and watching the Disney channel with his offspring. She might agree to help him out for one day, but not for the rest of the week.

His amazing children deserved better than a reluctant caregiver. He had to find an answer, and soon.

# BOOK ONE

*The more I traveled, the more I realized*

*that fear makes strangers of people*

*who should be friends.*

—Shirley MacLaine

# *Chapter One*

**Providence, Rhode Island**
**Wednesday, November 7**

When the cell phone on Andie Crystal's desk rang, her assistant stared as if her boss had received a call from beyond the grave. "Is that your cell phone?" Jasmine's wide eyes met her boss's. "In all the years I've worked for you, I don't think I've ever heard that phone ring."

Andie ignored the comment and picked up her phone, but the skin at the back of her neck prickled. Only a handful of people had her cell number, and most of them were her coworkers. None of the others would call unless they had news of a bona fide emergency.

She glanced at the number in the viewer, then told Jasmine they could finish the reports later. After tossing Andie another bewildered look, the assistant backed out of the office and closed the door.

Something inside Andie went still as she pressed the receive button. "Mr. Rueben?"

Her lawyer's baritone chuckle put her at ease. "Andie, how are you this morning?"

"Fine, but I was surprised to see your number on my cell. Is everything okay?"

"I'm not sure how to answer that." His sigh echoed over the airwaves between Providence and Chicago. "I'm calling for three reasons. First, I wanted to thank you for the nice birthday card. Getting older's no fun, but thoughtful people like you help take the sting out of the passing years."

Andie smiled. "After all you've done for me, remembering your birthday is the least I can do. I hope the celebration was fabulous."

"My wife and kids seemed to enjoy watching me sputter over all those candles—sixty-two this year. Soon my cakes are going to be a fire hazard."

Andie waited, knowing the man hadn't called to talk about his birthday.

"The second reason I called," he continued, "was to let you know we're putting your check in the mail today. It's not the windfall I wish we could send, but it'll be a nice addition to your retirement fund."

Andie moved to the window, which offered a view of a busy downtown street. "That's okay—I'm amazed every time I get a check."

"I'm not. TV Land loves the show, and in his cover letter Oliver mentioned that Nickelodeon just picked up the series. So it's a fair bet that you and your siblings will be earning residuals for months to come." He chuckled. "Everybody loves reruns."

Did they? Andie grabbed a hank of her hair and glanced at the ends to be sure the color was holding. She was blond in those reruns, and sometimes she suffered from nightmares in which her copper color washed away, leaving her with the pale hair of her teenage years . . .

"I hate reruns." She blurted out the words without thinking, then realized that her lawyer must think her awfully ungrateful. Embarrassment burned her cheeks as her words hung in the silence. "I mean—I wish—"

"I know you wish someone would lock those old episodes in a vault, but your mother depends on her residual income. I would imagine that your siblings don't complain about unexpected paychecks, either."

"I didn't mean to whine. Sorry about that. But those reruns keep the Happy Huggins alive, and as long as they're alive, the tabloids keep manufacturing wild stories. Just last week I saw a headline that said I'd been kidnapped by aliens."

"I can't believe people buy those rags." The lawyer snorted softly. "I know you're not ungrateful. You were always a good kid, maybe the best of the bunch. And that brings me to the third reason for my call—and I'm sorry to be the bearer of bad news."

"Did someone die or something?" Andie offered the question in jest, then slowly sank into her chair when the lawyer didn't answer. What was going on? Thomas Rueben rarely called; he usually mailed her checks along with a cover letter and his best wishes. He must have spectacularly bad news if he felt compelled to pick up the phone. The skin at her neck prickled again. Had something happened to one of her—

"It's your mother," he said, his voice flat. "Oliver said she hadn't been feeling well, so he finally got her to a doctor."

"Mom is sick?"

"Cervical cancer. The prognosis isn't good."

His news whirled in Andie's head, intelligible, specific, and complex, yet her brain reduced the report to one succinct conclusion: her mother was too stubborn to die on a doctor's schedule. She might be too stubborn to die at all.

"Andie? Did you hear what I said?"

The thought of her mother being terminally ill was so absurd Andie almost began to laugh. Mona Huggins, dying? She'd seen her mother fly in the face of network executives; she'd seen her bully her way into a bat mitzvah at the Beverly Hills Hotel so their band could play for a talent agent. The woman was half superhero and half politician.

"No way," she said. "No way my mom could be dying."

"Christy," he spoke the name slowly, as if to remind her that she had once been someone else, "denial is quite natural when one receives upsetting news. You've probably read about the stages of grief—denial, anger, bargaining, depression—"

"I'm not angry," she answered, her voice clipped. "And I'm not Christy Huggins, not anymore. You know that better than anyone."

"I know you're a sensitive young woman who's borne more than her fair share of grief. I know that years ago you divorced yourself from your family personally and professionally. But I also know that you care about these people, and though you may not realize it yet, you care deeply about your dying mother."

She pressed her hand over her mouth to squelch the sob that threatened to rip from her throat. How could this man— her own lawyer, for heaven's sake—call with news like this? She had finally managed to reach a place where she thought about her family only a few times a week, when she could almost resist reaching for the tabloid that reported on her sister's new baby or her brother's DUI arrest. She had worked so hard to put distance between her past and her new reality, but with one phone call Mr. Reuben had bridged that space and brought back all the pain . . .

She swallowed hard. "Cervical cancer." Her voice sounded thin and frightened in her own ears. "What do the doctors say?"

"They give her four to six weeks. I'm so sorry, Andie."

She gripped the armrest of her chair and waited until she had control of her voice. Mr. Rueben had caught her by surprise and yes, for a moment or two she'd spun in a cyclone of emotions. But she'd deal with them later. Alone.

Certain that her lawyer had been reluctant to make this call, Andie shoehorned a note of gratitude into her voice. "Thank you for telling me. I appreciate hearing about this before reporters break the story."

"Oliver's going public with the news next week. And Andie, there's something else."

His comment distracted her from dark thoughts of gossip journalism. "What's that?"

"Your mother wants to get the family together. She wants one last reunion . . . with all of you."

Andie heard his subtle emphasis on the word all, then she lifted her chin. "Impossible. I'm living with the aliens."

The lawyer's voice gentled. "Perhaps you should call —"

"I'm not calling her."

"I was going to suggest that you call Oliver. I'm sure he'd love to hear from you."

For half a minute Andie considered calling her former agent, then she shook her head. "He'd tell her I called, and somehow she'd find a way to ruin my new life."

"Your mother is not a malicious person."

"I know, I know, you don't have to tell me what kind of person she is. She may not be malicious, but she is ambitious, and her ambition ruined our family. I'm sorry, Mr. Rueben. I'm not heartless, really I'm not, but I have to protect myself. I'm not Christy Huggins any more."

He hesitated, then spoke in a gentle whisper. "But you are still your mother's daughter."

She sagged in her chair when his words struck a nerve. But he didn't understand everything she'd been through.

She *was* her mother's daughter. But she was also her father's daughter, and Cole's big sister.

And she could never forget that her mother was the reason her dad and Cole were dead.

Walking into the call center's operations room, Andie had a feeling that her bad morning was about to take a turn for the worse. The telephone bank, which usually churned with activity, seemed to hum with the fluorescent lights overhead. At least ten of the twenty morning operators were reading magazines; two were practically sleep-talking through their calls, and a half dozen bent over their desks with their heads tilted and their eyelids at half-mast. One of Andie's best operators, Jill Jones, had a customer on the line, but was clenching her stress ball so tightly her knuckles looked as if they were about to rip through her skin.

"Why's it so quiet in here?" Andie whispered to Gretchen Hinson, who was staring at the television on the wall.

"New on-air talent." Gretchen pointed to the screen. "This girl's a mess. She couldn't sell ice water in the desert."

A fluttering hand caught Andie's attention and motioned her over. "Why certainly, you may speak to my supervisor." Jill Jones's voice snapped with irritation. "One moment, please."

She lifted the microphone on her headset. "Can you handle this impossible woman? She has the IQ of a fence post."

Grateful that she could take care of at least one of the morning's problems, Andie stepped to an empty station and picked up a headset. "What seems to be the trouble?"

Jill shook her head. "Six months ago she ordered two jars of the face cream, used 'em both, and now she wants a full refund. She says the on-air hostess promised she'd look ten years younger."

Andie sighed. Sometimes the on-air talent got a little carried away with their sales patter. They weren't supposed to guarantee anything beyond what was offered on the cosmetics label, but they could go overboard when desperate to move products. "Did you explain the thirty-day trial period?"

Jill nodded. "She doesn't care. All she wants to do is scream profanities because she doesn't look like Jennifer Anniston."

"Okay, patch her over to me."

Andie put on the headset and took a deep breath as the customer's personal information flashed on the computer screen. "Good morning, Mary, this is Andie Crystal, sales supervisor for the Value Price Network. How may I help you?"

Customer Mary uttered a few choice words, then launched into a litany of complaints about New Dawn products. Andie looked at Jill, who was watching with undisguised glee.

"Because your trial period has expired I can't refund the purchase price," Andie explained when the woman finished her rant, "but I would be happy to send you a certificate for a jar of our rejuvenating face cream. Would you like that coupon sent electronically or through the mail?"

The woman sputtered a moment. "Is it guaranteed?"

"It is guaranteed to rejuvenate your skin by exfoliating the external layer. We can't guarantee that the result will be noticeable to others, but I'm sure you'll feel the difference."

The woman sighed and said email would be fine.

"Thank you, ma'am. Is your email address still princess-mary215@yahoo.com?"

Andie gave Jill an it's-all-settled smile. "I'll get that right out to you. Have a wonderful day, and thank you for calling VPN."

She pulled off the headset and dropped it on the desk.

"Thanks." Jill leaned forward to take another call. "I couldn't believe the mouth on that woman."

As Andie turned to walk back to her office, Gretchen bent over the back of her chair. "Hey, Andie. We're going to Chili's after work. Want to join us?"

"Sorry. I've got to get home to Sam."

"Sam always comes first." Gretchen winked. "When are we going to meet this mystery man of yours?"

"Maybe never." Andie gave her a wry smile. "He's shy."

"And a hottie, I bet."

"Of course."

"Some women have all the luck." Gretchen grinned, then turned to click on an incoming call. "Thank you for calling VPN, exclusive distributor for New Dawn Cosmetics. How may I help you?"

After leaving the call center, Andie slipped into her office and sank into her chair. A couple of clicks at the computer keyboard brought up a continually updated inventory spreadsheet. The New Dawn face cream dogged last night but was moving well this morning, probably because the spokesmodel pushed the product during the late morning time slot. Most of their viewers at that hour were 45 to 55, the age when women cared most about wrinkles and sagging skin.

Andie sent a note to her boss about promoting the sixteen-ounce exfoliation lotion in that time slot tomorrow. If they brought in three or four cases for a display, the old "pile it high and watch it fly" principle should spur enough sales to move the remaining six hundred bottles out of the warehouse.

She glanced over the updated sales report. Silk scarves had moved briskly the night before, proving again that women would buy accessories if a spokesmodel took the time to demonstrate different looks with them. Weed whackers dominated the midnight-to-two a.m. slot, testifying to the late-night pitchman's powers of persuasion. Andie couldn't imagine why anyone would shop for lawn and garden tools when most of the country was asleep, but neither could she understand why VPN set sales records on Thanksgiving, Christmas, and Easter. Her boss said it was because people were home with nothing to do but watch TV, but Andie knew the real reason was because people were desperate to feel connected. People who spent their holidays alone placed orders to feel like part of a national shopping family. She'd done the same thing at least a dozen times.

A silvery chime caught her attention. She glanced at her screen and saw an instant message from Miles Pearson, director of Human Resources. He wanted to know if she could come to his office ASAP.

Andie hesitated, her fingers hovering over her keyboard. Why would Pearson want to see her? Her department hadn't had any recent personnel trouble and her operators consistently scored high in employee satisfaction. She spent more time at the office than she did at home, so he shouldn't have received any complaints about her work ethic. She couldn't even remember the last time she took a sick day.

But why did she always assume the worst? She'd been in a negative frame of mind ever since Mr. Reuben's call, but she ought to be able to shake off her feelings of foreboding. She had committed her life to New Dawn products and the people at the Value Price Network had become her family. That other group, the people who shared some of her DNA, had no ties to Andie Crystal.

She took a deep breath to calm her jittery nerves. Maybe Pearson only wanted to suggest changes to the shift schedule. Maybe he had a niece or a nephew who needed a job. Her department didn't have any openings, but Janie Upchurch was due to take her maternity leave in a few weeks . . .

*No problem,* she typed in response. *See you in five minutes.*

◆

Andie's stomach took a nosedive when she rounded the corner. Miles Pearson's office sat at the end of the hallway, but she could see her new boss, Mitchell Walker, through the large window in Pearson's door. Walker wasn't the man who hired her when she was fresh out of college and more frightened than experienced—that would be Rich Gould, recently retired to Florida—but Walker was now president of the company and as rich as Midas.

She set her shoulders and continued on her way. No sense in borrowing trouble, as her mother used to say. If Walker or Pearson wanted to give her bad news, she might as well hear it. Bad news seemed to be the currency of the day.

She was about to rap on the window when Pearson lifted his head and motioned her in. After she opened the door, Walker thrust his big hand forward and grabbed hers in an overly snug grip. "Andie, let me be the first to say this is long overdue. Because we're all proud of you, I'm absolutely delighted that we're able to offer you this package."

His words brought an undeniable warmth to her face, but she had no idea what he was talking about. She managed a weak smile, then shifted her gaze to Pearson. The personnel director was also smiling, the edges of his two front teeth perched on his lower lip like a satisfied beaver's.

She crossed her arms and shivered—for some reason, Pearson's office was always ten degrees colder than the rest of the building. "Thank you, sir . . . but am I supposed to know what you're referring to?"

Walker grinned at Pearson, then reached behind her and gripped the doorknob. "I'm going to let Miles fill you in on the details. Just know this—the company's come a long way since your pioneering efforts. You deserve our thanks, and you're about to get everything you've earned."

Despite the assurance of his smile, his words sent a ripple of premonition up Andie's backbone. After Walker left, she fixed Pearson in a direct gaze. "Okay, Miles, what's going on? And why do I feel like I'm about to be fired?"

Pearson laughed. "It's nothing so drastic, Andie, so relax. Have a seat."

She slid into an empty chair as Pearson closed the door and

returned to his seat. He flipped open a folder, then clasped his hands and smiled at her.

Her pulse thumped in her ears.

"Andie," Pearson said, "it's come to our attention that in seven years of service to the Value Price Network, you've never missed a day of work. That's an amazing record."

She gripped the armrest of the chair, sensing trouble behind his smile. "Surely there's nothing wrong with having a strong work ethic."

"You've never even taken a sick day."

"Can't help it if I'm healthy."

"You're either lucky or you're the most dedicated employee we have." Pearson unfolded his hands and pressed them to the paperwork on his desk. "Not only have you never missed a day of work, you've never taken a vacation. I don't know how we allowed that to go unnoticed, since every employee is guaranteed a two-week vacation once they complete two years of full-time employment. With the additional day we add for every year of service, you've earned three weeks of annual vacation time."

All this fuss was over unused vacation days? She relaxed her shoulders. "Vacations aren't a big deal; I like my job. In the early days we were so busy I didn't feel right about abandoning the call center during peak hours, so—"

"And the boss appreciates your sacrifice." Pearson gave her a smug, better-get-with-it smile. "But VPN has moved beyond those pioneering years and we're trying to implement consistent policies across the board. Plus—" his smile dimmed— "we no longer need you to babysit the call center. Your assistant can oversee the operators when you're away, and I'd be surprised if she can't handle anything that comes up. Bottom line: we want you to take a vacation. In fact, once you leave work today we don't want to see you for another three weeks."

Her mouth went dry. "You're forcing me to take a vacation?"

"It was Walker's idea. To make it impossible for you to say

no, he's agreed to give you a bonus: an all-expenses paid trip. What would you say to a Hawaiian cruise?"

She stared at him. "I hate the water. I can't think of anything more awful than being imprisoned on a cruise ship for days."

She blurted out the lie without thinking, and realized she'd made a mistake when Pearson stiffened. She probably shouldn't have spurned such a generous gesture from the boss.

Pearson's features hardened. "I'd hardly call a cruise ship a prison. We thought you'd love the idea."

Because she couldn't give Pearson an honest response, she gave him an apologetic smile. "I know how generous the offer is, and I really appreciate the thought. But I can't take a cruise. I can't fly anywhere, either. I know you probably think I'm crazy and I know you could find a dozen employees who would happily accept Mr. Walker's offer — "

"They haven't earned a free vacation. You have." Pearson ran a finger over the right half of his mustache. "You say you're afraid to fly?"

Without much difficulty, she summoned up a shudder. "I'd have to be comatose before you could get me on a plane."

"Really." Pearson leaned back in his chair and regarded her with an analytical gaze. "This creates quite a problem. You see, Mr. Walker was horrified to learn that you haven't been taking annual vacations. When I reminded him that Rhode Island is one of a handful of states that requires a company to compensate workers for accrued vacation time upon termination — "

"Is he planning on firing me?"

Pearson lifted his hand in a gesture of reassurance. "Nothing like that, but the rule applies whether an employee is laid off or quits. Walker wants to settle accounts, as it were, so we're not hit with a huge payout when and if you ever decide to leave us. That's why he's sending you on a paid vacation. If you accept and take the time off, we won't end up owing you half the company when you're ready to retire."

She pressed her hand to her forehead as her thoughts whirled. Pearson was exaggerating, of course, but he had no idea what he was asking of her. She lived alone in an intentionally ordered world, she had crafted a quiet life in an unassuming town, and she worked behind the scenes at a company in the smallest state in the Union. She earned her college degree and MBA through online classes so she wouldn't have to mingle with curious students who watched too much television. She didn't want to leave her secure cocoon, not even to visit Hawaii or some other exotic place.

She'd seen Hawaii and she'd experienced exotic. Now she wanted to stay home.

"Miles." Andie lifted her head as her heart knocked against her ribs. "Honestly, I wouldn't know what to do on an expensive vacation. I enjoy my job and I'm happy staying put. Maybe I could give the vacation time to someone who needs it. One of my operators will soon be going out on maternity leave, so you could give my accrued time to her—"

"Can't be done; it's against policy. If I allowed you to donate vacation days, I'd have to allow everyone to do it and that would make a mess of things." He dipped his chin in a curt nod. "So no planes and no boats. Tell me, Andie, do you drive?"

Sarcasm wasn't going to help. "Listen, if you want me to take some time off, I can do that. I can stay home, read a few books, veg in front of the TV and rent a stack of movies—"

"The boss doesn't want to owe you for seven years of unpaid vacation time." Pearson's tone rang with finality. "He'll call me on the carpet if I don't come up with a package that allows us to pay off our liability. You've accrued eighty-five days of vacation time, so you need to accept a company-paid excursion and three weeks of paid time off."

She shook her head. "You don't have to worry. I'm not going to demand cash compensation when I leave VPN."

"You can't predict how you'll feel a few years down the road."

"I could put it in writing."

"And later you could contest your signed statement." Pearson closed the folder on his desk, then crossed his arms. "That's the bottom line, Andie. Do not come in to work tomorrow, and I'll send word when I've found a vacation that doesn't involve boats or planes. Meanwhile you might practice looking grateful, because Mr. Walker won't be happy if thinks you don't appreciate his generosity. In fact, I don't think he'll be happy until you're sending us postcards from some place warm and tropical."

Andie bit her lip as she walked back to her office. In all her years at VPN, she had never asked for special favors and never wanted special attention. All she wanted was to do her job, keep the boss happy, and make a decent living. All she'd ever asked of this company was to be allowed to live quietly under the radar. For seven years she'd been able to do that, so why did her new boss seem determined to make her miserable?

At four-fifty, as the on-air talent extolled the wonders of New Dawn Skin Lightener, Andie powered off the flat screen TV on her office wall, turned off the light, and walked toward the building exit. Buttoning her coat, she nodded to the security guard and stepped out into the chilly air.

At least a dozen people were already waiting at the bus stop, many of them engrossed in magazines, newspapers, or personal electronic devices. A homeless man sat on the bench, his odor reinforcing the boundaries of his personal space. A middle-aged woman stood nearby, resentment evident in her slit-eyed expression and the way she kept eying the empty end of the bench.

Andie slowed her step as she approached, then tossed the end of her scarf over her shoulder and pulled the knitted fabric over her lips to protect against the wayward glances of strangers. Once she had merged with the group, she folded her hands and faced the road, staring at the backs of her fellow passengers' heads. As the autumnal sun buried itself in the western horizon, everyone around her seemed intent upon getting home as quickly and uneventfully as possible.

Some of the women she worked with reported feeling uneasy in crowds, but Andie loved being part of the surging masses. No one noticed her; most people looked through strangers, not at them. Long ago she had learned—through watching a movie about Marilyn Monroe, no less—that celebrities could remain perfectly anonymous in a large group. Only when the celeb "turned on" the X factor that had made him or her famous did people stand back and take notice.

Over the years, Andie had learned to luxuriate in solitude. For the most part, anonymous people were not subject to being judged, second-guessed, photographed, Photoshopped, criticized, misinterpreted, nitpicked, blogged about, stalked, or idolized. They were left alone to be themselves, to find their own paths and follow them.

Like puppets on a single string the people at the bus stop turned to the left when a diesel growl rumbled in the distance. The College Hill bus approached, then pulled over to the curb and slowed with the hiss of air brakes. The crowd parted to let a few people off, then the group filed aboard.

Though it went against her self-protective instincts, Andie took an aisle seat and studied the people around her, a habit she'd developed since a teenage boy stole her purse two years ago. She'd learned that pickpockets focused on passengers who shut themselves off by closing their eyes or hiding behind a magazine; few would target a woman who was paying attention and apt to remember a face. So Andie rode home with strangers, hiding in plain sight, and no one recognized her.

She had been anticipating those solitary moments away from the office. Ever since hearing the news about her mother, she'd put off thinking about her, setting those concerns on a shelf until she could find some private time to sort through them. Finally, alone in the mass of tired travelers, she hoped to analyze the dull sense of foreboding that had hovered over her throughout the day.

"Excuse me." As the bus slowed, the young woman sitting next to her stood and pointedly stared at the aisle. Without meeting her gaze, Andie swung her legs out of the way, then slid into the window seat.

Autumn had reduced the roadside trees to skeletal branches and scarred trunks. The stark image, juxtaposed against thoughts of her dying mother, sent a sudden chill up her spine. Maybe she should wait to think about her mother.

Swaying in the stop-and-go rhythm of the bus, she turned her thoughts to the bizarre situation at work. In the early days of VPN, no one cared about manuals or procedures; they focused on moving product. The team came to work early and stayed late; everyone from the CEO to the receptionist hauled boxes and worked postage machines; they watched QVC and HSN and took pages of notes; they hired cousins and girlfriends and ex-husbands, eventually finding employees with the grit and determination to succeed in an extremely competitive field. No one talked about policies in those days; no one dithered over vacation pay or who-owed-what. The Value Price Network grew because the early employees invested their lives in the company.

But things had changed. Now VPN was publicly traded on the stock market; now they had a board of directors and a printed employee manual. Rich Gould, the fiery visionary who motivated the early team, retired to Florida, and Andie was one of the few original employees who remained at the company.

So how was she supposed to talk Walker out of sending her away? Her boss seemed determined to force her out of her comfort zone, but he had no idea why she dreaded the thought of a vacation. Andie wished she hadn't lied about being afraid to fly or take a boat, but she didn't think they'd understand why the thought of leaving the anonymity of a big city scared her silly.

Because Rich Gould was never a television junkie, she didn't think he'd ever seen her before she walked into the small office where VPN began its operations. By being careful and dependable — and by dyeing her hair and putting on a few pounds — she managed to forge a new life in a city where no one recognized her, no one hounded her for an autograph, and no one aimed a camera phone in her direction. If the Huggins family had gone the way of the Cowsills and the fictional Partridges, Christy Huggins might have been able to slip back into the mainstream of American life. But if what Oliver told Mr. Rueben was true, for the next several years her past would be airing nightly on at least two different television networks.

She pushed her bangs away from her face as the bus rolled up to her stop. Across the aisle, a woman in a business suit and track shoes stood, one hand wrapped firmly around the handle of her briefcase.

Andie stood, too, tucked her purse under her arm, and followed the businesswoman. A teenager at the front of the bus turned as they approached, quietly tucking his long legs into the short space provided for them. Andie thanked him with a smile as she headed down the steps, but he was swaying to a beat in his ear buds, oblivious to everything.

Ten minutes later, she walked up the sidewalk that led to her town house. Her flowerbeds were barren, the grass already winter brown. The earth was settling in for a long nap, and she'd been told to go on vacation.

Maybe a universal conspiracy had focused on her . . . because, as her mother used to retort, surely everything in the world revolved around Christy Huggins.

Andie snorted and lifted the lid of her mailbox. The effort netted a handful of bills and junk mail, but a package on the doormat might contain a book she'd ordered. She let herself into the house, then bolted the door and called for the love of her life. "Sam?"

A moment later her black-and-white cat came trotting into the foyer, his green eyes fastened on her as he meowed a welcome. "There you are." She scooped him up and stroked him from head to tail, then pressed her nose to his. The vibration of his purring sent a shiver over her skin. "I missed you today."

When Sam twisted in impatience, she put him down, then tossed her purse and the mail onto the foyer table. She and Sam walked together into the kitchen, where she opened a can of cat food while he wound around her ankles, purring so steadily she could feel micro-tremors all the way up her leg.

Once Sam was happily crouched before his bowl, Andie made a turkey sandwich, poured a diet soda, and moved into the living room. She set her food on a TV tray, then turned the radio to a station that aired political debates. While two hotheaded personalities harangued at each other, she settled on the sofa, took a bite of her sandwich, and opened the package from the bookstore.

She had just finished reading the prologue of her new novel when someone knocked on the door. For a moment she sat perfectly still, a half-chewed bit of turkey and bread in her mouth, then she set her book aside, swallowed, and tiptoed into the foyer. Through the peephole she recognized Sally Huffman, the older woman who lived in the adjoining townhouse. Sally was still wearing pastel scrubs, so for some reason she'd come straight from work.

Andie opened the door. "Sally? Is everything okay?"

"I hope so." The woman smiled, then squinted at an envelope in her hand. "Found a piece of your mail in my box. Don't you hate it when that happens?"

"Thanks." Andie took the envelope and groaned when she recognized the return address. "You could have pitched this one. I don't know why these companies keep sending me credit card offers. I can't stand the thought of being in more debt than I already am."

Sally chuckled. "Some months I swear my mortgage balance is going down by pennies instead of dollars." She tilted her head and looked past Andie into the living room. "Are you watching that Judge Rutner show? I love him! He's always arguing with the attorneys."

Andie shook her head. "I hate TV. You're hearing the radio. I turned it on for the noise."

"You do that? Me, too. Makes me feel less alone to hear voices in the house." Sally glanced at her hands. "I meant to thank you for the lotion you left by my door yesterday. I love it! Seems to be doing the trick for my skin. It gets so raw with all the hand-washing we have to do—"

"Let me know if you need more. I can get it unless—" she hesitated.

Concern flickered in Sally's eyes. "Something wrong, hon?"

Andie blew out a breath. "My boss wants to send me on a paid vacation. I don't want to go, but the personnel director keeps squawking about how the company doesn't want to owe me money when I retire."

Sally dropped her jaw. "Are you insane?"

Andie snorted, realizing how crazy she sounded. "I don't want to go through a lot of trouble. All that packing and sitting, and for what? You go away, you take pictures, you come home. But then you have to unpack and do laundry and put everything away again. I tried to explain that I'd be happy to take the time off and stay home, but they keep insisting—"

"I love traveling!" Sally's birdlike eyes focused on Andie's face. "I'd trade my favorite stretch pants for a free vacation. You can stay home and listen to the radio any time, but turning down a trip—that's not even logical."

Looking past her, Andie searched for a credible explanation. "Well . . . there's no place special I want to visit. And I don't have anyone to go with me, and who wants to travel alone? And there's Sam. I can't leave him for three weeks."

"I'll take care of the cat." Sally crossed her arms. "I'll watch your house, I'll bring in your newspapers and collect your mail. I'd love to help."

"You're busy; I couldn't ask you to do all that."

"You didn't ask, I'm volunteering. Go on a vacation; accept your boss's offer. This sort of opportunity doesn't come around every day."

Andie lifted her gaze to the sky, wishing she hadn't said anything about the trip. When she looked down again, a shade of sadness had entered her neighbor's eyes. "You know what they say—" her voice brimmed with weariness—"if you keep doing what you've always done, you'll get what you've always gotten."

"And that's supposed to mean . . .?"

"If you want your life to change, you have to do something different. Meet new people. Take a leap of faith."

"Who says I want my life to change?"

Sally's mouth twisted in something not quite a smile. "People need variety like they need air to breathe. Without it, you'll find yourself like me, stuck in a rut. So go on your trip, honey, and don't worry. I'll take care of everything you're leaving behind. I'd love to."

She spun on the ball of her foot and turned, forcing Andie to call after her. "Would you take the stupid trip for me?"

"I've already taken my vacation this year." Sally tossed the words over her shoulder as she walked toward her own front door. "Now it's your turn."

Before going to bed, Andie stepped into the small bedroom that served as her office and powered on her computer. She brought up her iTunes program, scanned a list of songs, and finally downloaded a karaoke version of "Somewhere Over the Rainbow." She listened to it, jotting down the number of beats between verses and the key change. Then she pulled the small microphone on her desk closer, opened her recording program, and clicked play.

As the instrumental accompaniment poured through her speakers, Andie straightened her spine, breathed properly, and sang, her voice filling the room with warm, vibrant sound. She closed her eyes as a tear slipped from her lashes and rolled down her cheek. Though her family's musical enterprise had brought an indescribable amount of pain and angst, she still loved the purity of music. So once a week her computer calendar reminded her of this task, a duty she took more seriously than her job. A weekly commitment she had not missed in thirteen years.

Over the final sustained chord she improvised a line about the lucky little bluebirds who could fly away . . . "so why can't . . . I?"

She remained silent for several seconds after the music stopped, then wiped tears from her cheeks and put on her headphones to listen to the final playback. She kept an eye on the levels as the recording played, then added a bit of reverb to the final note. She saved the file as an MP3 and attached it to an email addressed to BABYJANE@gmail.com.

*Dear Janey,* she wrote, *I hope you like this golden oldie. Makes me cry every time. Keep singing, sweetie.*

*Love,*

*Me*

She clicked send and waited for the reassuring whoosh of the computer, then powered down her machine and went to bed.

# Chapter Two

Despite Miles Pearson's warnings, the next morning Andie went to work and settled at her desk. No travel tickets had arrived on her doorstep the night before, and Pearson hadn't call with any sort of update. As far as she knew, life at VPN—and her part in it—was scheduled to continue as usual.

After glancing at the previous night's sales reports, she leaned back to watch the wall-mounted TV. The on-air hosts were running a promotion for body lotion, which would be followed by a promo for New Dawn's debut perfume, Desiree. Tiffany Moffitt, the network's most popular hostess, smiled as the cameras cut away for a commercial.

Andie turned to view her email inbox. Nothing from Walker or Pearson. Not much email at all, in fact.

She brought up a list of operators currently working in the call center. For November, when colds and flu usually decimated her crew, they were surprisingly well represented.

She glanced at the TV as the cameras went live again, and saw Tiffany arranging perfume bottles on a velvet-draped display

stand. "Anybody smelled this stuff?" She called, apparently un-
aware that her lapel mic was picking up every word. "I've got
roach spray that smells better."

Andie groaned as the director abruptly cut to an in-house
commercial. Call volume had been light so far, but traffic was
bound to increase as soon as Tiffany came back on the air. VPN's
customers, many of whom thought of Tiffany as a beloved
daughter, would call to assure her that she'd been forgiven for
the on-air flub.

They wouldn't, however, place much faith in Desiree
perfume.

Andie was trying to figure out how to counteract Tiffany's
gaffe when Miles Pearson appeared outside her open door, a manila envelope in his hand. He gave the door a perfunctory knock,
then stepped inside without an invitation. "I tried calling your
home—" he frowned— "and when you didn't answer, I figured
I'd find you in your office."

Andie shrugged. "I didn't hear from you last night, so I
thought I might as well come in."

"Sorry about that, but it took a little time to find the perfect option. So now you're under orders to go home, pack, and
get yourself on a train to Washington." He dropped the manila
envelope on her desk, then crossed his arms, his face glowing
with a self-satisfied smile. "I talked to my travel agent, and
she came up with a brilliant idea. We'll get you out of the cold,
you'll have a wonderful time, and there's nary a boat or plane
involved."

Andie stared at the envelope, but its blank surface offered no
clues. Still, her stomach dropped to the level of her knees. "Tell
me you're not sending me away for three weeks."

"Actually, we're not." He chuckled as if amused by a secret
joke. "This tour only lasts ten days, so if you really want a staycation in the comfort of your own home, you can do that when you
get back. But we expect you to be on your way this afternoon.

And we want a full report on your trip, including photos. You can email them. We'll be waiting."

She blinked at him, her mind spinning. Mr. Reuben's call, her mother's illness, this forced vacation . . . the combination was too much. But it was happening.

"I can't go. I don't live alone, you know, I live with Sam. I can't just take off and leave him—"

"That's why Mr. Mitchell said you can take a friend, if you want. Buy a companion ticket and charge it to VPN."

"A ticket to . . . where? Where are you sending me?"

"Maybe the question should be where aren't we sending you. Everything's explained in the brochure. You'll be going to Washington, Williamsburg, Charleston, Savannah, and St. Augustine, then you'll come home in a sleeper car. Hotels and restaurants are included. Tour busses, too. All arranged through Amtrak."

She gaped at him, speechless, until he gently grasped her wrist, lifted her arm, and dropped her hand on the manila envelope.

"Wait—you said this is a train trip?"

"Best idea I've had all month," Pearson said, practically hugging himself. "My travel agent says this vacation is top of the line all the way. You spend two days in each city, with short rides in between. I almost wish I were going myself."

She opened her mouth to protest again, but Pearson walked to the door, pulled her coat from the hook, and held it out. "You need to get moving, Andie. Your train leaves Providence at three-fifty and the boss wants you to be on it."

For one interminable moment her brain rebelled . . . then she stood, lifted her purse from her bottom desk drawer, and moved toward the door on legs that felt like wood. Despite her objections, her boss was sending her away. She would travel alone because she couldn't buy a companion ticket for a cat and she didn't have time to find someone who could leave town on a moment's notice. Even if she had time, she didn't have anyone to ask. Sally might go, but she needed to work and Andie needed her to feed Sam. Aside from the people at work, Andie had no other real friends.

She turned to slip into her coat, half expecting to hear the theme music from *The Twilight Zone* over the PA system. Who traveled by train these days? Nobody but commuters, as far as she knew. Business people flew; families vacationed in SUVs. Who chose to travel for long hours with a group of strangers?

On the other hand, this might be a good thing. With any luck, the passenger car would be mostly empty and the other travelers would be so focused on their destinations they wouldn't notice the woman sitting alone by the window . . .

"Have a great trip." Pearson sounded almost wistful as he settled her coat on her shoulders. "You're gonna have a wonderful time. You may not even want to come back."

She nodded as if agreeing with him. And though she'd fibbed about being afraid to sail or fly, she wasn't quite sure she could find the courage to step onto a train. Didn't those things derail sometimes? Who wanted to travel in a rolling shoebox?

Somehow Andie managed to accept that she would be away from work for three weeks, like it or not.

Before leaving VPN, she and Pearson established that Jasmine, her assistant, would oversee the call center and Alice Wheeler would make sure the payroll reports were filed on time. Judging from the enthusiastic farewells she received as she headed toward the front door, Andie wondered if anyone would even miss her.

After a quiet bus ride home, she sat on the edge of her bed and stared into her closet. Her suitcase stood against the back wall, mostly hidden by assorted sweaters, blouses, and skirts. The manila envelope with the train tickets and vouchers lay on the bed, but she'd barely glanced through the printed materials.

One thought kept running through her mind: why did she

have to go anywhere? VPN had fulfilled its obligation and purchased her tickets; no one would know if she didn't use them. No one was depending on her to fill a seat on the train; no one waited for her in any of those Southern cities.

At least she didn't think they did. The name Charleston snagged a shadowy memory, a fleeting thought that refused to surface. Did her family once play a gig in that city? Probably, but after a while all civic centers began to look alike. Did something significant happen in Charleston? A mistake onstage, a run-in with a photographer? She searched her recollections again, but the connection was too tenuous.

She didn't have to go anywhere. She could simply stay home and catch up on her reading, but the thought of lying around the house for twenty-one days made her cringe. She enjoyed weekends at home because she didn't get to spend much time doing domestic chores. If she had to stare at her walls for three weeks, she'd take to living in her pajamas, overeating, and refusing to put on makeup. After several days, she might become even more reclusive than she already was.

She couldn't forget that Thanksgiving fell within her three-week vacation window. Despite her frequent mentions of Sam, every year well-meaning people at work assumed she had nowhere to go and no family to help her celebrate the holiday. She spent most of November fending off invitations for dinners and parties. Though she appreciated people's thoughtfulness, she didn't want to be pitied. Once or twice she had considered accepting one of those invitations, but when she got too close to people they asked questions and she didn't like to lie. So when holidays rolled around she opened a can of sardines for Sam, sat down to a frozen turkey dinner, and told herself that she was one of the fortunate few who wouldn't have to deal with the strife and stress of the typical American family reunion. After her meal, she turned on the TV and watched one of the competing home shopping networks.

Why not forgo all that and go on a train trip? As Christie Huggins she'd traveled thousands of miles, but she'd never done any traveling as Andie Crystal. She'd never seen historic sites and waited in a queue as an ordinary person. She'd never checked herself into a hotel, stood in line for a cab, or carried her own suitcase. She'd never traveled coach class, nor had she ever ridden on a train. Sally was always saying that adding to one's life experiences was motivation enough for just about anything, so maybe she needed to try new things. And because the train tour would only take ten days, she'd have plenty of time to laze around when she got home.

Since Sally had already promised to take care of Sam, Andie couldn't come up with a practical reason not to go.

Other than the usual. The risk of being recognized always factored into her decisions, but surely that risk lessened with every passing day. Eleven years had passed since she stopped being Christy Huggins, and she had changed—she was older, her hair was a different color, and she no longer traveled with her singing siblings. No one would expect an ex-celebrity to be riding in a coach seat on an Amtrak train. Especially not one who had recently been abducted by aliens.

The thought of her siblings dredged up the memory of Mr. Reuben's call. The lump of guilt in the pit of her stomach hadn't dissolved overnight, so it wasn't likely to go away any time soon. If she stayed in Providence with nothing to do, her thoughts would turn toward the past, toward Mom and Dad, Charlie, Carma, Callie, Carin, and Cole . . .

If she didn't take this trip, she'd be home when the news about her mother's cancer broke. She doubted the major media would cover the story, but the tabloids and shows like TMZ would eat it up. If those articles ended up on the table in the break room at VPN, her co-workers would be discussing old photos of Mona Huggins and her musical family over their microwaved soups and Jenny Craig lunches. Did she want to be around when that happened? Maybe no one would notice the resemblance between Andie Crystal and Christy Huggins if she were a thousand miles away . . .

She plucked the brochure from the envelope with the train tickets. The cover featured a picture of a silver and blue train against a green forest and an azure sky. Inside, pictures depicted smiling people sitting around a linen-draped table in a dining car. Another photo revealed passengers reclining with open books in their laps. The unspoken message was clear: train travel was relaxing, roomy, and luxurious. The perfect mode of transportation for people who weren't in a hurry. The perfect thing for travelers who wanted to relax.

All right, then. She'd go.

A glance at the clock reminded her that she needed to get moving. Not only did she need to pack, but she had to write a note for Sally and enclose the key to her house. She had to leave cat food on the counter and check Sam's water bowl and tell Sally where she kept the cat litter. Then she needed to call a cab and hope he arrived quickly so she could get to the station on time.

As her blood surged with adrenaline, she strode to the closet and unearthed her suitcase, then swung it onto the bed. A thin layer of dust covered the leather-trimmed top, but otherwise it appeared to be in perfect shape. No dirt, no scuffs, no signs of wear on the little wheels.

Suitcases weren't supposed to look this good. Maybe it was time she broke hers in.

So . . . what did one pack to ride on a train? She glanced at Sam, who had decided that her open suitcase was the perfect place to stretch out. "You want to go with me? Maybe they have a cat fare."

His ears zipped back, then he sprang from the suitcase and landed on the floor. Andie guessed she wasn't the only one who'd prefer to stay home.

The tour itinerary said she'd have at least a full day to explore each of the southern cities along the route, but she had no idea what she would do in those towns. What did tourists do in Williamsburg? She supposed she could eat and shop no matter where she was. Eating out usually required dressy outfits, but tourists dressed for comfort. If Williamsburg was tourist-centered, any type of clothing would probably suit. Ditto for Charleston, Savannah, and St. Augustine.

She snapped her fingers, abruptly remembering Pearson's comment about wanting to see pictures. She could email really nice photos during the trip . . . if she could remember where she put her camera.

She finally found the camera bag in the spare room closet. The case was also covered in dust, but the Nikon—a digital SLR she won during a "name that song" call-in radio contest—was clean and would be ready to go after a battery charge. She hadn't taken more than three pictures with it, but she looked forward to using something besides the camera in her phone. She wanted to flood Miles Pearson's inbox with so many pictures he'd be sorry he ever uttered the word vacation.

She carried the camera into her bedroom and set it next to the suitcase. What else did one need on a train trip?

Clothes, of course, though it'd be a challenge to fit outfits for ten days into one bag. Maybe she should throw in some laundry detergent and hope she could find a Laundromat. She'd need pajamas. Toiletries, in case the hotels had lousy soap and shampoo. A bottle of vitamins and a bag of cough drops, in case she got stuck sitting beneath a vent and developed a sore throat. Her cell phone and charger, in case someone at work needed to reach her.

She tossed several items into the suitcase, then stood in the middle of the room and propped one hand on her hip, thinking. Clothes, camera, toiletries, vitamins. Comfortable shoes. Cell phone stashed safely inside her purse. Anything else?

She closed her eyes and imagined herself sitting in a seat by the window, her hands empty and her face exposed. If Southerners were as friendly as she remembered, she wouldn't be surprised if someone wanted to talk or asked where she was from. And while she'd never fault anyone for being friendly, her brain went numb every time someone asked about her past.

So she needed to take something that would help her look busy. If she were typing, people would assume she was working and leave her alone. With her iPad, she could even edit her digital pictures, pasting herself into snaps of a happy group or placing a handsome stranger on her arm. If she sent those photos to her call center crew, they'd buzz about them for a week.

And what they didn't know wouldn't hurt them.

She went into the spare bedroom and took her iPad and charger from the desk. She lifted her briefcase, removed the VPN printouts, and replaced them with her iPad, chargers for all the electronics, and ear buds. People would be even less likely to bother her if she was typing with earphones in her ears.

She was about to close her briefcase when she remembered the novel she'd started the night before. Computers were wonderful, but a book could transport her to a different world . . . and insulate her from the present one.

The novel went in the briefcase, too.

The cab dropped her at Providence Station with twenty minutes to spare. Situated beneath a gleaming silver dome, the stone building teemed with commuters who were heading home and trying to beat the downtown rush.

Andie's heels tapped the polished floor as she dragged her suitcase, purse, and briefcase through the large open area. Once she reached the line at the Amtrak ticket counter, she shifted her purse from the top of her suitcase to her shoulder, then glanced at her watch. Since she had no idea how much time she should allow between her arrival and her train's departure, she hoped twenty minutes would be enough.

Finally she reached the agent. She slid her tickets from the manila envelope and placed them on the counter. "I'm booked on a train leaving for Washington."

The agent examined one of the tickets, then peered at Andie over the top of her reading glasses. "You don't need to come to the counter; just take your bags to the baggage window. You'll be leaving from track two in about fifteen minutes."

Andie waited, expecting her to ask for ID or a confirmation number, but the agent only yawned and shifted her gaze to the next man in line.

"So . . . am I done here?"

Irritation flattened her smile as the woman pointed to a circular area in the center of the building. "You can wait over there until they call your train."

Andie grabbed her belongings and hauled them from the counter. The baggage window was exactly that—a large window manned by two uniformed women. As Andie approached they studied her luggage with sharp eyes.

One woman pointed to the tag on Andie's nondescript black suitcase. "You got your name, address, and phone number on that tag?"

"Um . . . almost. I don't give out my phone number."

"Then how are we supposed to call you if we find your bag where it shouldn't be? You gotta put your cell phone number on the card. Blank tags are on the desk; make sure you fill one out for every piece of luggage you're takin' on the train."

Andie wanted to ask how often a bag ended up where it shouldn't be, then decided she was better off not knowing. She gave the women a meek smile and moved out of the way so she could fill out bag tags without delaying the veteran travelers behind her. When other people walked up and left their luggage without being interrogated, she realized her inexperience made her stand out like a blinking beacon.

After filling out three new tags, she dragged her suitcase back to the baggage clerks. She lingered a moment to make sure they shoved her suitcase through a chute—something in her worried that her stupidity had so offended them they might "forget" to load her bag—then she walked toward the circular concourse where other passengers waited in cheap plastic chairs.

Located directly beneath the huge silver dome, the concourse was impossible to miss. The few passengers who weren't sitting were browsing inside the lottery store or lined up at the Cafe La France, where a woman in a hairnet sold pastries, coffee, and sodas.

Andie stepped into the concourse area and dropped into a chair. Less than a dozen people sat in the circle, so apparently she had arrived much too early. A security video played on an overhead screen; in it a uniformed Amtrak employee unzipped a woman's suitcase, glanced inside, then zipped it up and sent her on her way. If that was the standard security procedure, where and when did it happen? The video didn't say, but a smiling man assured her that Amtrak cared about customer safety, so all passengers should be prepared to show official identification after boarding.

She glanced at her watch again. Three forty-five, and still no sign of activity at the door labeled Track Two. A heavy woman with two preschool children trudged into the waiting area and herded her offspring to an open space beneath the video screen. A businessman carrying a newspaper, briefcase, and steaming coffee cup, entered and sat as far as possible from the woman and her children. A trio of teenage girls strolled into the circle, disturbing the quiet with high-pitched squeals. They dropped loaded backpacks on the floor and fell into the chairs, arms and legs twisting as they giggled and elbowed each other.

Andie crossed her legs and resisted the urge to glance at her watch.

The teenaged girls giggled, then ended one whispered exchange with riotous laughter, drawing attention from everyone in the waiting area. The girl with the heaviest eyeliner swept the circle of curious glances with a what's-it-to-ya look. Her eyes then locked with Andie's, and even after Andie looked away she could feel the pressure of the girl's gaze.

Her stomach twisted in the nauseating grip of déjà vu. The girl probably watched reruns of *Home with the Huggins* every night. In a minute she'd come over and ask if Andie would pose for a picture or sign her hand—

Andie gripped the strap of her purse, ready to run. She could hurry outside and hail a cab without going through any checkpoints; no one would even know she'd left the area. But her luggage, neatly labeled with her contact information, stood somewhere between the baggage window and a train. If she fled the scene, who knew when she'd get her suitcase back?

She glanced again at the teenage girl, who had lifted her hand in order to whisper to her friend. Andie blew out a breath and pulled her briefcase onto her lap. Maybe she was imagining things. Or maybe the girl merely thought Andie looked familiar, like someone she once knew. Maybe she'd never watched *Home with the Huggins* at all.

Andie picked up an abandoned section of newspaper, lifting it until her face was hidden by newsprint. She studied an ad for a Charleston hotel and again felt the familiar spark of a nebulous connection buried somewhere in her memory cells. She smiled at a few comics and squinted at reports from the stock exchange. She read disconnected articles that didn't penetrate her consciousness until the faint whistle of a train reached her ear.

A voice crackled over the loudspeaker: "Attention all passengers. Amtrak train #2171 Acela Express is now boarding on track two. Please make your way through the gate."

On legs that felt suddenly wobbly, Andie stood with the businessman, the teenaged girls, the mother, the children, and several other passengers. They gathered their carry-ons and moved through the door marked Track Two, then filed onto an escalator. With one hand holding her purse and the other gripping her briefcase, Andie rode the moving stairs until they dropped her onto a rough sidewalk that ran beside a set of railroad tracks. She was startled to discover that though she never heard anything but that one faint whistle, her train had already arrived.

Walking beside what appeared to be a never-ending column of cars, she followed the man in front of her, glancing at the silver and blue behemoth from the corner of her eye. She caught the words "first class," "cafe car," and "business class," painted on several cars, then the line of passengers turned. A uniformed employee—a porter, she supposed—stood at the base of built-in steps to help passengers onto the train.

She bit her lip and shifted the weight on her shoulders. As an elderly woman attempted to climb those steps, the attendant guided her elbow and encouraged her forward. When she reached the top, he lifted her small carry-on bag and tossed it onto the train after her.

Andie resisted the urge to rise on tiptoe to see if his toss knocked the poor woman over. The line moved forward, and soon she was standing in front of those silver stairs. Uncomfortably aware of the people waiting behind her, she struggled to maintain her balance and carry her bulky purse and briefcase up the stairs.

The attendant grabbed her elbow. "Where are you headed?"

For an instant her mind swarmed with city names, then she remembered her first stop. "Washington."

"Turn right once you're aboard," he said, so Andie did. Apparently there were no assigned seats on this train; she could sit anywhere in coach class.

She wandered through the car and noticed that most of the seats were already filled—and a disproportionate number of passengers seemed to be asleep, some dozing upright, some curled into fetal positions and taking up two seats. Sleeping children had draped themselves across their mother's laps; a couple of women were napping with their heads on their companion's shoulders. But not everyone slept: she spotted a woman reading a book, a man tapping on his computer, a teenage boy watching a DVD on a portable player. No one appeared to be socializing, and that observation sent a rush of relief coursing through her.

She dropped into the first available window seat, her purse and briefcase falling to the floor. She glanced around to see if anyone would challenge her for the spot, but no one did.

By the time Andie stashed her briefcase in the overhead bin, the train had rolled out of the station and picked up speed, rushing toward the next depot without any warning or fanfare. She was surprised she didn't hear any kind of announcement about safety procedures, but maybe that was out of consideration for the people snoring around her. Or maybe trains were simply a lot safer than planes.

Once settled, she looked around. Across the aisle, an old man was sleeping with his mouth open and his hands folded over his belly — where did he board this train? How long had he been asleep? And who would be responsible for making sure he woke in time for his stop?

Her questions were answered when a uniformed conductor came down the aisle. "Tickets," he called, pausing to punch printed cards along the way. Only after watching him punch a ticket and slip a card into the railing above a passenger's seat did Andie realize that he was marking each seat with a code for the passenger's departure point. So if a rider was asleep when the train neared his stop, someone should come along to wake him up.

Or at least she hoped someone would.

When the conductor paused by her seat, Andie handed him her ticket and offered her driver's license as well, since the security video had said she'd be asked to show her ID.

The man didn't even glance at her license. He merely punched her ticket, removed the largest portion, and handed her the stub. So much for railroad security.

Andie settled back and smiled. Without any help from an assistant, she'd made it aboard the train. She'd left VPN behind and was off on her first real vacation.

And apparently no one was going to peer at her identification and try to place her face.

At 10:05 p.m., right on time, Andie's train pulled into Union Station in Washington, D.C. With her heart in her throat she grabbed her purse, pulled her briefcase from the overhead compartment, and followed the others off the train, over a loading platform, and up an escalator. She stared upward, amazed at the stately grandeur of Union Station. She'd walked through huge airports, convention centers, and hotels, but she'd never seen anything like this ornate building.

She claimed her suitcase and dragged it through the gate area, the modern mall, and the grand lobby, where a gilded domed ceiling made her feel utterly insignificant. She had imagined that Union Station would be nearly deserted at this hour on a Thursday night, but dozens of detraining passengers, custodial staff, and tourists moiled throughout the cavernous space. Several people stopped to snap pictures of the elegant statuary while others exchanged noisy greetings. A cacophony of sound reverberated from the marble walls — laughter, shouts, the hum of rolling suitcases, the percussive sounds of hurried footsteps.

The sight of so many cameras reminded Andie of Miles Pearson, so she pulled her camera from her purse and took a picture of a carved statue set inside a gilded niche. She'd have to email this shot to Pearson as soon as she arrived at her hotel. He'd probably be astounded to learn she actually made it to the train station.

She dropped her camera back into her bag, grabbed her suitcase, and rejoined the flow of travelers through the mammoth building. She tilted her head, amazed at how different she felt traveling alone. She hadn't gone anywhere in the past eleven years, but as Christy Huggins she'd slept in a different hotel bed nearly every night. She was naive then, never giving a thought to all the logistical details that had to be arranged in order for her family to play in different cities. They moved around the world in a pampered bubble, surrounded by people who took care of everything from their travel arrangements to their hair, makeup, and wardrobe. Though Andie rarely saw them, members of the tech crew also traveled on the family's itinerary, but usually arrived early to take care of the lighting, sound, and stage setup. And always, no matter where the Huggins went, their agent Oliver Weinstein trotted ahead of them like a protective bullmastiff.

As part of the Huggins family, Andie never walked through the front doors of theaters, convention centers, or hotels, but was escorted through discreet VIP entrances into huge rooms where overloaded buffets offered food, bottled water, fruit juices, and any sort of soda she could want. Security guards stood near every door to keep the family safe while fans clamored outside the building. They rode in stretch limos with darkened windows; they flew in private jets. The television network portrayed the Huggins as an ordinary American family that happened to be musically talented, but they had stopped being ordinary the moment Andie's parents signed their first television contract.

Andie stopped in the middle of the cavernous station, the memory of her childhood passing through her like an unwelcome chill. Why was she thinking so much about the past? She was no longer Christy Huggins. She had no entourage and no travel perks. She was completely alone and walking through a world she had kept at arms length for years.

An incredibly noisy, confusing, busy world.

For an instant she was tempted to turn around and get on a northbound train, to head back to Providence and take the three-week staycation she'd talked herself out of. But only a child would be intimidated by something as simple as checking into a hotel, and she was no longer a child. She was thirty-one and a department supervisor at one of the nation's largest shopping networks. She was certainly capable of handling a solo trip to the nation's capital.

She gulped a deep breath, gripped the handle of her suit-case, and followed the streaming crowd as it flowed toward the massive doors at the front of the building. Beneath a portico she found a queue of people at a taxi stand. Perfect. She'd get a cab and go to her hotel . . . but which hotel was it? The travel agent had printed the name and address somewhere in her paperwork.

She stepped into the queue and fished the manila envelope from her briefcase, then quickly flipped through the assorted pages. Good—the voucher for Washington, D.C. She had a res-ervation at the Hilton Hotel on Sixth Street, near the convention center.

Behind her, a woman chuckled. Andie turned, fully expect-ing to discover that the lady behind her was either talking on the phone or sharing a joke with a companion, but she stood alone, too, and she'd been watching Andie.

"I've known that kind of panic." The woman's mouth curved in a sympathetic smile. "You get to your destination and sud-denly you can't remember where you're spending the night."

"I didn't even learn about this trip until this morning, so I'm not exactly up on the details."

Andie shuffled her travel papers and discreetly studied the woman behind her. She was older, probably in her early fifties, and wore dark jeans and a collared blouse beneath a traditional wool coat. She was dragging two suitcases, one piggybacked to the other, so she must be traveling for several days. Her hair had been cut in a short, no-nonsense style, and a decent-sized diamond winked at the woman's left hand. Laugh lines radiated from the corners of eyes that looked tired and a little sad. One of them was rimmed in beige makeup, applied too heavily and in the wrong shade.

One thing was certain—this woman wasn't in the cosmetics or entertainment business.

Andie held the hotel voucher between her teeth and stuffed the rest of her papers back into the envelope. When she'd finished sliding the envelope into her briefcase, she released the voucher and frowned at the bite marks at the top of the page.

"That could be interesting." The woman gestured toward the paper in Andie's hand. "The hotel clerk is going to think you got hungry."

"That reminds me—I could go for something to eat." Andie took two steps when the line moved forward. "Maybe once I get checked in."

"Traveling for business or pleasure?"

Andie gave her a wry smile. "Pleasure and business. My boss decided I needed a vacation, so here I am. You?"

The woman shifted her gaze to some distant place. "Escape." Her voice was so low Andie could barely hear it. "I needed to get away."

Not knowing how to respond, Andie forced a polite smile. "I hope you find what you're looking for."

"So do I."

A valet whistled, another cab roared off, and Andie stepped to the front of the line. The valet wasted no time in opening the next cab's passenger door, so she hopped in as he rolled her suitcase toward the back and heaved it into the trunk. She barely had time to set her briefcase on the seat before the driver slid behind the wheel and turned the key. "Where to, lady?"

"The Hilton," she told him, her voice brimming with pretend confidence. "On Sixth Street."

# Chapter Three

So . . . what was a girl do when she had an entire day to spend in Washington and no one to spend it with?

Andie tried to sleep late, but her brain was used to waking early, so at six she was awake, alert, and staring at the ceiling. As the sun rose over the nation's capitol, she stood at her hotel window and pulled back the drape. The Washington Monument towered in the distance, and at least a hundred museums, stores, and restaurants lay between her window and the towering obelisk. Having so many choices left her feeling paralyzed.

She let the curtain fall and moved to the desk, where her iPad had been charging overnight. She hadn't been to D.C. in years, so she hadn't seen the Holocaust Museum. Keenly interested, she searched for the appropriate URL and logged onto the museum site.

Her enthusiasm faded almost immediately. The Holocaust Museum was so popular that visitors needed a free ticket to enter—and though tickets could be reserved online, none were available for either day she'd be in town. She could request admission for Sunday, but thanks to Pearson's detailed planning, by Sunday morning she'd on her way to the next fabulous city where she could wander around bored and lonely.

Well . . . why not take her staycation in the hotel room?

She called room service and ordered a big breakfast—scrambled eggs, wheat toast, hash browns, a bagel with cream cheese, fruit plate, banana walnut bread, tea and orange juice. While she waited for her meal, she climbed back into bed and pulled her iPad onto her lap, then murdered a few minutes playing Angry Birds.

She answered the door in the plush hotel robe when her breakfast arrived. A woman in a black uniform wheeled in the cart, then lifted a brow. "You want your tray on the desk?"

"You can put it on the bed," Andie answered, pulling up the coverlet to smooth out the surface. "Thanks."

She checked her email while the woman placed the tray, then stood back. "Anything else, ma'am?"

"No, thanks."

Andie waited for the check, but the woman smiled instead. "You look awfully familiar. Didn't you used to be on TV or something?"

Andie pressed her lips together. "Or something. I work for the Value Price Network."

The woman shook her head. "That's not it. You used to sing. I remember you singing behind a piano."

With an effort, Andie kept her voice light. "Do you have something for me to sign?"

The woman snapped her fingers. "Christy Huggins! You're one of those kids from the Huggins Family."

Andie smiled. "My name is Andie Crystal. Sorry to disappoint."

She signed the check and added a generous tip, then waited until she heard the click of the lock before sinking back against the pillows. After waiting another minute to sure the woman hadn't returned, she crossed her legs, powered on the TV, and moved through channels until she found VPN. Tiffany Moffitt was extolling the wonders of Desiree perfume, but apparently she hadn't learned anything from her faux pas the day before. She held the bottle on her open palm and spoke of how marvelous the scent was, but Andie had seen Tiffany look more excited about a dental appointment.

Andie frowned and considered sending Jasmine an email . . . but no, if she worked on her vacation Pearson would probably hear about it. And he wouldn't be happy.

So she changed the channel, finally settling on one of the morning news programs. She ate slowly, making her breakfast last through three interviews, several chatty interludes, a half dozen clumsy segues, and a mini concert in Central Park. As the news program signed off, she glanced at the clock and realized that an entire day still stretched before her.

How was she supposed to enjoy ten days like this? She could watch TV and stuff herself at home.

She leaned against the headboard and chewed on her thumbnail as her thoughts drifted back to the last time she visited the Capitol. The Huggins family had been scheduled to play at the White House, but before the gig they were invited for a VIP tour of the Smithsonian. Some bigwig from the Institute came out to escort them through a couple of the museums — Andie couldn't remember which museums, but she did remember filming a short clip outside the first ladies' dresses and posing for still shots of her, Carma, and Carin ogling the Hope Diamond. The boys posed for pictures beneath towering dinosaur skeletons — would that have been at the Museum of Natural History?

She closed her eyes and studied the memory. Because they traveled so often, the details of most events tended to blur together, but the Washington gig had been unique. They had to go through extensive security checkpoints, handsome men in uniform escorted them from place to place, and the gravitas of the occasion awed even her mother. President and Mrs. Clinton were polite and gracious, but Andie was thrilled when Chelsea and her school friends rocked the East Room when the family played.

A flood of nostalgia swept through her, bringing with it other sights and sounds from her adolescence: music, laughter, irritated whispers, unexpected mishaps, her mother muttering orders between clenched teeth. During the six years her family lived in front of television cameras, Andie learned that Charlie couldn't resist a girl with a flirty grin, Carin hated hiding her intelligence beneath blond hair and a bleached smile, and Carma resented not being able to keep a dog. Because Oliver thought pets made the family more personable, on the show they had an Old English sheepdog. But as soon as the cameras stopped rolling, Blinkers went back into his portable kennel and his trainer hauled him away. Mom insisted that a live-in dog would ruin the carpets, but Cole once told Andie he thought Mom didn't like Blinkers because they loved him so much. "She's jealous," he said, his blue eyes twinkling above a cloud of freckles. "Mom can't stand competition."

Andie remembered stepping outside one afternoon as the dog trainer's van turned out of their gate and drove away. Carma stood on the porch, her arms crossed as angry tears streamed over her cheeks. When she sensed Andie standing beside her, she swiped the wetness away with the back of her hand. "When I grow up—" her voice sounded strangely adult for a fifteen-year-old— "I'm going to have all the pets I want and nobody's going to stop me."

That memory—unexpectedly unearthed—snagged the piece of information that had been eluding Andie for days. A couple of years ago she ran across an article about Carma's new baby in *People* magazine . . . and Carma's family lived in Charleston.

Charleston was a stop on the train tour.

Andie sat up, startled to realize that she could actually reconnect with one of her siblings. Because she'd believed she couldn't escape life as a Huggins unless she made a complete break with all things Huggins, she hadn't spoken to any of her sibs since she decided to disappear. They were adults now, with families of their own.

If she passed one of her sisters on the street, would she even recognize her? If she saw one of her brothers in a restaurant, would she find the courage to walk up and say hello?

She didn't know. Something in her hoped she'd be welcomed if she reached out to her siblings, but another part of her worried that they might not be happy about the way she cut herself out of the family. With her lawyer's help, she had walked away without looking back . . . at least not until now.

Andie chewed on the end of her thumbnail. She didn't know how Carma would feel if her long-lost sister showed up on her front porch, but she didn't have to make that decision now. She had several days to consider her options and other towns to explore. Beginning with Washington.

She took a deep breath, then swung her legs off the bed and headed toward the shower. She still didn't know how she would fill her day, but she wasn't going to sit in her room and eat herself into a coma. Especially since the server had recognized her and might already be spreading rumors.

Oliver always said the best way to scope out a new city was to hop on a tour bus and ride around. Andie was pretty sure Pearson had included a ticket for just such a bus in her manila envelope.

After a full day of sightseeing, Andie was worn out and ready to crash. She'd ridden the red, green, and blue routes of a double-decker bus; she'd toured the Spy Museum and visited the Ford Theater where Lincoln was assassinated. She'd snapped pictures of the Capitol, the Washington Monument, and more memorials than she could name, and she'd emailed all the photos to Miles Pearson's inbox. She'd snacked on cotton candy and Dunkin

Donuts; she'd lunched at Legal Seafood and bought bottled water from strangers on the street. She'd stared at bare cherry trees and longed for pink blossoms and she'd watched the changing of the guard at the Tomb of the Unknown Soldier and longed for international peace.

Now she was tired. And desperate for someone to talk to.

She wasn't really hungry, but because meals were comforting and routine, she asked the cabbie to drop her a block from the Hilton, certain that she'd find a restaurant on her way back to her hotel. Her walk led through the District's Chinatown, so she stepped into the first Chinese restaurant she came across. She wanted a quiet place to sit and something to put in her stomach. Plain rice would do.

A smiling Asian hostess approached her, menus in hand. "Table for one?"

"Please."

The hostess seated Andie at a table against the wall, and Andie sat so she could see the door. She liked facing the exit—the habit had become ingrained during her days of keeping a lookout for autograph-seeking groupies.

She glanced at the menu, ordered a plate of Kung Pao chicken, and sipped a cup of tea as the waitress scurried away. A group of Asian students occupied a large circular table in the center of the restaurant, all of them speaking Chinese—or so Andie assumed. She couldn't help noticing how modern they were, how American, even though they ate with chopsticks. She couldn't understand a word of their conversation.

Their chatter made her smile. Huggins family dinners used to sound like that—six children talking at once, all of them eager to capture Mom's or Dad's attention. As the eldest, Charlie would slouch in his chair, one arm draped over the back, pretending a cool aloofness Andie knew he didn't feel. Carin, younger than Charlie by a year, spoke with the self-consciousness of a budding woman who had recently become aware of her own beauty. She had always been more experienced than Andie, more successful and confident in a world of makeup, boys, and mysterious female rituals.

On Andie's other side, the youngsters clamored for their share of the group's attention: Carma, the animal-loving bookworm; Cole, the unexpected redhead with a killer smile; and Callister, the unanticipated child and the only one of the brood with a tin ear. Fortunately, Callie danced like Michael Jackson so no one ever noticed that his mic wasn't on.

Kids—Christy Huggins had always gravitated to the children in the audience, loving their warm spontaneity and boundless enthusiasm. She loved spending time with her younger sibs, finding more in common with them than with Charlie or Carin. And she and Cole had been, as their father always said, "closer than a tree and its bark."

Too bad Andie Crystal had no children in her life. She might have enjoyed them, too.

"One order, Kung Pao chicken." The waitress appeared at Andie's left and lowered a steaming plate to the table. "You okay here?"

"Yes, thank you."

She was about to spear a bite of chicken when an ear-splitting screech disturbed the comfortable atmosphere. Every diner, including the teens at the center of the restaurant, halted in mid-bite and turned toward a table near the front. A man, probably in his mid-thirties, sat there with two children, one of whom was standing on her chair and screaming at the top of her lungs.

Even as Andie winced, she felt a pang of pity for the kids' father. Cole had been a high-pitched screamer when he was little, and Mom had worried that he'd grow up to sing soprano.

The father lowered his head, probably to reprimand his children, but the little girl wasn't listening. The boy, who appeared to be a year or two older, stared up at his sister with obvious delight. The little girl stomped her foot; the father pointed to her plate. She shook her head, and then—to Andie's complete astonishment—she lifted her foot and kicked, catching the edge of her plate and launching most of her dinner toward her father's expensive-looking sports coat.

Andie stared, the teenagers giggled, and a woman across the room gasped aloud. Andie clapped her hand over her mouth as the red-faced father stood, swiped at his coat with a napkin, then lifted his daughter from the chair. He caught the waitress's eye and asked for the check in a voice heavy with forced calm.

The waitress ran toward the cash register while the man stuffed his daughter's arms into a lavender blue coat. The father jerked his chin at his son, wordlessly instructing the boy to put on his jacket.

As the waitress hurried over with their check, Andie joined the unspoken conspiracy initiated by the other diners. They returned to their meals as though nothing unusual had happened, though the teenagers kept sneaking glances at the father and his petulant little girl.

Once the small family had left the restaurant, Andie looked across the room and recognized the lady who'd stood behind her in the taxi line at Union Station. Andie waited a moment, wondering if the woman would look over and remember her, but she seemed focused on the menu.

Oh, well. Andie returned to the work of enjoying her dinner and thought about day two of the great American train tour. Tomorrow she would try to sleep late, she would rent a movie on TV, and she might do a little shopping in Chinatown. For fun, if she could squeeze it into her hectic schedule, she might watch an hour or two of the Value Price Network. Or she could order everything on the room service menu and see how long the staff took to deliver it.

After receiving the room service bill, Miles Pearson and Mr. Walker would think twice about sending her on another all-expenses paid trip.

# Chapter Four

Sunday morning Andie was up and dressed before sunrise. She checked out of the hotel and walked outside, buttoning her coat as she went. The concierge had called a cab, so Andie stood beside a streetlamp and shivered in a lonely cone of light as she looked for her ride. While she waited, the hotel doors slid open again and a woman stepped out—the woman from the taxi stand. This time she recognized Andie and chuckled as she walked forward. "Let me guess—you're going back to the train station?"

Andie crossed her arms as her teeth begin to chatter. "Y-yes."

"Would you mind if I shared your cab? The concierge said—"

"I'd l-l-love to."

The woman offered Andie a gloved hand. "I'm Janette Turlington."

Andie pulled her hand free and shook Janette's. "Andie Crystal. Nice to meet you."

The taxi's arrival interrupted their small talk. They helped the driver stack their suitcases in the trunk, then slid into the backseat for the short ride to Union Station. The eastern sky brightened on the drive, and Andie's spirits began to rise as shadows evaporated from the downtown streets.

Janette smiled as they pulled into the circular drive in front of the station. "Where are you headed this morning?"

This time Andie didn't have to consult her paperwork. "Williamsburg."

"Really? Me, too."

Andie wanted to ask if they would be on the same train, but just then the cab driver announced that they'd arrived. They split the fare, got out, and gathered their belongings. Andie turned to Janette, assuming that they'd walk in together, but the older woman waved goodbye and sauntered toward a coffee shop while Andie stood on the sidewalk feeling . . . lost.

She was being silly. Why should she feel like an orphan just because a nice woman went on her way? They weren't friends; they were barely acquaintances.

But after two days alone in Washington, Andie had enjoyed connecting with someone, even if only for a moment.

She set her briefcase on top of her suitcase and dragged both into the grand lobby. She had assumed that the place bustled around-the-clock, but only a few people moved through the massive vestibule. The shuttered restaurants and shops loomed around her, and dense silence absorbed the sound of her heels on the polished floor. The solitude reminded her of apocalyptic movies in which Washington was depicted as haunting and deserted in marble emptiness. She half-expected a flesh-eating mutant to emerge from behind one of the elevated marble statues and sweep down on her.

She quickened her pace and hurried through the tiled tunnel that led to the ticket counter. She smiled at the gate agent and pushed her suitcase toward the scale. "Good morning. I'm going to Williamsburg."

"Okay." The woman tapped Andie's luggage. "Sorry, but

there's no baggage service on that train. You need to take all your luggage with you."

Andie gaped at the agent. "You mean . . . I have to drag this onto the train?"

The woman responded with an automatic smile. "Thousands of people do it every day."

"Which train, exactly?"

"The Northeast Regional, departing out of Gate H. Turn right and keep walking; you can't miss it."

Still stunned by the revelation that train travel sometimes meant taking your luggage with you, Andie moved away as directed, noticing that activity had picked up since she entered the building. Gate H was across from a Ben & Jerry's and adjacent to a McDonalds, where the breakfast crowd had already formed a long line. Her stomach gurgled at the thought of a hot sausage biscuit and a cup of coffee, but the line was long and she didn't want to risk missing her train. Security must be tight in the nation's capitol, and she had no idea how long it would take to drag her bags through a checkpoint . . .

She stepped into the gate area and took one of the few available seats, noticing another video about security procedures playing on wall-mounted monitors. A clock on the wall marked the time, and before too long an announcer spurred the waiting crowd into action: "Attention all passengers. Amtrak train #67 Northeast Regional is now boarding on track 25. Please make your way through Gate H."

Andie rose with the others and pulled her rolling suitcase through a pair of double doors. Because she'd stacked her briefcase and purse on her suitcase, when she pulled the heavy load onto the escalator riser behind her, their combined weight shifted forward and nearly shoved her onto the man in front. Her mind filled with the image of luggage-laden travelers toppling like dominoes, but sheer desperation gave her the strength to hold herself upright on the tediously slow journey downward.

Finally the escalator spat its riders onto a sidewalk that ran between a series of railroad tracks—more tracks than Andie had ever seen in any one location.

As she followed the other travelers, she realized that the Northeast Regional was not as upmarket as the train she'd taken earlier. There were no first class cars, no business class cars, and no baggage car—just coach cars and a single cafe car. A uniformed attendant helped passengers board near the rear of the train, then he heaved their suitcases aboard, leaving the riders responsible for finding a place to stow their bags. After boarding, Andie found herself boxed in by her suitcase and the man in front of her, but attendant called, "Just inside the door you'll find an empty space for luggage. Store your bags there and keep the line moving."

The vacant space was actually inside the door and past the restrooms, but Andie finally found it and stowed her suitcase. Then she wandered through the crowded car until she discovered an available seat and dropped into it. At least she had managed to end up in the right place at the right time.

Once again, the train pulled smoothly away. Andie leaned back as the train rolled through a dark tunnel that must have run beneath Union Station, then she blinked when light flooded the car again. As they headed into the Virginia countryside, she looked out and searched for familiar landmarks, but all she could see was gray sky and trees painted in the muted colors of late fall.

Several people still shuffled in the aisle, probably trying to find a convenient place for their luggage and personal belongings. Andie closed her eyes to block out the distraction.

Rocked by the steady rhythm of the rails, she drifted into a shallow doze.

◆

Andie had been steadfastly trying to avoid the necessity of using the public restroom on the crowded train, but her pea-sized bladder wouldn't let her wait until she arrived at her destination. She would have to make her way down the entire length of the aisle to reach the restrooms at the back of the car.

Walking on a train, she discovered, wasn't as easy as it looked. On a plane you might encounter the occasional bump, but on a train you had to adapt to a steady side-to-side movement as well as the occasional bump and jostle.

Though she had hoped to leave her seat without attracting attention, Andie found herself lurching along like a slaphappy drunk. More than once she had to grab the headrest on a nearby seat to keep from falling, and none of the passengers resting on those headrests appreciated having their heads reclined without warning. She murmured "Excuse me" at least a dozen times, tripped on three straps dangling from backpacks or purses, and woke a half dozen sleeping passengers.

Her reward for all her trouble? A long, narrow restroom with a smelly toilet, a push-button sink, damp toilet paper, and wadded paper towels strewn randomly over the floor.

After returning to her seat, for the first time Andie studied the man riding next to her. White whiskers on his upper lip trembled as he breathed in and out, his arms were crossed, and his hands firmly tucked into his armpits. Probably in his sixties or seventies, the old man slept like a baby, leading Andie to believe that he must be a frequent train traveler.

Leaving her neighbor to his nap, she extended the footrest beneath her seat and discovered that it wasn't quite long enough for her to stretch out. She could either bend her knees and ride like a gigged frog or let her feet dangle over the edge. Since neither position was attractive or comfortable, she lowered the footrest. Maybe she shouldn't sleep. Maybe should pull that novel out of her briefcase, or turn on her iPad and see if she could catch a wireless signal from some passing coffee shop . . .

She went for the book. She'd read the first two paragraphs of chapter one when an ear-splitting yell yanked her from the story.

For an instant she was convinced terrorists had commandeered the train, but after peering down the aisle she spotted a little boy and girl running toward her as if the devil were giving chase. She looked past them, expecting to see a frustrated parent in hot pursuit, but she saw no one.

She braced herself as the kids ran by in a whoosh of energy. Someone's little darlings had escaped and were running loose.

Curious, she looked up and down the aisle, but none of the awake adults seemed to be missing children, and none of the sleeping adults appeared young enough to have small children. Could they have come from another car?

The thought of young kids venturing into the dangerous junction between two cars spurred Andie to action. She stood, intending to find the children and ask where they belonged, but she hadn't taken more than a step when she heard heavy steps approaching. She turned and saw a uniformed Amtrak employee coming down the aisle.

Her nerves tensed when the man fixed his gaze on her, and for a moment her mouth went dry — did he think those were her kids?

"Excuse me, miss."

She waited, expecting some sort of reprimand, then she realized he wanted nothing more than permission to pass. She stepped aside, then stared when he stopped at the seat directly behind hers. A dark-haired man sat there, a man who'd been quietly murmuring into his cell phone ever since boarding at Union Station.

"Sir," the grim-faced conductor said, "may I speak to you for a moment?"

Maybe the porter's mission had nothing to do with the children. Curious, Andie dropped back into her seat. She knew eavesdropping was rude, but why would a conductor seek out a passenger? Had the man behind her boarded without paying? Had he used a counterfeit ticket? Or had someone informed security that a dangerous fugitive had boarded the train?

The passenger told whoever was on the phone that he'd call again later. "Someone here needs my attention," he said, his voice calm and reassuring, "so hold the fort, okay? See you in a few days."

Andie glanced over her shoulder, hoping to catch a glimpse of the man's profile. He sounded far too sophisticated to be an escaped convict or a terrorist, but he could be guilty of some white-collar crime. Extortion, maybe? Embezzlement?

The man stood and moved into the aisle, giving Andie and everyone else a better view of the unfolding situation. The passenger wore a long-sleeved shirt and tie, the uniform of a professional man, and he was at least five inches taller than the Amtrak conductor. Andie smiled when she realized he'd stood to employ an effective bit of body language—intimidation through superior height. She'd read all about subliminal messages and body blocks in one of her business textbooks.

The man gave the conductor a polite smile. "May I help you?"

The conductor lifted his chin. "Sir, I believe you boarded with two children, is that right?"

"Yes."

Andie lifted a brow. So this was about the children. If he was supposed to be caring for those two wildcats, he wasn't doing a very good job.

The conductor showed his teeth in an expression that wasn't a smile. "Where are your children now?"

"They've gone in search of a restroom." Without glancing around, the passenger braced himself on the railing of the overhead baggage compartment, another intimidating posture. "Have my children broken one of your rules?"

"Actually, sir, you have. We require children to be supervised by a parent at all times. If they need to use the restroom, you should safely escort them to the back of the car."

"Really." The man glanced right and left, as if he could will his children into appearing. "They're not babies; they're eight and six. Fully capable of finding their way to a restroom and back."

The conductor gripped the radio hanging from his belt. "No, sir, apparently they are not. The cafe car attendant has corralled them in the lounge. She's holding them until you come pick them up."

"I see." The father pulled a money clip from his pants pocket. "Am I going to have to pay a fine to get them back?"

The conductor's face darkened to an uncomplimentary shade of maroon. "There's no fine, sir, but we don't allow children to run loose on this train. We are not going to release those kids until you take custody and remind your children that train cars are not playgrounds. It's not safe for children to run amok on a train."

At the word amok, the dark-haired man straightened and narrowed his gaze. Fascinated, Andie stared at the father's face, which shifted from calmly self-possessed to unquestionably perturbed. His last expression struck a chord in her memory—she knew this man. She'd seen him and his children at the Chinese restaurant in Washington.

"I beg your pardon—" the father's tone chilled— "but my children have never 'run amok.' They are constantly supervised and exceptionally well-behaved."

Remembering the flying dinner plate, Andie choked on a cough.

To his credit, the conductor didn't argue, but took a half-step back and extended his hand toward the front of the car. "If you please, sir. After you."

A current of whispering flowed through the onlookers as the father straightened his shirtsleeves, adjusted his tie, and walked toward the front of the train without once needing to support himself on another passenger's seat. After he left the car, other people leaned into the aisle and made comments to their neighbors—a couple of people laughed, but six or seven prac-tically growled. One woman didn't bother to lower her voice: "Did you see those two brats runnin' up and down the aisle? Un-leashed terrors, both of 'em."

"I don't know about that." Andie met the woman's eye and offered a peacemaker's smile. "The boy reminds me of my kid brother. He wasn't a brat, just high-spirited."

The woman snorted. "High-spirited today, hoodlum tomorrow."

Andie straightened her spine. "I beg your pardon, but that is definitely not true. My little brother was one of the best kids you could ever meet. He would be one of the finest men I know—if he hadn't died."

When Andie's voice cracked, the woman lowered her gaze and looked away.

Andie slumped in her seat as a wave of remorse flooded over her. She hadn't meant to mention Cole, hadn't wanted to play his death as a trump card in a petty argument. He'd only sprung to mind because something about that little boy reminded her of him, maybe the spark in his eyes or the sly mischief in his smile . . .

Andie reclined her seat and returned to her novel, but soon her eyelids grew heavy. She was about to stop reading when she sensed a subtle shift in the atmosphere. People were craning their necks, so she looked toward the front of the car, where the man and his children had reappeared.

The little girl—who could have been a windblown angel with her brown eyes, round cheeks, and long, tangled hair—skipped in Andie's direction, jostling people as she passed. The boy fol-lowed, his lower lip jutting forward, his reluctant steps heavy on the carpeted floor. The father wore an expression of frustrated discomfort as he herded his offspring back to their seats with a stuffed animal tucked beneath his arm.

When he arrived, he gripped his children's shoulders and pointed to the two empty spaces behind Andie. "That is where you sit," he said, his voice strong and resonant. "Roman, Emilia, into those chairs you go. Now, if you please."

The kids obeyed, settling into their places with a flurry of kicks and jostling elbows. Peeking through the gap between her seat and her companion's, Andie couldn't help noticing that though both children wore designer clothing, the boy's shirt was wrinkled and the little girl's blouse was stained with something that looked like grape juice.

When the children had finally settled, the father pulled two packages of M&Ms from his pocket and tossed a bag to each child. The girl pursed her mouth when she caught the brown bag, and looked as though she might protest—

Andie gripped her armrest, bracing for a scream.

But quick as a flash, the boy exchanged his yellow package for the brown bag in his sister's lap. "Emilia doesn't like the chocolate ones," he told his father. "She likes peanut, I like plain."

The little girl smiled, her dimples winking as she ripped the top of the yellow bag with her teeth.

Andie relaxed, then sneaked another glance at the man in the aisle. What sort of father didn't know what candy his kids liked?

The dad sighed and looked around, obviously aware that other passengers were watching with undisguised interest. For an instant a look of sad weariness passed over his face, then he seemed to collect himself. "Let those with perfect children—" his stentorian voice carried over the hum of the moving train as he smiled— "cast the first stone."

He sank into the empty seat across from his kids. Not wanting to turn and stare, Andie found herself studying his polished leather shoes, one of which had been thrust into the aisle and into her peripheral vision. When he shook open a newspaper, she had to wonder—was he truly interested in the news of the day or was he, like her, using his reading material as a shield?

After a moment, she exhaled a sigh and crossed her arms. Whatever the man's motivation, he had nothing to do with her.

He and his kids would probably get off at the next stop and she'd never see them again.

She closed her eyes and hugged her book to her chest. Sometimes, when she considered the ramifications of everything she'd done to establish a safe distance between Christy Huggins and Andie Crystal, she deeply regretted not being able to enjoy her nieces and nephews.

But not today.

Andie wasn't sure how long she slept, but before reaching full consciousness she felt a hovering presence — and opened her eyes in time to be blinded by an unexpected flash.

After a moment of painful squinting, she found herself staring into the face of the brown-haired girl who had been sitting behind her. No longer hugging her stuffed animal or eating M&Ms; the child was pointing a digital camera straight at Andie. "I know you." She grinned over the top of the seat formerly occupied by a teenage boy. "You're Christy Huggins and you sing on TV."

Andie blinked the remnants of blindness away, more than a little disconcerted to have been discovered by a pint-sized peeper.

"My name is Andie." Her voice emerged in a sleep-encrusted croak. "And I'm not on TV. I'm on a train."

"I love Christy and Cole and Carma and Carin and Charlie Huggins," the little girl insisted in a singsong lilt. "And Hannah Montana, Justin Bieber, and Selena. I love everyone who sings on TV."

"Emilia." The father's voice rumbled from across the aisle. "You shouldn't invade other people's privacy. Get back to your seat, please, or I'll have to confiscate your camera."

Ordinarily Andie would have assured the man that his daughter had done no harm, but the child's perceptiveness left her flustered . . . and a little worried. The girl obediently walked back to her seat, and a moment later Andie glanced behind her and saw that the child had pulled a coloring book from a pink backpack.

Maybe that would hold her attention for a while.

Across the aisle, the father leaned over his armrest and waved for Andie's attention. "You'll have to forgive my daughter — she imagines herself a celebrity photographer. Last week she thought she saw Hannah Montana at the grocery store."

Andie worked up a tentative smile. "At least she's not spotting Elvis on every corner."

"Right." He laughed. "Well, sorry if she woke you. My children are a little wound up. Excited about the trip and all."

As if to prove him right, the boy appeared in the aisle, having clambered over his sister. At close range he bore an amazing resemblance to his dad. They shared the same chin, dark hair, and brown eyes. Parentheses marked the father's mouth, however, giving him a look of determination, yet shadows moved in his eyes. Andie recognized those dark shades, having glimpsed them in her own face. They were the shadows of loss.

She reached out and touched the boy's arm. "You remind me of my little brother. He was my favorite person in all the world."

The boy blinked at her, his eyes alight with the same spark of intelligence that had lit Cole's.

"Anyway," the father said, "I apologize if my children bothered you."

"They aren't a bother. They're just high-spirited." She studied the boy, the girl, and the father. The empty seat next to the man raised a question: where was the mother of these children?

The boy tugged on his father's sleeve. "Dad, can I please have my game?"

"May you have your game? Yes, you may."

The father stood and began to rummage through the overhead bin, tossing smaller items onto his seat as he searched for whatever game the boy wanted. Andie watched as the dad dropped a child-sized jacket in Washington Redskins colors, a folded trench coat, its buckles swinging free, and a small lavender blue coat with black velvet trim—

The sight of that pretty little coat brought a smile to Andie's face. Judging from what she'd witnessed at the Chinese restaurant, the Redskins ought to audition that little girl as a kicker.

"Here." Dad uncovered a navy blue backpack and handed it to his son. The boy unzipped it, pulled out some kind of handheld electronic gizmo, and settled back into his seat.

As the father stuffed all the paraphernalia back into the storage bin, Andie forced herself to make polite conversation. "Are you on a family vacation?"

The man glanced over his shoulder and nodded. "I'm taking the kids to visit my mother in Charleston. I thought about flying, but I get to spend so little time with these two, I thought we'd do something special. Make a few memories while we can."

"Are you from the District?"

"I work in Washington, but we live in Virginia. We'll be spending a couple of days in Williamsburg before moving on."

A nebulous realization began to form in Andie's brain. The odds were astronomical, but if this family wasn't on the same tour, what were the chances they would board in D.C. and visit Williamsburg before going to Grandma's house?

"Did you, by chance—" she smiled—"purchase a ten-day train tour through the South?"

The man's preoccupied expression morphed into one of surprise. "You, too?"

When she nodded, his surprise faded to relief. "And here I thought I'd be desperately lacking for adult conversation over the next several days." He extended a broad palm into the aisle. "Matthew Scofield."

Andie accepted the second handshake she'd been offered that day. "Andie Crystal."

He released her hand and pointed to his daughter. "That's Emilia, and the handsome kid sitting by the window is Roman." At the sound of his name, the boy lifted his gaze from his game, his face brightening as he grinned. She grinned back, finding it hard to imagine how any kid with so much life in his eyes could be named after an empire long relegated to dusty ruins.

She gestured to the empty seat. "Is your wife traveling with you?"

Matthew's gaze shifted to empty space. "I lost my wife just over a year ago. The kids have had a nanny since losing their mother, but last month Nessa went back to Ireland to marry her sweetheart. We've tried babysitters who haven't worked out, so we haven't quite decided what to do next."

"I'm so sorry."

Their conversation ceased as a heavy woman in navy pants and a white shirt approached from the rear of the car. "Tickets," she said, clicking a hole punch as she stopped beside the Scofields' seats. Still standing, Matthew pulled three tickets from his pants pocket. The conductor ripped off the body of the tickets and handed Matthew the stubs. Before moving on, she wrote WBG on three narrow cards and slipped them into niches above the family's seats.

Andie handed the woman her ticket, knowing better than to hand over her driver's license as well.

"Williamsburg," the woman murmured, writing the station code on a slip of paper. She placed it in the slot above Andie's head and moved on.

Andie caught Matthew's eye. "Can you believe how lax the security is? No one checked my suitcase even in Washington."

"And not a metal detector in sight." He chuckled and sat on the armrest of his seat. "After all the fuss they put you through at airports, riding the rails is sort of refreshing."

"Christy, Christy." Emilia's brown eyes appeared over Andie's headrest, then she folded her arms and began to sing the theme song from *Home with the Huggins*: "If you need a friend, if you need a smile, come to the Huggins' house for a while . . ."

"Like I said, too much TV." Matthew ran his hand through his hair. "Emilia, if you don't use your inside voice, a lot of tired people are going to be upset with you."

The girl's voice trailed away, then her big brown eyes focused on Andie. "She doesn't mind, Daddy, 'cause it's her song. She's Christy Huggins."

An alarm clanged in Andie's head, but Matthew Scofield appeared oblivious to the effect of his daughter's words. "Don't mind her," he said, shrugging. "I tell her not to watch so much TV, but it's hard to monitor their activities when I'm at work. Since Nessa left, I've had a terrible time finding reliable babysitters."

Andie didn't care about his babysitting problems, but she was desperate to change the subject. "What do you do?"

"I'm a lawyer." The corner of his mouth quirked in a wry smile. "Immigration law. So if you ever need a nanny, I could put you in touch—"

Without warning, his precocious daughter leapt from her seat and landed in his arms, announcing that she had to go to the bathroom and he had to take her.

Andie smiled and looked away, more than willing to let the conversation end.

Her stomach began to rumble when they were still an hour away from Williamsburg. While she didn't think the train had a dining car, she kept seeing people walk by with hot dogs, mini-pizzas, and something that looked like a collision between a bagel and a slab of Velveeta. None of the food looked very appetizing, but the aromas proved irresistible.

She pulled herself from the security of her seat, settled her purse on her shoulder, and walked toward the front of the train as best she could. When the train lurched to the right, she reached out to brace herself and ended up clawing the shoulder of an elderly man. He winked and gave her a knowing smile. "The trick to train walkin'," he said, "is to keep your feet shoulder-width apart and sort of teeter-totter as you go. That'll keep you upright as you get along."

She nodded her thanks and took his advice, moving forward with one hand outstretched as she rocked from left to right. The method wasn't the most graceful way to traverse a train, but at least she was making steady progress.

She traveled through two other passenger cars without mishap, though she nearly yanked the ear buds from a teenage boy whose rock music buzzed like an agitated beehive. She shuddered as she hurried through the junctions where the cars connected—warning signs reminded her that standing in those spots wasn't safe. She couldn't help but imagine what might happen if the cars separated while someone stood in the gap.

She exhaled a sigh when she finally entered the cafe car, a long rectangular space dedicated to a snack bar. Several tables and benches stood against the opposite wall and a queue of people waited patiently for food.

A woman stood ahead of her in the snack line, but Andie didn't look closely until the woman placed her order. "I'll have a hot dog," the lady told the girl behind the bar. "And a diet soda."

Her accent sounded familiar, and when Andie leaned forward she recognized the woman from Union Station and the taxi. What was her name? Now that they were no longer shrouded in pre-dawn gloom, she could see that her taxi companion looked more rested than she had the first night they met. Her dark pants were wrinkle free, her hair neatly styled, and her tailored shirt probably came from Talbots or Ann Taylor. Her left eye, though, still looked as though it had been smeared with makeup that wasn't doing a good job of camouflaging the bruise beneath it.

She had said she was traveling to escape . . . was she running from the guy who'd given her that black eye? Andie's fingers curled into a fist as she considered the sort of man who might hit a woman as genteel as this one seemed to be. What kind of brute was he?

When the woman turned, Andie flashed a quick smile and hoped her thoughts weren't written on her face. "Small world, huh?"

The woman blinked. "Andie?"

"And you're . . . Annette?"

"Close enough—Janette. Did you come in search of breakfast, too?"

"Yeah. Though I was kind of hoping for bacon and eggs."

"Afraid you'll have to find an official dining car for that— and this train doesn't have one."

The girl behind the counter pulled a cellophane-wrapped hot dog from the microwave and dropped it into a box tray, then set a can of diet Pepsi next to it. "Anything else?"

Janette squinted toward the candy display. "Maybe a bag of Skittles?"

"You want the red bag or the orange?"

"What's the difference?"

"Beats me."

Janette sighed. "Red, then. I know I like those."

The girl tossed a bag of candy into the tray, then took the proffered cash. Janette lifted her cardboard tray and moved toward the baskets of condiments at end of the counter.

"I'll have a burger and a bag of chips," Andie told the cashier. "And a bottle of water, please."

While the girl microwaved the burger, Andie helped herself to a cardboard tray and looked around for Janette, who had taken a seat at one of the tables. Maybe, like Andie, she'd grown tired of staring at naked trees outside the window.

After paying for her food, Andie slid onto the bench opposite her new acquaintance. "I hope you don't mind if I join you, but I'm getting tired of the view from my seat. I brought a book with me, but where I'm sitting there are too many distractions to read."

"I know. I thought I would use my travel time to do some deep thinking. Instead, I take naps. Lots of them." A quick smile flashed across Janette's face, then she bowed her head for a moment. Andie watched, bemused, until the woman lifted her head and bit into her hot dog.

Okay—the woman was religious and prayed before meals. As long as she didn't preach or insist Jesus was a Republican, they ought to get along.

Andie ripped open a packet of mustard and squirted the contents onto a gray slab of processed beef.

Janette wiped her mouth with a corner of her napkin. "Where are you from, Andie?"

"Providence. Rhode Island."

"And you're traveling to . . . ?"

"Williamsburg, for now. This trip is my boss's idea of a wonderful vacation. I told him I'd rather stay home, but he seems to think I need to see America before I go back to work."

Janette chuckled. "I don't know how you're going to see the country from the train. I've been riding the rails since Little Rock, I haven't seen much besides trees and industrial districts."

"You didn't go sight-seeing in Washington?"

She shook her head. "I slept. Like a dead woman. I must have been more exhausted than I realized."

Andie took a bite of her burger and studied the woman across the table. She'd watched enough Dr. Phil and Oprah to know that grieving or depressed women often slept too much. They did it to escape, and Andie understood escape. She'd been perfecting the art for years.

With an effort, she swallowed the mediocre burger. "You came all the way from Arkansas?"

Janette nodded. "I rode more than thirty hours on the first leg of this trip, and I had to sleep sitting up. Aside from swollen ankles, I didn't mind too much. Getting away was worth the aggravation of puffy feet."

Because she didn't want to pry, Andie ripped open her bag of chips and searched for a safe, unobtrusive question. "So where are you getting off?"

"Williamsburg, same as you. But I don't have a clue what I'll do when I get there."

"Neither do I." Andie smiled, aware of how stupid her answer sounded. "The company gave me this tour package—ten glorious days exploring the Southern seaboard. But so far it's felt like ten days of figuring out how to entertain myself in a hotel room."

Janette laughed. "Tell me about it. I bought the same package."

"You chose it? On purpose?"

She shrugged. "First thing I saw that appealed to me. More than anything, I wanted to leave town for a while." Her eyes cleared, as if her thoughts had sharpened. "You know, there are some interesting sites in Williamsburg. The College of William and Mary is lovely, plus there's a mile of buildings from the original settlement. The shopping's good, too."

"You've been there?"

"Years ago . . . but I think I'll enjoy seeing it again." She gave Andie a confident smile. "If you want company in Williamsburg, give me a call. I'd be happy to show you around—if I can remember where to go." She pulled a business card from her wallet and pointed to the number at the bottom. "That's my cell phone. If I have the phone turned off, leave a voice mail and I'll call you back."

Andie glanced at the dark print: Janette Turlington, Manager, Community Christian Thrift Store. "You manage a thrift store? I'll bet that's interesting."

Janette's lips twitched with amusement. "It can be—you wouldn't believe some of the donations that come in. But I like to think we provide an important service—not only do we help people clean out their basements, but we provide inexpensive goods to the community. Plus, after paying our full-time employees, all our profits go to organizations who feed the poor."

"Your work sounds a lot more admirable than mine. I'm in sales, too—but sometimes I think most of our customers are bored women. And our products aren't exactly inexpensive."

"Let me guess—cookware?"

"Not quite."

"Clothing?"

"Cosmetics, mostly, on the Value Price Network. And though I'd never admit this in public, the goop we sell for $90 a jar isn't much better than the stuff you can pick up for ten bucks at the corner drugstore."

"Thanks for the tip. I'll keep it in mind." Janette popped the last of her hot dog into her mouth, washed it down with a swallow of soda, and dropped the Skittles into her purse. She lifted her cardboard tray. "Good to run into you again, Andie. Don't forget to give me a call if you want company in Williamsburg."

"Are you sure? If you have other plans I wouldn't want to intrude—"

"I have no plans at all, and I'm tired of sleeping." A note of relief echoed in her voice. "For the next few days, absolutely no one is depending on me for anything."

# Chapter Five

The Williamsburg depot reminded Andie of Disney World—the charming, traditional building featured Victorian spindles and cream colored arches that supported swaying fern baskets. A uniformed attendant stood on the brick sidewalk, his blue eyes intent as he waited to welcome arriving passengers.

Maneuvering through the crowded aisle, Andie gathered her luggage and hauled her belongings down the steps. On the sidewalk, as she stacked her briefcase and purse on top of her suitcase, she saw Matthew Scofield calling out warnings to his children as he organized his family's bags.

Giving the family a wide berth, she gripped her suitcase and strode into the depot, heading straight for the front door. According to her itinerary, she had a room reserved at the Hampton Inn, and at that moment she could think of nothing more relaxing than being horizontal on a comfortable mattress for an hour or two.

She was at the curb, waving at a taxi driver, when Matthew and his children appeared behind her. "There's Christy," the little girl squealed.

Andie resisted the impulse to cut and run. "My name is Andie." She made the correction with a smile. "And you're Emilia."

Her father stepped to the curb. "Are you at the Hampton, by chance?"

Andie suppressed a groan. "Um . . . yes."

"I thought you might be, since we're on the same tour. Want to share a cab?"

Several objections leapt to the forefront of Andie's mind, but Roman had already opened the back door to her taxi and Emilia was climbing in.

Andie bit her lip and looked at the cabbie, an elderly man who had just grabbed her suitcase. "You know the Hampton Inn on Richmond Road?"

"Of course." The driver, who barely came up to her shoulder, flashed a big smile. "You and your family on vacation?"

"We're not—"

"Close enough." Matthew patted the old man's shoulder. "Thanks for the help."

They rode to the hotel together, Andie flattened against the door on one side of the cab, the lawyer squashed against the other. Between them, Roman sat ramrod straight in order to look out the windows, and Emilia clutched her stuffed animal and gazed at Andie as if she were Hannah Montana, Selena Gomez, and Justin Bieber all rolled into one.

"If you need a friend, if you need a smile," she sang, her stare burning holes into Andie's face, "Come to the Huggins' house for a while . . ." She leaned closer, bracing herself on Andie's knee. "Don't you want to sing?"

"Your kids seem to have enjoyed the train," Andie said, struggling to divert the girl's focus. "Do you all have exciting plans for Williamsburg?"

Roman tugged on his father's sleeve. "Dad! The lady's talking to you."

"Hmm? Oh." The lawyer turned from the window and

glanced at his children as if he was a bit frightened by the prospect of being alone with them. "I don't know what we're going to do for the rest of the day. I hear the hotel has an indoor pool, so I imagine that's where we'll go first."

The boy's head whipped toward his sister. "Did you hear that, Emilia? We can go swimming!"

"If you want to." Matthew's mouth tightened and his throat bobbed as he swallowed. "I have to make some phone calls, but I'll watch while you swim. How does that sound?"

Andie thought his plan sounded like something invented by a man reluctant to leave the office behind, but what this family did or didn't do was none of her business.

"Daddy, I don't know how to swim." Emilia's voice thinned to a plaintive whine. "You have to get in the water and teach me."

"I have to make calls, honey. I have clients."

"But I don't know how to swim. What if I drown?"

"You won't drown. I won't let you."

The girl held up her threadbare stuffed animal. "What if Walter drowns?"

Walter, Andie realized, had to be Emilia's lovey, her favorite toy. When she tilted her head to see the animal better, she discovered that the toy she'd assumed to be a bear was actually a dinosaur. At one time he must have been plush and attractive, but the years had worn his fur away and someone had broken his neck. His oversized head flopped from side to side, his felt tongue had split, and two empty circles were all that remained of what must have been button eyes.

Matthew Scofield stroked his daughter's hair. "Walter won't drown, Emilia. He doesn't like the water."

"He does!"

"No, I don't think he does. Dinosaurs don't swim. You can check the fossil record."

Emilia's mouth puckered into a frown. Before Andie could be asked for her opinion, she turned to look out the window.

Dozens of brick colonial buildings were sliding by, reinforcing the impression that they had traveled back to colonial times. She knew very little about Williamsburg, but she suspected that the city building code required every structure to utilize bricks and shuttered windows on the facade. All the local restaurants — even the astoundingly numerous pancake houses — featured colonial exteriors.

Ten minutes later the cab pulled beneath a portico attached to a handsome hotel: brick, of course, with shutters at the tall rectangular windows. Andie hopped out the left side while Matthew Scofield tumbled out of the right passenger doorway and attempted to herd his energetic children toward the hotel entrance.

"Thanks for sharing the cab," Andie called, slipping the driver her share of the fare plus a tip. "And have a nice visit. 'Bye, kids."

Matthew looked up as if he was about to say something, but just then Emilia yanked on his sleeve and screeched for his attention. While the lawyer tended to his daughter, Andie slipped inside and beelined toward the reservation desk. On her way through the lobby, though, she spotted a tabloid newspaper on a coffee table, a bold headline centered on the front page: Mona Huggins Near Death; Children Gathering at her Bedside.

Reality swept over Andie in a powerful wave she could no longer resist. Mr. Reuben's call had disturbed her, but seeing the truth spelled out in bold black newsprint brought the truth home in a way nothing else could.

Every disaster in her life had been trumpeted in a headline. Cole's death. Her parents' divorce. Her father's death. Charlie's stint in rehab. Callie's drug arrest. Even her own "disappearance."

She turned away from the coffee table, head lowered, as a cloud of anguish and guilt threatened to engulf her.

◆

Worn out by travel and haunted by the thought that her mother's illness had made the national news, Andie spent the afternoon locked away in her room. She'd been thinking a lot about her family in the last couple of days, and pain squeezed her heart every time she imagined her brothers and sisters gathering around her mom's hospital bed. If it hurt so much to think about them, how much more would it hurt to join them?

She sat on the edge of her bed and did a quick survey of the entertainment-focused programs on TV. None of them mentioned the Huggins family, so the tabloid reporters were way ahead of the others in covering her mother's illness . . . unless the major networks had decided to ignore Mona Huggins altogether.

She powered off the TV and closed her eyes, realizing that not even media silence could dispel the cloud hanging over her head. She didn't know if she was feeling depression, sadness, despair, or a mixture of all three, but the air in the room felt stale and she was desperate to get outside. She needed to go for a walk, she needed to talk to someone, anyone who could take her mind off all things Huggins. But who did she know in Williamsburg?

She had only two names on her list, four if she counted the kids. She pulled Janette Turlington's card from her wallet and picked up her cell phone. Should she call? Janette might be out, but if she was also feeling adrift, maybe she'd welcome some company.

Janette answered on the first ring. "Hello?"

"Hi, it's Andie. I hope I'm not disturbing you."

"Of course not." Her voice warmed Andie's ear. "Did you get checked into your room okay?"

"Everything's fine. Listen, I wondered if you want to go get something to eat. The Hampton doesn't have a restaurant, so we'll have to walk unless you want to call a cab—"

"Great idea. I'm at the Quality Inn right next door."

"Then you probably saw the Olive Garden just down the road. Shall I meet you outside your hotel so we can walk over? Say . . . in fifteen minutes?"

A few minutes later, Andie buttoned up her pea coat and waited for Janette in a patch of fading sunlight. As the shadows of evening stretched across the parking lot, the streetlights came on and the cars on the highway faded to twin dots of white and red lights. The air chilled, the wind turned brisk. Andie realized her cheeks would be chapped if she had to wait much longer.

She was beginning to wonder if she'd been stood up when she saw Janette approaching, her arms crossed over her chest, her head wrapped in a bright gold scarf. She wore her red coat and rubbed her arms as if she were freezing. Her mouth curved in a smile when she saw Andie.

"Sorry I'm late." Her eyes seemed unusually shiny. "I got held up. Lots of phone messages."

Andie peered at her, sensing that something had gone wrong. This was not the confident woman she met in the cafe car — either she'd been crying or she wasn't feeling well. She had that feverish, bright-eyed look Andie's younger siblings used to get whenever they were coming down with something. The makeup around her eye looked even worse than usual because the bruise had faded from black to green and purple. Cheap makeup wasn't going to disguise that colorful combination.

Andie didn't feel comfortable asking a virtual stranger why she looked bruised and wet-eyed, so she held her tongue. "Don't worry about it. Want to start walking?"

They moved out of the parking lot, neither of them talking as they crossed to the sidewalk. Janette took long strides for a woman, and Andie found herself working hard to keep up. She was accustomed to walking, but Janette, who was probably old enough to be Andie's mother, was definitely in better shape.

Andie made a mental note: spend more time on the treadmill.

They were both out of breath by the time they arrived at the restaurant. Dozens of people clustered around heaters in the outdoor waiting area, and Andie feared they'd have to go elsewhere. But Janette breezed through the doorway and gave her name to the hostess.

"There's a twenty-minute wait," the girl said, slouching over her seating chart. "Unless you want to eat at the bar."

Janette lifted a brow and glanced at Andie for confirmation, then nodded to the hostess. Andie worked at unbuttoning her coat as the hostess led them to a spillover area where a high counter ran the length of a solid wall. The waitress dropped laminated menus on the tiled countertop and left.

"This okay?" Janette asked.

Andie nodded. "Whatever. I'm starving, so I don't care where we eat."

They climbed onto stools at the counter, then picked up the menus. Andie would never have wanted to eat in front of a plaster wall if she were dining out with co-workers, but this was merely a meal of convenience, a way to keep another traveler company.

Janette and Andie both decided on soup and salad, and placed their orders with the frazzled waitress who finally appeared with glasses of water. As the server hurried away, Andie smoothed her jeans and sipped from her glass. Living alone had taught her to be comfortable with solitude, so she often found herself uncomfortable with small talk. But Janette didn't seem to pose a threat. She hadn't mentioned Andie's resemblance to anyone on TV, nor had she remarked that Andie looked familiar. Maybe she'd never heard of the Huggins family.

Andie sipped from her glass again. She figured they should talk, but what should they talk about? When her gaze fell on Janette's wedding ring, she decided to take the initiative. If she asked the first question, maybe she could open up the topic of Janette's bruised face. Maybe the woman was desperate to talk, if only someone would provide an opportunity.

Andie took a deep breath and lowered her glass. "I see that you're married. Do you have a large family?"

At the mention of the word family, Janette's lips thinned. "I have a husband—" her voice sounded strained—"a really good man. And we have a daughter. That's it, just the one child."

Andie hesitated. Whenever she had to conduct an interview at work, she usually asked a prospective employee about her family and spent the rest of the allotted time murmuring in agreement. Most people loved to talk about their spouses and children, rarely even realizing that the other person wasn't adding much to the conversation. But Janette, apparently, wasn't like most people.

Andie waited for Janette to say something else, but the woman only pulled the straw from her water glass and dropped it on the counter, then proceeded to drink as if she were dying from thirst. Andie kept waiting, expecting more details about Janette's husband or daughter, but the woman didn't volunteer another word.

Andie could understand why Janette might not want to talk about the husband who'd hit her. But why wouldn't she talk about her daughter? She hadn't mentioned the girl's age, what she was doing, whether or not she had a family of her own . . .

Crossing her legs, Andie searched fruitlessly for the waitress and decided that she'd simply have to change the subject. If Janette wanted to keep quiet about her family, maybe she'd be willing to talk about her job. Maybe, like Andie, she was centering her life around her work.

"So you manage a thrift store." She returned her gaze to her companion. "I'll bet you've picked up some interesting stories in your work."

"Oh, yes." Janette's expression relaxed as the waitress came over with their salads. "Most people think my job is easy, but it isn't. Mainly because I have to manage a team of volunteers."

"Volunteers aren't easy?"

Janette raised her gaze to the ceiling. "Heavens, no. They're a trial."

Andie shifted to face her, honestly surprised by her response. "I work in customer service, so I deal with difficult people all the time. But my complainers have paid for a product, so they can be ticked about anything from the quality of a face cream to the packaging it came in—"

"Oh, I get complaints from customers, too," Janette said. "People who get upset because they paid fifty cents for a shirt, took it home, and stained it when they washed it with a marker in the pocket. I can handle the customers. It's my staff that gives me fits."

"How so?"

Janette groaned as she lifted the serving tongs. "Since my people are volunteers—" she filled Andie's plate with salad— "I can't fire them. But because they're not paid, they think they have a right to take anything they see on the shelves. We lose a lot of stock—a lot—to our staff, because they're always pilfering. I keep trying to tell them that these goods have been donated to bring in money for community programs, but either they don't hear me or they don't listen. Don't get me wrong—most of them are angels, hard-working and generous, but some of them are genuine rascals. The rascals drive me crazy."

"I know what you mean," Andie assured her. "Once I saw that one of my call center operators had tucked more than ten tubes of New Dawn Sunscreen in her purse. When I asked why she thought she was entitled to them, she said, 'Why wouldn't I be?'"

Janette shot Andie a quizzical look, so she explained her work at the Value Price Network. "I started on the ground floor," she finished. "I worked every single day the doors were open, and that's why I'm on this train trip. My boss decided it was time the company showed its appreciation."

"Could have been worse." Janette picked up her fork and

stabbed a green pepper. "They could have sent you to some place like the Galapagos Islands."

Andie laughed. "Actually, the Galapagos aren't a bad idea. Peace and quiet, not a lot of people—"

"You must be an introvert."

"Maybe. I like people, I just . . . well, I like peace and quiet more."

"I think I understand. Excuse me a moment." ·

As Janette prayed over her food, Andie welcomed the break in conversation, not wanting to explain how her previous life had left her shattered and overexposed. If Janette wanted to think of her as a recluse, that was okay. But just because she liked peace and quiet didn't mean she didn't care about people. She cared plenty about her employees, her job, and her cat. She cared about her family, though it broke her heart to think about them, and she cared about the battered woman who sat across from her. If Janette had left home to escape, surely she needed someone to talk to. And who better than a virtual stranger?

"By the way—" Andie cast Janette a sidelong glance when she lifted her head— "you haven't mentioned why you're on this trip."

Janette took a bite, not looking at Andie until she had swallowed and used her napkin to dab at her mouth. "I did tell you." She picked up her knife and fork. "I needed to escape."

Andie was about to joke that Janette hadn't given much her of an answer, but at that moment the waitress came toward them with two steaming bowls on her tray. As they pushed their salad plates aside to make room, Janette chattered brightly about how good everything was. She ladled up a spoonful of soup and tasted it, then rolled her eyes in exaggerated pleasure.

Andie sighed, understanding more than Janette realized. The older woman would rather talk about soup and salad than explain her reasons for coming on this trip. Maybe she'd open up later, but she didn't want to talk about anything personal just yet. Maybe she didn't trust Andie, or maybe she felt they didn't know each other well enough.

Andie stirred the concoction in her bowl, breathing in the scents of pepper and sausage. "I love this stuff. I could eat it every day."

"Me, too." Janette's eyes flashed in gratitude—not for the soup, Andie would have wagered, but for the change of subject.

She tasted the fragrant broth. After swallowing, she found Janette studying her with an intense expression. "You remind me of someone." Her brows drew together. "I can't figure out who, but it's someone I either know or knew a while back."

"I have one of those everyday faces." Andie stirred her bowl again and braced herself for the inevitable. "Everyone says I remind them of someone—a cousin, an old friend, someone in a movie—"

"But it's not only your face—even your voice sounds familiar. A minute ago you laughed, and I had a moment of déjà vu."

"I read something about that the other day." Andie propped her elbow on the table. "According to this one scientist, déjà vu occurs when a current situation matches a fuzzy memory stored in the brain's hippocampus. It's sort of like thinking you recognize someone in a blurry surveillance tape, but you're not really recognizing them. You just think you are."

Janette lifted both brows. "You read a lot of science?"

"I read all kinds of things." Andie waved to catch the waitress's attention. "Can we get our check, please?"

Janette pulled her napkin from her lap, then set it by her empty bowl. "I guess I'm at the age where everyone looks like someone from the past. When you're more than halfway to a hundred, I suppose it can't be helped."

"Maybe."

The waitress brought the check and they pulled out their wallets to divvy up the bill. They didn't talk much on the chilly walk back to their hotels, but when they parted, Andie found herself thanking Janette with complete sincerity. "I wouldn't have come out by myself, and I'd have gone crazy if I'd stayed in my room," she said. "So thanks for coming along."

She hadn't come on this trip intending to make a friend, but she'd stumbled upon someone with secrets of her own. If they could respect each other's boundaries, they might actually enjoy the journey ahead.

◆

The weekly tabloid, *Celebrity Chatter*, was still on the coffee table when Andie came through the hotel lobby. Since no one seemed likely to claim it before the cleaning crew came through, she grabbed the paper and continued to the elevator, then headed directly to her room on the fourth floor.

Once she was safely locked in for the night, she fell onto the bed, switched on the lamp, and turned to the article about her mother:

### Mona Huggins Near Death; Children Gathering at her Bedside

Mona Huggins, mother to the brood which starred in the nineties reality show, *Home with the Huggins*, has been diagnosed with cervical cancer, her agent announced last week. Oliver Weinstein, who represented the family through seven seasons on the Entertainment Television Network, released a statement saying that Huggins had been undergoing treatment for several months, but had reached a point where "no further treatment is advisable. We have notified the Huggins children and expect them to rally around their mother as she enters her final days."

The musical Huggins, commonly considered the reality version of the Partridge Family, frequently earned top ratings while the show aired from 1995-2001. Weekly episodes featured the parents and six children as they struggled to maintain a balance between their personal lives and their jobs as professional performers. The child stars enjoyed the celebrity granted to teen idols, licensing their likenesses to be showcased on dolls, board games, and karaoke machines. The production consistently ranked in the top ten cable shows until a tragic 2001 accident caused a permanent rupture in the family. After an auto crash in which sixteen-year-old Cole Huggins died, the family dispersed, the older children retreating into private life while Mona Huggins struggled to maintain control of the family's accumulated assets. Chester Huggins, the family patriarch, divorced his wife in late 2001 and moved to Kansas, where a year later he died from a coronary event.

Mona Huggins filed for bankruptcy in 2004, but was allowed to keep the spacious family home that had served as a setting for the TV reality series.

Where are the Huggins children now?

- After struggling with alcoholism and spending time in rehab, Charlie Huggins married his long-time girlfriend, Bettina (fans may recall her appearing sporadically on the show), and moved to Houston, where he is a web designer. He and Bettina are raising three children, none of whom sing. When reached by telephone, he would not comment on the news about his mother.
- Carin Huggins graduated from Harvard and settled in Boston, where she manages a bank. She never married and could not be reached for comment.
- Christy Huggins, the lead vocalist for the family, disappeared not long after the series went off the air. Several sources have claimed she is living under an assumed name in Ireland, where the family spent one autumn

filming a Christmas special. No one has been able to verify her current location.

- Carma Huggins attended UCLA. She married a veterinarian and lives in Charleston, SC with her husband and two children.

- Callister Huggins, the youngest of the surviving children, remained with his mother after the show's cancellation. Now 25, he frequently attends acting auditions and reportedly sleeps in his van when away from home. He told a Chatter reporter, "Of course, we're all terribly upset about Mom, but we're going to do all we can to make her last days memorable."

When asked if the network would consider filming a deathbed reunion as a Huggins homecoming event, agent Oliver Weinstein would only say, "Stay tuned."

Andie greedily devoured the details about her siblings, but Oliver's comment—if what she'd read could be trusted—left her feeling nauseous. If her mother was truly at death's door, she couldn't imagine anything more tasteless or invasive than inviting cameras to film her final days. As kids, they'd grown up with cameras in the house, and in no time they learned how to put on a "show face" and play to the invisible audience. Her younger siblings were even more camera-conscious than Andie, able to switch from their honest faces to their show faces in a microsecond.

In her last moments, how could any woman prefer false faces over honesty?

Oliver couldn't have been serious when he spoke with this reporter. Surely not even Callie would want to use their mother's death as an opportunity to thrust himself back in the spotlight.

Andie pushed the idea away and savored the updates on her siblings. She could have asked her lawyer for news about them at any time; he would have made the necessary inquiries and reported back. But caution kept her from asking—caution and concern that one of them would learn where she was and reveal her new name to the press. Once exposed, all the work she'd done to walk away from Christy Huggins would be pointless. She'd be jettisoned back into a life she never wanted and into a celebrity she despised. Nothing could persuade her to risk her hard-won freedom, not even contact with her brothers and sisters.

She never would have believed a copy of *Celebrity Chatter* could bring unexpected delights. She smiled and ran her finger over the names of her siblings. So . . . Charlie married Bettina after all. She knew he wanted to, but Bettina would never have married him if he kept drinking. Andie knew she could have read all about his drinking and rehab in some gossip magazine, but they had a habit of using random facts to fabricate scenarios that weren't at all accurate.

Charlie living in Houston . . . that was a surprise. Then again, he had always loved the Lone Star state, saying everything in Texas was bigger and better than anywhere else. She wouldn't be surprised if his kids wore cowboy hats to school. Three kids— boys or girls or both? She shook her head, regretting that the tabloid hadn't provided more details.

Carin . . . when they weren't on camera or on stage, she'd always buried her nose in a book. Andie wasn't surprised to learn that Carin ran a bank, and she was sure her sister's bank was the best in the area. Years before, when Andie read about her sister's graduation from Harvard, she'd wondered how many reporters tried to snap photos of Carin as she trekked back and forth across the Cambridge campus. With the paparazzi nipping at her heels, no wonder Carin never married. What kind of guy would put up with all that?

Carma still lived in Charleston, and that was good news. Apparently she and her husband had made a permanent home for their children. But how could Callie still be in LA? Andie was only a little surprised to learn that he'd stayed with their mother; as the baby of the family he was always ducking responsibility. Since he was only fourteen when the show ended, he might feel like he somehow got short-changed since he hadn't enjoyed all the attention the older kids received. Mom must have kept him close, feeding his dreams of stardom and paying his bills while he searched for celebrity, never realizing that fame meant nothing once the lights had gone dark.

Because the lights did go dark. Whether suddenly or gradually, curtains fell, shows were cancelled, relevance faded, and celebrity dimmed. Oh, people would still know your name and face, but they only wanted to touch a reminder of what you'd once been. They cared nothing about what you really were, the mature person you had become.

For a few years the Huggins were America's favorite clan, a real-life musical family with more than its fair share of children, talent, opportunity, wholesome good looks, and love.

But everything America—and Andie—believed about the Huggins family shattered the moment a semi plowed into their SUV.

Andie closed her eyes on the memory of that wet, horrific night. Callie and Cole were close, but none of the kids had been tighter than Andie and Cole. Her little brother depended on her, and that night she let him down.

But at least she didn't kill him.

# Chapter Six

As the elevator doors slid open the next morning, the aromas of baking waffles and brewing coffee enticed Andie to the hotel's crowded dining area. Wide windows ran the length of the pleasant room, and through them she could see the indoor pool shimmering serene and empty.

On her side of the window, solo diners occupied several breakfast tables—mostly men and women in business suits, eating with newspapers in hand while their eyes occasionally flicked toward the wall-mounted television airing the morning news. She had expected to see more tourists, but at this time of year most children were in school. Matthew Scofield must have pulled some strings to get his kids out for a vacation.

Yet not everyone was traveling on business. A group of older ladies crowded a round table in the corner, and the lawyer from the train sat with his children in the center of the room—at least, he was trying to sit. The moment his rear came anywhere near the chair, either the boy or the girl asked for something else, and Mr. Lawyer rocketed off to get it.

Andie smothered a smile. The sight of Matthew Scofield with his kids reminded him of how she and her siblings had kept both parents hopping up and down for one thing or another. Her mother had always maintained that it was her responsibility to cook the meal; Dad had to take care of silverware, plates, drinks, condiments, and napkins, none of which he ever completely remembered. All of that changed, though, once the TV cameras arrived. Meals became picture-perfect, though they were never really quiet.

Torn between the attraction of good memories and the horror of bad ones, she lowered her gaze and walked toward the breakfast buffet.

Scofield bumped into her — literally — at the waffle machine. For a moment he stared blankly, then he grinned. "Sandy!"

"Andie," she corrected him. "And you're Matthew."

"Right. Well, excuse me. Didn't mean to run you over."

She nodded toward his table. "I see your kids are keeping you busy."

He lifted his gaze to the ceiling as if appealing to a higher power, then exhaled a heavy sigh. "I have come to the conclusion that our nanny was underpaid. I don't know how she coped."

Andie filled a paper cup with waffle mix from the dispenser. "You might try letting your kids get things for themselves."

"Allow my kids to mingle with innocent people? You have to be kidding."

She shrugged as she lifted the lid of the hot waffle maker. "I'm sure most of these people have kids of their own. They're used to dealing with mayhem."

He shook his head, then raised a brow. "Do you have kids?"

"No — but I was one of a half dozen. Early on I learned how to fend for myself."

"Six kids?" he groaned. "And I thought two were a lot to handle. I don't know how your parents ever got anything done."

For the first time in years Andie felt tempted to explain just how much her parents accomplished with hard work, six kids, and a few musical instruments, but Matthew had already moved to the orange juice dispenser.

She poured the lumpy mix onto the waffle iron, lowered the lid, and turned the handle to start the timer. While she waited for the clock to tick down, she noticed that the lawyer had returned to his table and appeared to be clearing the area in front of the fourth chair. He couldn't be making space for her . . . or could he?

Any lingering doubts vanished when the little girl — Emilia — caught Andie's eye and waved, a picture of winsome appeal. Andie smiled and waved back, though something in her heart sank. She had hoped to spend the day in a state of slothful uselessness, maybe lazing around her room until noon, then walking to one of the dozen or so pancake houses they'd passed on the drive to the hotel. She wasn't sure why Williamsburg had so many pancake houses, but if the locals kept all those places in business, someone must have a delicious pancake secret.

The timer on the waffle maker beeped, so Andie flipped the handle, pried her creation out of the iron, and drenched the resulting pastry with syrup. After grabbing a cup of coffee, she stepped into the dining area, where Emilia was flapping her arms and calling Andie's name — her former name. "Christy! We're over here!"

Every eye turned as Andie forced a smile and walked toward the family's table. "Good morning." She slid her plate into the empty space. "And my name isn't Christy."

"Her name is Sandy." Matthew frowned at his daughter as he pulled out the chair for Andie. "How would you like it if she called you by the wrong name?"

"I'd like it." Emilia pushed hair out of her eyes with syrup-coated fingers. "She can call me Walter if she wants."

"Andie." She sat in the empty chair. "My name is Andie."

Roman tipped his head back and laughed, apparently

delighted by the fact that a limp piece of waffle was protruding from his lower lip and coating his chin with syrup.

"Roman." Matthew folded his hands. "Keep your food in your mouth, please."

The boy slurped the errant bite into his mouth, swallowed, and grinned at his sister. "Walter is your dinosaur. You can't have his name."

"Why not?" Emilia hopped out of her chair and picked up something on the floor, rising a second later with the worn-out stuffed animal in her hands. She tucked it under her arm, but angled her body so Andie couldn't miss seeing her toy.

Sprinkling a spoonful of powdered sugar over her waffle, Andie smiled at the little girl. "How is Walter doing today? He looks like he's ready for an adventure."

Her goofy response wasn't very imaginative, but Emilia grinned and even Mr. Buttoned-down Lawyer seemed surprised. Or grateful. He wore a sports jacket and dress pants, so he must not be the vacation type any more than she was. But if he was doing this train tour for his kids, maybe he deserved credit for his good intentions.

"So tell me, Andie," he said, cutting a piece of sausage with a plastic knife and fork. "Why did your parents pick that name for you?"

They didn't, but she wasn't about to reveal details that didn't matter. So she gave him a mostly true answer. "Someone special to me—to my family—was named Andrew. So Andie seemed like a name that would honor him and still work for a girl."

Matthew nodded, but Emilia hijacked the conversation by tugging on Andie's sleeve. "What are you doing today? We're going to the Williamsburg."

The shiny traces of syrup on her cuff brought the ache of sweet memories to Andie's throat. She swallowed hard and tried to focus on the child next to her instead of the children in her memory. "I thought we were already in Williamsburg."

"She means the historical area," Matthew said. "We're taking a cab over to see the restored village. You should come with us." He waggled both brows in a pitiful Groucho Marx imitation. He looked so silly that even though Andie didn't want to laugh, she couldn't help it.

Matthew grinned. "I understand there are several unique shops, restaurants, even a theater. Lots to do over in the historic area. We'll have fun."

Andie didn't want to encourage him, so she concentrated on cutting her waffle. "I hadn't really thought much about my plans for the day."

"Then you have no conflicts. Come go with us—I promise you and Roman and Walter—" he winked at his daughter—"will have a good time."

Andie bit her lip and watched Roman, who was pasting Cheerios to his sticky chin, and Emilia, who was desperately trying to do the same thing. The sight of them—so innocent and natural—unlocked another buried memory and freed it to flutter through her mind. How many mornings had Callie and Cole joked like this at the breakfast table? How many times did Mom tell them to cut it out because the camera crew had arrived? Too many to count.

She shivered in vivid recollection. Since coming on this trip, every hotel room, every conversation, and every stranger reminded her of something about her brothers and sisters . . .

When Emilia squealed because one of her Cheerios fell into her yogurt cup, Andie blinked the images of the past away. "I tell you what—" she gestured to the pool behind the windows— "you guys go to historical Williamsburg. When you get back, I'll go swimming with you. That way your dad can get some of his work done."

Shock flickered over Matthew's face. "I couldn't ask you to do that."

"Why not? I like kids. And I like swimming."

"Really." He blinked, then recovered quickly. "Swimming—doesn't that sound great?" he grinned at his kids, then turned to Andie. "We'd still like you to come with us. If you don't have other plans, that is."

She studied him, trying to figure out if he sincerely wanted her company or if he was hoping to rope her into nanny duty. When he gave her a sly smile, she wondered if he'd read her mind.

"I'd love to have another adult along," he said, calmly extending a warning hand into the space through which Emilia and Roman had begun to toss Cheerios at each other, "especially someone who's as good with kids as you are. But I'm not looking for a babysitter. I'm looking for grown-up company."

Andie lowered her gaze and dragged a bite of waffle through a puddle of syrup, torn between the undeniable appeal of touring with a nice family or sitting alone watching pay per view. But before she could reach a decision, her phone rang. Surprised, she drew it out of her purse and recognized Janette's phone number. She glanced at Matthew. "Excuse me a minute."

Janette apologized for calling so early, then said she was still thinking about going to the historic part of town. Would Andie like to come along?

A smile tugged at Andie's lips. "You get your wish and then some," she told Matthew. "Today you'll have two adults for company."

Andie told Janette that they'd pick her up in front of her hotel, and promised to see her soon.

After shivering up and down a mile-long street of historic buildings, the small touring party was more than ready for a lunch break. Andie was willing to eat anywhere that offered both chairs and food, but Matthew insisted on whipping out his smart phone and finding the highest rated restaurant within walking distance. "The Blue Talon Bistro," he said a moment later, grinning as he slipped his phone back into the pocket of his sports coat. "Come on, gang, it's only a block away."

Andie glanced at Janette, half-hoping she'd protest that she was too tired to walk another step, but once again, the older woman had outlasted Andie. Smiling, Janette took Emilia's and Roman's hands and led the way, practically skipping over the brick sidewalk.

Andie watched them go, more than a little envious of their energy. "I thought I was in good shape, but apparently I don't get as much exercise as I ought to."

Matthew slid his hands into his pockets. "You work for a television network? Doesn't being a TV star keep you busy?"

His question struck like a blow to the center of her chest, and her forearms pebbled with gooseflesh. For an instant Andie was convinced that he'd learned her secret, then she remembered that earlier she'd mentioned VPN.

She smiled in relief. While impressed that Matthew could remember the little bits of information she'd shared, she didn't want him to get the wrong idea about her job. "I'm not the on-air talent," she said. "I don't have anything to do with programming, either, just sales. I oversee the operators who call the 800 number for orders or customer service. It's not at all glamorous."

"It's one of those shopping channels?"

"You've probably seen it. We have hours devoted to women's products, an hour devoted to the kitchen, and a couple of hours for selling home and garden tools. Books get an hour in the middle of the night—probably because my boss thinks only insomniacs read any more—and we give an hour before sunrise to men's toiletries. That's when we figure most men are awake and getting ready to shave."

Matthew laughed. "Sounds like you're more active than I am. I spend all day either behind a desk or in my car, so I have to put in an hour at the gym just to stay halfway fit. But the gym's an hour away from the office and about twenty minutes from my house, so that means even more time away from my kids." A frown settled between his brows. "I didn't have this problem when . . . when Inga was with us. My wife was a wonderful mother, and she gave me the time I needed to get everything done. After we lost her, Nessa did a good job of being there for the kids. But since she's been gone . . ."

His voice trailed away. Because Andie wasn't comfortable following that particular conversational thread, she tugged on another string: "How long have you been without a nanny?"

"Four weeks. Four weeks of babysitters who aren't up to the job." The corner of his mouth drooped. "I know you're probably wondering how I'm going to cope with my kids if I can't survive more than a month without help. Trust me, I've been wondering the same thing. That's part of the reason for this trip—I need to get my childcare arrangements settled."

Andie studied him, wondering how he could possibly arrange for childcare while on vacation. Then again, he was on the phone all the time. Maybe he was checking with an employment agency, or seeing if anyone had responded to a classified ad . . .

"They're great kids, you know," she said. "Imaginative, fun, and creative. You should be proud of them."

"I am—and I love them more than I can say. But there are times, especially lately, when I wonder if I'm even capable of giving them what they need to grow up. When Inga and I got married, I had my life all planned out. Then she died, and now I'm not sure what I'll be doing next week."

Andie was wondering how she could ask about Inga's death without seeming rude, but then they turned a corner and found themselves standing in front of the Blue Talon Bistro, a striking brick building painted in shades of sage green and Williamsburg blue. Brilliant red impatiens spilled from tall pots near the door, exuding a colorful welcome despite the autumnal chill in the air.

Matthew hurried ahead and held the door; Janette informed

the hostess that they were a party of five for lunch. They followed the young woman to a round table, but Matthew excused himself and took the children to wash their hands.

Janette and Andie sank into seats and accepted menus from the hostess. After she moved away, Janette lowered her menu and took off the big sunglasses she'd been wearing all morning. Though the weather was sunny, Andie hadn't felt the need for shades. Then again, she wasn't trying to hide a black eye.

Janette leaned forward, her mouth curving in a sly smile. "So . . . what do you think of Matthew?"

Andie narrowed her eyes. "You're not match-making, are you?"

"Are you not available?"

She shook her head. "Not terribly interested. I have too many other things on my mind. So does Matthew, apparently."

"But you've been thinking about him." Janette picked up her menu again. "He seems like a nice young man. And those kids are adorable."

"They are. But they're also a handful."

"Anyone with a little patience could deal with those children. They're only acting up because they're desperate for their daddy's attention."

Andie lowered her menu as Janette's words seeped into her brain. Could she be right? Matthew had handed his kids over to a nanny for the past year, so no wonder he didn't know them very well. But surely he could get closer to them if he tried to. If he wanted to.

"You know—" the beginning of a smile tipped the corners of Janette's mouth— "I could offer to stay with the kids tonight if you and Matthew wanted to go out for dinner."

To Andie's extreme annoyance, a blush burned her cheeks. "I'm sure Matthew doesn't want to have dinner with me."

"I think you might be surprised. I've seen him watching you."

Andie shrugged. "It's polite to pay attention when someone is talking to you."

"It's not that he looks at you, it's the way he looks at you. I may be a few years past my prime, but I remember the look that means a man is interested."

Andie took a wincing little breath. Could Janette be right? She had given up on dating so long ago that she no longer felt sure of herself. Since most of the call center employees were women and most of the company execs married men, her love life wasn't exactly brimming with prospects. A few years ago she tried corresponding with a couple of different guys she'd met through an online dating service, but those relationships never went any further than the computer screen.

And it wasn't like she had a lot of dating experience. Once *Home with the Huggins* began to air, Charlie, Carin, and Andie went from being ordinary teenagers to teen celebrities. No one wanted to date the ordinary Huggins, but everyone wanted to be seen with a TV star. Andie endured more than one date with guys who were all about getting photographs with her featured on TMZ or posted on Facebook; not one of them cared about her as a person.

And then there was her prom. The memory brought back a shudder, causing Janette to lift a brow and ask if Andie was feeling chilly.

"I'm fine," Andie assured her. "Just having a muscle contraction."

The mere thought of the prom fiasco was enough to make her want to hide under the table. Joshua Barnett, a school friend from long before the Huggins kids dropped out to be tutored, called to ask Andie to his prom at Hollywood High. Since they had known each other since second grade, Andie figured it'd be okay to accept. She was foolish enough to think Josh might actually like her, since he'd known her back when she wore braces.

When Oliver heard Andie mention that she was excited about going to the dance with Josh, he decided that an episode of *Home with the Huggins* should feature Hollywood High's senior prom. That meant the Huggins Family had to play for the event, Andie's parents and siblings had to come along, and every reporter, cameraman, and paparazzo in the universe had to show up to record what turned out to be the greatest humiliation of Andie's life.

She might have enjoyed the dance if Josh hadn't been such a jerk. But after fawning all over her in front of the cameras, after bringing her roses and kissing her cheek when he greeted her, after escorting her into the hotel ballroom and leading her onto the dance floor while all the world watched, Josh excused himself and left her with Cole. She thought her date had only gone to talk to some friends until a tabloid reported the story the next day: Christy Huggins' Disastrous Date. Apparently Josh went in search of Tiffany Buckholder and found her out by the hotel pool. While a cameraman filmed from several yards away, Josh and Tiffany talked for a while, then shared a romantic slow dance, even making out for the camera they pretended not to see. Snippets of Josh and Tiffany's encounter would later be edited into footage of Andie and Cole sitting by the punch bowl, laughing and talking about how much fun they were having.

A few weeks later, on *Home with the Huggins*, all of America watched as Joshua slobbered all over Tiffany while Andie leaned toward Cole and whispered that she might actually be falling in love. The video editor added subtitles to be sure no one missed a word.

That night Andie learned a lesson about dating. She became convinced that if any of the Huggins kids were to actually fall in love, they'd have to meet someone who had never watched *Home with the Huggins*. If Charlie hadn't met Bettina before the cameras began to roll, Andie didn't think they would have ever gotten together.

"You know, Janette—" she took a deep breath— "thanks for the offer, but I'd rather not complicate things on this trip. All I want to do is make it through the next several days so I can get my boss off my case."

Janette smiled. "That's okay. I understand."

Did she? Andie doubted it, but she wasn't going to explain why dating had never been an option for her. Even as Andie Crystal, she'd never reached the point in a relationship where she felt she could be completely honest with a man, open enough to tell him about her past and reveal who she used to be. She was always afraid she'd see his eyes light with interest, hear him say that she needed to capitalize on her past and use it to rebuild her music career, or write a tell-all book and make a fortune—

No, thank you. Sometimes the past needed to remain in the past.

Did her siblings have the same problem? Since Carin wasn't married, she must have faced the same struggle. Carma apparently found a nice man and settled down, but Andie would bet her bottom dollar that Carma's husband wasn't involved in the entertainment industry. If he were, he'd be fighting to get Carma on the cover of *Entertainment Weekly* or *People* magazine, to keep her name in the news and get her on *Dancing with the Stars* or *Celebrity Apprentice* . . .

What sort of life had her little sister managed to create? How did she find a way back to normal?

Andie pretended to stare at the menu while her thoughts churned. She didn't know her siblings, not any more. After so many years apart, she would like to see them again. She wished she could spend real time with them, but to do that she'd have to return to a spotlight she hated and a lifestyle that never agreed with her. She'd have to reveal her hiding place.

She cast a sideways look at Janette. "Do you stay in touch with your siblings?"

The older woman's brows rose into perfectly matched

triangles. "I wouldn't say we are close. For one thing, we live in different states, and we're busy with families of our own. Plus— well." She shrugged. "Let's just say there's a lot of water under the bridge."

"If you had an opportunity to visit a sibling you hadn't seen in a long time, would you go?"

Janette gave Andie a curious look. "Well . . . yes. I think I would."

"Even if . . . if something traumatic had torn you apart? Would you go knowing that you might have to address that issue all over again?"

Janette nodded thoughtfully. "Yes, I would. If things got too painful, I could—you could—always leave again."

Andie bit her lip, then give Janette a lopsided smile. "So . . . is it a sister or a brother you're thinking of?"

"A sister. Older than me."

"Do you talk often?"

She sighed. "We're different. My husband and I have had to deal with things my sister and her husband would never understand. They have perfect children, you see. While we—well, sometimes I have to remind myself that I've never met anyone who's actually perfect."

She looked away, lashes fluttering, and Andie took a sharp breath when she realized Janette was about to cry. Andie's innocent question had touched on something painful, something buried deep beneath the varnish of middle-aged respectability . . .

Maybe they had more in common than Janette realized.

The older woman turned her head, touched a fingertip to the corners of her lashes, then wiped her wet finger on her napkin. Now she was tapping the skin around her left eye, the one camouflaged in makeup, and for some reason Andie felt compelled to tell her that she didn't have to worry about hiding her injury. Not any more.

"I know," Andie whispered. "About the black eye."

Janette stiffened, then held her hand over her poorly disguised bruise. "Is it that obvious?"

"I don't think Matthew or the children have noticed. But I sell cosmetics."

Silence stretched between them, then Janette sniffed and cast a quick glance in Andie's direction. "I know what you must be thinking, but my husband didn't do this."

Andie pressed her lips together. "Okay."

"It's not something I can talk about."

Andie searched Janette's face, looking for the truth. Janette didn't seem the sort of woman who would lie even to protect her husband, but if she'd run into a door or a tree, she would have no reason to hide anything.

Something wasn't right. But Andie didn't want to pry.

"We'll consider the subject closed." She smiled and picked up her menu again. "The chicken and mushroom crepes look good. I had waffles for breakfast, but something tells me these crepes won't be anything like what I cooked up at the free breakfast bar."

"I'm thinking macaroni and cheese." Janette swallowed hard. "This place claims to be famous for comfort food, and nothing's more comforting than mac and cheese, especially on a chilly day like today."

The children's arrival saved them from further awkwardness. Matthew seated Emilia and Roman, then dropped into the chair between them. "Lunch is on me, ladies," he announced. "It's a small price to pay for the pleasure of your company — and your help with my kids."

They placed their orders. And while they ate, laughing at the children and gingerly sharing bits of information and personal history, Andie realized that they had become a sort of family — loosely knit, of course, but connected nonetheless. If they remained together for the rest of the trip, she might have enjoyed this forced vacation.

But guilt and responsibility had been hounding her, and the nascent sense of family around the table reminded her of what she needed to do.

She would have to leave the party just as it was beginning.

On Tuesday morning Andie was pleased when she met the Scofields in the lobby and Matthew suggested they share a cab from the hotel to the depot. As she studied the itinerary she realized this would be the longest of all the train trips. Their journey would take them from Williamsburg north to Richmond, where they would disembark and hop aboard a train heading south to Charleston. Before they arrived at the next destination, they would have spent almost ten hours riding the rails.

She hoped Matthew had packed something to entertain his kids.

They caught the Northeast Regional and settled into seats for the relatively short trip to Richmond. Janette took the window seat next to Andie and was dozing by the time the train began to roll. Roman and Emilia fell asleep almost as quickly, which meant they were still worn out from yesterday. After lunch, they had gone back to the hotel, where Matthew sat in a corner making phone calls while Andie and the kids played Marco Polo in the pool. She was pretty sure she still had water in her right ear.

She leaned forward to speak to Matthew, riding in the seat in front of her. "So, did your kids sleep well last night?"

He groaned and leaned into the aisle. "I wish. They were up half the night with stomachaches. Roman even threw up."

"Oh, no! Do you think they're getting sick?"

"I think they ate too much. Remember all the free samples they got at the Peanut Shop? My boy's eyes have always been bigger than his belly, and he doesn't know how to slow down. After eating everything from candy-coated sunflower seeds to chocolate-dipped pecans, I think his stomach demanded some time off."

Andie smiled and reclined her seat, grateful that the kids were recovering. She ate too much herself yesterday, but who could have predicted that colonial Williamsburg would offer such good food?

They detrained — Andie loved that word — in Richmond, and sat in molded plastic chairs for about an hour before hearing that the 89 Palmetto train was approaching the station. Having learned that trains do not linger at their stops, Andie gathered her carry-ons, then helped Emilia slip her arms through the straps of her pink backpack. Matthew finished a call on his cell phone while Janette helped Roman stuff his Skipbo cards back into the box. Finally they were all ready to file aboard the next train.

Matthew might have hoped his kids would sleep on this leg of the journey as well, but by that time Roman and Emilia were wide-eyed, restless, and hungry. After stowing their belongings over their seats, the group made their way to the dining car and scrunched into a booth. Janette and Andie ordered salads, the kids asked for hot dogs, and Matthew chose a veggie dish, though Andie was certain he'd rather be eating the Angus beef burger. After they finished, Janette suggested that they move to one of the tables in the cafe car, where they wouldn't be in the way of other hungry passengers.

Two weeks before Andie would never have believed that she'd spend an entire afternoon playing Skipbo on a train, but she enjoyed every minute of it. She helped Emilia plan her strategy, but Roman needed no help at all — like his father, he proved to be a whiz at the game, and volunteered to show Janette how to play her cards. As they challenged each other to successive rounds, Andie realized that the two rambunctious kids weren't being rambunctious at all. Janette must have been right about the kids wanting to spend more time with their dad.

"Matthew." Janette shifted the cards in her hand, then smiled at the man across the table. "I'm not trying to be critical, but your children look a bit disheveled. Do you let them dress themselves?"

Matthew glanced at Roman and Emilia, then tilted his brow at Janette. "Don't those outfits match?"

"I'm not referring to the colors, but to the condition. Roman's shirt is as wrinkled as a raisin, and Emilia's blouse looks as if she yanked it out of a suitcase."

The corner of Matthew's mouth twisted. "Maybe she did."

Janette exhaled a melodramatic sigh. "Dressing children isn't difficult. Most clothes are permanent press, so all you have to do is set out at night whatever the kids want to wear the next day. Wrinkles will practically fall out, especially if you hang things in a bathroom."

A reluctant grin tugged at the lawyer's mouth. "We'll try to do better. Won't we, kids?"

Emilia squeezed her stuffed dinosaur. "Walter says yes, Daddy. He doesn't want to look dis-shoveled."

As the game continued, Andie couldn't help remembering the hours she and her siblings played Rook over tables in various private jets. Cole might have played around the clock if he'd been allowed to. She used to catch him and Callie playing long after they were supposed to be asleep, and not even Charlie could beat Cole when he was on a roll.

When Janette won yet another round, Andie pretended to glare at her as she gathered the cards. "I don't understand how you could get so good at this in one afternoon. An hour ago, Roman had to teach you how to play."

"He had to remind me." Janette propped her elbow on the table and rested her chin on her hand. "My family used to play a lot when our daughter was younger."

"You have a daughter?" Friendly curiosity shone in Matthew's eyes. "You didn't mention—"

"She's grown up—or trying to be." Janette lowered her gaze to the cards Andie was tossing into piles on the table. "She's twenty-five."

"Yep, that's grown up." Matthew gathered his cards. "I was nearly finished with law school at that age. What's your daughter doing?"

When Janette didn't answer, Andie wondered if she'd heard the question. She didn't look at Matthew, but kept her attention focused on her cards.

"Janette?" Andie bent to catch her eye. "Everything okay?"

Janette dipped her head in an abrupt nod. "Sorry, wasn't paying attention. So who opens this round? Is it my turn?"

"Emilia goes first." Andie smiled at the little girl. "Are you ready to draw five?"

As Emilia counted aloud and withdrew five cards from the center pile, Andie intercepted Matthew's gaze and lifted a questioning brow. Something had upset Janette, Andie would bet her last dollar on it, but from the blank look in Matthew's eye Andie knew neither of them had a clue how to make things right.

Back on the train, Andie found herself sitting next to a teenage boy who had closed himself off from all conversation by putting on his headphones and closing his eyes. An attendant found seats for Matthew and the kids in another car, and Andie lost sight of Janette a few minutes after boarding.

Sitting alone, with no one to talk to, a feeling of nostalgia washed over Andie, reinforcing the decision she'd made earlier that morning. She hadn't yet mentioned her plan to anyone, but when they arrived at the Charleston depot, she would tell her new friends goodbye. Instead of going to the hotel where she had a reservation, she would take a cab to her sister's house and see if Carma would put her up for a night or two. After a short visit, Andie would return to the train depot and continue with her Amtrak itinerary.

She wasn't expecting Carma to welcome her with open arms, but this detour should at least give Andie something new to discuss with Janette.

Darkness had settled over the landscape by the time they pulled into the station. Without waiting for Matthew or Janette, Andie grabbed her carry-ons and stepped off the train, then proceeded immediately to baggage claim. The Charleston depot wasn't nearly as attractive as the one in Williamsburg, but she barely had time for a quick glance before retrieving her suitcase. She knew Matthew, Janette, and the kids would take a while — they had to button coats, visit the restrooms, and check out the vending machines. By the time they gathered at baggage claim, Andie could be on the road.

Though she was strongly tempted to make a clean get away, she couldn't leave without a word. So she grabbed her suitcase and rolled it over to the small alcove where Matthew, Janette, and the kids had gathered around a snack machine.

"I'm going to say good-bye for now," she told them, ignoring Matthew's and Janette's stunned expressions while Andie smiled at the children. "I have a friend in Charleston, so I'm going to surprise her with a visit."

"You didn't call first?" A line appeared between Janette's brows. "What if she's not home?"

"Then I have a reservation waiting at the Hampton, so I'll call a cab. If you don't see me at breakfast tomorrow, you'll know I found a bed for the night."

Matthew slid his hands into his pockets, his expression echoing Janette's concern. "At least take our cell numbers in case you run into trouble."

"I have Janette's number, but I'm sure I'll be fine." Avoiding Matthew's gaze, she gave the group a cheery wave and strode toward the front door. They were kind to worry about her, but they didn't have to. After all, they weren't family, and they were barely friends. At this point, Andie wasn't sure she had any family at all.

She hailed the first cab in line and handed the driver a slip of paper with information she'd gleaned from the Internet: Felix and Carma Paraskevas resided at 87 Maiden Lane, Charleston. She'd have to speak to Carma about doing something to hide that information—it shouldn't be so readily accessible.

And as the cab pulled away, she glanced over her shoulder and saw Matthew, Roman, and Emilia on the curb, their faces following her. She turned and closed her eyes, reminding herself that those people were practically strangers. They meant nothing to her, but she shared a history with Carma.

She mentally rehearsed her opening line: "Carma—it's me, your big sister." Or "Long time no see, Carma, it's Christy."

How would her sister react? Carma had been only eighteen when Andie left California, and she knew very little about what Carma had been doing in the intervening years. Obviously, she married and moved east, but Andie had no idea how she met her husband, if she went to college, or if she was happy as a wife and mother . . .

As the cab traveled deeper into the heart of the old city, Andie peered out at tree-lined streets and realized that Carma and her husband had to be doing well. This part of Charleston was filled with historic homes, some two or three stories tall, shaded by live oaks and adorned with side porches that ran the length of the structure. From what Andie could tell in the street-lit gloom, most of the houses were white with black or dark green shutters. Like Williamsburg, historic Charleston apparently had a dress code.

The cab stopped in front of a stately home crowning the top of a hill like the ornament on a wedding cake. Andie paid the driver and stood on the sidewalk as he set her suitcase on the curb. "Before you go—" she turned—"do you have a card? I may need to call you back."

"Sure thing, lady." The man fished a business card from his pocket and placed it in her palm. "Want me to carry your suitcase up to the porch?"

Andie looked at the intimidating stone steps, then considered the quiet street. "Let's leave it on the sidewalk. If my timing is bad, I'll need to go to a hotel, and there's no sense in hauling that heavy thing all the way up only to turn around and bring it down again."

The driver touched a finger to the brim of his cap, then got into the taxi and pulled away. Andie watched his taillights disappear in the distance and felt a sizable portion of her courage vanish with him. What was she doing here?

Before tackling the stairs, she looked carefully left and right, searching the lamplit street for parked cars with people sitting in them. The paparazzi used to linger outside the Huggins' house for hours, waiting for any opportunity to photograph family members walking the dog or checking the mail. Andie didn't suppose Carma got much attention from the press any more, but their mother's story had been in the news, so one never knew who might be lurking in the shadows . . . or maybe she was just being paranoid.

Satisfied that no one was watching the house, Andie climbed the stone steps, then walked up the wooden stairs leading to the entrance. Tall shuttered windows lined the front porch and a brass doorknocker gleamed in a solitary nimbus of porch light. A pink tricycle stood in the corner, so apparently Carma had a little girl who liked to leave her toys out.

Strewn toys, a happy sign of an ordinary family. Thank goodness.

Andie knocked, then stood back and held her breath. The sound of footsteps followed an interval of silence, then the door swung inward and Carma stood in front of her. Andie would have known her sister anywhere, even though her hair had been cut short and she'd gained weight over the years.

Carma widened her eyes and caught her breath. "Can I help—oh my goodness, Christy?"

Andie opened her arms and Carma flew into them, hugging her so fiercely that Andie struggled to catch her breath. Carma finally released her, but kept an iron grip on Andie's hand as she dragged her inside.

"I left my suitcase at the bottom of the hill." Andie pointed over her shoulder. "I didn't know whether you'd be home—"

"Good grief, you can't leave it there. Felix! We have company."

A chair scraped over a distant floor, then a man appeared in the kitchen doorway—dark haired, dark eyed, and attractive. Older. He stared at Andie, puzzled, and his frown deepened when Carma said, "It's Christy! My sister."

He sucked at the inside of his cheeks for a moment, looking from Andie to his wife. "You said she'd left the family."

"Obviously, she's back. Her suitcase is on the sidewalk—could you bring it up, please?"

Carma might have been too flustered to remember her manners, but Andie's brother-in-law wasn't. He extended his hand, his dark eyes searching hers. "Felix Paraskevas. It's nice to finally meet you."

"Andie Crystal." She shifted her gaze to meet Carma's bewildered eyes. "I changed my name."

Felix strode toward the door as Carma's mouth opened in a silent gasp. For a moment she stared, then she blinked and gestured toward the kitchen doorway. "We were having dessert. Come on in, let me fix you something. Have you eaten dinner?"

"I ate on the train."

"On the—you were on a train? Good grief. You want dessert? Coffee?"

"Coffee would be great. Thanks."

Andie sat on a high-backed wooden chair as Carma bustled around the red and green kitchen. This was obviously a family home, decorated with loving touches and splashes of color. Children's drawings and magnets blanketed the refrigerator while plastic mats covered the oak table. The place looked nothing like the home they grew up in—after the camera crews arrived.

Andie nodded at the pictures on the fridge. "Your kids—I saw a birth announcement in *People*."

"That would have been Kalliope's. We have two girls—Kalliope, who's seven, and Ritsa, who's four. They'll probably come storming in at any minute."

Andie accepted the coffee cup Carma offered. "Unusual names."

"They're Greek, of course. Felix likes traditional names." She pulled a platter off the counter and set it on the table. "Baklava? I made it myself."

"You bake?"

"I do lots of things. I bake, carpool, clean, and I run a small catering business."

"I'm impressed. But no thank you on the baklava. I've been eating way too much lately."

"Well, you look great with a few curves. You need cream for your coffee? Sugar?"

"I'm fine, Carma. I don't want to do anything but talk."

"After all these years, now you want to talk?" Carma sank into the nearest chair and gazed at Andie with wide eyes. "But I'm really glad you came. I have so many questions, I hardly know where to begin."

Andie sipped the coffee and braced herself for whatever Carma might ask. "I don't blame you for being curious."

"Okay, then. What in the world are you doing here? Where have you been all these years? And why did you change your name?"

If she had to ask, she probably wouldn't understand. But Andie wanted to be a good sport. "I didn't want to be Christy Huggins any more. I wanted to find out who I really was."

"But like it or not, you are Christy Huggins."

"I might have been Christy Huggins, but that girl became something I'm not. The girl who stood in front of the microphone all those years — she wasn't happy there, but she couldn't let anyone know for fear of disappointing the family."

"But you were so good at it. It's not like anyone else could have pulled off the lead."

"I wish someone could have. Truthfully, Carma, I've never liked crowds, public performances, or traveling. I tolerated all that, but after the accident I didn't see any point in continuing. I didn't want to pretend anymore, and I didn't want to be involved in anything that might get anyone else killed."

"You can't blame the group for —"

"If we hadn't been a group, odds are that Cole would be alive today. We'd all be ordinary people. And I'm pretty sure we'd all be a lot happier."

Carma's chin quivered. "Mom says the accident changed you. She says you blame her for everything."

"The accident changed everything but me. The only good thing that came out of losing Cole was the producers' decision to cancel the show. I was glad. That's when I knew I'd finally have a chance to be myself — or figure out who I was supposed to be."

Carma studied Andie, brows working above her thoughtful blue eyes. "When you went off to find yourself . . . did you ever think about how your leaving would affect the rest of us? We'd just lost Cole, then Dad left. Then you vanished."

Andie was stunned to see honest anguish on Carma's face. "I didn't mean to hurt you. I didn't want to hurt anyone."

"But you did. And I'm not talking about the show, I'm talking about the family. Callie and I looked up to you. We knew Charlie would eventually get married and Carin would go off to college, but we thought you'd be there for us, especially after we lost Cole. But you disappeared and scared all of us to death. We worried for days, then Mr. Rueben called to say you were safe,

you were fine, you just wanted to live on your own for a while."
She stared, unspoken pain alive and glowing in her eyes, and for
the first time Andie realized that she might have caused more
hurt than she suffered.

"I'm sorry." Unable to bear the pressure of Carma's gaze,
Andie ran her finger along the outer seam of her jeans. "I was
grieving for Cole. I was upset about the divorce. I was twenty
years old, plus I had my own money and my own lawyer. I knew
I could survive on my own, and I had to leave. But since Mom
would never let me go without a major battle, it was easier to just
. . . walk away and not look back."

She waited, fearing another gentle rebuke, but they were distracted by the sound of the front door opening and closing. Her
suitcase had arrived.

Carma wiped wetness from her lower lashes, then stood and
leaned into the kitchen doorway. "Can you take that upstairs,
hon? You can put it in the guest room."

Her husband didn't answer, but Andie's suitcase replied in a
thump-thump-thump as Felix hauled it up the steps.

Finally Carma looked at her again. "I don't blame you for
leaving," she said. "I was eighteen that year . . . if you had asked,
I would have gone with you."

Andie gaped at her sister, tongue-tied, and considered what
might have been. They could never have pulled it off, two Huggins hiding in plain sight, but it was comforting to know that
Carma understood why Andie left.

"I forgave you a long time ago," Carma added. "The others . . . well, Callie's the only one who still holds a grudge. He
blames you for sinking the good ship Happy Huggins. I think
he's bitter because the money ran out by the time he was old
enough to appreciate it."

Not knowing how to respond to that, Andie said nothing.

"So." Carma leaned back and smiled. "Why are you here?"

Andie shook her head. "You won't believe it. I'm on vacation.

A train tour, of all things."

"You're traveling alone?"

"I do everything alone these days." A grin lifted the corner of Andie's mouth as she thought of Matthew and Janette. "Well, mostly alone."

"I thought maybe you'd come because of Mother. You've heard the latest?"

"My lawyer told me about her cancer." Andie wrapped her hands around her mug and stared into the dark liquid. "I was sorry to hear that she's terminal."

"So you're planning to go see her?"

The question stung, but Andie knew the topic would eventually arise. She drew a deep breath and met her sister's piercing gaze. "I have a new life."

"Is that a no?"

Andie pressed her lips together as a flush of misery darkened Carma's face. "How can you say that?"

"I told you, I have a new life."

"But she's the only mother you'll ever have."

"I can't help that." Andie blew out a breath. "Has she changed?"

Carma looked away, tucking a wayward strand of hair behind her ear. "Life's worn her down. She had to declare bankruptcy, you know. She makes ends meet by selling autographed eight-by-tens from the glory days."

"She sells pictures of us? Of Cole?" Andie's stomach churned at the thought of her mother profiting from a photo of her dead son. Years later, she was still leeching off her kids.

Carma nodded, but she wouldn't meet Andie's gaze. "Our success . . . it's all she has left. A bunch of old pictures, a garage full of costumes, and a few boxes of videotapes. You can't blame her for clinging to a time when she was on top of the world—"

"I don't blame her for that. I blame her for always being more focused on celebrity than on her children." Andie thought she had managed to put the pain of the past behind her, but her sister's comments ripped open a seam barely stitched together. Tears stung Andie's eyes and her hands began to tremble. This is not the visit she wanted to have. "I'm sorry. I didn't come here to talk about the past."

"Why did you come?" Carma asked, her voice quiet and probing. "I'm happy to see you, honest I am, but I'm surprised. Stunned, actually."

Their heads turned when a high-pitched chattering interrupted the conversation. Andie looked toward the staircase and saw two little girls launch themselves from the second step, landing on the wooden floor with solid thumps before they ran into the kitchen.

They stopped short when they saw her. The oldest girl, a curly-haired beauty, stared at Andie with mirror-bright eyes as her mouth opened in a small O.

Carma drew the youngest girl onto her lap and threaded her fingers through a tangle of silky curls. "This is Ritsa, and that—" she pointed to the gaping girl— "is Kalliope. Girls, this lady is your Aunt Christy."

"But you can call me Aunt Andie." Andie bent forward, her elbows resting on her knees, and smiled at the older girl. "I'm happy to meet you, Kalliope. Did you draw the pretty pictures on the refrigerator?"

The child's eyes grew even wider, but she managed a terrified nod before ducking toward the security of her mother's arms.

"They're not really shy," Carma said, drawing Kalliope close, "but you surprised them. You surprised all of us." She gave each girl a kiss on the forehead, then asked if they'd come downstairs for a cookie. Turning from Andie, they babbled brightly, explaining that they were having a tea party in Ritsa's room.

"You'll need something to eat, then." Carma stood and wrapped two snicker doodles in a napkin. "But bedtime is in half an hour. So finish up your tea party and then brush your teeth."

She gave the napkin to Kalliope, along with a warning to share with her sister, and the two girls scurried back to the stairs. Andie watched them go, and smiled when Ritsa peered at her through the railings, keeping a careful watch as she climbed.

Andie's heart twisted as she watched them go. If she hadn't cut herself off from the family, she could have been collecting hugs and kisses for years.

"I think I understand why you're here." Carma dropped back into her chair. "You came because you heard about Mom. Do you want me to give her a message or something?"

Andie gave her a grim little grin. "I came because my train happened to be going through Charleston. And since I don't know anyone else in town . . ."

"I'm the best you could do?" Carma smiled, but accusation underlined her words.

"I didn't mean it like that. I didn't even remember you lived here until after I was on the train. Once I realized you were close by . . ." Andie shrugged, uncomfortable with the lie she was about to tell. "Of course I wanted to come. You're my sister."

The image of Kalliope and Ritsa peering through the staircase spindles floated before her eyes, then shifted to a memory of her and Carma doing the same thing the day Mom brought Callie home from the hospital. He had been a surprise to all of them, but Christy, Carin, and Carma had fought over the right to hold and kiss him . . .

Memories. They weren't all bad.

"Being your sister has never counted for much before this." Carma tilted her head. "Callie and I have talked about how in the space of a few months we lost Cole, then Dad, then you. We lost the show. We'd get out of bed and not know what to do with ourselves since no cameras were coming and no concerts were on the calendar. We had these gaping holes in our lives—"

"Someone should have introduced you to the real world." Andie set her coffee cup back on the table. "Look honey, it may sound cold-blooded, but I've never believed in trying to patch up things that were flawed in the first place. If I'd stayed around, you know Mom would have tried to get me behind the microphone again. She would have stopped Carin from going to college, she wouldn't have let Charlie get married, and she wouldn't have wanted you to go to school. She would have kept the happy Huggins alive for as long as she could."

"You don't know that."

"I know Mom was never happy unless she was on camera or on stage. When I first heard about her cancer, I felt terrible, but then I read that Oliver might be trying to film a deathbed family reunion. That's horrible. It's unthinkable."

Carma's face brightened in a flush. "It wasn't Oliver's idea, it was Mom's. She keeps saying she wants to make a documentary like the one Farrah Fawcett did in her last months. Oliver got the network to agree to a Huggins reunion special, but only if Mom can get the entire family together again."

"That's impossible. Cole's gone. Dad's gone."

"The entire surviving family. She's called all of us to see if we knew where you were. Oliver's even been phoning agents in Europe and Canada, thinking that maybe you left the country." She raked a hand through her hair. "They've promised Mom a burial plot at Forest Lawn Cemetery, somewhere near Michael Jackson's mausoleum. She's crazy excited about that."

Andie stared, too stunned for words. Their mother didn't want to be buried near her son? Cole was buried in the Hollywood Forever Cemetery, home to dozens of departed stars, musicians, writers, producers, and directors. Mom would get plenty of visitors in Hollywood Forever, but apparently she'd rather have Michael Jackson's spillover than enjoy eternal rest beside her son—

Biting back sharp words, Andie crossed her arms. "My lawyer mentioned something about a reunion, but I told him I wanted no part of it."

"I thought you might feel that way." Carma released a bitter laugh. "Carin and I have tried to convince Mom that the next few weeks should be private family time, but she says privacy has no place in the life of a star. She wants to share her story so other people will know about this disease. She keeps insisting that a documentary will help women all over the world."

"She'd say the same thing if she were dying from a gunshot wound. Face it, Mom is an exhibitionist. She's addicted to celebrity, and she can't imagine dying outside the spotlight."

"Would you begrudge her a last wish? You don't know how hard the past few years have been for her. No one wants an interview, the CDs don't sell, and Oliver takes days to return her calls."

"You make her sound like Norma Desmond."

Carma lifted her chin. "She's our mother and she's dying. We need to be with her."

"I have no intention of being a part of the Huggins' finale." Andie curled her hands into fists. "Especially not if cameras are involved."

"Honestly, Christy—how can you be so bitter?"

Her remark made Andie hesitate. She didn't remember her younger sister being so intuitive. When she left home, Carma was focused on boys, fashion, and music. Since then, she'd developed a feminine intuition far more perceptive than their mother's.

But in this case her instincts were dead wrong.

Andie uncrossed her arms and leaned toward her sister, hoping to make her understand. "I'm not bitter. Bitterness implies anger, and I'm not angry, not anymore. I'm a different person now. I'm a woman who's learned that she doesn't like the spotlight, doesn't need the cameras, and doesn't want to go back to a life where we were hounded by the paparazzi and didn't have a minute to call our own. We couldn't look for a restroom in a public place without being followed by cameras, don't you remember? Every time we wore a new dress, someone would criticize us for being extravagant, vain, or trashy. I left that life behind, and I can't go back to it. I won't go back. Not even if Mom wants us to give a command performance."

Carma shot her a withering look. "Okay, so maybe you're not bitter. You're just heartless."

That retort stung worse than anything Andie had heard, but she didn't think she'd be able to change her sister's opinion. "If I'm heartless—" she looked at her hands— "it's because my heart broke the day Cole died. I loved that boy, and every time I think about that poor cameraman—about his kids never seeing their daddy again—" she stopped when her voice clotted. Carma already knew those things.

Her sister didn't rebuke her again. Instead she stood, took Andie's empty coffee cup, and carried it to the sink. "How long can you stay?" The iron had vanished from her voice. "I'll put you in the guest room. There's a bath down the hall."

Andie lifted her head. "Thanks. And I almost forgot, but today's Wednesday, right? I need a computer."

Carma blinked. "Sure, there's one in the office."

"I need to record a song." Andie gave her sister a wry smile. "I'll try to sing softly."

"What on earth?" Carma tilted her head, surprise on her face. "I thought you were out of the music business."

"I am. But do you remember meeting Janey Caudill, one of the superfans? We met her in Albuquerque."

Carma shook her head.

"Come on, her mother brought her backstage before our concert. She was mentally handicapped. Her mother was too old to take care of her anymore, so when we met her she'd just put Janey into a group home. Janey was really sweet, and kept telling us that she was our biggest fan in the whole wide world."

Carma's forehead wrinkled, then she shrugged. "I don't know how you remember things like that."

"I remember Janey because we became pen pals, of a sort," Andie said. "I started sending her songs every week because her mom said she loved to hear me sing. At first I sent her cassette tapes, but now I just record something and email it to her."

"Does she write back?"

"Sometimes a nurse will answer for her." Andie smiled. "I usually get a 'thank you' and an 'I love you.' The nurses say she looks forward to my songs every week, so I wouldn't want to let her down."

Carma frowned and crossed her arms. "Can you explain why you cut all ties to your family, yet you kept up a relationship with some handicapped girl? That's not even logical."

Andie shrugged. "I doubt Janey remembers who I am. But she loves music, and I love singing for her. She's the only one I sing for these days." She bit her lip as a current of melancholy flowed through her, then she looked up at her sister. "Do you miss it? Not the travel or the crowds, but the music?"

Carma laughed. "I don't have time to miss anything. My family keeps me busy."

"Well." Andie spread her hands. "My job keeps me busy. But singing for Janey scratches an itch. She keeps me sane."

Carma's frowned deepened into a look of puzzlement, then she shook her head. "Anyway. You're welcome to stay as long as you like. I'll have to leave you a key, though, because we're leaving town day after tomorrow."

"You're going somewhere this week?"

"We're going to Los Angeles. I spoke to Mom's doctor this morning. He said she won't last longer than four or five more days."

Andie sat still, blank and shaken. She'd been relying on false information. Her mother didn't have four to six weeks; she had four to six days. She might have leaked the wrong information to the press so the network would have time to process their footage, find performance clips, and edit the assembled materials to an hour-long program before announcing her death.

Or maybe life itself as responsible for the discrepancy. People didn't always die on schedule . . . not even Mona Huggins.

"I can stay until you leave," Andie told Carma, standing. "Then I have to get back to my train."

# Chapter Seven

Andie rose early to eat breakfast with her sister's family, careful to stay out of the way as Carma readied her girls for school. Kalliope, Carma told her, was in second grade; Ritsa was in preschool. And after the girls were on their way, they could enjoy some quality sister time . . .

Once Felix left to drive the girls to school and head for his veterinary office, Carma dropped into a chair at the cluttered breakfast table.

"So." She lifted a discarded piece of buttered toast, the first morsel she'd had a chance to eat. "What do you want to do today?"

The last thing Andie wanted was for her sister to squire her around town. She would have been happy to sit on the sofa and talk, but apparently Carma wanted to play hostess.

"I'll do whatever you want to do," Andie told her. "Really, I'd just like to catch up. I want to hear about how you met your husband and what it's like to have a family."

"I can't believe you haven't gotten married." Carma took a bite of the toast, then set it down and gathered the dirty dishes on the table. "Aren't you interested in starting a family?"

Andie smiled at the Crayola-colored pictures on the refrigerator door. "Of course I'd like a family, I've just never had time. I got in on the ground floor of a shopping network, and I've had to put in a lot of hours—"

"But the company's doing okay?" Carma set the dishes on the counter, then opened the dishwasher. "What's stopping you now?"

Andie shrugged. "I don't know anyone I'd like to marry."

"Maybe you should meet some new people."

"Maybe." Andie sipped from her third cup of coffee, then lowered her mug. Any more caffeine and she'd be likely to leap out of her skin. "Do the paparazzi ever bother you here?"

Carma turned, a startled look on her face. "Are you kidding?"

"I never kid about those pests."

Carma chuckled. "I haven't seen a photographer around here in ages. They stopped coming the year I got pregnant. A shot of me carrying all that extra weight must not have been worth much on the tabloid market."

"How do you maintain your privacy? Don't people recognize you?"

Carma laughed as she rinsed a saucer and placed it in the dishwasher rack. "I've gained forty pounds and aged eleven years since our show was cancelled. Plus, I was younger than you when the show aired. No one recognizes me any more." She narrowed her eyes and studied Andie. "You haven't changed that much. I'll bet people recognize you even as a redhead."

"Sometimes they do. Most of the people I work with never watched the show, so I don't worry about them. Kids, however, are a different story. The other day a little girl on the train woke me up singing the Huggins Family theme song."

"I'm surprised anyone remembers it."

"You're forgetting about TV Land and Nickelodeon. The happy Huggins may live forever in reruns."

The irony in her words—and the fact that Cole was no longer living—brought pain, like a fist squeezing the base of Andie's esophagus. She fell silent and studied the morning paper as Carma rinsed and stacked, then wiped the kitchen counter.

When she was finished, Carma dried her hands on a dishtowel, gobbled the last bites of the toast, and said she needed to run upstairs to shower and change. "After that," she said, "we'll go out. I know some great shopping places downtown, then we can grab some lunch."

Andie gave her a whatever-you-want smile and let her go about her routine. After watching half an hour of the VPN morning show, she followed Carma upstairs, thinking that she might gather a load of laundry and ask if she could use her sister's washer and dryer.

Midway up the staircase, Andie's gaze fell on the dozens of framed photographs lining the wall. She'd barely glanced at them last night, assuming them to be pictures of Carma with her husband and children, but the morning light revealed them to be pictures of people Andie knew. She studied a photo of a middle-aged couple on a farm—the man's ruggedly handsome face seemed familiar, but her jaw dropped when she realized she was looking at Charlie and Bettina. The next photo featured Carma standing next to a woman with intelligence and strength etched into every line of her face: Carin. Another picture presented younger versions of Kalliope and Ritsa sitting in a young man's lap—and he had to be Callie, their uncle and Andie's youngest brother. Finally, she spotted Carma, Felix, and their children with a thin, dark-haired woman whose pronounced cheekbones emphasized the aura of melancholy emanating from her dark eyes: Andie's mother.

The old feelings of grief surged in her consciousness like a rogue wave that spun her into a deep pool of memory and loss.

Those people were her family, yet being with them was sheer torture, especially after Cole died. If not for the cameras, if not for the fame, they might have grown old together. She might have portraits like those on her walls.

Her stairwell featured photos of boring landscapes. Instead of sharing her home with children and a husband, she had a cat.

She had made certain choices, and she couldn't regret them now. She had been the lead singer, the cog that held the band together, and her decision to run freed all of them. If she hadn't made those choices, their mother might still be controlling their lives. If she hadn't found the courage to run away, Carma might not have Felix or those darling girls.

Andie continued up the stairs, gulping deep breaths so she'd seem calm and relaxed when she spoke to her sister. When she approached the master bedroom, however, she overheard Carma talking to a friend on the phone. She was canceling a lunch date, something Andie hadn't asked her to do.

Andie stepped into the room, waved for Carma's attention, and told her not to change her plans. "I have another friend in town," she explained. "I can meet her for lunch."

Carma covered her phone. "I thought you didn't know anyone in Charleston."

"I made a friend on the train. I can call her."

"But I can have lunch with Brittany almost—"

"I didn't come here to upset your plans. Go on, have lunch with your friend. I'll meet you back here later in the afternoon."

When an expression of relief crossed her sister's face, Andie knew she'd made the right choice.

She would forget about doing laundry. She stepped into the guest room and took her cell phone from her purse, then dialed Janette's number. She had no idea what Janette had planned for the day, but if Matthew and the kids wanted to swim at the hotel, she might be desperate for company.

Thankfully, Janette answered right away.

"Hi, it's Andie. I thought maybe we could meet for lunch and a bit of sightseeing this afternoon."

Relief threaded the woman's voice. "Are you okay? I worried about you all night, afraid your sister wouldn't be home—"

"She was, and everything's fine. But my sister has plans for lunch, so if you'd like company today—"

"Of course; I'm already dressed. Where shall I meet you?"

"How about at the first booth at the marketplace? My sister says it's downtown, right off Market Street. But you can ask anyone and they should be able to point you in the right direction."

"I'll be there. Around noon?"

"Sounds great. See you soon."

Before Carma could whine about not being a better hostess, Andie called a cab, which arrived fifteen minutes later. She gave her sister a hug, told her to enjoy her day, and promised that they'd catch up later.

◆

The cab dropped Andie at the Charleston market a few minutes before twelve . . . where Janette, Matthew, and the kids were waiting. The lawyer, overdressed in a wool jacket and tie, smiled a welcome and ran his fingers through his daughter's hair when Andie looked at them. Janette gave Andie a light, welcome embrace, but Roman was focused on his camera, reminding Andie that she needed to send Miles Pearson a few shots of horse-drawn carriages for his collection.

After greeting everyone, Andie looked at Janette and lifted a brow, asking in female shorthand if she was indulging in a bit of matchmaking. "Imagine meeting all of you here."

"Matt and his family were kind enough to keep me company at breakfast." A whisper of pink crept across Janette's cheeks. "Since I had no plans, they asked me to join them downtown." She gave Andie a look that clearly said, *What was I supposed to do, ask them to get lost at lunchtime?*

And apparently it was *Matt* now, not *Matthew*. At this rate, by the time they reached St. Augustine they'd be planning to exchange Christmas cards.

"Are you ladies ready for lunch?" Matthew joined them at the curb and grabbed each of his offspring by the hand. "There's a little seafood restaurant a couple of blocks to the east. They might have a kids' menu."

"I want a hamburger." Roman tugged on his dad's arm. "A big one."

"I want grilled cheese." When her father didn't respond, Emilia ratcheted up the volume. "I WANT CHEESE!"

Janette grinned, and Andie shrugged as if to say *kids will be kids*. Then she looked at Matthew and said she didn't care where they ate, any place was fine. So he led the way, dragging his hungry children forward while Andie and Janette tried to keep up.

Once the women were a safe distance behind Matthew, Andie whispered to Janette: "Our lawyer friend isn't using you as a babysitter, is he?"

"Heavens, no." She shook her head. "I love kids, especially when they're that age. My daughter was a delight when she was small." She drew a breath as if she would say something else, then pointed to a store window. "Would you look at that nautical lamp! I could spend all day window shopping in this place."

Once again Janette had abruptly changed the subject, but this time she'd left Andie a clue about her daughter. The little girl was once a delight but apparently was a delight no longer . . . What could have happened to change things?

Andie was out of breath from Matthew's brisk pace when they reached the restaurant, a quaint building with a chalkboard menu, exposed brick walls, and hand-painted murals on the few remaining bits of plaster. Everything about downtown Charleston seemed designed to reinforce the city's reputation as a historic site, but this building appeared genuinely old.

The hostess seated them and gave the children paper place-mats and a pair of crayons. Emilia set Walter on the table next to her, then asked the waitress if the dinosaur could have a crayon, too. The hostess obliged, dropping a red crayon by the thread-bare animal. As the kids busied themselves drawing pictures, the waitress arrived with water. She smiled, introduced herself, and set glasses on the table, but when she reached Janette, she accidentally spilled the glass. Water splashed over the table and splattered Janette's chest.

"Aaaaack!" Janette shoved her chair back, trying to escape the ice-cold waterfall streaming over her placemat.

"I'm so sorry." The flustered waitress picked up the glass, then hurried away for paper towels. Matthew and Andie tossed their napkins on the spill, sopping up the water as best they could. The waitress returned a moment later, her cheeks blazing as she apologized again and mopped up the mess.

When the water was gone and Janette had been given a dry placemat and napkin, the embarrassed girl stood beside their table with her notepad. Everyone placed their orders, then the waitress left.

At that point Matthew excused himself and took his cell phone outside to make a call. The women watched from the window as he paced on the sidewalk, emphatically gesturing as he talked.

"Poor man finds it hard to leave his work at the office." Janette's gaze drifted toward the children. "No wonder these little darlings are always trying to get his a-t-t-e-n-t-i-o-n."

Emilia dropped her crayon and handed Andie her placemat. "I drew this for you."

"You did?" Andie took the page and studied it. "I love the colors. It's really beautiful . . . but what is it, exactly?"

A dimple winked in Emilia's cheek. "It's us in a carriage." She pointed to a row of round heads, each dominated by a half-moon smile and two dot-eyes. "That's you and Daddy and Miss

Janette and Roman. And that—" she placed her finger on a figure that looked like a watermelon with stick legs— "is the horse pulling the buggy."

"Ohhh, I see. It's a lovely picture."

"Thank you." The girl settled back in her seat. "It's for you to dismember me by."

"Dis—oh. Well, thank you again, it's a nice keepsake. Every time I see it, I will think of you."

Emilia looked at her brother's incomplete picture, then tilted her head to look up at Andie. "We're going to Grandma's house soon. Daddy says we'll be there in a couple of days."

Andie made a quick calculation. "Does she live in Savannah?"

"Uh-huh. Daddy says she has a big house with a room for Roman and a room for me. Daddy says Grandma's town has nice schools where they let you paint with your fingers and play on the playground."

"Really." Daddy certainly had been saying a lot about Grandma's house, but why would he mention the schools? Andie cut a glance to the window, where Matthew was still gesticulating at the unseen caller on his phone.

She stretched her hand toward Roman. "Are you drawing a picture, too?"

The boy, who had made only a couple of marks on his placemat, let the crayon fall from his fingers. "I'm too tired."

"Didn't you sleep last night?"

Emilia answered for her brother. "He's sleepy because Daddy let him stay up to watch Power Rangers on the movie channel."

Janette arched a brow. "Does Daddy always let Roman do whatever he wants?"

Emilia nodded. "Daddy doesn't care when we go to sleep. Nanny Nessa cared, though. We had to be in bed by eight. Sometimes the sun was still shining when she tucked us in."

Andie acknowledged Emilia's indignation by blowing out her cheeks, though she could imagine the relief their nanny must have felt when eight o'clock rolled around. These two were a handful at the best of times, and when they were at their worst . . .

God help their next nanny.

When the waitress brought their drinks, Andie folded Emilia's picture and slipped it into her purse. Talking to Emilia and Roman reminded her of Carma's children, and she couldn't forget that her sister's family was flying to California tomorrow. Carma would see their other siblings—all of whom Andie missed—and their dying mother. Though Andie couldn't say she missed her mother, she certainly didn't hate her. She wasn't happy about her mother's illness, and she didn't want anyone to think she was bitter—

But she couldn't imagine any way of going to California without exposing her new life to the dangerous influences of the past.

"Janette—" she propped her head on her hand, shielding her face from the children's view—"I could use some advice."

Janette snorted softly. "I'm not sure I'm the best person to talk to."

"You seem to have a lot of common sense."

She barked a laugh. "You don't know me that well."

Andie smiled, refusing to believe Janette wasn't the calm, sensible woman she appeared to be. "Still, would you mind if I laid out a hypothetical situation for you?"

"Hypothetical?"

"Mostly."

Janette closed her eyes, and when she opened them again, she appeared resigned. "Okay. Go ahead."

Andie drew a deep breath. "Suppose I came from a big family and my mother had an addiction of sorts. Once her addiction got her into some trouble that pretty much destroyed our family. Dad left us and after that, once we were old enough to leave home, most of us kids went our separate ways."

"Your hypothetical situation doesn't sound all that unusual."

"Maybe not, but let's say there's a wrinkle. What if I've just learned that my mom is dying. I've worked really hard to establish a new life away from my family—most of them don't know where I'm living or what I'm doing. But my sister is going to see Mom before she dies, and she's trying to convince me to go, too. I would go if I thought I could just drop in and see her, but you don't know my mom—everything with her ends up being a production. If I go and all the family's around, I'll be caught up in that old life again."

When Andie's voice broke, Emilia looked up from the picture she was coloring, her little forehead pleated with concern.

Andie flashed the child a wavering smile, then turned back to Janette and lowered her voice. "Am I being a total monster if I stay away? My sister seems to think I'm being heartless, and maybe I am. But there was a time when I got up every morning and asked God why he hadn't done something about my mother. Now I don't know what I'm supposed to do. I want to do the right thing, but what is that?"

Janette tilted her head and looked intently at Andie. "This situation doesn't sound hypothetical."

Andie shrugged. "Can't help that."

"So you're being honest." She took a deep breath. "Let me make sure I understand—your mom is an alcoholic?"

"Her addiction isn't drugs . . . it's a lifestyle. One I want nothing more to do with."

Janette gave her a wry half-smile. "You wouldn't believe the ideas running through my head. Were you in the mafia? Running from a coven? Maybe you were part of a cult that abused children in bizarre satanic rituals."

Andie laughed aloud. "I hope you're kidding. Our situation isn't that dramatic, but it was unusual."

Janette looked past her, thought working in her eyes. "Well . . . first, I don't think God has struck your mother with an illness because of your prayers. He can do anything, of course, but when we ask him to punish someone who's hurt us, we usually don't realize that only his mercy prevents us for being punished for the times we hurt others. None of us is perfect, Andie—not your mom, not you, not me."

"I never said I was perfect." Andie lifted her chin. "But I've never been able to understand why God put me in a family with a mother who could be absolutely toxic."

"I don't know why, either." Janette's voice softened. "But you're a lovely young woman—pleasant, thoughtful, and good-natured. You must have picked up a lot of good qualities from your family, even your mom. I've watched you with Matt's kids—you're very patient with them, and you had to learn that from someone. Maybe you were exposed to hurtful influences, but you were also exposed to goodness. Surely your mother had something to do with that."

Andie drew a deep breath. "I know you're religious."

"I'm a Christian."

"So you probably think I should go see Mom and turn the other cheek or something?"

Janette smiled. "I don't know if cheek-turning is called for, but perhaps you should go see her. Maybe you have a right to stay away, but having the right to do something doesn't mean it's the right thing to do. I have the right to be rude to our waitress when she spilled water all over me, but I'd rather bless her than hurt her. You don't owe your mother a visit, but what would it cost you to bless her with kindness?"

That radical thought stole the breath from Andie's lungs. What would it cost to visit her mom? Everything. Her identity. Her privacy. The new life she'd managed to create out of the jagged shards of the old.

"Maybe 'bless her' isn't the right phrase to use with a young person." Janette frowned. "Maybe I should have suggested that you should do her a solid or cut her some slack."

Andie choked back a hysterical laugh. "Doesn't matter what you call it. I don't think I can go. It'll cost me too much."

"No one can make you do anything you don't want to do." Janette's voice dropped to a soft whisper. "But why don't you pray about your choice?"

Andie gave her a half-hearted smile. "You think God cares about my decision?"

"He cares about everything . . . especially the situations we can't handle ourselves. Or so—" Janette's voice cracked "—I've always heard."

Andie leaned forward, about to ask what was upsetting the older woman, but Janette shook her head and refused to meet her gaze.

All right, then. Janette's problems were still off limits.

Andie lowered her napkin to her lap as the waitress approached with a platter of food. Matthew wandered in, his cell phone tucked into his coat pocket, and for once the kids were quiet as they eyed the heaping plates.

Janette turned back to Andie as the waitress set the plates on the table. "I once had a friend who hurt me deeply," she said, lowering her voice as she laid her hand on Andie's arm. "We had been close, but I didn't speak to her for years after she lied about me. Then I heard that she'd lost her husband, and a little voice inside told me to go see her. I didn't want to go. I wouldn't care if I never saw her again. But that little voice kept hounding me, so I drove over to her house."

Janette fell silent as the waitress lowered a plate before her, but as soon as the girl moved away, she leaned closer to Andie.

"I went, and my former friend's eyes lit up when she opened the door. She hugged me like I was a long lost sister, and smiled as if she'd completely forgotten about our falling out. And while I sat on her sofa making small talk, I kept thinking that I had the right to confront her about how she'd wronged me. I wanted to confront her and I wanted an apology. But I had a loving husband

at home, and my friend was living alone in a house full of memories. I realized I could never beat her up about something that
happened years before. She might not even remember it."

"But as I said good-bye, she grabbed my hand and clung to
it like a drowning woman. 'I'm so sorry,' she said, beginning to
cry. I thought she was finally about to apologize and set things
right, so I stopped at her door. 'I'm so sorry,' she said again, 'that
you've held a grudge and kept us apart for so long.'"

When Matt asked for the catsup, Andie passed it without taking her gaze from Janette's face. "What'd you say to that?"

A small smile tweaked the corner of the older woman's
mouth. "At first my anger flared — how could she blame me for
our estrangement? Then I wanted to laugh. Some people are
simply blind, Andie. They only see what they want to see, and
they're not going to change because life hands them a tragedy.
But they don't have to make us suffer. We can accept them, forgive them, and move forward. So that's what I did."

"Do you still see her?"

"We have lunch every couple of months — when I'm in town,
that is." Janette gave Andie's arm a final pat, then turned her attention to her salad.

Watching Emilia tackle her grilled cheese sandwich, Andie
couldn't help feeling a small pinch of jealousy. Life was so simple
for children. When she was young, her biggest gripe had been
being forced to watch Cole and Callie when they played in the
backyard. Such a simple task, but as a kid, she'd resented being
asked to do it.

She'd give anything if she could be asked to handle that responsibility again.

Because her train left at an unearthly hour on Thursday morning, Andie dressed in the dim light of a bedside lamp. When she
was ready, she called a cab from her cell phone, not wanting to
wake Carma's family on the day they'd be flying to Los Angeles.

She had just finished lugging her suitcase downstairs when the stairwell light came on. Carma appeared on the landing, wrapped in a white terrycloth robe.

"Are you sneaking away in the middle of the night?" She spoke in a stage whisper as she padded down the stairs.

"I'm sorry. I didn't want to wake you."

At the bottom of the steps, Carma threw her arms around Andie and held her for a long moment. She hadn't rebuked Andie for deciding to return to the train, and that simple kindness brought tears to Andie's eyes.

Carma released her, then wrapped her hands around the newel post, her eyes gleaming beneath the overhead light. "Can I tell the others I've seen you?"

"Sure. Tell them I miss them. And who knows?" Andie forced a laugh. "Maybe I'll show up on one of their front porches someday."

Carma grinned, then her brows knotted. "And what should I tell Mom?"

Andie hoisted her purse onto her shoulder and exhaled a deep breath. "Tell her I love her."

"I will." Carma studied her for a long moment, then her cheek curved in a wistful smile. "If Cole were dying in that hospital room, would you fly out to see him?"

The gentle question snapped like a whip.

"Totally unfair." Andie kept her voice low, but she was sure Carma could see the hurt she'd inflicted. "Cole isn't with us any more . . . and that's Mom's fault."

Carma's face rippled with regret, then she stepped away to unlock the front door. "Don't stay a stranger," she said as Andie rolled her luggage onto the porch. "Write me. Call me. Visit us again sometime."

"I will." Andie stood her suitcase upright, then looked out over the dark street, searching for oncoming headlights. A car was approaching from the north, and at this hour it was likely to be her cab.

"You be good." Andie hugged Carma again. "And take care of my beautiful nieces, okay?"

Carma nodded and rubbed her nose. Andie knew that gesture; Carma always did that when she was about to burst into tears.

Andie gave her sister another smile and a wave, then thumped her way down the porch steps.

The Silver Meteor was scheduled to depart Charleston at 5:06 a.m., and dawn was still hours away when the cab pulled into the depot. Andie paid the driver and waited until he unloaded her suitcase, then she grabbed the pull-up handle and hesitated. Through the depot windows, she saw several other passengers: slow-moving women with sleeping children in their arms, an old man dozing in a wheelchair, Matthew Scofield with his kids, and Janette checking her suitcase at the baggage window. Soon the train would pull in to disgorge a few riders and take on a few more.

Should she be one of those travelers? Should she obey her instincts and continue south with her new friends? Or should she follow her conscience and head to the airport?

The question shimmered in the soft glow of a streetlamp, and something in the quiet reminded her of the morning she woke for Cole's funeral. Before sunrise she had crawled out of bed and tiptoed to her bedroom window. Squinting out over the lawn where she and Cole had played together, she saw dozens of glowing red orbs — burning cigarettes — behind the iron bars of the gate. Even at that hour, a horde of photographers and reporters had gathered, all of them waiting for some marketable sign of the Huggins family's grief: a soul-shattering cry, the glint of tears on a cheek, a trembling hand, evidence of faltering steps. Like vultures they perched and preened, cackling to each other, their movements crunching the gravel. Then, like now, the predawn hush magnified every sound.

Now the predators were gathering outside the Cedars-Sinai Medical Center in Los Angeles, where her mother waited for death. If she went to California, she would be unwillingly exposing the most private parts of her soul to the marauders who collected evidence of human pain and packaged it for the pitiless masses. She could be filmed for a television special she wanted no part of, and subjected to the media scrutiny she had hated for so many years.

Bless her mother with kindness?

Janette Turlington meant well, but she did not know what Andie knew, she had never walked where Christy Huggins had walked. And Andie would not willingly go down that path again.

She gripped the handle of her suitcase and dragged it toward the doors of the depot.

◆

"If you need a friend, if you need a smile, come to the Huggins' house for a while . . ."

Because she'd been dozing, at first Andie assumed the theme song was embedded in the fabric of her nightmare. But she opened her eyes and found herself on a moving train, in a window seat, yet that blasted song kept playing . . .

She looked across the aisle, at Roman and Emilia. Like so many others on the train, Roman was asleep and curled under a blanket, but Emilia sat upright, Walter the dinosaur under her arm and a new DVD player on her lap. Andie had been with Matthew when he bought portable players for the kids, but she didn't notice which DVDs the kids had picked out.

She groaned as reality hit. Apparently Emilia bought the *Home with the Huggins* boxed set. Andie might have to hear Huggins music all the way to Savannah.

"Emilia!" She leaned across the aisle. "Didn't you get headphones for that thing?"

The girl blinked at Andie as the overhead reading light painted a soft halo over her brown hair. "I don't know."

"I'm sure it came with headphones. Maybe they're in your backpack."

Emilia shrugged and returned her attention to the DVD player. On the screen Andie saw her siblings singing on a staircase, lined up like ducks in a shooting gallery.

She sighed. Emilia's pink backpack was nowhere in sight, which meant it had probably been stored in the overhead compartment along with Roman's and Matt's stuff. Matt was sleeping in the seat in front of Andie, and she didn't want to dig through his belongings without asking permission. But to ask permission, she'd have to wake him, and she didn't want to do that, either.

Though the music woke her, it didn't seem to be bothering anyone else. After glancing around to make sure, Andie leaned back and closed her eyes. The theme song ended as the program settled into an episode. Cole's pre-adolescent voice carried across the aisle, followed by Charlie's baritone rumble, then she heard her mom explaining that they had a gig, so they'd better learn the new song. Andie didn't have to look to know they were gathering in the garage as Mom passed out charts and they assumed their places. And then, through the marvel of selective editing, the Huggins family played the song without a single mistake, every note pitched perfectly and every rhythm precise.

Just as the sound engineer and video editor produced it.

Though her memories were tinted with cynicism and regret, the music remained fresh. As irresistible as forbidden fruit, the song called to her:

I wouldn't be who I am without you.
I wouldn't be what I am, it's true —
I wouldn't know how to get along, I wouldn't know real love,
So come on brother, sister — we've got to make it through.

Lift up your hands and be my brother,
Lift up your voice, my sister, too —
We'll sing a song unlike any other,
'Cause I couldn't be who I am without you.
No, I wouldn't be who I am without you.

Suddenly Andie was singing in her head, whispering the words, breathing in rhythm, holding the high notes only she could reach. With her eyes tightly closed, she felt her brothers and sisters around her. She heard Charlie riffing on the bass and Carin playing the drums, she saw Carma smacking her tambourine while Cole stood at the microphone, his voice harmonizing with hers. She sensed the keyboard under her fingertips and felt the stretch through her tendons. At stage right she saw her mother on the guitar, her smile inspiring them with confidence and urging them to do their best.

And for the moment, captured by the music, Andie was a Huggins again, a musician, a performer . . . and she liked it. Carried along by the power of the music, she felt every chord change, every sustained note, every thump of the drums. She believed the message, she inhaled it and lived it and clung to it, because they were a family, they were the Huggins, and they had each other. They had only each other, because since the show had gone on the air they found it nearly impossible to develop friendships outside the family circle. New friends didn't value them for who they were, but as what a Huggins might do for them, so the sibs depended on each other for companionship, advice, friendship, and fun . . .

Unbidden and unexpected tears slipped down Andie's cheeks as the music brought her long-neglected family back to life.

# Chapter Eight

She was stumbling through a fog-filled landscape while a little girl clung to her hand and a female voice asked: If Cole were dying in that hospital room, would you fly out to see him?

Ouch. Her eyes flew open when something hit her head. Emilia stood on the armrest of the seat next to Andie, tossing things in every direction—

Andie picked up a small plastic football that had appeared in her lap.

Mindful of the sleeping people around them, Andie tugged on the bottom of Emilia's sweatshirt. "Sweetheart, you need to get down. What if you fall?"

"I need my coloring book. I want to show Grandma how good I can color."

"I'll get it for you." Once she'd helped Emilia down, Andie reached for the pink backpack containing the little girl's toys, books, and DVDs. She handed it over, put the football, a coat, and a book back in the overhead bin, then dropped into her seat and looked out at the eastern horizon. The sky had brightened considerably since they left Charleston, but the sun still hadn't made its appearance.

A conductor came down the aisle, studying the destination cards above their seats and waking those who were to get off in Savannah.

"You were talking." Emilia pulled out one of her coloring books. "You were saying, 'Go, go, go.' Were you dreaming about a race or something?"

Andie shivered and pulled the edges of her sweater together. "I don't think so."

The announcer said something unintelligible over the intercom, but most of the Savannah passengers were already preparing to detrain. Several had begun to take suitcases, hats, and duffel bags from the overhead bins while a female attendant moved down the aisle collecting pillows and blankets.

Emilia stopped coloring and looked out the window. Together she and Andie watched the depot appear, then the train stopped. Behind them an attendant opened a door and lowered the stairs. Andie stood as Matthew rose from his seat, shaking off sleep like a dog shaking himself dry.

"You wait here for your daddy," Andie told Emilia as she moved into the aisle. "He'll want to hold your hand as you get off."

"Can't you hold my hand?"

Andie turned away from those earnest brown eyes. "You need to wait for your Daddy."

Once again Andie was the first of their little group to detrain, and once again she beat Matthew and Janette to the baggage area. She claimed her bag and settled her briefcase atop the load, then strode through the terminal, dodging the woman with the Welcome Home, Michael! sign, the young man waiting with a single red rose, and other bright-eyed relatives standing on tiptoe in their eagerness to greet family members.

Once outside, she breathed deeply of the fresh air as her

half-formed decision bloomed to fullness. She had a family, too. And they were gathering in California.

She gripped her suitcase and headed toward a sleepy-eyed cabbie at the taxi stand.

"I need to go to the airport," she told him, leaving her suitcase beside his trunk as she opened the taxi's back door. "As quickly as you can get there, please."

"Whatever you want, lady." He hurried to the rear of the car. While he loaded her bag, Andie used her phone to search for available flights to Los Angeles.

She was terribly tempted to look over her shoulder, but she didn't want to see Matthew or Janette or one of the children. She hated goodbyes, and she didn't know if she'd ever see those people again.

But Janette would realize where she'd gone, and she'd explain things to Matthew.

Maybe she'd be back in a few days and rejoin her friends for the trip to St. Augustine. Maybe she wouldn't make it back at all. But Janette would tell Matthew that Andie had done the right thing.

As for Roman and Emilia . . . Andie blew out a breath. She'd exhibited bad manners by rushing off without saying goodbye, but she was nobody to them, not really. Only a brief acquaintance, a lady they met on the train. She doubted they'd remember her for long, and that was a good thing.

Because her decision to leave was so tenuous she couldn't risk one of their smiles changing her mind.

Andie caught an early morning flight from Savannah to Atlanta, then boarded a jet that flew from Atlanta to Los Angeles and touched down at noon.

As she waited at baggage claim, she dialed Janette's cell phone, but her call went straight to voice mail. Because she was no good at goodbyes, her words came out in a solid string, as if they'd been glued together: "Janette-I'm-sorry-I-didn't-say-anything-but-I-am-going-to-see-my-mother.    Thought-you'd-understand. Tell-Matt-and-his-kids-goodbye-for-me.  And-by-the-way-Emilia-was-right.My-name-was-Christy-Huggins-before-it-was-Andie-Crystal. Sorry-to-be-so-secretive. Thanks-for-everything."

She disconnected the call and slowly exhaled. She didn't know if Janette had ever heard of the Huggins Family, but it really didn't matter. At least Andie hadn't left her with a lie.

By one o'clock, she was twenty-four hundred miles from Savannah and on her way to Hollywood. The cab driver gave her a strange look when she told him where she wanted to go, but within an hour he turned through the gate and slowed, glancing from left to right.

"You want me to let you out someplace special?"

"Turn right," she told him, "and I'd like you to wait. I shouldn't be more than a few minutes."

He drove slowly down the narrow access road, squinting at ornate monuments in the Forever Hollywood Cemetery. "I don't get much call to come out here." He stopped to gawk at the mausoleum on a small island in the center of a man-made lake. Fountains plumed above the water and a solitary visitor walked over the floating bridge.

The cab driver turned to Andie. "You thinkin' 'bout bein' planted here?"

"Not any time soon." She pointed to a side road. "You can pull over and wait there."

When the cab stopped, she got out and took a moment to check her bearings. If memory served, this was section seven. Cole's marker lay to the left, right next to Vampira, aka Maila Nurmi, gothic actress and star of *Plan Nine from Outer Space*.

Something within her went silent when she discovered her brother's resting place. The slab over his gravesite was still shiny, but some of the engraving had filled with dull residue from grass clippings, fallen leaves, and dust. Someone should pressure clean the stone.

She sank to the small bench at the foot of the grave and read the inscription: *Cole Andrew Huggins, Jan. 4, 1985–Aug. 31, 2001. Son, Brother, Friend. We wouldn't be who we are without you.*

Anguish rose inside her and broke forth in a sob. "I'm sorry I stayed away so long. I'm sorry I've never told anyone that you're my brother. Most of all, I'm sorry nobody knew how really wonderful you were even away from the cameras."

She closed her eyes as the memory of that awful August night swamped over her. They had finished a gig at the Beverly Wilshire—a bar mitzvah for some movie director's kid—and Andie wanted to go see the movie *Pearl Harbor* with Charlie and Carin. Cole wanted to go with them, but because Andie knew the movie would be a tearjerker and she didn't want Cole to make fun when she cried, Andie insisted that he ride home with Mom.

When he didn't give her a hard time about not being left behind, she should have realized that he'd thought of a way to take the sting out of the situation.

Carma would later tell Andie the entire story. While Charlie, Carin and Andie stood in line for the theater's last showing, Cole begged Mom to let him drive home. Though most kids Cole's age had been driving for months, he hadn't had many opportunities to get behind the wheel. At sixteen, he was still driving with a learner's permit, and under the terms of that provisional license he was allowed to drive at night only if accompanied by another licensed operator over 25.

As their van driver prepared to leave with the sound equipment, Mom asked if Carma and Callie could ride with him. Cole strutted around with Mom's keys dangling from his thumb, obviously eager to drive her Lexus. As the responsible operator, Mom should have taken the front passenger seat, but, thinking that footage of Cole behind the wheel might be useful for the show, she called the cameraman, Hank, out of the van and asked him to film Cole driving. Oliver, the family's agent, joked about the risk of riding with Cole in rainy weather, then hopped in the equipment van.

Both vehicles pulled away from the Beverly Wilshire a few minutes after eleven. From the van behind Mom's vehicle, Carma saw Hank pointing the camera at Cole as he drove with one hand on the wheel. Every once in a while, Hank turned to get a shot of Mom, who was apparently making comments from the backseat.

Because Cole had to be thinking about the camera, because he kept his right hand low to avoid blocking the shot, because Mom wasn't beside him where she might have been able to shout a warning, because the roads were wet and Cole inexperienced and because a speeding black Escalade roared up from an obscure two-lane side road, he never saw the threat, never sensed the danger, never knew what hit him.

His mother walked away from the accident, traumatized but unhurt.

But Andie's beloved younger brother died on that dark and wet road, and so did Hank—father of two little boys and husband to Marianne, whose life had centered around her sons, her husband, and the macramé purses she sold every Saturday at the Santa Monica flea market.

Carma, Callie, and Oliver saw everything from the van.

The footage in Hank's camera never aired, and neither did the footage of Cole's funeral. After a flurry of retrospectives and teary tributes, the television audience said goodbye to Andie's brother and the network said goodbye to *Home with the Huggins*. Why? Depending on who you asked, answers ranged from "Because the Huggins were supposed to be a happy family, and happy families have no business being sad" to "Sorrow is incompatible with the established brand."

Andie believed the network dumped the show because the outworking of the family's grief would be too painful to be considered entertainment. America valued happiness and prosperity, but after Cole's death her family had little happiness or prosperity to share. Years of repressed disagreements erupted between her parents and spewed flames over the rest of the kids. Chester Huggins left the family, and after a few months of quiet preparation, so did Christy.

"I'm so sorry, Cole." The words clawed at Andie's throat as she forced them out. "I should have let you come to the movie with us. Or I should have stayed behind to drive. I would have talked Mom out of inviting Hank, so no one would have been distracted and you'd still be with us."

Fresh tears sprang up from a buried river as she pressed her hand to her mouth and stared at her brother's grave. Yes, if Cole were dying in a hospital bed she would go see him. She'd do anything for him, Dad, Charlie or Carin, Callie or Carma . . .

And she would visit her mother. Because even though she had spent years blaming her mom for the accident, she had also blamed herself.

Andie knelt at the foot of the grave, brought her fingertips to her lips, then pressed her hand to the polished granite that bore her brother's name.

The woman at the Cedars-Sinai reception desk gave Andie an odd look when she asked what room Mona Huggins was in, but she dutifully turned to her computer. After a moment, she pressed her lips together. "I'm sorry, but that room is closed to visitors. Immediate family only."

Andie considered pulling out her driver's license for ID, then remembered that it wouldn't help. "I am family. I'm her daughter."

"Which one?"

"Christy."

The nurse, who was definitely old enough to have grown up with the Huggins family, studied Andie as if matching her face to photocopied memories. "All right," she finally said. "That's room 402. Elevator's at the end of the hallway to your left."

No one seemed to think it unusual for Andie to pull a large piece of luggage through the wide hospital hallways, but this was Los Angeles, the national headquarters for cosmetic surgery. Maybe the staff was accustomed to the sight of people hauling suitcases in preparation for facelifts and other surgical alterations that required long-term private recovery.

She waited for the elevator, then waited again when the doors opened and a pair of orderlies wheeled out an empty gurney. She stepped aboard and put her luggage in a corner, then pressed the button for the fourth floor. Before the doors closed, a middle-aged man in shirt sleeves and dark jeans hurried into the car, nodded at Andie, and pressed the four again.

While the elevator rose, Andie studied the big black bag hanging from the man's shoulder. A laminated tag dangled from a corner, the word PRESS emblazoned in black letters. A reporter would be carrying a small notebook, maybe a digital recorder. Only cameramen and photographers carried bags that size.

With her senses on full alert, Andie followed the man through the fourth floor hallway and slowed her stride as he neared room 402. Sure enough, he strode into the room without knocking, emerging a moment later with the bag on his shoulder, a camera in his hand, and a grin on his face. "Can I get a cup of coffee somewhere around here?" he called to an aide at the nurse's station. She gestured to the left, and the man walked away.

He hadn't even hesitated, the brazen bully. She hoped someone inside had prevented him from getting a shot.

Andie hurried forward and knocked on the same door, then tiptoed inside the private room. A curtain had been pulled around the bed, so she stood her suitcase in a corner and pulled the curtain back.

Her mother lay silent on her pillows, her frame shrunken to a nearly skeletal state. Her face, once round and full, was nothing but angles and bones, tent poles beneath stretched canvas. Her eyes were closed, her lips parted, her hair pale and sparse. Downy wisps barely covered the pink skin of her skull, and blue veins outlined her flesh like a roadmap of worry.

Andie's oldest brother, Charlie, slept in a nearby chair, his long legs crossed, his head thrown back, his eyes closed. A folded newspaper rested in his lap and one arm dangled at his side. Fragrant bouquets adorned every horizontal surface—a dresser, a nightstand, even the wheeled overbed table against the wall.

Andie's mother slept, too.

Andie stepped toward the bed and waded into a deep pool of what might have been. If her mother had been gifted with a different temperament, if she had been less attracted to glitter and gold. If she had been content to be a soccer mom, if Andie had been able to adopt her mother's dream as her own. If Mom hadn't let Cole drive in the rain, and if Andie had been able to forgive her sooner . . . they might have been a different pair. They might be one of those mother-daughter duos who shared every secret and every sorrow. They might have been the best of friends. They might have been together for the last eleven years, instead of separated and out of touch.

Memories closed around Andie and filled her with a longing to start over. Janette had been right—her mother had been a source of grief, but Andie would never have had the life she'd led without her mom. She wouldn't have her siblings, her memories, her talents, or her history. She wouldn't have had her precious Cole.

The memory of Janette's words washed through her, pebbling her skin like the touch of a phantom spirit: *Some people are simply blind, Andie. They only see what they want to see, and they're not going to change just because life hands them a tragedy. But they don't have to make us suffer. We can accept them, forgive them, and move forward.*

Why not move on? In running away from her past, was she placing far too much emphasis on it? In refusing to see her family, was she wallowing in grief and resentment? Janette had found freedom from the past in rekindling a friendship. Maybe it was time Andie found freedom by reestablishing her family relationships.

She bit her lip. Carma hadn't hidden her identity, but she'd found a way to build a normal life with a husband and family. Apparently Charlie and Carin had done the same thing. Callie was the only one still living in Hollywood and still yearning for the spotlight. Because he couldn't move forward.

In a silence marked only by the squeaking of a cart moving in the hallway beyond the door, Andie forgave her mother for everything. She reached for the hand closest to her, the one not attached to a machine or an IV line. She didn't want to wake her mom, but at her touch the spider-webbed eyelids fluttered. Her mother's eyes opened; her head turned. A lost look filled Mona Huggins's face as she studied Andie. "Who . . . who are you?"

"It's me, Mom. It's Christy." The name she hadn't used in years rolled off her tongue, and at the sound of it something moved in her mother's eyes.

"Christy Diane?"

Andie nodded.

"My Christy is a blonde."

"Not anymore, Mom." Andie lifted a hank of her hair. "Blondes might have more fun, but redheads are remembered."

"Christy." The thin hand tightened around Andie as a smile lifted the sunken cheeks. "I knew you'd come."

"I'm here." Andie glanced toward the window saw that Charlie was still sleeping. This might be the only time she had alone with her mother, so she might as well say what she'd come to say.

"Mom?"

"You came."

"Yes, I did. I came because I wanted to tell you that I'm sorry for staying away so long. I know I hurt you, and I feel terrible about that. It was . . . wrong of me."

Mom's smile trembled as her eyes softened. "But you came."

Aching with regret, Andie leaned forward and kissed her mother's cheek. "I'm here, Mom. And I'll stay . . . as long as you need me."

A corner of her mother's mouth pulled into a slight smile. "Lift up your hands and be my brother," she sang, her voice dissolving into a thready whisper.

As her mother's eyelids lowered, Andie braced her arms on the bed railing and continued the song: "Lift up your voice, my sister, too. We'll sing a song unlike any other, 'cause I couldn't be who I am without you."

She turned the catch in her voice into a small cough and went on: "No, I wouldn't be who I am without you."

"Who are you?" The male voice was sharp and brimming with anger. Andie turned and saw her youngest brother, Callister, standing next to the privacy curtain. He'd grown up since she last saw him.

"Callie? My goodness, you've grown a yard."

"Sweet heaven, could it really be you?" The sternness left his face as he set coffee cups on the overbed table and wrapped Andie in a bear hug. As he held her, Andie couldn't help but remember what Carma said about Callie still holding a grudge. Maybe he did, but this hug felt sincere.

By the time she pulled away and turned, Charlie had awakened. He was staring at Andie as if he was seeing a ghost. "Christy? I don't believe it."

"It's me, Charlie."

"Come here, kiddo." He stood and hugged her, too, then kissed her on the cheek for good measure. "She'll be so glad you came. She hasn't said much, but we all know she's been waiting for you."

"I've already spoken to her." Andie glanced toward the bed,

but her mother's eyes were closed. "She was awake a minute ago. She knows I'm here."

"Good." He slipped his hands into the pockets of his jeans. "She keeps telling the crew not to film anything until you arrive. Then she wants a shot of all of us around her bed—" His voice cracked. "I can't believe we're losing her. I can't believe any of this."

He shuddered, his face lined with weariness, and Andie nearly staggered with guilt. She should have been around to carry part of the burden; she should have come sooner. Charlie, Carin, Carma, and Callie were still her brothers and sisters. No matter how painful the past, she loved them. They had never done anything to hurt her, but their love and laughter had pulled her through trying times. She could stand in front of thousands and sing, not because she loved the attention, but because she knew her siblings were depending on her. They were all members of the same team.

Charlie straightened, palmed tears from his face, and regarded her with a disbelieving look. "Good grief, girl, where have you been? We looked everywhere for you. Mom even hired a private detective."

She gave him a simple smile. "I got a little lost. I was never out of reach—Oliver stayed in touch with my lawyer, and Mr. Rueben kept me in the loop. If something important had happened to any of you, I'd have known about it."

Callie gestured to their sleeping mother. "You don't call this important?"

"I knew about it. But I wasn't sure I wanted to come until this morning."

"Not want to—" Charlie folded his arms. "How could you not want to come? Our mother is dying."

"I . . . thought I needed to make a new life for myself."

"So you threw the old one away?"

A low moan interrupted their conversation. Charlie and

Callie rushed to opposites sides of the hospital bed and bent in tender concern.

"Mom." Charlie's hand fell to her shoulder. "Are you in pain? Should I call the nurse?"

"Cole." She exhaled the name in a ragged whisper.

Charlie gestured to Andie. "Did you see? Christy's come home."

Her eyes opened and shifted from left to right, then focused on Charlie's face. "Christy's here?"

Andie cleared her throat. "Right here, Mom. At the foot of your bed."

"I thought . . . I thought I saw Cole."

Charlie stroked her hair. "You must have been dreaming. But Christy's here."

When Callie pushed a button, the head of the bed rose. Andie stood rooted in place, a dozen different emotions colliding as she waited for her mother to recognize her again.

The blue eyes reached out and found her, then settled on Andie's face, the pupils growing smaller as she stared. "Christy." Her cracked lips spread in a smile. "I knew you'd come."

Andie managed a small nod. "Carma and her family are on their way, too. They should be here soon."

"Everybody will be here." Mom moved her thin fingers, her thumb tapping each one as she counted. "Charlie, Carin, Christy, Cole, Carma, and Callie. All six of you." She shifted her gaze to Callie and patted his hand. "Don't worry, son. Call the crew; tell them we're all here. Warm up your voice like I taught you. Nobody will turn you down after this."

Andie fought back tears. Was her mother completely delusional? Mr. Rueben had mentioned something about a network deal, but surely Charlie and Callie wouldn't want to go through with it.

She looked at Charlie. "Is she lucid?"

Charlie shook his head. "Mostly. The network promised

to pay for the funeral if they could get exclusive footage of the Huggins family reunion. Apparently they hope to use it in a retrospective."

"And you think this is a good idea?"

"It's what Mom wants." Callie moved away from the bed and looked at Andie, his eyes narrow and gleaming. "Her story is every bit as fascinating as Farrah's. Since the production needs a narrator—"

"You and Mom have already decided that you'll narrate her story." She pinched the bridge of her nose and turned away, feeling as though she'd stepped into a nightmare. This sort of thing could only happen in California . . . and maybe only in her family. She had forgiven her mother, but how could she deal with this sort of craziness?

She turned, about to question her brother's sanity, when her thoughts hit a brick wall. What would it matter if someone filmed the family at her mother's bedside? The photo would be a blip in a newspaper; a video might make a two-minute spot on *Entertainment Tonight*. Any producer crazy enough to even want to produce a special would focus on the early days, not on the pitiful sight of a dying woman in her bed.

And maybe, just maybe, the sight of five children gathered around a dying woman would spur someone else to visit their dying relative.

Photos of Andie with her sick mother would strip away her privacy—anyone who cared enough to put facts together would realize that Andie Crystal and Christy Huggins were the same person. And so what?

A flash of comprehension ripped through her protective cocoon. So what if people discovered the truth? Nothing would change, nothing at all. Only the most desperate of tabloids would even be interested in such an old story.

And if in the months to come a child like Emilia happened to spot Andie on the street or a train or a bus, and if that little girl happened to sing the Happy Huggins theme song, Andie would only delight her by singing along. What could possibly be wrong with that? After all, she'd been sending songs to super-fan Janey for years.

Andie blew out a deep breath and dropped her purse into the empty chair. A beautiful arrangement of roses sat on the bedside table, and as she bent to inhale the fragrance, she spotted a small black square among the long-stemmed flowers. Curious, she extended a finger and pushed another blossom aside, revealing a cord attached to the square. Puzzled, her gaze followed the cord to a rectangular tissue box on the same table.

She picked up the cardboard box, shook it slightly, and felt the weight of a hard object inside.

She knew what it was; they'd sold the same type of hidden cameras on VPN. With a gadget like this, intruders didn't even have to be in the room to infringe upon the Huggins family's privacy.

Sighing, she looked at her brothers. "Did you two know about the camera tucked into these roses?"

Charlie's face screwed into a question mark, but Callie's expression remained locked in neutral—a dead giveaway. He not only knew, he may have set it up. "What camera?"

Andie leaned on the bed railing. "The one connected to the battery in the tissue box. I don't think filming our mother like this is the best idea in the world, but if she gave her permission I don't suppose there's much I can say."

"Callie?" Charlie gave him a perplexed look. "Have you lost your mind?"

"Oh, come on." Callie gave them a wintry smile, a weak attempt to persuade them that a hidden deathbed camera wasn't miles beyond the boundaries of good taste. "Think of all Mom's done for you. Think of all her dreams that were never fulfilled—"

"Think of all the dreams that were," Andie countered. "She had a husband and kids who loved her, she traveled throughout the world, and for a while she controlled a financial empire. Instead of regretting everything she lost, why doesn't she focus on everything she had?"

A sudden thought jutted into her consciousness—a memory of Janette's face. She almost felt like she was channeling the woman, saying the sort of things Janette would say . . .

Callie opened his mouth to speak, but Andie held up her hand, silently urging him to be quiet.

She hadn't come for the cameras; she'd come for her mother. She wanted to—how did Janette describe it?—bless her. Honor her. She wasn't sure she knew how to do that, but she knew what Janette meant. And because she wouldn't be who she was if not for her family, she needed to support them during this time. No matter what it cost, no matter how much it hurt, because it was the right thing to do.

After her mom had passed away, she wouldn't have to stick around for the press. She would, however, stay around for her family.

Andie inhaled a deep breath and slowly released it, calming her stormy heart.

"I won't complain about the cameras if Mom wants them," she told Callie. "Film whatever you want. But when this is all over I want us to go back to the house and talk. We need to catch up and spend some time together. After all, we're a family."

Charlie and Callie stared as if they'd never seen her before . . . and she didn't suppose they had ever seen her as a mature woman. In the passing years she'd learned to be independent, and she was a stronger person than the girl who fled years before.

But in the last few days she'd learned lessons that would impact the woman she would be in the future.

# BOOK TWO

*Rowe's Rule: the odds are five to six
that the light at the end of the tunnel
is the headlight on an oncoming train.*

— Paul Dickson

# Chapter Nine

**Savannah, Georgia**
**Thursday, November 15**

After checking to be sure the luggage and the kids' backpacks made it into the trunk of the cab, Matthew herded his offspring into the backseat and slid in beside them. He leaned forward and gave the lady driver his mother's address, then frowned at a prominent warning sticker on the dashboard: $250 cleaning fee if you yack in our hack.

If his colleagues could see him now.

Though the sun had barely risen above the flat line of the horizon, he settled back to survey his surroundings as the cab negotiated the curves of long-forgotten roads at the edge of Savannah's industrial district. Early morning fog still blanketed the ground and a thick hush lay over the earth.

A shame, really, that the romance of train travel died at some point in the mid-twentieth century. Most of the depots they'd passed on this trip had been neglected outposts at the fringe of their respective towns, aging buildings sequestered near junk-yards and automobile graveyards. For the most part, his fellow passengers had been college students and senior adults, people for whom airline travel must be too expensive.

He grimaced, remembering his colleagues' reactions when he mentioned his plans to take a train to visit his mother. "You're going by rail?" Don Giles, a partner at his firm and Matt's closest office mate, had regarded him with incredulity. "Why on earth would you do that?"

Matt shrugged. "I'm doing it for the kids. They've lost their nanny, and they'll soon be facing a major change in their situation. I thought a train trip might be educational and give us quality time together."

"You know the Cortez case comes up next month. The firm is counting on you to score a home run, pardon the pun, and the Nationals—" Don whistled. "Let's just say I'd hate to disappoint thousands of baseball fans."

Matt laughed. "Don't worry, I'll take care of Vito's immigration problems. I've found the names of a couple of witnesses who can testify that his life would be threatened if he's sent back to Mexico. We can get his visa extended."

"Just make sure you stay on top of it. The Nationals want his case settled in time for spring training."

"Don't worry. I'll have lots of time to read on the train. And along the way, I'll give my kids an experience they'll never forget."

That's why he bought cameras for the kidlings. Photos, he'd discovered, kept memories alive in a way nothing else could. Without tangible reminders, too many precious moments faded into memory and became lost in the clutter of life.

Even now he found himself wishing he'd taken more photos of Inga, for his sake and his children's. The kids had a few pictures of Nessa, whom they had liked immensely, and he hoped they had managed to capture a few shots of Andie and Janette. If his plans for Savannah worked out, he would be unlikely to ever see those ladies again.

Roman held his camera now, aiming at only-God-knew-what through the window. Matt peered through the glass, but saw only trees, grass, weeds, and the occasional overturned shopping buggy. He squeezed his son's shoulder. "What'd you shoot, buddy?"

"A bed, Dad. Under that bridge—" he pointed to the overpass behind them— "I saw a mattress and a big pile of stuff. Do you think someone lives there?"

Matt did, but how could he explain the problem of homelessness to an eight-year-old? "Did you see anyone living there?"

Roman shook his head.

"Then it might have been only a pile of trash. Some folks are too lazy to haul stuff to the dump, so they leave it wherever they want to."

"They shouldn't do that." Disapproval edged Emilia's voice. "That's messy. Nessa hated messes, and so did Mommy."

"I don't think your grandmother is too fond of them, either. So keep that in mind, will you, when we reach her house?"

The lady driver pointedly cleared her throat. She hadn't said a word since Matt gave her the address, so he caught her eye in the rear view mirror. She wasn't smiling.

"Is there a problem, ma'am?"

"Maybe some folks don't have no car to haul stuff to the dump." She shifted her gaze to the road. "Or maybe some folks don't have no home to live in. Did you ever think of that?"

"Thank you." He spoke in his most authoritative voice, tactfully reminding her that he was the parent of these children. They had years to learn about poverty and homelessness, and he didn't want to spoil their innocence at this point. He didn't want them to grow up the way he had.

Already he could feel the pull of this place. When the cabbie's dialect wrapped around him, all the hours he'd spent practicing standard English pronunciation slipped away like morning fog. He was glad the train tour only allowed two days in Savannah. If he stayed much longer, he might find a few *y'alls* or *fixin' tos* stowed away in his vocabulary.

"Eww." Emilia turned to him and pinched her nose. "What's that smell?"

"Smells like barf." Roman curled his upper lip. "I think I'm gonna hurl."

Matt gave him a grim smile. "The word is vomit, and you're not going to do it. The smell will pass in a minute or two."

"Roman always barfs at bad smells," Emilia informed him. "Nessa always told him to step outside and breathe some fresh air."

Once again Emilia had reminded him that the nanny knew his children better than he did. But he was learning.

"Fresh air, huh?" Matt put the window down as the driver eyed him in the mirror again.

"Outside air gonna make it worse," she volunteered. "The dump do smell bad when the sun heats up all that garbage. Just be glad we're not passin' by in the heat of the day—it stinks worse then."

Roman climbed over Matt and stretched for the open window, his mouth open while gagging sounds came from his throat. The driver's sticker flashed through Matt's mind—$250 cleaning fee if you yack in our hack—and he refused to owe this woman money just because his son had a highly suggestible stomach.

He put the window back up. "You are not sick, Roman. Sit up straight, please, and close your mouth. Try to think of something pleasant until we're away from this part of—er, the dump."

The lady driver thrust out her lower lip but said nothing as they continued over the twisting road. Eventually the air sweetened and Matt spotted signs of civilization: a stoplight, a pair of dilapidated wooden houses, a seedy convenience store. People were stirring; a woman walked to the mailbox on a shoulder-wide strip of bare dirt; a man stepped onto his front porch in bare chest and boxer shorts to verify the arrival of a new day.

The people who lived in this area were as poor as the people in Thunderbolt. Matt closed his eyes and saw himself walking to school on the dusty fringe of a two-lane highway, second-hand high tops flapping around his ankles because he couldn't afford shoestrings. He'd shiver in the chill until a vehicle passed by, then he'd lift two fingers and exhale a steaming breath, feigning the casual indifference of a young thug out for his morning smoke.

His kids had never walked to school . . . and if he had anything to do with it, they never would.

The driver took a ramp onto the interstate and drove in heavy morning traffic for a while, then the cabbie slanted toward the exit that would deliver them to the Bellewood development. Matt's mother had lived in Bellewood for ten years; long enough, he hoped, to feel that she belonged. Behind them, the rising sun finally crowned the horizon, spilling sunshine over what was certain to be a glorious day.

Matt stretched his arm along the back of the seat and inhaled a deep breath, feeling like a man who had sprinted through a painful race and was finally nearing the finish line.

Emilia straightened to make herself tall enough to see out the window. "Beautiful houses." As usual, her opinion was overly generous. "Grandma lives in one of these?"

"She does." Matt smiled, remembering the day he brought Momma to this subdivision, led her to an empty lot, and handed her the blueprints. After fifty years of living in the same tiny wooden house, she couldn't believe she would soon be leaving Thunderbolt for Bellewood, a suburban development where every tidy brick home featured front porch pillars, a garage, central air conditioning, tile floors, and at least two bathrooms.

"That the place, mister?"

When the taxi driver pulled to the curb, he recognized the

stately live oak shading Momma's front porch. "This is it. How much do I owe you?"

He slid several bills from his money clip while the kids scrambled out of the backseat. They sprinted up the driveway and Matt let them go, happy to stay behind and help the cabbie unload their luggage. Let Roman and Emilia ring the doorbell and surprise the bejabbers out of his mother. She'd be delighted to see them.

And if all went according to plan, she would never want to let them go.

◆

"Lord, have mercy!" Still in her flannel pajamas, Matt's mother wrapped the kids in a bear hug, then came after her son. "What are y'all doin' here?"

"Surprise, Momma." He returned her hug and gave her a peck on the cheek. "We took a train trip, and guess where we ended up?"

"I can't believe it!"

"You might as well, 'cause here we are."

He followed her into the house, dismayed to realize how easily he was falling back into the rhythms and cadences of the South. Momma wouldn't even notice if he slipped into old habits, but his co-workers would snort coffee through their noses if he dropped a y'all into a conversation.

After Momma whipped up a breakfast of pancakes and eggs, Matt and the kids gathered around her table and dazzled her with their ability to make a home-cooked meal disappear in no time. In between bites, Emilia told her grandmother about Andie, Janette, and the marathon Skipbo game they'd played in the cafe car. Roman bubbled over with stories of how big the train was, how delicious candy-coated sunflower seeds were, and how much he liked his camera and DVD player.

Momma lifted a brow at this last bit, silently letting Matt know she disapproved of gadget expenditures. Rather than launch a lengthy defense, he turned sideways and munched on the last piece of bacon.

Momma had sprung from a social stratum where children made toys from sticks and cast-off milk cartons. His kids wouldn't know what to do with a stick, and they'd be more likely to recycle a milk carton than play with it. He was raising upper middle class children, and nothing occupied a modern child better than an electronic gadget.

When every last morsel had been devoured, Matt grabbed the TV remote and stretched out on the sofa while the kids played in the wide backyard and Momma cleaned the kitchen. He kept one ear cocked for the sound of unexpected screams, realizing that his kids might not know how to climb trees or safely jump from a swing in motion, but he found it hard to hear anything over the dishes rattling in the kitchen. He watched the morning news, massaged his aching feet, and remembered that he ought to pull clothes for tomorrow from their suitcases. He stood, about to get the luggage, then he remembered where he was . . . and that Momma would happily iron anything that had wrinkled.

Smiling, he sank back to the sofa and took out his cell phone to make sure he hadn't missed any important messages. Don Giles had texted the dates for the Cortez case, but Matt's secretary would enter those in his calendar. Rookie pitcher Vito Cortez would require all his attention once Matt returned to the office, but the first hearing wasn't until December second, so he'd have plenty of time to prepare once this trip was finished. If all went according to plan, he'd have even more time than usual to devote to his client. He needed to locate his witnesses, travel to interview them and obtain affidavits, and talk to the Mexican authorities. The INS didn't extend visas to convicted drug users, but if Matt could vacate Cortez's youthful conviction and convince the authorities that the threats on the pitcher's life might actually serve as a strong incentive not to associate with drug dealers, the Washington Nationals wouldn't have to worry about their star rookie.

Finally, silence replaced the noise in the kitchen. The door opened, a stream of light poured into the quiet living room, and his mother dropped into the oversized easy chair. She leaned back, used her apron to wipe sweat from her temples, and breathed a sigh.

Matt peered at her. "Are you okay, Momma? You look a little worn out."

Her smile drew her cheeks up like curtains. "I'm fine. Just glad y'all are here."

He powered off the TV, aware that precious time was fleeting. He might need to do some last minute shopping for the kids, so it'd be advantageous to settle the arrangement as soon as possible. Once he returned home, he could get the kids' clothes boxed up and shipped in no time.

"You want anything?" he leaned toward her. "Want me to get you a Coke? A fresh cup of coffee?"

She closed her eyes. "Coffee's all gone."

"So I'll make some more."

"You don't know how."

"Sure I do. You put water in the well and coffee in the filter."

She opened one eye and squinted at him. "My coffee pot is aluminum and sits on top of the stove. I brought it from the old house."

She had a point—though Matt remembered the old coffee pot, he didn't think he'd ever used one that didn't plug in and practically operate itself. As a kid, he'd watched Momma make coffee every morning, but those details were buried with dozens of other memories he would rather not unearth.

He should get her a modern coffeemaker for Christmas. One of those one-serving models with the handy cups. No fuss, no bother, no waste.

"Momma—" he softened his voice and slanted toward

her— "I need to tell you what's going on. About why we're here."

She opened both eyes. "You didn't come to see me?"

"Of course we did. But there've been some developments in my life—"

Her face split in a broad smile. "Don't tell me. You're gettin' married again."

He blinked. "No. No, no. Whatever gave you that idea?"

She gave him a shrewd glance. "It's been over a year. You're bound to be lonely."

"I don't have time to be lonely, Momma, and I'm not looking for another wife. But I'm sure you've heard me mention Nessa—"

"That girl who talks funny?"

"She's Irish, Momma. Our Irish nanny. She's been wonderful for the kids. She got them through that hard time, got all of us through a time when I didn't know which end was up. Somehow she kept me on schedule and held our family together."

Momma flapped her hand in a half-hearted wave. "I remember her name bein' on last year's Christmas card. She was in the family picture, wasn't she?"

"The kids insisted. Anyway, Nessa had to leave us. She went home to marry her sweetheart, and she's going to stay in Ireland."

A tiny spasm of surprise widened Momma's eyes, then she shook her head. "That's too bad. Maybe you should have married her."

Matt blew out a breath. "It was never like that. And she was engaged."

His mother's brows knit with concern. "Will you get another nanny?"

"That's the thing. Since the kids are school age now, I thought we could get by with after school care. For the last four weeks I've been getting them out of bed every morning, making sure they're fed and dressed, and taking them to school. I've hired a couple of different babysitters to pick them up and help them with their homework."

"Sounds like a good plan. So how's it working?"

"It's not working at all." He sighed and ran his hands through his hair. "Getting the kids dressed and out the door is harder than I thought it would be. And last week, Roman was sick for two days, which meant I was trapped at the house trying to find a sitter while my associates scrambled to cover for me at an immigration hearing. I nearly got slapped with contempt of court, I ruffled feathers at the firm, Emilia was late for school, and I couldn't even manage to get my sick son to our family doctor—" he hung his head. "That's when I realized that part-time care won't work for us. My kids need someone to look after them full time. They need someone who'll be there when they're sick, someone who can pick them up when necessary and take care of them until I'm available. One babysitter wanted to go home every night at six, but I often need to stay at the office until eight or nine. I can't be a good lawyer and a good father. I've had to learn that truth the hard way."

The air in the living room thickened with the silence of concentration. Matt focused on the important things he'd gone there to say, and his mother seemed focused on listening. Good. This might have been the most crucial presentation he'd made all year.

Matt hauled his gaze from the floor and returned his attention to the little woman in the easy chair. "That's why I asked the partners for some time off. That's why I told the kids we were taking a trip to see Grandma. I thought we could make some wonderful memories on the journey, so I gave them digital cameras to make sure they'll never forget. I want them to be able to look at those photos and remember that their father loved them enough to spend several days cooped up on a train when he could have been working."

He smiled, hoping his mother had intuited where he was heading, but she only stared at him, her face composed and still.

"What I'm saying, Momma, what I'm asking, is this: will you

be the caregiver your grandchildren desperately need?"

To his great surprise, at first his mother showed no reaction. Then her mouth opened in a round O and her brows rushed downward in a distinct V. "Will I what?"

"Will you help me by taking the kids for a few months? I know you love them, and they adore you. They'd like Savannah, and they could transfer to the local schools. I'd come down as often as possible for weekends and holidays—"

Momma's eyes appeared to be at risk of falling out of her face. "You want me to raise your kids?"

"Not raise them—at least, not forever. Because I'm making a mess of things, I need you to take them off my hands for a while."

"For how long?"

There it was, the question he'd been dreading. He stifled a wince. "It would be wonderful if you could take them for the rest of the school year. Or at least until I can find the time to locate a suitable live-in nanny. But that could take a while, as I'll soon be tied up with a huge case that might last several months."

His mother sprang up like a jack-in-the box. "Matthew Levi Scofield, are you insane?"

He snatched a quick breath. "Momma, you know how hard things have been for me since Inga died. I've lost my wife."

"I think you've lost all your sense, too. I'm your mother, not your children's."

"But you love my kids."

"That I do. But you do, too, or at least you should. You're their father, Matt, and not having a wife doesn't let you off the hook. They need you to bring them up."

"Wait a minute, Momma. Other grandparents have stepped in to help rear their grandkids. Nearly all my clients have children who are in the care of aunts or grandmothers—"

"That's because nearly all your clients are locked up and waiting for their deportation hearings. They don't have a choice in the matter. You do."

He stared at her, his heart pounding, then he slid to the edge of the sofa. "That's just it, Momma, I don't have a choice, either. If I'm going to keep my job, if I'm going to do the work I was hired to do, I can't be a full-time parent. There simply isn't enough time."

She crossed her arms and sat back down. "Everyone has twenty-four hours in a day, son. You just need to restructure your priorities."

"It's not that simple."

"Why isn't it?"

He stood and strode to the window, his frustration building as he looked out over the leaf-strewn lawn. His mother must think lawyers put in tidy nine-to-five office hours, that they had an army of staff to assist with their jobs. She was right about the staff, but she didn't know about his firm's directive to submit twenty-three hundred billable hours per year or hit the street . . .

"Momma—" he whirled around to face her— "you don't understand the pressure I'm under at work. The partners expect me to put in a seventy-hour workweek—that means I'm at the office from seven in the morning until nine at night. I leave the house at six and get home at ten. If it weren't for weekends, I wouldn't even see my kids. Can you imagine how I felt when I realized that my children knew Nessa better than they knew me?"

Momma sank into the curve of her chair, her gaze focused on the base of the coffee table.

"I love my kids, Momma, and I hate the thought of them being raised by a succession of babysitters. Wouldn't it be better if family raised them? Someone who understood them? Someone who really loves them?"

Momma's chin quivered, and beneath her blank expression a suggestion of desperation glimmered in her eyes.

"Please, Momma." He stepped closer and held out his hands. "I'm begging you. Will you take my children for the rest of the school year? I'm not asking you to move; they can stay here with you. I'm not asking you to provide for them; I'll send money to cover anything they need. What I am asking is for you to give them the love they deserve. Be the one who'll teach them the difference between right and wrong, and encourage them the way you always encouraged me. Most babysitters don't care about my children's character, but you do. You raised me, and while I'm not perfect, I think you did a darn good job."

He waited, silence stretching between them, until his mother tipped her head back and met his gaze. "Maybe I didn't do such a good job," she said, her voice throaty and rough. "If I'd done better, you wouldn't be thinkin' about runnin' out on your kids."

"I'm not running out on them."

Her face crumpled with unhappiness. "I know it's not easy being a big-time lawyer and having two little kids, but nobody says you have to work for that fancy firm. You could come to Savannah and open an office here, maybe practice some other kind of law."

"It's not easy to switch careers, Momma. I can't change my area of expertise on a whim. And to come here, I'd have to take the Georgia bar exam."

"You're smart, you could pass any exam they give you. And why would you have to switch areas? We have immigrants down here, and I reckon they need lawyers as much as anyone up where you are. You should move to Savannah."

He groaned and massaged his temples, understanding where the discussion was headed. Momma might take his kids, but if she did, the favor would have an infinitely long string attached . . . to his ankle. After a few months, she'd reel him in, inexorably pulling him back to Savannah.

He knelt on the carpet beside her chair. "Momma, it wasn't easy to get where I am today. Coming from nothing the way I did, I had to work harder than any of my peers. My firm wouldn't have even looked at me if I hadn't graduated at the top of my class."

"Savannah could use another smart lawyer. Here you could find work that won't keep you busy fourteen hours a day."

"If I moved here, I couldn't make the kind of money I'm making in Washington."

"You wouldn't need that kind of money in Georgia. You could find a nice house in this neighborhood, a place with a good educational system. I could watch the kids after school, and you could pick them up at suppertime—"

"Momma, you're not seeing the big picture. If I'm going to realize my full potential, I need to mingle with the movers and shakers and policy makers. And I can only do that in Washington. That's where the power base is located."

Momma gripped the armrests of her chair. "Well, then. Maybe you'll never see things my way, and that's okay. Young people ought to have minds of their own. But you should know this, Matthew—I'm not going to be mother and father to your kids, not as long as you have breath in your body. Those two angels are heaven-sent gifts for you to love and protect. I'm not going to steal your blessings."

"You wouldn't be stealing them. I'd be loaning them to you."

The old chair creaked as she pushed herself up. "I'm glad you came to visit, Son, and I'm always happy to see my grandbabies. But I hope you can find something to do this afternoon because I have plans. I'd better get dressed now."

Before he could ask where she was going, she headed toward her bedroom, leaving him alone in the silence.

Still kneeling on the carpet, Matt stared at her empty chair. This was not the reaction he had expected. He thought she'd have questions. He anticipated her bringing up possible problems, and thought she might offer to move to Washington.

He never once considered the possibility that she'd flatly refuse his request. Like a novice lawyer who puts a hostile witness on the stand without knowing what she will say, he assumed too much and prepared too little.

He'd lost his case. He'd failed his clients.
And he didn't have a backup plan.

"You know, you really should have called first, Matthew."

Momma made this announcement in an iron voice, and the restrained fury in her eyes surprised him. He looked up from the sofa and saw that she had showered and changed into a purple velour jogging suit. She was already carrying her purse.

"I'm sorry, I didn't know you had plans." He straightened his spine, feeling like he'd just had his hand slapped. "If you want to go out for lunch, I could get the kids and we could meet—"

"I'm on a bowling league." She lifted her chin as though she expected him to dispute her. "Every Tuesday and Thursday, 11:30 sharp, we bowl three games. If I'd known you were coming—"

"It's okay, Momma, we'll be fine until you get back. I'll feed the kids cereal or something for lunch."

"I don't have any cereal."

This snippy tone was unusual . . . and so was the anger. What had he done to upset her to this degree? He ought to be furious with her for refusing to help his children.

He gave her a tight smile. "No big deal, Momma. After that huge breakfast, the kids aren't likely to be hungry. So go bowling. If the kids get hungry, I'll scrounge around and see what I can find to eat. We can always make sandwiches." He lifted a brow. "Surely you have peanut butter and jelly."

She gave him a stiff nod, then crossed the room and dropped her hand to the doorknob. "I've got to get on the road."

He shifted his attention to the TV. "Go ahead, have fun. We're not going anywhere."

"How long are you staying?"

He looked at her, surprised by the question. "You're acting as though you don't want us here."

"Of course I want you." Her eyelids fluttered as she forced a smile. "I'm delighted to see those adorable children. But I have a life, Matt; I have friends."

"I'm glad you do." He nodded toward the doorway, still mystified as to why she was behaving so strangely. "Go out with your friends, have fun."

"But you didn't answer my question—how long are you staying?"

Her insistence forced him to consider an answer. He had planned to leave the children with her; he had hoped to take a jet back to Washington after making sure they were settled. But if he couldn't change his mother's mind, he might as well fall back on already-existing arrangements.

"We'd like to spend tonight and tomorrow night with you, if that's okay. After that . . . well, our train leaves early Saturday morning, and I have to be on it to make it back to Washington in time to prepare for my next case. Do those plans work for you?"

She cut a glance toward a calendar hanging on the kitchen door, then nodded. "I'll have to juggle some appointments, but I can do that. There's peanut butter in the pantry and jam in the fridge. You take the guest bedroom, and put the kids in my sewing room. You'll find extra pillows and blankets in the upstairs hall closet, along with a couple of sleeping bags, if the kids would like to use those. Clean towels are under the bathroom sink. I'll be back in a couple of hours."

Matthew nodded, stupefied, and watched from the window as his fifty-eight-year old mother stepped outside and jogged down the front stairs.

# Chapter Ten

After Matt's mother left for the bowling alley, the kids came inside looking for a snack. Certain that he was raising children with bottomless pits where their stomachs should be, he pulled himself off the couch and scouted for food. Momma didn't have much — did she eat out all the time? — but he found a box of soda crackers in the pantry. He handed a small stack to each child, reminding them to be sure to eat at the table.

The kids made a game out of eating crackers, sliding the squares past their chomping incisors like planks being fed to a buzz saw. Crumbs flew right and left, but Matt was more concerned about his mother's state of mind than a few crumbs.

He slid into a chair and studied his offspring, waiting until the chewing game stopped and he had their full attention. "Sometimes," he finally began, "surprises aren't such a good thing. We surprised Grandma, and I think she's a little perturbed by our arrival."

"What's pre-turbed?" Emilia asked, her mouth stuffed with dry crackers.

"It means upset." Matt pressed his lips together. How honest should he be with his kids? He didn't want them to think he was dumping them, but the situation would be easier if they were excited about the possibility of living here. "We don't want to upset Grandma, okay? We want to be extra-nice to her because she loves us. So let's mind our manners while we're here, and let's be careful about her things. No running in the house, no shoes on the sofa, and always remember to flush."

Roman chomped the corner off a cracker and asked if Grandma had any peanut butter. Matt stood and crossed to the pantry, then set the jar on the table.

While the kids smeared peanut butter on their crackers, he took their luggage from the foyer and carried it upstairs. The air on the second floor was musty and stale, and a glance at the thermostat revealed the reason: Momma had turned off the heat pump. Because her bedroom was downstairs, he suspected she didn't often climb the steps. Still, he was glad she had the extra space.

He set the kids' bags in the sewing room where Momma stored everything she couldn't assign to any other area. On a quick survey of the room he found a single twin bed, dusty record albums, cassette tapes, a sewing machine, a portable cassette player, a mini-trampoline, dozens of books, a few board games, and a treadmill with dust on the track. His kids would probably consider this room a museum.

He dropped his suitcase in the guest room, a small space blooming with floral patterns and rose pink carpeting. Before heading back downstairs, he turned on the heat pump, grateful to hear the fan kick on and begin circulating the air.

"Hey, kids!" he called over the stairway railing, "Grandma's got games and books in the closet up here."

A moment later the stairs vibrated from the pounding steps of small feet. Once the kids started exploring Grandma's treasures, Matt figured he deserved a few minutes of personal time.

Leaving the kidlings to amuse themselves, he went downstairs, kicked off his shoes, and got horizontal on the sofa. A few clicks of the television remote landed him on ESPN, and he was happy to discover that his mother had finally had cable installed. He surfed through the sports channels and tried to ignore the occasional thump from up above.

When a particularly loud thump was accompanied by the sound of breaking glass, he sat up and wearily turned toward the staircase. "Roman? Emilia? What are you two doing?"

"Daddy! Roman broke a lamp!"

So much for his warning to be careful around Grandma's things.

Matt groaned and dropped his head back to the sofa, then realized that his mother wasn't around to take care of the situation . . . and neither was anyone else. Which meant he had to get off the couch, go upstairs, and clean up the mess before one of the kids opened an artery.

He took the stairs two at a time and found his children in the bathroom. Apparently Momma had positioned a small lamp on the back of the toilet — a dangerous place for any electric device — and one of the kids accidentally knocked it onto the tile floor. The lamp was smashed, the cord still plugged in, and they were surrounded by plumbing fixtures and running water —

In how many ways could one room spell death trap?

"Out." He pointed toward the door while bending to unplug the cord. "Go back to the sewing room and find something to do."

Emilia lingered near the doorway, Walter the dinosaur tucked firmly under her arm. "Grandma doesn't have toys. She doesn't even have video games."

"You can make up your own game. Play something with Walter."

"Walter doesn't know how to make up a game."

Matt turned, heat flooding his face. "Just get out of here, will you?"

Emilia's lower lip quivered. She stared at him, her fingers twisting, then she turned and ran, her sneakers squeaking on Momma's polished wooden floor.

Matt closed his eyes as a mantle of guilt threatened to smother him. He shouldn't have yelled, he didn't mean to snap at her, and he had to be the worst father in the world. All of which only proved that he wasn't meant to raise children. His mother was far more suited for the job, so why couldn't she see it?

He picked up the largest shards and dropped them into the bathroom trashcan, a ridiculously ornate glass receptacle trimmed with gold. Since when did his mother begin decorating with so many fragile objects?

Irritable and unhappy, he carried the body of the ruined lamp downstairs and tossed it into the tall kitchen trashcan, then paused. He didn't think two children could make much of a mess with crackers, but the table was littered with crumbs and smears of peanut butter. The open jar was still out, the knife inside, and an undeniable handprint marked the place where Emilia sat. What'd she do, spread peanut butter with her fingers?

That mess would have to wait; a more urgent disaster demanded his attention. He opened the pantry door, searching for a broom and dustpan, and was momentarily distracted when the security system chimed—someone had come through the front entrance. That someone had to be his mother, home to save her kingdom.

He gritted his teeth. Why couldn't she have stayed away until after he'd cleaned up the mess?

"Momma." He pulled his head out of the pantry and greeted her with a smile. "What'd you bowl?"

"Two-thirty five." She set several grocery bags on the counter and frowned at the open pantry door. "Didn't you find something to feed those kids?"

"They ate crackers. But something upstairs got broken, so I was looking for your broom and dustpan."

"Something broke? All by itself?"

"It might have had a little help. But I'm sure it was an accident."

"Anyone get hurt?"

"The kids are fine, but one of your lamps was DOA. I'll get you another one, but I've got to sweep up those little pieces before someone walks in there with bare feet—"

Before he could move, Momma ducked beneath his arm, yanked the broom from a niche, and charged up the stairs, broomstick like a lance under her arm. He was tempted to tell the kids to step away lest they be run through, but apparently they had already realized they'd be better off waiting in the sewing room.

Though he was likely to be about as helpful as a blind eyewitness, Matt climbed the steps after his mother.

Momma stood in the bathroom doorway, one hand at her throat, the other choking the broom. She regarded the remaining ruins with mournful eyes. "My poor Princess lamp."

Matt squeezed her shoulder. "I'm really sorry. What's a princess lamp?"

"Princess House is a brand of crystal. I wouldn't expect you to know anything about it."

He ignored the slap at his knowledge of glassware. "So where do I get a replacement?"

"You can't get a replacement; that lamp was discontinued years ago. I found that one on eBay."

He blinked, struck dumb by the news that his mother had learned how to navigate an Internet auction. Only five years before she'd thought computers were Satan's playthings.

He reached for the broom. "Let me do this."

"I've got it."

"Mom, the kids are my responsibility."

"But it's my bathroom—and I've watched you clean. This is one time good enough won't do. I don't want those children cutting their feet on slivers you didn't take the time to get up."

Sighing, he lifted his hands and backed away. Momma set to work, her broom slapping the baseboards as she scraped slivers into submission.

Not knowing what else to do, Matt stepped into the sewing room and saw his children sitting side by side on the bed. Both were as wide-eyed as jackrabbits.

He made a parting motion and sank into the space between them. "Emilia, I'm sorry I was cross with you."

She snuggled under his arm. "That's okay, Daddy. You were pre-turbed."

Roman leaned in closer. "Is Grandma mad?"

"She's concerned, that's all. She doesn't want you to cut your feet on the glass."

Emilia peered up at him. "Will she make us leave?"

"Do you want to leave?"

"No . . . but we might have more fun with Miss Janette and Miss Andie."

"I'm sure they have plans of their own."

"Can we meet them at the hotel?" Roman asked. "Can we go see them?"

Matt shook his head. "Grandma's feelings would be hurt if we left now. As long as we're in Savannah, we belong at Grandma's house."

They listened until they heard the crystalline chink of shards falling into the glass trashcan, then they braced for trouble as Momma exited the bathroom, her broom in one hand and her fancy trash can in the other.

"All clear." She barely glanced at the three of them before striding toward the stairs. "You can use that bathroom now. I'm going downstairs to clean up the mess in the kitchen. I still have groceries to put away . . ."

She stomped down the stairs, muttering under her breath. Matt looked at his kids. "Either of you need the bathroom?"

They shook their heads.

When the sound of Momma's steps had faded away, Emilia tugged on Matt's sleeve. "I want to go watch the Huggins."

"Your DVD player's over there, in your backpack."

"Not those ones—I want to watch them on TV."

"The older shows." Roman stood. "They're on Nickelodeon, but not until four o'clock."

Emilia slipped off the bed and followed her brother. "I want to watch Miss Andie."

"Andie's not on—" he began, then he remembered that Emilia kept confusing Andie with a singer from the old show. He probably ought to explain that their new friend worked behind the camera, not in front of it, but since they'd probably never see Andie Crystal again, why not allow Emilia to enjoy her little fantasy?

◆

By five o'clock, whatever problem had been bothering Matt's mother had been apparently resolved. For the last hour and a half she'd kept herself busy in the kitchen, rattling pots and running water in the sink. When the scent of fried chicken wafted into the living room, Matt's hopes were confirmed: Momma was cooking a full course Southern dinner. Tonight they would partake of dishes as delicious as anything prepared by Savannah's famous Paula Deen.

"Come on," Momma finally called, stepping into the hallway as she wiped her wet hands on her apron. "Y'all come on into the kitchen and take your places at the table. Matty, make sure those kids wash their hands, okay?"

Roman giggled as he came down the steps. "Daddy, she called you Matty!"

Matt pointed toward the downstairs bathroom. "That's

because she's my mother. Now march to the sink, both of you, and wash up. Don't touch anything else!"

While Roman and Emilia scrubbed for supper, Matt meandered into the kitchen and took the chair at the head of the table. He caught his mother's eye and gestured to the gleaming white plates on plastic placemats. "New china?"

"New to you, maybe." She set a heaping bowl of mashed potatoes near his place. "I've had them five or six years."

She swept back to the stove as his children appeared in the doorway. Matt seated them on opposite sides of the table, then dropped a paper napkin into each of their laps. "Company manners," he reminded them. "No burping during dinner. No eating with your fingers. If you need help, let me know."

"I can't cut meat." Emilia croaked out the words in an attempt to whisper. "Nessa always cut it for me."

"I'll help you."

Roman didn't say anything. He was too busy staring at all the food Momma had prepared.

Matt slid back into his chair as Momma came toward the table again, this time carrying a platter of fried chicken stacked on paper towels. She placed it in the midst of the dishes already on the table: green beans, macaroni and cheese, mashed potatoes, buttermilk biscuits, fried okra . . . a veritable feast.

Matt folded his hands, pleased to realize that for the first time in a long time, he and his kids would eat the evening meal together like a traditional family. Because of his crazy work hours, they haven't eaten together since before Inga died.

"Momma, this looks delicious." He gave her his most appreciative smile. "We don't eat nearly this good at home."

"It's the least I could do, seeing as how I only see y'all a couple of times a year." She dropped into her chair, then counted the dishes on the table. "I forgot the honey for the biscuits. Or would you kids rather have jam? I have homemade cherry preserves, or strawberry —"

"Don't get up." Matt caught her gaze and held it. "We can use butter. You need to relax and enjoy the meal with the rest of us."

Momma swallowed hard, then snatched her napkin and spread it in her lap. Matt picked up his fork, about to spear a steaming chicken breast, but halted in mid-reach when his mother bowed her head and folded her hands.

Grace before every meal. The ritual had been part of their supper routine even when Matt and his mother had precious little to be thankful for. Though now she had all she needed, apparently she hadn't given up the practice.

She closed her eyes. "Matthew, will you lead us in giving thanks?"

He bowed his head and folded his hands, but the traditional words couldn't get past the boulder in his throat. He knew he could make something up, but he didn't want to demonstrate hypocrisy in front of his children, nor did he want to pray to a God who would take his wife without reason or warning.

Matt coughed, then held his hand to his throat as if he were coming down with a cold. "Why don't you do it, Momma?"

"All right."

He watched from beneath lowered lids as Momma gripped her hands more tightly. Even when they were butting heads and he considered his mother the meanest woman on earth, Matt never doubted that heaven heard his momma's prayers.

"Dear Heavenly Father—" her voice shaped itself into reverent, hallowed tones— "I thank you for bringing my precious ones safely to this house. Please bless Matthew, and Roman, and Emilia, and help us to have a joyful time together. Thank you for giving us life, and thank you for allowing these precious young ones to grow up safe and happy. Bless this food now to our bodies, and help us love each other more than we love ourselves. I can ask these things because Jesus is my Lord. Amen."

She looked up and smiled. "Now we can eat. Roman, take that chicken leg and eat it with your fingers. Emilia, honey, there's a leg for you, too. Good thing chickens have two legs, isn't it?"

Emilia looked at Matt. "Daddy, can I eat with my hands?"

"Do whatever your Grandma says. When you're at her table, she knows best."

He sat back and smiled, leaning on the armrest of his chair as he watched Momma fuss over his kidlings. She might have been annoyed when they arrived without warning and she might have been irritated when the kids broke her lamp, but she was a natural nurturer, and she loved his kids to death. Once she realized how desperate he was, she'd change her mind about keeping them. She'd come through, if not for his sake, then for the sake of his children.

At least he hoped she would.

In the upstairs bedroom Momma reserved for guests, Matt lay on his back and stared at the ceiling. The hall clock had just chimed the half hour and he couldn't sleep—nor could he remember the last time he was in bed at ten-thirty.

Despite the twin bed in Momma's sewing room, both kids were zipped into sleeping bags, thrilled to be "camping out" on Grandma's carpeted floor. From his bed Matt could hear the soft, steady rhythm of their breathing, and something about the sound evoked a sense of melancholy. Was this the closest his children would ever come to a camping trip? His mother wasn't likely to take them camping, but neither was he, not with the hectic pace of his life.

Roman and Emilia really needed to stay here in Georgia. They'd have more fun with his mother than they could ever have with him.

Still, he thought the kids would agree that they'd had a good day. Once they settled the problem with the broken lamp, they spent the afternoon relaxing and playing catch in the backyard. Later, while the kids watched that Huggins show they were so crazy about, Matt went upstairs and pulled a pad and paper from his briefcase. Strategy, he wrote across the top of the page. How to Convince Momma to Keep My Kids.

He pondered the problem for quite a while, cataloging his assets and liabilities. Without a doubt, his strongest asset was Momma's love for his children. What grandmother didn't adore her grandkids? So while they were with her, he would encourage them to listen to her stories and compliment her cooking. It helped that they were brown-eyed, adorable, and looked a lot like he had when he was their age. Every time Momma saw one of them smiling up at her, she'd be reminded of him . . . but maybe that wasn't such a good thing. He got into a lot of trouble as a youngster, and frequently had to go outside and break off a switch for a spanking. Momma didn't agree with most contemporary child-rearing experts. She had a healthy respect for the Bible and interpreted scriptures quite literally, including the pronouncement that he who spared the rod, spoiled the child.

She knew more about child rearing than he'd ever know. Another asset he could use to make his case.

As to liabilities, well, Momma tended to worry too much. She might be worried that he'd prove to be like his father and fail to provide for his children, so if he had to chart out a budget and promise a regular amount in child support, he would do that. She might be anxious about their education, but he could afford to send them to the best private school in Savannah. She might be afraid the kids would be too much for her to handle, so he could speak to the kids about behaving better while they were here.

Another liability—he'd miss the kidlings once he was gone. Probably more than he ever thought he could.

After dinner that night Momma pulled out some old photo albums and showed Roman and Emilia pictures from Matt's childhood, an activity the kids found interesting for about ten minutes. She made an effort to point out the only picture ever taken of Matt with his father—a Polaroid snapped about two days before the man ran off. Emilia stared at the infant in the unfamiliar man's arms, then looked up at Momma. "Who's that baby?"

"That's your daddy."

"He didn't have much hair."

"I know. I loved him anyway."

Roman tapped the man in the photo. "Who's he?"

"That's Levi, your grandpa. Your daddy's daddy."

"Why doesn't he live here with you?"

Momma ruffled Roman's hair. "I don't know where he is, child. But I miss him every day."

Emilia tilted her head. "Do you miss us when we're gone?"

"I miss you something fierce. And I ask God to look after you."

Matt didn't say much as Momma interacted with his children—he didn't want to press her about her decision, and he didn't want to argue in front of the kids. She had probably interpreted his silence as pouting.

She could think what she liked, but his mother's refusal to help had left a welt on his soul. Not only was he stunned to realize she could refuse to care for her grandchildren, but how could she possibly be so ungrateful? Because he didn't want to start his own family while still owing Momma for everything she'd done for him, for five years he religiously set aside twenty percent of his paycheck, earmarking it for Momma's house. When he finally saved enough for a decent brick home on a half-acre, he flew down here, scouted the area, spent two days with a builder, and purchased this lot.

Inga had been thrilled to help with the house project. Matt could close his eyes and see her, shining with expectation and faintly nauseous with morning sickness, bending over a drafting table as she chose fixtures, cabinets, and carpet colors for his mother's new home. Matt believed Inga loved the idea of giving Momma a house as much as he did. They differed, however, in their motivations: Inga wanted to present a gift to her mother-in-law; Matt viewed the house as payment on an outstanding debt.

After the home was finished, Matt furnished the house and hired movers to transport the few pieces of furniture Momma wanted to bring from her tiny wood-frame home in Thunderbolt. On moving day she was so excited, Matt thought she might end up in the hospital with heart palpitations.

Why wasn't she still grateful? She continued to enjoy the benefits of her improved situation. She was living a new lifestyle in a better neighborhood. And she had no financial worries—every year Matt paid the taxes and replaced any appliances that had worn out. He also gave her an annual allowance for upkeep and utilities. If it weren't for him, Momma wouldn't have this house or anything in it.

Though the lawyer in him wouldn't hesitate to point this out, the son in him didn't want to be petty. He didn't want her to feel indebted—she had earned every square inch of this place. She brought him up without help from anyone, unless you counted the people who ran government welfare. She raised him on pork 'n beans and dented cans from the thrift store, on powdered milk and tuna fish. She took in ironing and made quilts from scraps she bought at the Goodwill; she canned corn and green beans and tomato sauce. Her callused fingers worked around the clock in order to provide him with new clothes, decent shoes, and schoolbooks; she pushed him to read and study until he earned a college scholarship and his Juris Doctorate. She made him the man he was, and for that he owed her.

Yes, Momma did everything she could for him . . . which is why he couldn't understand why she didn't want to help him now. She got all choked up whenever she talked about him raising two motherless children, so her reasons for turning him down couldn't be based on any lack of compassion. So why did she tell him no?

His momma was not selfish. He remembered sitting at the dinner table and watching her offer him the best portions of meat. If a chicken or pot roast didn't stretch enough to last the week, she'd say she wasn't hungry and leave him to finish whatever remained in the refrigerator. He'd never been that unselfish.

Matt rolled onto his side and searched for other reasons why she might have said no. He doubted she was placing her social life above his children, unless . . . could her reasons have something to do with a man? Momma wasn't even sixty, so she was far from elderly. Maybe she was interested in some guy on her bowling team and didn't want to give up her afternoons. He tried to imagine her turning away from his kids to hang on some man's arm, but he couldn't get that picture to focus. Momma hadn't chased men when she was younger, so why would she do it now? She might be opinionated, stubborn, and frugal to a fault, but she wasn't the type to put romance above her family.

He could only come up with one answer for Momma's refusal: she was so irritated with him for showing up unannounced that she wanted to teach him a lesson about being presumptuous. If that was the case, she'd let him stew a while, then she'd soften and tell him she'd changed her mind.

But on the off chance that he was wrong, he would enlist the children's help: tomorrow they needed to be extra careful, extremely well behaved, and as polite as they could possibly be. They had one more day to spend with Momma in Savannah, then Matt had to head either to the airport or the Amtrak station. If all went well, the kids wouldn't be going with him.

But . . . He swallowed hard and burrowed under the covers, rubbing his bare arms. His wife had been gone over a year, yet he still found himself reaching for his phone to call Inga in the middle of the day. In the middle of the night he still turned to her side of the bed when he woke and wanted to share his thoughts.

Though he never spent much time with his children before Nessa left, they'd been growing more accustomed to each other over the last month. How many weeks would have to pass before he stopped watching and listening for their little voices?

# Chapter Eleven

Matt woke to the scent of lilacs — probably some fabric softener or spray Momma used on the sheets — and sat up, groggily listening for the kids. When he heard nothing but silence from the sewing room, he threw off the covers and lumbered into the hallway. Both sleeping bags were empty, but voices and cartoon sound effects rumbled from the television downstairs. Good — the kids had made themselves at home. They were feeling comfortable.

He was about to go back to bed for another half hour or so, but the aroma of bacon drifted up the staircase and his stomach growled. Something was sizzling in a frying pan, and suddenly a Southern breakfast seemed far more appealing than catching a few more zzz's.

He pulled on a pair of sweat pants and a T-shirt, ran his hands through his hair, and jogged downstairs. The kids were sprawled on the carpet in front of the television, and through the kitchen doorway he spied his mom at the stove, wooden spoon in hand.

"Morning, kids." He moved past them, then tugged on

Momma's apron string. "Um, that smells delicious."

She tossed a smile over her shoulder. "I wanted to send y'all out with a good breakfast in your bellies."

He staggered to the table and dropped into his usual chair. "What would you like to do today? We're up for anything."

She lifted the skillet and spooned scrambled eggs onto four waiting plates. "I know what I'm doing today—I have a women's missionary meeting at church. We're assembling Christmas boxes for orphans in Guatemala."

Matt settled his chin in his hand, not certain he'd heard her correctly. "The orphans aren't going to take all day, are they?"

"They might." She uncovered a pot and ladled out generous helpings of steaming grits. "We have a lot of boxes to fill."

"I thought you said you were going to juggle your appointments."

"I did—I was home for dinner last night, wasn't I? But I can't juggle this meeting today. Too many people are involved and I'm a team leader."

For a moment he considered persuading her to cancel her plans, but the attempt would be counterproductive. He wanted her to see that caring for his children wouldn't entail a drastic change in her daily routine, so he couldn't ask her to adjust her schedule. "Okay, then." He tented his hands. "Ordinarily the kids would be in school on a Friday, but since they're not, do you have any suggestions about what we could do while you're at the church?"

She dropped the lid back on the pot. "Downtown's got lots to see. You could go have lunch at Paula Deen's."

"Why should I eat at some tourist joint when I could eat lunch with my mother?"

"Because you can't eat lunch with me. I'm eating with the church ladies." She said this in a light voice without any edge, and her attitude was completely relaxed . . . not at all the reaction he expected.

"Let me get this straight." He propped an elbow on the table. "The kids and I travel five days to pay you a surprise visit, but you plan on going about your business as usual."

"I might have made other arrangements if I'd known you were coming." She looked directly at him, bracing one hand on her hip. "You didn't give me any advance notice, Matty. Is it fair to expect me to drop everything and cater to your whims?" She shook her head. "Honestly, sometimes you act so smart and grown-up, but at other times you behave like a spoiled little boy. I don't know what to do when you're like that—you're too big to turn over my knee."

She didn't yell, she didn't stamp her foot, she didn't even raise her voice. But his mouth dropped open as shame siphoned the blood from his head. He didn't understand how a woman who barely came up to his shoulder could make him feel like a ten-year-old, but Momma certainly had the gift.

He drew a deep breath and began again, starting with a contrite apology. "I'm sorry, Momma. I'm sorry I didn't tell you we were coming, and I understand why you felt you had to go bowling yesterday. But now you know we're here, so I was hoping you'd find a way to spend the day with me and the kids."

She shook her head again. "It's not just the schedule. It's everything."

"Like what?"

"Like you sitting around and expecting me to do everything for you."

"Is this about the cracker crumbs on the kitchen table? I was about to clean up that mess when you came in—"

"It's not about the cracker crumbs. If you can't see what I'm sayin', well . . . you just can't see." She picked up a plate loaded with crisp bacon, then dropped strips onto each of the four plates. "I should be back around four. We can do something tonight, if you want. Maybe go out to eat."

She set the empty dish next to the sink, then bent to draw a pan of biscuits from the oven. He was hoping she'd offer to cook dinner again—he and the kids had had their fill of restaurants, and nothing beat his mother's cooking. But apparently she figured that yakking with the church ladies would wear her out.

Bottom line, he wasn't willing to make promises if she wouldn't do the same. "The thing is, Momma, I'm not sure when we'll make it back because I have no idea what we'll end up doing. But I'm sure we'll find some way to amuse ourselves."

Still unruffled, Momma dumped the biscuits into a basket, then covered them with a clean towel. "Those trolley cars are nice—you can hop on and off any time you like, and there's lots to see. So go, have fun, enjoy yourself. Let the kids take lots of pictures with those fancy cameras."

He dropped his head into his hands as Momma set the biscuits on the table and called the kids to breakfast.

After Momma dressed in another jogging suit and went off to huddle with the church ladies, Matt got himself and the kids ready for a day of sight-seeing. He showered, then pulled on jeans, a sweatshirt, and tennis shoes, clothes he usually wore only around the house. The kids yanked stuff from their suitcases and dressed themselves, and he groaned when he saw their wrinkled shirts and pants. He thought Momma would be around to take charge of the kids' clothes, but obviously he miscalculated . . .

He found himself at a complete loss when Emilia brought him a hairbrush and a blue ribbon.

She trailed the silky strip across his palm. "I want to wear a pony tail like Christy Huggins."

He blinked at her. "Honey, I don't know how to make a pony tail."

"It's not hard. You just take the hair—" she grabbed hers in her fist— "and tie a rubber band around it. Then you put on the ribbon."

Of all the women in his life—friends, secretaries, mother, wife—none of them seemed to be around when he needed them. He was tempted to flatly refuse, but his daughter's lower lip was already edging forward.

So he got up and went into the kitchen where he scrounged through Momma's drawers until he found a rubber band. Then he sat on the sofa and called his daughter. He brushed the tangles from her hair, eliciting several irritated squeals. Though his hands felt unusually huge and clumsy, he somehow managed to get a rubber band around the silky strands. Then he tied the ribbon around the band and pulled it tight, only to hear Emilia yelp again.

"Daddy, you're not doing it right."

"Do you want me to take the rubber band out?"

"No!" She turned and backed away, torn between glaring at him and admiring her reflection in the front window. It wasn't the world's smoothest ponytail, but as long as Emilia was satisfied . . .

He would have been happy to stay at the house and prepare for the Cortez case, but he ended up calling a taxi because he'd promised the kids they'd do something special.

Roman's knees knocked back and forth as they waited in the living room. "What are we going to do? Are we going to a movie?"

"I want to get candy," Emilia announced, her arms wrapped around her tattered dinosaur. "Walter wants Junior Mints."

"I'm not sure what we'll do, but I am certain we'll have fun. Do you have your cameras?"

"I don't want to carry mine," Emilia said. "It's heavy."

"Yeah," Roman echoed. "It's too heavy to carry around all day."

So much for making memories.

When a yellow cab pulled up to the curb, Matt herded the kids toward the door and pocketed the spare key. "Let's see what kind of adventure we can find."

After a ride over the interstate, the cab dropped them at the trolley stand on River Street. The kids hopped over the old cobblestones while he got in line to buy all-day trolley tickets. He didn't care about seeing anything specific in downtown Savannah, but the trolley car was usually s nice ride. Best of all, if the children saw something they like, they could get off and take a look; if they didn't, they could ride around for a couple of hours.

"Why, Matthew Scofield. Imagine meeting you here."

He turned, surprised to see Janette Turlington in the line behind him, a discount coupon in her hand. Though he suspected the effort would be wasted, he looked for Andie, too. No luck.

Janette must have read his mind. "Looking for Andie?"

He glanced back at Janette, who looked better than usual this morning. The shadow under her eye had lightened considerably, and the lines between her brows had disappeared. "Hey, good to see you. And yeah, I thought you and Andie were the dynamic duo."

"Andie has a sick relative in California, so she left for the airport just after we arrived in Savannah. She wanted me to tell you good-bye."

"Oh." Matthew smiled even as his heart sank. Andie Crystal had been an interesting young woman, and she'd seemed to actually enjoy his kids. He hadn't realized the idea of not ever seeing her again would be so disappointing.

He smiled at Janette and pointed toward the ticket counter. "Deciding to take a spin through Savannah?"

She grinned. "I thought this would be a good way to spot interesting places I might want to visit when I have someone to share the experience with me."

"You can share it with us. I thought the trolley would be a good option in case it rains." He gestured to the gray sky looming above. "At least we'll have a roof over our heads."

When he stepped forward, he couldn't help noticing a young couple he'd seen at the train station. The girl, a blonde of about eighteen or nineteen, hung on the arm of her companion, a leggy young man with scraggly hair and the faint beginnings of a beard.

The young man saw Matt and lifted his chin in recognition. "Dude."

Matt raised his chin in return. "Hey."

"I remember them," Janette whispered as the line moved forward. "He had a guitar stuffed up in the overhead bin."

"That doesn't surprise me."

"Daddy, here comes the trolley!"

Roman and Emilia scampered out of the road as a red and green trolley car pulled up, a driver at the wheel and a dozen or so passengers staring out the wide windows. The cashier hustled to move them through the line; Matt handed her his credit card and told her he'd take four tickets, two adults' and two children's. Janette stammered in pleased surprise when Matt invited her to join them, then they hurried toward the trolley, sandwiching the kids between them as they climbed the steps.

"By the way," Matt told Janette, "I know the kids' clothes are wrinkled. I forgot about setting their things out."

Janette laughed. "By the end of the day we'll all be in need of a good laundry service."

The driver slowed his canned patter long enough to glance at their tickets as they filed past him. "Come on, folks, welcome aboard. This is trolley stop eleven, if you want to come back here later."

Roman and Emilia slid onto one of the wooden benches. Since the benches had no seat belts, Matt sat behind his kids, figuring that he'd be able to grab a shirt collar if one of them decided to dive through the open window.

Janette sat next to Matt, and the young couple from the train moved to the back of the car. Soon, like the others on board, they were a captive audience listening to the polished prattle of Driver Don, who proudly informed them that he'd spent eighteen years operating a trolley car. "And let me remind you," he said, glancing in the rear view mirror as he rang his bell and pulled away from the curb, "our rules forbid smoking, standing while the trolley is in motion, and alcohol . . . unless you're going to offer me a swig."

The driver tittered at his own joke, but Matt stared out the window, his mood drooping like the tattered clouds hanging over the city. Though a Washington lawyer should be handle any kind of pressure, he had never been good at shaking off his mother's disapproval. The sharp things she said at breakfast were still with him, stinging his conscience like nettles.

Nothing was going according to plan, yet his time in Savannah was running out. Last night he went to sleep convinced that Momma would come around, but now he wasn't at all sure he could count on her. Unless something changed, tomorrow morning he'd be boarding the train with his children, which meant he'd probably spend the rest of this so-called vacation on the phone with a nanny agency. They might be able to email names and referral letters, but Matt wouldn't be able to meet with prospective nannies until they got home. Then he'd have to steal valuable time from the Cortez case to conduct interviews. If the partners sensed that he wasn't giving Cortez 100 percent of his time and effort, they'd pull the file. They had to pull his case when Inga died, and even though his situation garnered sympathy from all the partners, everyone at the firm understood that one failure was excusable, two were unforgivable.

Apparently oblivious to his pensive mood, Janette nudged his arm. "It felt odd not to see you and your children at breakfast in the hotel. Are Roman and Emilia enjoying Savannah?"

He shrugged. "We haven't seen much of the city. We spent all day yesterday at my mother's house. Fortunately, the kids have no problem entertaining themselves as long as there's a TV around."

Janette clicked her tongue in a gentle tsking sound. "I

always wonder if television isn't doing our kids more harm than good. The other day I read that shows like Sesame Street actually encourage children to have short attention spans. I don't have little ones now, but I do remember that my daughter always complained of being bored. I used to be amazed when she'd say that because I was never bored as a kid. There was always a book to read, a flower bed to dig in, neighborhood kids to play with . . ."

Matt couldn't imagine this woman crawling around in a flowerbed, not even as a child. He didn't consider Janette old, but she and his mother must have grown up in the same world.

Janette folded her hands over the purse in her lap. "I was surprised to see you today. I thought you'd be spending all your time with your mom."

Matt couldn't stop a wry smile. "I thought so, too, but my mother has a fantastically busy social calendar. She had a meeting planned for today, and I couldn't persuade her to skip it. Apparently the orphans of South America are more important than her own grandchildren."

Janette gave him a puzzled look. "I'm sure she didn't mean to make you feel unwelcome. Wasn't she glad to see you?"

"Sure, for about ten minutes. Then she went off to play for her bowling league."

Janette chuckled. "She sounds like an active lady."

"She's a lot more active than I realized. I never pictured her sitting around knitting socks, but I never dreamed she'd develop into a social butterfly, either. She rarely went anywhere when I was growing up, but now I'm beginning to wonder if she ever stays home."

"Most seniors like to be as active as they can be. How old is your mother?"

"Fifty-eight, I think."

"That's hardly what I'd call senior. Your mom is barely middle aged."

Matt swiveled his eyes toward her. "You're kidding, right?"

"Not at all. Fifty is the new forty. It's not old."

"It feels old."

"When you're fifty it won't."

"To the right—" the driver's intercom crackled overhead— "you'll see the statue of James Oglethorpe, founder of the Georgia colony and the city of Savannah. A devout man, Oglethorpe did not allow the importation of slaves or strong drink, making Georgia the only southern colony in which slavery and booze were illegal . . . until Oglethorpe died, that is."

"He sounds like a good man," Janette said. When Matt lifted a questioning brow, she clarified: "I'm talking about Oglethorpe, not the driver."

They rode in silence for a while, then a thought struck Matt: Janette was a woman, and unless he was way off, she was close to his mother's age. Maybe she could help him see what he'd been missing.

"Janette, may I ask you something?"

"Of course."

"My mother . . . yesterday we had a conversation that's left me feeling as though I barely know her."

The suggestion of a smile played at the corner of Janette's mouth. "What do you mean?"

"First, I should probably explain that I lost my wife a little over a year ago."

Janette's face contracted in a small grimace. "I'm so sorry. Was she ill?"

"She choked on a sandwich when no one was around to help."

Janette's expression morphed into a mask of horrified sympathy. "How awful for all of you. I'm so sorry."

He looked away, overcome, as always, by a flood of frustrated helplessness. "I can't tell you how many times I've beaten myself up for not hiring a maid or a housekeeper, someone who would be at the house all day. Now even my kids know how to do the Heimlich maneuver."

"Those poor babies." Janette pressed her hand to her chest as her eyes brimmed with tears. "Please, go on."

So he told her about their adjustments, about Nessa, the unreliable babysitters, and his idea to approach his mother about caring for his kids. He even told her about providing Momma with a house, a place with plenty of room for two small children.

"So . . . you feel she owes you?"

He shook his head, startled by her perception. "I'm not saying that. Our balance sheet is clean, neither of us owes the other anything. But if Momma loves her grandkids, I thought surely she'd want to take them in instead of having me hire a babysitter who would only think of my kids as a job. I don't want to hire someone who'll only keep an eye on them; I want to engage someone who will invest in them, correct them, encourage and teach them . . ."

"You want to hire a mother. Who wouldn't?" Janette's gaze drifted toward the front of the trolley, and for an instant Matt wasn't sure she was still listening. Her eyes grew cloudy and abstracted as she stared into the distance. "Some people," she said, her voice soft, "sacrifice a great deal in order to parent their children. If you're not willing to make the sacrifice, maybe you shouldn't be a parent."

He blinked, bewildered by the change in her tone. "I'm willing to sacrifice. And I don't want you to think I dislike being a father. I love my kids."

"I believe you do." Janette lowered her gaze, her lashes shuttering her eyes. "But now that your wife is gone—"

"I can't raise them alone." He spread his hands in a helpless gesture. "I don't know how to take care of two little ones and succeed at my career. I asked my mother to pitch in and she said no. She didn't even ask for time to think things over."

Janette remained quiet for a moment. When she lifted her head, her gaze was clear and sharp. "Maybe she had a problem with the arrangement you suggested. Did you offer to let her live with you?"

"She wouldn't want to do that. She loves her home and she hates the area around Washington. My momma's a southern girl."

Janette laughed. "Virginia's not exactly New York City. It's south of the Mason Dixon line."

"But it's not her home. If I moved Momma, she'd be leaving her house, her friends, her community and her church. The change would be hard for her. That's why I thought bringing the kids to Savannah would be the best solution."

Janette gripped the bench in front of them as Driver Don swung wide around a corner. "I don't know what to tell you, Matthew, but you need to keep one thing in mind."

"What's that?"

"You sprang this on your mother?"

"Not exactly. I waited until after breakfast."

Janette released an unladylike snort. "You sprang it on her, so you can't expect her to give you an answer right away. Even if she were willing to take your kids, she'd have to think long and hard about how her life is going to change. Taking responsibility for two young kids at fifty-eight? I'm a few years younger than your mom, but I wouldn't want that job."

He gave her a sidelong look of disbelief. "Not even for your grandkids?"

"I don't have grandchildren . . . and probably won't, at least not for a long time."

"But you have an adult daughter —"

"My daughter may be twenty-five, but she's a long way from motherhood. She's still living at home with us."

Matt chuckled and crossed his arms as Janette's odd mood shift began to make sense. "Can't get that little bird to leave the nest, huh?"

"Can't get the little bird to do much of anything." Janette smiled, but the smile didn't reach her eyes. "Let me know if your mother does decide to take your children. If she's ready to run a boarding house, I'd be willing to pay her to raise my kid."

The trolley halted as Driver Don launched into a lecture on the famous Pirate House Restaurant. Janette listened attentively, but like the smoke from a steaming locomotive, Matt's thoughts drifted over a track he had already traveled.

◆

October 4, 2010 began like any other Monday. Matt woke, showered, and dressed. Drank a cup of coffee, downed a piece of toast and two tasteless fiber bars because Inga was always fretting about the state of his digestive system. Stopped by the bedrooms to kiss Inga and the children. At 7:03 he grabbed his briefcase and headed out into a crisp morning, certain that he wouldn't cross his threshold again until after dark.

The day was completely, utterly ordinary. Wholly unremarkable, which still surprised him when he considered that the date had been branded into his heart along with his children's birthdays and his anniversary. He spent the morning in a client meeting; he spent his lunch hour reading briefs. He was about to pop into Don Giles's office when his secretary forwarded a call from John Masters. He didn't recognize the name until the man identified himself as the principal at Forest Edge Elementary School.

Had one of his kids done something bad enough to merit a call from the principal? Matt glanced at the clock: 3:45. Inga always picked up the kids at 3:15, so they were probably home by now.

"I'm calling on behalf of your children," Masters said, a note of concern in his voice. "They're still here at the school. We've tried calling your wife, but she doesn't answer."

Matt pursed his lips, confused and mildly irritated at the interruption. "I'm so sorry. My wife must have been caught in traffic—"

"We've tried Mrs. Scofield's cell number, but she doesn't answer that phone, either." The principal's voice remained steady. "I thought perhaps you might know if she made alternative arrangements for Roman and Emilia to be picked up."

Alternative arrangements? Inga always picked up the children. If she'd found herself in a jam she would have called Matt, knowing he'd send his secretary or another trusted employee to take care of the kids.

"You tried the house?" Mr. Masters might have already mentioned this, but Matt was so flustered he couldn't remember.

"We did."

"And no answer?"

"We left several messages on the machine, but Mrs. Scofield hasn't returned our calls."

Matt picked up a pencil and flipped it between his fingers. He was preparing for an important hearing and Inga knew he didn't have time to play taxi. But if she didn't answer the phone or meet the kids at school—

Something cold slid down his spine, prickling his skin and evoking a shudder, but Matt pushed the foreboding away. This probably meant nothing; Inga had been late before. An accident on the freeway could tie up traffic for hours . . . but Inga didn't need to take the freeway to reach the school. Still, if she'd been out shopping she might have been on the highway when an accident occurred.

He glanced at the television and considered turning it on. The local news station always reported major accidents. Then again, if there'd been a major accident, someone in the office would have heard about it. Bad news always traveled fast.

"I'll send my secretary to get the kids," Matt told the principal. "Thank you for calling."

He stepped into the outer office and asked Mrs. Wilson if she'd mind picking up his children. "After that, you can go on home. Might as well call it a day."

She smiled and said she'd be happy to do that, so Matt left her powering down her computer and clearing her desk.

He sank into his office chair and struggled to remember what he'd been about to do before Masters called. He wanted to ask Giles something, but what?

He fished around for his lost thought but came up empty. Mrs. Wilson was taking care of his children, but Inga remained incommunicado and that wasn't like her.

Matt picked up his phone and punched in his wife's phone number. No answer. He dialed the house and listened as his wife's voice instructed him to leave a message and ended with "Have a good day!"

His day had taken a nosedive. Clearly, he wasn't going to get anything done until he found out why Inga wasn't answering her phone. If she forgot to charge it, if she left it on the kitchen counter, or if she and her girlfriends let time slip away while they lunched, he might have to convince her that they needed a nanny.

Resisting a rising wave of unease, he stuffed his case file in his briefcase and headed toward the parking lot, consoling himself with the fact that he could work at home once he'd spoken to Inga. With any luck, he wouldn't have to count the afternoon a complete loss.

The drive home was strikingly unremarkable, banal in route and routine. The oppressive heat of summer had dispersed; the refreshing bite of autumn hadn't yet turned bitter. He drove with the windows open and the radio on, taking advantage of spare moments to record thoughts about his current case on a digital recorder. At the back of his mind, though, a niggling worry clamored for his attention.

Matt pulled into the driveway a few minutes before five. As he stepped out, he glimpsed his secretary's car approaching from the north end of the street. His throat tightened when he saw two small heads in the backseat. His children were about to come home . . . to what?

He pulled out his keys, but the front door was unlocked. Prickles of premonition nipped at the back of his neck as he stepped across the threshold. Inga never went out without securing the house and setting the alarm. He called her name, but heard only the faint echo of his voice as it bounced in the high-ceilinged foyer.

"Inga?" Aware that his children were on their way, Matt peered into the living room, then strode to the office. No sign of her. He walked through the dining room and into the kitchen. A half-eaten sandwich sat on a plate on the counter bar, but the chair lay sideways on the floor. A glass of watery tea stood near her plate, next to a crumpled napkin. Had there been some kind of struggle? He saw no signs of blood, but neither did he see his wife.

He turned to the opposite counter, where his wife's designer purse sat beside a grocery list. Beneath a picture of puppies and kittens she'd written don't forget M's shaving cream. Another note, starkly pale against the dark granite countertop, lay several feet away by the phone. He couldn't read it from where he stood, so he moved past the kitchen island, turned the corner, and found Inga lying motionless on the floor.

A rise of panic threatened to choke off his breath. His throat worked, but his tongue refused to form words. The bones in his legs gave way, dropping Matt at his wife's side like a useless sack of skin. He stared at her face: blue-lipped, one cheek dark and mottled, the other as pale as paper. She looked nothing like the warm and beautiful woman he'd kissed goodbye that morning.

"God, help me." Somehow Matt managed to stand and grab the phone. He pounded 9-1-1 and gasped as a woman came on the line. He told her he needed help, he gave her the address, he shouted that she should hurry —

He hung up and slid down a cabinet, closing his eyes. This couldn't be happening. In a moment he would wake up, he would open his eyes and find himself in bed or asleep on the sofa in his office. He shouldn't have had the pastrami at lunch; he shouldn't have overindulged. His conscience was punishing him for being irritated when the principal called; he should have known better than to think she would let shopping come before her children . . .

Blood slipped like cold needles through his veins when he heard the front door open. His children's innocent voices echoed in the foyer, their light conversation a striking contrast to the raw sound of his breathing. "Mom?" Roman called. "Hey Mom, where were you?"

The sound of their voices sent a surge of adrenaline through Matt's blood. He stood and intercepted the children at the entrance to the dining room. "Come on, kids." He placed his hands on their shoulders and steered them away from the kitchen. "Mrs. Wilson's going to take you for ice cream."

His secretary cast him a startled look.

"McDonalds." Silently he pled for cooperation as he met her gaze. "Take an hour, maybe more, get these guys a snack. Please. And . . . maybe you should call me before you bring them back."

In that moment, only one thing mattered: he couldn't let his children into the kitchen. He couldn't let Roman and Emilia see their mother on the floor like that; he couldn't allow that sight to supplant all the lovely memories they'd made with their mother. Besides, if the house was a crime scene, none of them should be inside. By touching the doorknob, they might have already ruined some piece of crucial evidence . . .

Mrs. Wilson pulled her keys from her purse and plastered on a stiff smile. "Come on, kids, I know where the closest McDonalds is. Let's go get a cone. If you're really hungry, I'll even spring for Happy Meals."

Matt followed her to the front door, buckled the kids into her car, and watched in numb horror as his secretary pulled away.

Within three minutes, the ambulance arrived, with the police not far behind. The EMTs made a valiant effort, but Matt overheard one of them remark that they might as well be trying to jump-start a dead horse. Rigor had already set in, indicating that Inga had been dead for between two and four hours. A cop made notes, a forensics investigator took pictures, and Matt watched everything from behind the counter, his mind and body frozen in place.

An EMT pulled him away as others put Inga in a body bag and zipped it up, then lifted the bag onto a gurney. "Mr. Scofield?"

When he didn't respond, the man placed his hand on Matt's shoulder. "Mr. Scofield, you don't want to watch that. It'll be better if you remember your wife alive."

"Why?" Matt lifted his gaze. "Why is she . . . not alive?"

The man hesitated. "This is unofficial, of course, but it looks like she choked on her lunch. The timeline fits, and we found an obstruction in her windpipe."

Details in the kitchen suddenly made sense: the half-eaten sandwich on the table, the melted ice in her glass, the toppled kitchen chair, which, the EMT pointed out, might indicate that she tried to perform the Heimlich maneuver on herself. Failing that, she reached for the tablet and pen she kept by the phone, finding time to scrawl out one last note before she lapsed into unconsciousness. Her message? I love you.

"Why didn't she call 911?" Strangling on a sob, Matt picked up the phone, which still lay on the counter where he'd dropped it. "Why'd she write a note when she could have called for help?"

The EMT released Matt's shoulder. "When people panic, reason goes out the door. And if she was choking she wouldn't have been able to speak."

"But the emergency operators would have known the address, wouldn't they? The 911 system is able to access addresses."

The guy had shaken his head. "Your wife might have forgotten that fact. Or she wanted to write the note first. We'll probably never know what she was thinking."

Matt had never been able to understand why his wife choked to death, but he did know what she was thinking: she wanted her family to know she loved them. She gave them a world of comfort in three little words.

And for a long time after the funeral, those words—that fact—was all Matt cared to remember.

# Chapter Twelve

"Along this street," Driver Don intoned, "you'll see a row of pastel-colored town homes commonly known as 'Rainbow Row.' These buildings date from the late 1800s, so they are among the newer structures in the Old Fort District."

Janette tapped Emilia on the shoulder, then pointed to the colorful townhouses. "Aren't those pretty? They remind me of Southern girls in lacy summer dresses."

"Can we get off, Daddy?" Emilia turned to Matt, her face alight. "Can we walk over and see the houses?"

Why not? When the trolley stopped, Roman and Emilia scampered to the front and hopped down the steps; Janette and Matt followed at a more sedate pace. When they reached the sidewalk, Matt looked around for something to do—surely there was an ice cream shop or an antique store or some other commercial establishment in this part of town.

Janette noticed the look on his face and laughed. "Relax, Matthew." Her expression reminded Matt of his mother. "Just walk with your kids and have a good time. This is a lovely area."

His kids didn't want to walk with him; they wanted to walk with Janette. They gripped her hands and set off, strolling in front of the Rainbow Row houses, studying the pastel walls and matching shutters in hues of blue and pink and green and yellow. Matt didn't care for pastels and he wasn't particularly interested in architecture, so he walked behind them, his hands in his pockets, his eyes focused on the trio in front. How did the woman charm kids like that?

He listened as Emilia looked up at Janette and babbled about a doll she had at home. Even Roman, who once refused to wear a yellow shirt Nessa bought him, waited for his sister to finish and then told Janette about a pink house in his neighborhood.

Matt watched as Janette listened, her head tilting to catch every word, her lips pursed in thought, her hands welded to those of his children. She wasn't auditioning for a nanny position and she certainly wasn't trying to dazzle him, but he was impressed nonetheless. Janette and Andie always seemed to know the right thing to do and the right way to respond to Emilia's chatter and Roman's persistent questions.

Were some people natural parents? If he didn't know otherwise, he would have guessed that Janette had reared several children. Inga was like that—an intuitive mother—and he used to marvel as she held their babies to her breast, mother and child bonding in moments that left him feeling outcast and alien. Women, he'd decided, had a biological advantage—not only did a woman create children from the core of her being, she also nourished them. Though Inga had occasionally complained about the hassles of breast-feeding, Matt knew she treasured the intimacy between mother and child. She would never have admitted it, but he suspected she enjoyed knowing that her babies depended on her in a way they would never depend on him.

So why'd she have to go and choke on a chicken sandwich? He closed his eyes against the unwelcome rise of anger in his chest. A grief counselor had warned that he would experience anger, along with depression, bargaining, and denial, but the emotions could still catch him by surprise. Eventually, the counselor promised, Matt would reach acceptance, a kind of emotional plateau where he did not experience hot spurts of anger and loss . . .

Janette and the children stopped before a particularly ornate building—the structure appeared to house three separate homes, delineated by shutters in colors of blue, pink, and green. A narrow front porch ran along the first floor, the owners' privacy guarded by delicate railings and cream-colored spindles that looked like frosting on the side of a wedding cake. His daughter was staring at the home with open-mouthed awe. Something in this sight touched her, but he was clueless as to why she found it so appealing.

He stood on the sidewalk, jingling the change in his pocket, as Emilia announced that she'd like to live there. "Can we move into that house, Daddy?" She glanced back at him. "We could have the blue part, Miss Janette could take the pink part, and Miss Andie could live in the green part."

He smiled the suggestion away. "That wouldn't be practical, honey. I work in Washington—how would I get to work if we lived here?"

"You could take a jet," Roman suggested. "A big jet would get you to work on time."

Matt shook his head. "Sorry, kiddo, but I'm afraid that wouldn't work. By the time I fought the traffic, got to the airport, flew to Washington, fought the traffic again, and made it to the office, the day would be over. Not a very realistic plan."

Roman lifted his chin. "You don't have to come home every day. We could see you every once in a while."

"Is that . . . I mean, would you be okay with that?"

Roman shrugged, then turned and tugged on Janette's hand, leading the woman and his sister farther down the sidewalk. Matt followed, knowing that he had somehow said the wrong thing and hurt his son's feelings. Lately he seemed to hurt or annoy someone every time he opened his mouth, but Roman's reply had hurt Matt. Had he been so absent from his children's lives that they didn't even want to see him?

He never experienced that kind of insecurity when Inga was with them. On the other hand, in those days he'd been content to let her do everything for the kids.

He exhaled slowly, remembering the gray season right after his wife died. For two days he had walked around in a fog, but friends stepped in to help him out. Momma flew up to be with him, and several of the partner's wives brought over casseroles, flowers, and coffee urns. One of them suggested a nanny agency; he hired Nessa on her recommendation. With Momma at the house and Nessa on her way, he didn't have to think about being a father. He didn't want to think about anything.

Despite all that coffee, every night Matt fell into a deep, dreamless sleep. He thought he was subconsciously preparing for the funeral—an event he steeled himself to endure with constant reminders to be strong, be a man—but after the funeral he found the following weeks far more draining. For days he dragged around the house, frequently finding himself unable to concentrate or remember small details.

He had known grief before—or at least thought he had. Inga's father passed away not long after they were married, and he comforted her as she cried and talked about how much she'd miss her dad, her only surviving parent. But after a few blue days she managed to put her sorrow aside and get back to the business of living. Matt was sure he'd be able to do the same, but just when he thought he might be able to carry on a normal conversation with a neighbor or colleague, an unexpected wave of grief would knock him down and pull him under.

Nessa, newly arrived from Ireland, took charge of the children and pretty much left Matt alone, but after a week of wandering in a fog, he convinced himself that work would solve his problem. He yearned for the procedural routine of his caseload because at the office he knew what to do and what to expect from others.

But the partners weren't exactly keen on welcoming him back.

The firm had reassigned the case he was handling at the time of Inga's death. When he returned to work two weeks later, the partners expressed their reluctance to give him a new one. "You need time to grieve," Don Giles told him, but Matt had no idea how he was supposed to do that. So he went to his office and sat at his desk; at six he went home and sat in his easy chair. At eleven he went to bed and dreamed of Inga. He heard her deep-throated laughter, he saw her teasing smile, he listened to her smooth voice as she asked about the children, the house, and her flower garden. They walked together by a crystal lake, they lay together on the beach; he felt her breath on his cheek right up until the moment she vanished like a windblown candle flame.

He dreamed of his wife every night, and one particular dream haunted him. He was standing on a train platform with Inga and the children. When a flashing silver train pulled in, his wife scampered up the steps and lingered in the open doorway as the train began to pull away. Matt grabbed Roman and held him up, urging Inga to take him, but she simply waved goodbye and smiled until Matt could no longer see her.

That dream had been replaying in his brain for months. On some nights he urged Inga to take Emilia; other nights he tried to jump on the stairs as the train moved out. But he was too clumsy, his feet too leaden, and the children weighed him down. Inga always slipped away, leaving him scraped, sore, and responsible for the crying children abandoned by the tracks.

On mornings after he had dreamed of Inga, he opened his eyes beneath a dense cloud of guilt—the exact feeling he'd experienced on the few occasions he and Inga had quarreled. He turned to her side of the bed, ready to apologize, and found nothing but empty space and an untouched pillow.

Then he remembered.

He remembered why he was always cold, why there were extra blankets on the bed, why a nanny lived in the guest room upstairs, why he'd lost twenty pounds, and why he'd been billing more hours than usual.

He remembered why he walked around in a cocoon of disinterest and often felt that he had cotton stuffed in his ears.

He remembered why his house seemed empty when he came home from work, even though he knew at least three people were upstairs or in the kitchen.

The heart of his home had disappeared.

He supposed every individual grieved in his or her own way, but he didn't grieve while sitting, working, or even dreaming. He felt the pang of loss most keenly in the morning when he woke.

In his college days, he would never have imagined that he might come to depend on a woman for happiness. But then he fell in love with Inga's spunk and the sweetness she lavished on him. She loved the idea of being a lawyer's wife, and at their wedding they promised to support each other come what may. She adored their children, and seemed to instinctively know what to do in any emergency. Her loss had left a hole in their lives, a gap he hadn't been able to fill.

In some ways, Roman and Emilia seemed to accept their mother's death more easily than he had. For that, he was sure the credit went to Nessa—she had done a remarkable job of easing their fears and answering their questions. In her charming Irish brogue she told Roman and Emilia that God had called their mother home, but they shouldn't worry because God Almighty "always kept his hand on wee motherless children."

Though Matt wasn't religious, he didn't object to Nessa's explanations. And one evening when his children asked why their mother had gone away, he told them to ask their nanny, who had a better grasp on the situation than he did.

Nessa had given him a startled look, then shook her head. "I am deeply sorry for your loss. But perhaps 'tis true that I know more about grief." Her hand fell on Roman's brown hair. "They say Ireland is the land of tragedy and sad mothers. The world is filled with sad children, too, yet don't you worry. God circles them with his angels and holds them in his hand."

Months later, Matt thought Nessa was joking when she told him she wanted to go home. He had come to think of her as part of the family, as necessary to the functioning of his household as the refrigerator and microwave. When she explained that she wanted to marry, he considered sponsoring her fiancé so the young man could come to the United States and get a job in the area.

But Nessa made it clear that her heart lay in Ireland, not the U.S. She was going home, she said, "to marry a lovely fella called Liam" and work on his family dairy farm.

So she left and the procession of babysitters began. The first wore black and had piercings in her nose, eyebrow, and thumb; the second flirted with Matt so openly that even the kids realized her priorities were out of order.

After a frustrating month, he seized upon the most logical idea: why not entrust his children to a woman who'd already demonstrated that she knew how to raise little ones? His mother loved his kids and she would do a marvelous job with them.

Or so he had thought . . . until yesterday.

"Look, Daddy." Roman stopped before a metal plaque at the Mulberry Inn Hotel. He rose on tiptoe and ran his finger over the engraving, sounding out words to read the inscription. Matt stepped forward, about to read it for Roman, but Janette gently plucked at his sleeve and shook her head.

Matt crossed his arms as an inner voice assured him she was right; once again he had made a mistake. When he did what came naturally, he was almost always wrong.

Becoming a father had been easy. Being a father felt like an unending series of blunders.

When another trolley car came around the bend, Matt was more than ready to move on.

When the trolley pulled up to a square with a shady park, Roman spotted a stunning white fountain in the distance. "Daddy! Can we get off and go see the water?"

Matt glanced at Janette and lifted a brow. She probably thought he was asking if she minded stopping there, but what he really wanted was her approval: should a good father say yes?

When she smiled and stood, he nodded at Roman. "Let's go." He followed the children off the trolley amid several other riders who felt a need to stretch their legs. Among them was the young couple from the train—the blue-jeaned girl and her boyfriend must have gotten off at another stop and caught up to them.

This time, instead of greeting them with a nod, Matt smiled and extended his hand. "I believe we're traveling on the same train tour. I'm Matthew Scofield, and this lady is Janette Turlington."

A dimple appeared in the blonde's cheek. "I'm Violet." She took his hand with an uncertain grip. "And this here's Beverage. We've seen you guys around."

Janette blinked. "I'm sorry, did you say Beverage?"

The young man grinned. "Yeah. Been called that my whole life."

"Okay, then. Enjoying the trip?"

"Yeah, sure." The young man thrust his hands into his pockets and nodded toward a food cart on the other side of the street. "But when I saw the sign for hot pretzels, I had to get off. I'm hungry."

Emilia and Roman zeroed in on the pretzel cart. "Daddy, can we get one?" Roman asked.

"A huge one," Emilia echoed. "With big salt on it."

Matt was about to refuse, not wanting to spoil their appetite for lunch, but Janette gave him a lighten-up look. "A warm snack would be good on a chilly day like today." She tempered her expression with a smile. "The kids could split a pretzel and still be hungry for lunch in a bit."

Honestly, could the woman read his mind?

Matt slid a five dollar bill from his wallet and pressed it into Roman's hand, then apologized to Janette. "I hate to leave you here alone, but I need to walk them across the road. Would you like a pretzel, too?"

Janette shook her head. "No, thanks. I don't need the calories."

"Hey, we'll take the kids." The blonde from the train—Violet—grinned at Roman, then looked to Matt for permission. "I'll walk the kids over and bring them right back."

Matt studied the girl and her boyfriend, trying to decide if they looked trustworthy. His initial inclination was to decline her offer, but lately his instincts had been anything but reliable. He didn't want to be a spoilsport and they were on vacation . . . plus, he could sit and keep an eye on them without any problem.

"Okay—but kids, you come straight back here once you get your pretzel. We'll go to the fountain together."

He watched as Roman and Emilia took Violet's hands. They walked to the street crossing, then dutifully waited for the light to change.

What was it with his children and female strangers? Were they so in need of mothering that they'd go with any woman who smiled at them?

He looked at Janette, about to ask her opinion, but she was engrossed in a brochure.

"Forsyth Park," she read aloud, "is the largest and oldest park in Savannah, spanning thirty acres. The exquisite white fountain at the south entrance was purchased from a New York mail order catalog and erected in 1858."

"You can buy fountains from a catalog?" Matt turned to survey the structure providing the park's focal point. The enormous circular structure, composed of a large center basin surrounded by spraying jets, was impressive.

"Want to get comfortable?" Janette pointed to the wide path that led to the distant fountain. "We can sit on one of those benches and wait for the kids."

They wandered a few feet down the path and settled on a bench in the shade of a sprawling live oak. A noisy mob of people walked past, the latest tour group arriving by trolley car. "By the way—" Janette locked her hands over her bent knee— "your children are adorable. I hope you enjoy them while they're young."

Her voice sounded clotted, as if some strong emotion was choking her voice, but her meaning eluded him. Was she implying that he didn't enjoy his children, or that they wouldn't remain adorable?

He cleared his throat. "Am I to infer that kids aren't so much fun when they're older?"

She grimaced. "Maybe some kids are. But we didn't know how tough parenting could be until Annalisa graduated from high school. The past few years have been worse than all her childhood and teenage years rolled together."

He was about to ask what she meant when he saw Violet running toward them, an expression of horror twisting her face. Her boyfriend wasn't with her, and neither were his kids.

A dozen scenarios flashed through his head: One of his children had been hit by a car, Beverage had kidnapped Roman, Emilia was choking on a chunk of soft pretzel—

His heart pounded like a speed bag against his sternum. He didn't remember standing, but suddenly his sneakers were slapping the pavement as he ran toward Violet. She met him on the path and glanced over her shoulder as she gasped for air.

"Violet? Where are my kids?"

She pushed hair out of her face. "We bought pretzels, and I walked them . . . from the pretzel cart to the crosswalk," she said, her voice ragged. "The kids wanted to go see the fountain. I told them we had to wait for Beverage, but—" Her gaze darted from left to right as she searched the crowd.

"What?" Matt waved his hand before her eyes, reminding her to focus. "Where are my children?"

She swallowed hard. "That's just it, I lost them. A trolley pulled up to the corner and a bunch of people piled off. By the time that mob thinned out, the kids had—I couldn't see them."

Janette was suddenly standing beside Matt. She placed her hand on Violet's arm, and something in her touch seemed to calm the girl. "Take a deep breath and let's figure this out. Where's Beverage?"

Violet pointed across the street. "He's going up and down the other side, looking for the kids. We tried calling them, but we don't know their names—"

"Roman." Matt rasped out the word. "Roman and Emilia."

Without waiting to hear more, he surveyed the park. If a trolley had unloaded a group, some of those people would have crossed at the crosswalk. Roman and Emilia could have easily blended with the crowd. Roman wanted to see the fountain, so the odds were good that he was on the park side of the road.

And he wasn't going to waste time debating the matter.

"Excuse me." Leaving Janette and Violet, he strode across the wide expanse of grass, each step longer and faster than the one before. He scanned the crowd, listening for the sound of his children's voices, hoping to catch sight of a boy with brown hair or a girl with a messy ponytail and a blue ribbon. Janette walked at his right, her quick steps swishing through the grass, while Violet kept pace at his left, her breathing punctuated by hiccupped sobs.

Once they had traversed the large open area, Matt swerved toward the paved path leading to the famous fountain. Strolling visitors crowded the walkway, so he quickened his pace in case one of those visitors was a kidnapper with Roman and Emilia in tow. One brown-haired boy looked very much like Roman from behind, so Matt jogged forward and grabbed his arm. The boy yelled as Matt whirled him around, but the child wasn't his son. "Sorry." Matt gave the boy's startled mother an abashed look, then shaded his eyes and continued his search.

Janette gripped his wrist and stared up at him. "Slow down a minute, don't panic. The kids wanted to see the fountain, so let's go there first. If we don't find them on the way, we'll call the police."

"We need to split up." Matt caught Violet's eye. "Young lady, you stay here. If you see the kids, grab them and don't let go. Then call me on my cell." He took a business card from his wallet and slapped it into her hand, then headed toward the splashing fountain. Though Janette had to be ten or twelve years his senior, she had no trouble keeping up. Matt looked at heads, bodies, and faces as they moved forward, but his kids must be playing hide and seek . . .

How was he supposed to find them in a crowd on thirty acres? And what was he thinking, allowing them to go off with virtual strangers? Maybe he'd become too trusting; he assumed Violet and Beverage were like Janette and Andie, as if only responsible and caring people rode the train. But what kind of parents named their kid Beverage? He was probably from some horrible cult, and right now he was trying to stuff Matt's kids into the trunk of a car . . .

Matt walked faster, grateful that Inga wasn't with him. She'd be frantic with worry. But if she were here, none of this would be happening. Inga would never let a stranger take the kids anywhere. She wouldn't even want to take them on a train.

If something happened to his children, he would have no one to blame but himself.

He quickened his pace, striding toward the fountain on the verge of a run. He moved ahead of Janette and stopped when he reached the wall of the huge white basin. He probed the water. Nothing beneath the surface but sodden leaves and pocket change. At least his kids hadn't drowned.

Janette caught up to him, breathless and red-faced. He glanced at her and swallowed hard, struggling to maintain control. "Your kid ever do this? Get lost in a crowd?"

"Every kid does it at least once." Her voice was grim, her lips tight. "Why do you think parents get gray hair?"

Not knowing what else to do, Matt gestured to the path encircling the fountain. "I'll go right, you go left, and we'll meet on the other side. If you see the kids, you have my permission to tackle them and tie them to a tree."

Janette set off, her jaw jutting forward as she swerved between strolling couples and dog walkers. Matt followed the right side of the circle, breaking his stride to run around an older couple walking an apparently arthritic canine. He didn't see his children anywhere near the paved path, and from where he stood he could see for almost half a mile. The walkway stretched across the grassy area and wound through a stand of trees . . .

His heart stopped. Unless his eyes were playing tricks on him, Roman and Emilia were sitting on the gnarled roots of a live oak, stuffing themselves with what he presumed was a giant pretzel. Emilia still had Walter tucked under her arm, and Roman looked perfectly content.

After such an abrupt shock, his heart began to beat double fast, a genuine aerobic workout. From somewhere off to his left, Janette released a cry, then both of them ran toward the tree like a pair of dogs after a rabbit.

He reached the kids first, collapsing on the grass in front of them as his legs turned to marshmallow. Emilia's face and hands were smeared with mustard and Roman had yellow on his chin, but otherwise they looked fine. "Roman, Emilia." Matt blinked at their messy faces. "I didn't know you liked mustard."

Roman shrugged. "Only on pretzels."

"Oh." Matt inhaled a deep breath, torn between anger and exultation. What should he do next? He glanced at Janette, who smiled at him with a you-can-handle-this look on her face.

He hoped she was right.

He crossed his arms and regarded his children with a stern gaze. "Why did you run away from Violet and her boyfriend?"

"We didn't run away." Roman gave him a puzzled look. "I told the dude we were going to eat by the fountain."

"The dude?" Matt's inner alarm clanged. "What dude?"

Janette put forth a more reasonable question. "Are you sure Beverage heard you say you were going to the fountain?"

Roman shrugged and took another bite of mustard-covered pretzel.

"I think he heard us," Emilia said, a pea-sized glob of coarse salt sticking to her chin. "I heard Roman tell him, then we walked over here. We weren't being bad, Daddy."

Not being bad . . . of course they weren't. Matt pulled both of them into an exasperated embrace. "I thought I'd lost you. Don't ever, ever walk away like that again."

Emilia patted his cheek. The tiny sound of her "I'm sorry, Daddy," brought a lump to his throat.

He held them, his eyes closed, until they began to squirm. "Listen, kids—" he squeezed their arms— "you don't know how frightened I was. I didn't know where you were, and I was afraid something had happened to you."

Emilia's face twisted. "Something bad?"

Matt shook his head, not wanting to fuel her imagination with horrible possibilities. "I was afraid because you were lost. I didn't know where to find you."

"We weren't lost." Roman's eyes brimmed with confidence. "We knew you'd find us."

Something in his declaration melted the ice that had been flowing through Matt's veins. Did Roman really have that much faith in his father? If only Matt could be as sure of himself.

He finally released the kids and pushed himself to a standing position. Janette moved closer, a relieved smile on her face. She looked at him, then pulled a tissue from her purse. "Here."

He blinked the wetness from his eyes. "It's okay."

"No, you're not. You have mustard on your cheek."

A moment later Violet and Beverage hurried toward them, their faces flushed. "Wow." Beverage propped his hands on his knees as he bent to catch his breath. "That was scary. I thought I was about to, I dunno, have a heart attack or something."

Violet dropped her hand to her boyfriend's shoulder and released a nervous laugh. "I thought we were going to get arrested. I've never lost anyone's kids before."

Matt rubbed the back of his neck and looked at them, at a complete loss for words. Maybe they should have been more responsible, but how could he blame them when he'd let the kids go with them? He should have known better. He was their father.

Gripping his kids' shoulders, Matt took the first deep breath he'd enjoyed in the last ten minutes. "Thanks, everyone, for helping me look for them. And you two—" he bent to look into his children's eyes—"never wander away from the person who's watching you. You stay with them until they're ready to move on; you don't go anywhere without permission."

Roman hung his head and Emilia pressed her face against Matt's leg. He doubted they'd ever wander off again, but with children, who could tell?

"I guess we'll see you around." Beverage gave his girlfriend a look of relief, then linked his hand with Violet's as they walked away.

When Matt felt wet stickiness on his fingers, he looked down and discovered that his palm was smeared with mustard. If he didn't take care of the problem, all their clothes would be stained before day's end.

At least he'd had the foresight to wear jeans.

He turned to Janette. "Did you see any sign of public wash-rooms on our mad dash across the park?"

"Over there, I think." She pointed to a bandstand about a quarter mile away. "Didn't the brochure say something about new facilities?"

"I don't care if they're old facilities. As long as they have soap and a sink."

The sun peeked out from behind a cloud as the four of them strolled across the field, crunching the remnants of summer grass. Matt was suddenly glad Janette had come along—she could take Emilia into the ladies' room and make his daughter presentable again. He'd take care of Roman.

Roman and Emilia skipped in front, both of them covered in mustard, salt, and pretzel crumbs, both of them laughing and happy. Emilia talked to Walter, and Roman answered in a deep voice Matt had never heard before.

"He's pretty good." Janette nodded at the boy. "Maybe you have a future ventriloquist on your hands."

"Or even an actor." Matt studied his children, suddenly aware that he might not have many more opportunities to see them playing like this. If he left the kids with his mother, she'd be the one who noticed their budding talents, heard their creative play, and laughed at their funny conversations . . .

Yet nothing worthwhile was gained without sacrifice. If Roman and Emilia were to go to the best colleges and have the future he wanted for them, he needed to remain in Washington and focus on his career. Ivy League schools were expensive, and social connections had to be made and maintained.

"Has your heart stopped pounding yet?" Janette asked.

He managed a weak smile. "Almost."

"Same here. They say it's good to get your heart pumping every once in a while."

He answered with a grateful nod. And as they walked, he couldn't help wondering why this woman, who didn't even know them a month ago, was so willing to help with his children while his own mother refused.

He had to be missing something . . . but for the life of him, he couldn't figure out what it was.

At lunch, Matt dropped his napkin into his lap and studied his children's expectant faces. "We've ridden the trolley and seen a lot of things that grownups like. What would you guys like to see?"

Roman and Emilia looked at each other, Emilia looked at Walter, then all three of them turned back to Matt. "We dunno," Roman said.

"Dunno," Emilia repeated.

Matt looked at Janette for inspiration. Though he had grown up in the area, he'd never played the part of tourist. In his younger years, he and his mother couldn't afford to go sightseeing in the ritzy historical area. He supposed he could take the kids on a tour of Thunderbolt and show them the rickety house he'd grown up in, but that wouldn't be fun for anyone.

Janette pressed her napkin to her lips and smothered a smile. "Despite what Roman said earlier—" she lowered her voice— "more than anything your children want to be with you. But why don't you ask our waitress about activities for children? A lot of families vacation here, so there has to be something nearby."

As always, Janette's suggestion proved to be perfect.

An hour later they climbed out of a cab at the Lazaretto Creek Marina, where Captain Tom conducted dolphin tours on his bright blue boat. As they walked over the long dock that led to the loading area, Matt had to admit this idea felt like a winner. Though the wind was cool, the sun felt warm on their faces and the kids were practically dancing with excitement. Neither of them had ever seen a dolphin in the wild, and Matt was grateful for the opportunity to expand their horizons.

He thought he might even enjoy the trip himself.

He bought four tickets at the weathered welcome booth, then they crossed a gangplank to board the blue boat. Roman led the way to the back, where they sat on a bench beneath the fluttering canopy. When the boat had filled, the crew cast off while Captain Mike, clad in a white skipper's uniform, lifted his microphone and informed this guests that for the next ninety minutes they'd be heading toward Tybee Island and circling a lighthouse, where they were certain to see dolphins and might even spot a dolphin family.

"You kids be careful and don't lean over the edge of the boat," he cautioned, acknowledging that most of the parents had given the outer seats to their children. "We'd hate to have to pluck any-one out of the sea on a fine day like this."

As the engine shifted from a low putter to a growl, Matt leaned back and relaxed. Emilia and Roman sat up straight, their eyes focused on the sparkling water, hoping for a glimpse of something wonderful.

Matt stretched his arm over the back of the seat and allowed himself to drift into a haze of self-recrimination. Somehow, prob-ably by sheer luck, they had barely avoided a tragedy at the park. One or both of his children could have been kidnapped or taken by some lunatic. They could have been hit by a car, trampled by a horse-drawn carriage, or knocked over by a distracted jogger. They could have faced danger at so many points—

"Smile, Matthew." Janette raised her voice to carry over the roar of the engine. "Your kids want you to enjoy this, so put whatever's troubling you out of your mind."

He closed his eyes and leaned toward her. "I can't stop think-ing about what might have happened today."

"Nothing happened. Let it go."

"But I messed up. I'm no good at parenting. No matter what I try to do, I end up making mistakes. You're a natural; even Violet was better with children than I am."

"I have more experience, that's all. And Violet made a huge

mistake. She should never have lost sight of those kids."

"Still . . ." He shifted his gaze as the boat hit a wave and water splashed over the side, making his children squeal. After making certain they were all right, he cast Janette a questioning look. "Is there a school where the curriculum includes lessons in fatherhood?"

Her eyes softened with an emotion that looked too much like pity. "Your children are six and eight years old, so you have time to grow. You've already learned more than you realize."

He snorted. "I'm so far behind. I never spent much time with my kids until — well, until now. But most of the fathers I know hardly ever see their children. And most of the mothers act as though fathers aren't necessary. Two women in our office have had babies through artificial insemination with anonymous donors. One of the guys made a crack about those kids not knowing their dads, and one of the mothers said fathers only get in the way. I was shocked to hear her say that, but I've gotta tell you, most of the time that's how I feel. Like I'm only in the way."

Janette pushed her windblown hair out of her eyes. "Is that why you want to give your children to your mother?"

Her conclusion startled him, but maybe she could see what he'd been unable to figure out. "I want what's best for my kids. I want them to be happy. And yes, I think they'll be better off with someone who knows how to raise children. That's not something they teach in law school."

Janette rubbed her arms as a slow smile crept across her face. "Matthew, parenting is something you learn by doing, and okay, maybe you're off to a late start. But you have started, and that's a good thing. From this point, all you have to do is read a few books, talk to a few parents, and say a few prayers . . . better yet, say a lot of prayers. Learn how to let your heart lead you. But most of all, talk to your kids. They'll teach you what you need to know."

Easy for her to say. In their time together, Matt had observed that Janette was devoutly religious, deeply maternal, and apparently a perfect mother. But she didn't really know him. Or his world.

"Straight ahead," Captain Tom rumbled, his amplified voice cutting into their conversation. "See those ripples in the water? We've got a pod of dolphins off the starboard bow, and for you land lubbers, that means off to the right. I think—yep, I'm sure—we're looking at a mama and her baby, among others."

Emilia and Roman stood; for safety's sake Matt pressed them back into their seats. A flush of pleasure warmed his face when they gasped at the sight of the sleek gray bodies breaking the surface and running alongside the boat.

And while the sight of swimming dolphins was amazing, Matt found the look on his children's faces unforgettable.

# Chapter Thirteen

By the time they dropped Janette at her hotel and made it back to Momma's house, the front porch light was blazing. The kids piled out of the taxi and ran for the door while Matt paid the driver and followed them up the hill. Roman and Emilia were exhausted from their busy day, so he hoped they'd go to bed early and sleep like babies.

Meanwhile, he was bracing for the most important conversation of his life. He had one last chance to convince his mother to take charge of his children, but he'd taken comfort in the fact that he was a professional persuader. He had assumed too much when he first broached the subject with Momma; he'd launched a half-hearted argument, caught her off guard, and put her on the defensive.

But tonight would be different. She'd had time to think about their situation, and he'd had time to prepare a formal strategy. Tonight he would approach the matter as if he were preparing to stand before a judge. He would employ Aristotle's rules of rhetoric and use *ethos*, *logos*, and *pathos* to win his argument. Credibility, reason, and emotion—in the hands of a master, those tools could accomplish miracles at a judicial hearing. Perhaps they could do the same in his mother's living room.

The kids stopped at the front door. Roman stood on tiptoe as he worked the doorknob, but Momma must have thrown the deadbolt. Emilia kept slapping the doorbell, so after a moment Momma appeared and hugged the kids before they steamrolled their way into the living room. She waited, holding the door until Matt caught up, but the smile she gave him was not as enthusiastic as the one she'd given the kids.

"Hello, son." She patted his back when he embraced her. "Did y'all have a nice day? I thought you'd be back sooner."

"We got caught up in dolphin-watching. We took a boat out to Tybee Island."

"Sounds like a full day."

"It was. We went to the Savannah museum, played around the fountain at Forsyth Square, and ate pretzels with mustard, most of which is now decorating the kids' clothes."

Momma made a face and led the way into the house. "You want me to wash those dirty things? Mustard stains, you know, and you don't want to tote dirty clothes all the way back to Virginia."

He hesitated. Was his mother reminding him that she planned on sending them away tomorrow?

"Would you mind doing a load of laundry for me?" He gave her a tentative smile. "I hate to ask you to work tonight, but since the train leaves early in the morning—"

"I'd be happy to do it." She closed the door behind him and put on the deadbolt, already locking up for the night. "What are grandmothers for?"

He arched a brow. Part of their job description might include stepping in when a parent desperately needed help, but he wasn't going to raise the issue now. Later, when the kids were settled in their sleeping bags, he'd present her with his revised argument.

Obeying their empty stomachs, the kids had tramped into the kitchen. Matt followed, and was surprised to discover an empty dining table. Even though she'd said she wanted to go out to eat, he had expected another home-cooked meal, a dinner with mashed potatoes and gravy and fried something-or-other . . .

"Are you cooking, Momma?"

She shook her head. "I hardly ever cook these days. Seems like such a waste when it's just me."

"But there are four of us."

"I'm too tired to even go out to eat, so I was thinking we could order a pizza. The kids like pizza, don't they?"

They did, but they ate it all the time. Matt was hoping for something a little more traditional, but he wasn't going to argue or make demands. Not now.

He gave her a compliant smile. "Whatever you want will be fine with us."

"All-righty, then. Why don't you order the pizza and I'll get those kids in the tub."

His spirits rose at this sign of nurturing behavior. He'd been thinking that the kids would get dirty during dinner, but if Momma wanted to scrub the children now —

His mind filled with the image of her kneeling beside a bubble-filled bath, singing goofy songs as she made shampoo antlers out of their hair and draped bubble beards over their chins . . . evidence that her long-dormant maternal instinct was kicking in.

Go, Grandma, go.

He took his smart phone from his pocket and brought up the app for a pizza chain. He found a franchise less than five miles away, which meant they'd deliver in less than thirty minutes. He called and ordered a large pepperoni pizza, the kids' favorite, then settled into the recliner, picked up the TV remote, and punched on the power.

A half hour later, Roman and Emilia raced into the living room, their faces clean and bright, their bodies clothed in clean, unwrinkled pajamas. Did Momma already go through their suitcases and wash their clothes? She hadn't appeared yet, but he could hear the rhythmic thump of the washing machine in the basement.

When the doorbell rang, Roman raced to answer it. "Pizza's here!"

Matt paid the delivery guy, then carried the box to the kitchen table. His mother didn't say much as they ate and the kids babbled about their day. When the pizza was gone, Matt leaned back, arms crossed, and watched Momma use her napkin to wipe two childish faces and plant a kiss on each forehead. "Go brush your teeth," she said, "then zip yourselves into your sleeping bags. I'll come read to you in a minute."

Roman frowned. "But we don't have any books."

"Don't you worry—before you get into bed, look in the box on the floor of the closet. I saved all of your dad's books from when he was a little boy. Pick out the ones you like best, and I'll read them for your bedtime stories."

The kids scrambled from their seats and ran upstairs, their bare feet pounding the steps. Matt smiled and rested his chin on his hand. "You've made their night. Books are the perfect ending to a good day."

"I wish I could do this more often." Momma picked up the empty pizza box, folded it, and slid it into the tall kitchen trashcan. "It's a shame I don't get to see them but once or twice a year."

Did she realize she was setting herself up? Maybe this final argument would be easier than he'd anticipated. Or maybe she'd been mulling his proposition and was about to tell him that she'd had second thoughts . . .

"Momma." He lowered his arm and reached out to her. "Will you sit down for a minute? We need to talk."

"Yes, we do. But I promised to read to those kids, and if I keep them waiting they'll fall asleep. I know they're tuckered out." She moved toward the hallway, then lifted a warning finger. "Tell you what—you finish cleaning the kitchen, then meet me in the living room. We'll talk there."

She'd get no argument from him. As she left, Matt stood and put their empty glasses in the dishwasher, then pushed the chairs under the table. What else? A smear of pizza sauce marked Roman's place, so Matt grabbed a wet dishtowel and wiped the plastic tablecloth, reliving memories of when he used to help Momma clean the kitchen at the Thunderbolt house. That kitchen was smaller than this one, it lacked a dishwasher, and the four painted metal cabinets squatted beneath a chipped cast iron countertop . . . they'd come a long way since then.

When he couldn't find anything else to clean, he draped the dishtowel over the edge of the sink and went into the living room. He dropped onto the sofa and turned on the TV, but lowered the volume so it wouldn't distract from the conversation he and his mom were about to have.

Momma's voice floated down the stairs, accompanied by his children's musical laughter. She was reading *Ferdinand the Bull*, so he waited, straining to hear the story of the bull that didn't like to fight. After Ferdinand, Matt propped his head on a pillow and listened to *Mike Mulligan and His Steam Shovel* and the tale of *Curious George*.

His eyelids were as heavy as lead when Momma's hand squeezed his shoulder. "Matty?" She chuckled. "Did I put you to sleep, too?"

"Um, I'm awake." He sat up and gave her a drowsy smile. "I enjoyed listening to you read."

"You should have come upstairs and joined us."

"That's okay." He cleared his throat. "I wanted you to have some private time with the kids." He waited until she settled in her favorite chair, then he braced his elbows on his thighs.

"Momma, I want to thank you for putting us up the last couple of days. I realize I should have called first. I know we inconvenienced you, dropping by unannounced like we did, and I'm sorry."

His mother waved his apology away. "Don't worry about it, son. You can always drop in on family."

He waited, letting her words reverberate in the quiet. "You've always said that if you can't count on family, who can you count on?"

She fixed her gaze on the flickering television. "That's right."

"That's why I was hoping I could count on you now, Momma. To help me take care of the kids."

Her eyes sharpened as she shifted her gaze. "I'm glad you brought that up, son. I've had all day to think about what you said yesterday."

He struggled to keep his smile in check. "I'm glad. Because I wanted another opportunity to explain our situation."

She nodded, her expression blank, so he launched into the *ethos* part of his argument: establishing his credibility.

"You know I'm a successful lawyer. I'm not sure you realize just how successful I've been over the last few years. The firm trusts me. They've noticed how I've proven myself. I've brought them a lot of money and a lot of good will. Just the other day one of the managing partners assured me I was a valued part of the firm. He hinted that they might soon offer me a partnership."

His mother squinted. "What does that mean?"

"Bottom line, it means I'll make more money and I won't be under so much pressure to record billable hours."

"Money's not everything, son."

"It's more than you know, Momma. I want my kids to go to the best colleges, and do you know how much that will cost? A lot. I want my kids to have a solid future. I don't want them growing up in a place like Thunderbolt."

Her chin wobbled. "I didn't realize your growing up years were so awful."

He groaned. Now he'd hurt her feelings, and he never meant to. "They weren't awful, but I want better for my kids. Is that a crime?"

"Congratulations, then. Looks like you're on your way." Her voice had chilled, which meant he'd better move into the *pathos* part of his presentation.

"I know you know—" he paused as a genuine lump moved into his throat—"how hard the last year has been. Inga's accident happened so suddenly, at times I've wondered if my family would survive. The kids have adjusted as well as anyone might expect, but I'll be honest, Momma—sometimes I want to stay in bed all day because the pillow still smells like my wife. Inga was the love of my life, and no one can replace her in my heart or the hearts of my children."

His eyes brimmed with honest tears, but Momma stared at the carpet, her face perfectly blank. Since when had she become such a master at hiding her feelings?

And now, *logos*. An appeal to reason. This time he wouldn't offer her a choice between yes or no, he'd offer Virginia or South Carolina.

"That's why we need you so much. I know I sprang this proposal on you without warning, and I neglected to mention all the possible options. If you don't want to take care of the kids down here, I could move you to Virginia. You could keep your house, of course, even rent it out while you live in our guest room. If that's too small, I'll build on another wing, whatever you want. You can find a new church, make new friends, join a new bowling league—maybe even learn to like snow. Our seasons are beautiful, even prettier than what you'll see in Savannah."

He waited, silence stretching between them, while she appeared to study the carpet design. After a long moment, Momma looked at him with unshed tears in her eyes. Maybe she hadn't quite mastered the art of concealing her emotions.

"Today I spent a lot of time thinking about you and the kids, Matty. I realized that you don't understand why I can't take your kids like you want me to. It'd be an imposition for me, sure, and I'd have to change everything about my life, but that's not the reason I won't do what you're askin'. Not here, and not in Virginia."

Shock flowed through Matt as he met her gaze. He never dreamed she'd turn down both the options he offered.

"The first reason I have to say no," she continued, "is because sometimes parents have to practice what they call tough love, even with adult children. I'm not refusing because I don't love those two kids upstairs—I love 'em to death, and if you were to die tomorrow, I'd be on the first plane to go get 'em. They're precious to me."

"But—"

"Let me finish. I'm not gonna take those kids because it wouldn't be fair to you. You're their father, and I think you were handicapped in the beginning because your wife let you off the hook when it came to your kids. Inga was a lovely girl, but she let you get away with too much. Losing her was a tragedy, but you continued to get away with not being involved in your kids' lives because you hired a nanny who took care of everything for you. The truth, Son, is that no one has required you to be the father you ought to be. No one can make you be a daddy to your kids, and even though you may go out next week and hire another nanny, you'll only be cheating yourself. One day you'll look at Roman and Emilia and realize that you don't even know them. Those kids will smile and stick their hands out for a check, because that's all they've ever gotten from you. They won't ask for your love or your opinion, because they'll have no use for those things. They won't want you, they'll only want the things you can provide."

He sat, slack-jawed with amazement, because his mother had just unloaded more heartfelt sentiments than she'd uttered since their arrival. She'd made herself abundantly clear, and though he didn't agree with her conclusion, one thing was certain: she was dead set against helping him raise his kids.

He had utterly failed. "Well, Momma—"

"I'm not done, Matty." Annoyance struggled with humor on her face as she stared at him. "That was just the first reason I'm tellin' you no. The second reason is because you're like a proud rooster, all puffed-out and crowin' about being king of the mountain without realizin' that you're standing on a dunghill. You're too set on bein' a self-made man. You see yourself as the captain of your own soul, and don't you think I know you bought me this house because you think you've managed to pay me back? You can't pay me back for bein' your momma, and it's silly to even try. You pay the debt to your parents not by writing checks, but by investing in the next generation. You pay it back by lovin' your own children."

He sank into the old sofa, feeling as small as a flea. He hadn't felt this thoroughly scolded since Momma caught him stealing dollar bills from the cookie jar emergency fund.

Somehow he mustered the courage to whisper, "Are you finished?"

"One more thing."

He gripped the armrest of the sofa, resisting the urge to say uncle.

"The third reason I'm not taking those children is because I suspect you've kept yourself so busy that you haven't taken time to properly mourn your wife."

He released the sofa, eager to score a point. "That's not true. I grieved—"

"No, son. Grief happens, whether you want it to or not, but mourning is something you do. It's active; it's intentional. It's the way you say goodbye, the way you pick yourself up and move

forward. You've never said so, but I get the clear feelin' that after Inga died you handed your kids off to that nanny and threw
yourself into your work, never takin' the time you needed to
mourn your loss. If you didn't do it, your kids didn't get to do
it, either. So that's the last reason I can't take those children from
you. They need to be with you so your family can say a proper
good-bye to your wife."

She tucked her hair behind her ears, then folded her hands in
her lap. "So there, son. Now you've heard the reasons why I'm
not gonna take your kids."

He sank back against the sofa, feeling himself compressed
into a shrinking space between the weight of his mother's argu-
ments and his feeble presentation.

"Momma, you should have been a lawyer."

When he looked up again, an annoyed but forgiving glint
filled her eyes. "I'm content to be a lawyer's momma." A smile
tugged at the corner of her mouth. "And I pray every night that
God would heal your broken heart and bind it to your children's. Because those young 'uns are delightful. Roman is sweet
as peaches and Emilia is as smart as a tree full of owls. But if you
don't change your priorities, you'll never know them. And one
day you'll wish you'd done things differently."

Matt wiped his damp palms on his jeans, then drew a deep
breath. "I guess I'd better see to that laundry." He stood. "You
need me to do anything around the house before I go?"

Momma rose from her chair, the top of her head reaching
only to his shoulder, and smiled, featherlike laugh lines crinkling
around her eyes. "Thanks for askin', Matty. Just wake me up
before y'all leave in the morning. I can't say goodbye without
getting one more hug and kiss from my grandbabies."

◆

That night Matt dreamed a dream so real, so wonderfully
ordinary, that he didn't want to wake up. He came home from
work, entered the house, and heard the clang of pots and pans in

the kitchen. He walked through the dining room and found Inga at the stove, an apron around her trim waist and a smile on her face. He put his hands around her waist and she leaned against him, then turned her head and looked at him with love shining in her eyes. "I thought you'd never get here." She dropped a lid on a steaming pot. "I've been waiting a long time."

He sank onto a barstool, marveling that she hadn't changed. She looked so beautiful, so real, so present.

"I've been waiting for you, too." His voice was as rough as sandpaper. "Things are falling apart . . . because you held our family together."

"Matthew Scofield." She underlined his name with reproach. "You are the foundation of this family and our children's father. Nothing you do is as important as raising them." Her eyes softened as her mouth curved in a smile. "You will be a wonderful dad, Matt. Once you make up your mind to do something, you always do it whole heartedly."

His eyes stung in an onslaught of unexpected tears. He lowered his head to dash the wetness away and when he looked up again, he was alone in the kitchen, a solitary man staring at a pair of unattended saucepans. He pressed his palms to the countertop, gripping at the dream, but though he tried to summon Inga again, the cool granite beneath his fingers transformed to the warm softness of cotton sheets.

Matt sat up and stared into the darkness, well-aware of who and what and where he was. He was a widower who hadn't taken the time to mourn his wife. A workaholic lawyer. And a prideful father who had been desperately trying to avoid his responsibilities to his children.

Thick quiet filled the sleeping house, but he could hear the deep breaths of his kids across the hall.

Momma was right. He didn't know how she managed to read him, but her intuition was infallible. Maybe one day he'd know his children as well as she knew him.

He had learned a lot about Roman and Emilia since boarding the train, but he'd also learned a lot about himself. Though he'd always thought of himself as a courageous, hard-working, inventive lawyer, he'd been a cowardly, lazy, and unbelievably unimaginative father. Like a little boy who signed up for a paper route and then decided he didn't want to get up early every morning, he'd run home to Momma, hoping she'd step up and do his job for him.

No wonder his kids were attracted to Andie and Janette—women had provided most of the parenting his children had received. They didn't remember the occasions he changed their diapers or rocked them while reading a legal brief. They wouldn't recall the nights he stumbled through the darkness to give them a drink of water or chase away a nightmare. By the time they reached their toddler years, he had decided that he needed his sleep, so Inga took over those nighttime duties.

These thoughts ushered in a new realization, along with a chill in the pit of his stomach: his children didn't know how much he loved them.

Words of love had never come easily to him. And from a child's perspective, he doubted his actions had ever demonstrated it. What was it Inga used to say? "Children don't spell love L-O-V-E. They spell it T-I-M-E."

Except for this train trip, when had he last spent uninterrupted time with his kids?

He slipped out of bed and crossed the hallway, then stepped into the bedroom where his children lay in sleeping bags on the floor. The glow of a nightlight revealed Roman resting flat on his back, his chin lifted to the sky, his hands fisted even in sleep. Emilia slept in the fetal position, one arm curled around Walter, her thumb tucked into her mouth.

Matt tilted his head. He thought Emilia gave up sucking her thumb long ago. This might be a regression, a way to comfort herself. But why did she feel the need for comfort?

Tomorrow and the day after and the day after that . . . He'd do his best to find out. To understand his son and daughter. To show them how much he loved them.

The heater clicked on, sending a welcome warmth through the room. Matt sank to the floor and sat cross-legged, content to watch his precious ones sleep.

Because they had to catch an early train, Matt and the kids woke before Saturday's sunrise and packed their freshly-laundered clothes. Though Roman was irritable and Emilia mumbled like she was still half-asleep, somehow Matt got them out of their pajamas and into the kitchen for a bowl of cereal and a glass of orange juice.

Though he'd told his mother that she didn't have to get up with them, she stood in the kitchen, too, watching them with crossed arms and watery eyes. She hadn't said much since coming out of her bedroom in her nightgown and slippers, but Matt figured she'd said everything she wanted to say the night before.

"Okay, kids—" he glanced at his watch— "the train leaves at 6:50, so we'd better call a cab and put on our coats."

"You don't have to call nobody." Momma looked directly at him. "I'm takin' you to the station."

"You don't have to. It's so early and you're not dressed—"

"Give me a minute and I'll be ready. No sense in you wastin' good money on a cab."

She stalked toward her bedroom, her slippers slapping the vinyl floor. He helped the kids into their coats, buttoned them up, and unlocked the front door. By the light of the moon and a solitary streetlamp he took the kids outside and buckled them into Momma's car, then returned for the suitcases and backpacks, which he loaded into the trunk. By the time he had everything in place, Momma had come out in tennis shoes and yet another warm-up suit. Her breath steamed in the air as she crossed the frost-dusted lawn and slid behind the wheel.

No one spoke on the way to the station. Matt glanced at the backseat, certain that both kids had fallen asleep, but they were sitting ramrod straight, their eyes wide, their faces alternately lit and darkened by passing shadows. The sky had begun to brighten in the east, but he didn't think the sun would rise until their train had left Savannah.

If he were more mystical and metaphorical, he might find that fact significant.

At the station, he pulled the luggage from the trunk while Momma unbuckled the kids. She hugged each of them, then walked over and threw her arms around Matt.

As he held her wiry frame, he wondered why they always seemed to be at cross-purposes. He loved his mother and knew she loved him, but no matter what he did or how well he did it, he always seem to fall short of her approval. Why was that?

"Thanks for putting us up," he said when she released him. "I'll call you when we get home."

"Son—" she hesitated, her eyes softening with seriousness. "I hope you know I'm proud of you. I'd do anything for you. And if you can't find anyone to keep Roman and Emilia—"

"You don't have to worry. I'm going to work it out. Somehow."

Momma's chin quivered, then she bent to tweak the end of Emilia's nose. "You be a sweet girl, okay? Keep reading so you'll grow up to be as smart as your daddy."

She stepped toward Roman and placed her hands on his shoulders. "You're a very special young man. Take care of your sister and never let anyone hurt her."

Roman nodded, then he and Emilia watched as Momma got into her car, gave one last wave, and pulled away without looking back. Instinctively, Matt knew why she hadn't looked at them again—she was crying.

When the car pulled out of the parking lot and disappeared behind a stand of trees, Emilia burst into tears. Alarmed, Matt dropped to one knee to examine her. "Honey, what's wrong? Are you sick?"

When she didn't answer he turned to Roman, whose lower lip was quivering. "Son, what's going on?"

Roman looked at Emilia, who wiped her nose with the back of her hand and clutched Walter tightly.

"We heard you and Grandma last night," Roman finally said, his voice wavering. "We know you want to get rid of us, but Grandma won't let you."

"Get rid of — oh, no." Matt felt his heart contract as he reached out and drew them into a close embrace. "I don't want to get rid of you. I was only trying to find someone who could look after you while I'm at work. I thought Grandma might be the right person."

Emilia pulled back and looked at him, tears gleaming beneath the silken fringe of her lashes. "Don't you want us anymore, Daddy?"

The question pierced his heart like a dart. He didn't know how he would work things out, but he would find a way to be the father Inga would want him to be. The kind of dad who spent bucketloads of time with his kids. The kind of dad he should be, no matter what.

"I want you," Matt told them, pulling them closer. "I want you now and forever because I'm never going to stop loving you."

They didn't reply in words, but their little arms tightened around his neck.

# BOOK THREE

*When the whistle blew*
*and the call stretched thin across the night,*
*one had to believe that any journey*
*could be sweet to the soul.*

— Charles Turner

# Chapter Fourteen

**Savannah, Georgia**
**Saturday, November 17**

Though habit urged Janette to look around the station for signs of a familiar face, she refused to do so. Why should she set herself up for disappointment? Andie was with her family in California, and even though Matt said his mother had refused to go along with his plan, Janette doubted the woman resisted him for long. At this very minute she was probably making breakfast for her grandkids while Matt tried to book a flight back to Washington.

Which left Janette to take the last leg of the journey alone.

The knowledge twisted inside her, evoking an unexpected feeling of loneliness. She swallowed the sob that threatened her throat and tried to focus on the business at hand. She couldn't help but find it ironic that she had started her journey looking forward to solitude; now she dreaded it. She was going to miss her traveling companions.

She checked her suitcase at the baggage counter, then walked through the double doors that led to the train tracks. Most of her fellow passengers waited inside the warm terminal, but she needed to get used to being alone. Her little vacation-from-life would end in two days, then she had to decide whether she should go home or simply . . . go. Start a new life somewhere else, someplace where she wasn't a wife or a mother, but only a middle-aged woman ready to live the second half of her life free from messy emotional entanglements.

The speaker above her head crackled as a railroad employee disturbed the predawn quiet with an unintelligible announcement. The reason for his interruption soon became clear: the train was approaching, its shrill whistle annihilating the silence and rattling her eardrums. One more train ride, this one from Savannah to Jacksonville. She would enjoy two more days riding the rails, then face a moment of decision.

Janette gripped her small bag and walked forward, coming within several feet of the tracks. The train whizzed past her, finally slowing, and silver stairs dropped from a nearby coach car. She nodded at the uniformed attendant and strode forward, ticket in hand. He helped her aboard and pointed her in the right direction. She walked through the aisle, carefully avoiding the protruding arms, legs, and feet of sleeping passengers.

She shoved her carry-on bag into the overhead bin, then dropped into her assigned seat and fished her compact from her purse. After glancing around to make sure no one was watching, she opened the compact and centered her left eye in the mirror, tilting the glass so she could study the top of her cheek. Eleven days after the incident, the swelling had gone down and the bruise was scarcely visible, even in the unforgiving glare of the overhead light.

Tomorrow she might look normal again.

She put her compact away as an elderly woman stopped in

the aisle and gestured to the empty chair next to Janette. "I believe this is my seat."

Janette moved her purse from the seat to the floor. "Make yourself at home."

The woman sat and arranged her skirt around her, keeping her purse on her lap. She smoothed her gray hair, which was pulled tight in sort of a no-style style, and tilted her seat back, then leaned forward to bring up the footrest. Amazingly, she was so short her feet didn't hang over the edge.

Janette drew her sweater closer and smiled. "You must travel a lot."

"Every weekend." The woman slipped both arms through the straps of her purse, binding it to her body. "I ride from Savannah to Jesup one weekend, then come back the next."

"Visiting relatives?"

She nodded. "My children pass me back and forth like a hot potato. But I don't mind. It's the only way I ever get to see 'em."

She closed her eyes, a sure sign that she'd like to sleep, so Janette took the hint and looked out the window. The sun hadn't yet risen, but the station glowed with electric light. A handful of people waved as the whistle blew and the train pulled away, leaving the station porter on the sidewalk, red-faced and sweating in his wool uniform.

Janette reclined her seat and closed her eyes. Because the alarm clock had rung so early, she ought to catch up on her rest. Or maybe she should think about bracing herself for the end of her trip. She'd enjoyed these days away from the powder keg she called home, but she couldn't ride the rails forever.

Though she often wished she could.

She was drifting on the edge of sleep when she heard a familiar squeal followed by a child's laughter. She sat up and turned, searching the back of the car, and saw Beverage and Violet standing near the restrooms, their arms wrapped around each other. Young love, shallow and bright. What would they do when this trip ended? Stay together or go their separate ways?

She finally spotted the Scofields on the opposite side of the train. Matthew was sitting in the uncomfortable center of a double seat, a child on each side. Roman and Emilia had pillowed their heads against his chest, while Walter's long neck draped over Matt's stomach. Emilia was walking her fingers over the buttons on Matthew's dress shirt while Roman giggled at her antics.

So — Matt's mother had held her ground. Janette lifted a brow, wondering what had transpired between the two of them, then she smiled. The kids looked so sweet, so angelic — she caught Matt's gaze, then twiddled her fingers in a friendly wave. He tipped his head toward the children and mouthed they need to sleep with a bemused look on his face.

He was learning.

Feeling less alone, Janette snuggled into her seat, placing the thin Amtrak-issued pillow between her shoulder and the window, then sat up as a hot flash warmed her skin. She peeled her sweater off and dropped it by her side, then fanned herself with a magazine from the seat pocket. A smile twisted her mouth when the woman next to her began to snore. If she really traveled every weekend, it was no wonder she'd mastered the art of sleeping upright. Had she found a cure for menopausal power surges?

Janette closed her eyes as the heat faded away, but she couldn't sleep. The thought of returning home had awakened a vivid memory that now floated across the back of her eyelids. She saw herself in her own kitchen, she read the hand-stitched sampler hanging over the window, words from her favorite psalm: The boundary lines have fallen for me in pleasant places. She breathed in the aromas of oregano and sausage; she heard herself humming as she prepared a pot of Italian wedding soup for the neighborhood's annual progressive dinner. She lifted her head at the thump of quick steps on the stairs — her daughter was coming down, her face flushed and her eyes narrow.

Annalisa swept into the kitchen and sat on a barstool at the counter, then clamped her head between her hands. "I'm bored."

"You could read a book," Janette suggested, working hard to keep her voice level. They were expecting company within the hour, and she didn't want to upset the delicate balance between Annalisa calm and Annalisa enraged. "I read a good one the other day. It's on the bookcase in the living room."

"I don't want to read one of your stupid books!" Annalisa spread her fingers and peered through them like an animal in a cage. Then, without warning, she dropped her hands and released a stream of profanity, cursing Janette, the progressive dinner, her father, even the Lord.

Trembling, Janette turned and gripped the edge of the sink, her heart shriveling. Of course it had started again. Whenever they planned something special, even something as casual as having a few friends over for dinner, Annalisa did something to draw attention to herself. It was as though she couldn't stand to be anywhere but in the dead center of her parents' focus, their activities, their lives —

And how could she spew that kind of profanity after they'd taught her about Truth, after they'd loved her and taken her to church, after they'd been as firm and gentle as they knew how to be? Janette knew the girl was pushing her buttons, hitting where she knew she'd elicit the most powerful reaction.

Despite the saying on the sampler, this was not a pleasant place.

"Harry!" Janette raised her voice, shouting to be heard above her ranting daughter. "Harry, can you come here?"

"Why are you calling him?" Annalisa's voice had gone ragged with fury. "Why don't you ever want to talk to me?"

"I'd be happy to talk to you —" Janette kept her voice light and turned to face her daughter — "if you are willing to speak in a rational tone. But I'm not going to argue with you because I have a dinner to prepare. The neighbors are coming—"

Annalisa slid closer to the hand-painted soup tureen Janette had set on the counter. Sharp intention formed in her eyes, but before Janette could move, Annalisa's fingertips pressed against the sloped side of the beautiful pot Janette used only on special occasions, the one she waited six months to buy on sale because it was too expensive at full price—

Annalisa slapped the tureen. Though Janette cried out and moved to intercept it, the dish slid across the countertop and fell onto the tile floor, shattering into a hundred pieces. Annalisa stood, lips pressed together in grim satisfaction, hands on her hips, eyes narrow as she waited for her mother to react.

Janette couldn't stop herself. Fueled by a hot spurt of anger, she stalked toward her daughter, wooden spoon in hand, ignoring the crunch of glass under her slippers. Her stomach knotted and the kitchen blurred before her eyes, wood and glass and dinnerware rattling in a seismic shift. Janette pulled back her arm, ready to smack her daughter's hand with the spoon, but Annalisa's fist flew forward, slamming into Janette's eye socket with the force of welterweight's punch.

Janette bent at the waist and covered her face, shaking like a bull stunned by the slaughterer's blow. Her spoon fell amid the shattered pottery as Janette's eyes overflowed. Harry entered the kitchen, his eyes wide as he surveyed the damage, and Annalisa's fist swung around to punch him, too.

But Harry had always been strong. Janette peered through the fringe of her bangs and saw him catch Annalisa's arms and secure them in a vise grip. "Hold on now." He spoke in an even tone, trying to calm her down. "What do you think you are doing?"

Annalisa screamed, her normal voice distorted by rage. "Mom was going to hit me."

Janette lifted her head, knowing she'd reached her breaking

point. Everyone, their counselor said, had a limit. No one had to take everything a wild child dished out.

She drew a deep breath and forbade herself to tremble. "Don't question her, call the police." Her words tumbled out in a determined rush. Their daughter hated them and was out of control. What would stop her from coming into their bedroom and stabbing them in a murderous rage? They didn't keep guns in the house, but they had knives and scissors and hammers, any one of which might be a convenient weapon in their unpredictable daughter's hands—

"Call the police." Tears streamed over Janette's cheeks as she stared at Harry, begging him to act. "Please, honey, I can't take this anymore. I can't live like this; I can't walk away and pretend this never happened. She punched me. That's battery. She's an adult; old enough to know better."

Harry winced. "Are you okay?"

"No, I'm not. I think I'm going to have a black eye."

Harry's gaze locked on their daughter. "Why'd you hit your mother?"

"She started it!"

"What did she do?"

"She was about to hit me!"

Pulse pounding, Janette clenched her jaw. "I admit I was about to smack her with a spoon." She couldn't believe she had to defend her right to react to her daughter's lunacy in a way that would get the girl's attention. "Look at what she did." She pointed to the shattered tureen, the brightly painted pieces glinting on the tile floor. "But this is about more than a broken bowl. She was going off again, saying the most vile things—"

Harry was still holding Annalisa's wrists. "Why'd you break your mother's bowl?"

"Because she told me to read one of her stupid books!"

A hysterical laugh bubbled up from Janette's throat. "What kind of reason is that?"

"Come with me." Harry gripped Annalisa's arm and led her into the den, where a familiar script would play out yet again. Janette knew the lines by heart—Harry would try to reason with their daughter, Annalisa would rant, Harry would respond calmly, then Annalisa would rant some more. Finally, through sheer persistence, Harry's patience would outlast their daughter's rage and Annalisa would calm down.

Janette knew her husband was trying to take care of the problem. He was giving Janette time to clean up the kitchen, fix her face, and get the soup ready for their guests. She also knew that in an hour, maybe two, Annalisa would morph back into a reasonable person. By the time the neighbors arrived she might actually be civil. She might come out and talk to their neighbors, behaving as if nothing at all had happened. Or she might decide to sit in her room and stare at the wall.

For years Janette had picked up the pieces, patched holes in walls, and pretended that their daughter's behavior wasn't reprehensible. But after being punched in the face, she couldn't pretend any more.

How was she supposed to go to work with a black eye? How was she supposed to look at her friends and act as though nothing had happened? She could make up a story about Henry elbowing her in his sleep, but she didn't want to lie.

Their daughter had dominated their household for years, but she had never been a physical threat until now. The situation at home wasn't improving; it was growing worse. They'd tried counseling, they'd tried talking to Annalisa, they'd tried discipline. But how could you discipline a twenty-five-year-old woman? What did you do, ground her for misbehaving? You could kick her out, but what if she had no place to go? What if she refused to leave?

As difficult as their situation was, Janette knew she and Henry were not alone. She'd read blogs and articles written by other distraught mothers. She'd talked to other women, and she'd become convinced that thousands of parents with twenty-something children were quietly dealing with drug addicts, kids with absolutely no financial restraint, and unexpected grandchildren. Even kids who finished college were likely to boomerang back to their old bedrooms with stuff they collected through four years at expensive schools where they partied and learned skills for careers that did not exist in the current job market.

What did parents do when they couldn't take it any more? In all her reading and talking, Janette had never discovered a good answer.

So eleven days ago she turned off the stove and left the soup for whichever neighbors showed up at their house. As Harry tried to reason with Annalisa, Janette went into their bedroom, pulled a suitcase from the closet, and opened it on the bed. Ignoring the tears that poured from her wounded eye, she counted out a half dozen pairs of underwear, socks and shoes and toiletries. She grabbed several blouses, three or four pairs of slacks, and two pairs of comfortable jeans. Then she zipped the suitcase and picked up her purse. After cleaning out the emergency fund in her lingerie drawer, her wallet held over $1200, plus two credit cards. Her cell phone was fully charged.

And her car waited in the garage.

All she wanted—all she still wanted—was to get away, clear her head, and come to some sort of a decision about what she needed to do. Because one thing was obvious . . . unless something changed drastically, she couldn't go on living in that house.

The train whistle blew, pulling her from the pool of memory and reminding her that they were nearing another station. Too soon for Jacksonville, though, so she didn't have to open her eyes.

But after St. Augustine, she would have to make a decision. This train tour would end and she was out of money. A responsible wife and mother couldn't run away forever.

So she either went home, or she stopped being a responsible wife and mother.

◆

Unable to sleep, Janette walked down to the cafe car for a bottle of orange juice and a cellophane-wrapped version of an egg-on-English muffin, then carried her box tray back to her seat. Her traveling companion had awakened, and she graciously lowered her footrest so Janette could slide back into her spot.

The woman eyed the English muffin in Janette's tray. "That smells good."

Janette lowered her tray table and cast a sideways glance. "Would you like some? I could cut this in half."

The woman chuckled. "You need to eat your own food."

"I'm not that hungry, honest. I'd be happy to share."

The older woman pursed her lips, then nodded and reached for her tray table. "Then I don't mind if I do. Thank you kindly."

Cutting through a microwaved English muffin with a plastic knife wasn't easy, but Janette finally managed to do it. She set half of her breakfast on a napkin and dropped it on the woman's tray. The lady pulled her chair upright and began to eat with an admirable appetite.

"Before you started traveling back and forth—" Janette figured she might as well make small talk— "did you live in Savannah or Jesup?"

The woman chewed for a moment, then swallowed. "Neither. I'm from Greenville."

"South Carolina?"

"Born and bred there. Raised six children there. They're all scattered now. One's in Atlanta, one in Savannah, one in Richmond, one in Montgomery. My two oldest daughters are in Jesup, and they'll be picking me up at the station this morning."

"That's nice." Janette took a bite of her own sandwich. Not too bad, if you were starving. Which, unfortunately, she wasn't.

"You got kids?" The woman lifted a quizzical brow, and though her question was completely harmless, she'd broached a topic Janette would rather not discuss.

She lowered her sandwich and wiped her mouth with her napkin. "I have a daughter. She's grown."

"She still live at home?"

Janette reached for her juice. "She does."

"She go to college?"

"Annalisa . . . wasn't interested in college. Her father and I tried to talk her into it, but she didn't want to go."

"She have a job, then?"

Janette gave the woman a thin smile. "Annalisa works part-time at a pet store."

"Bet she likes that. My oldest girl loves dogs, has a bunch of 'em at her house. Two big 'uns and two little 'uns."

"Really."

The woman tilted her head and studied Janette more intently. "My questions upsettin' you?"

Janette winced. Her frustration must be written on her face. "I'm not upset. Not with you, that is."

"Then what's bothering you, honey? You look like you've got the weight of the world ridin' on your back."

Something about her question—or maybe it was the com-passionate look in her eyes—ripped at a seam in Janette's heart, unleashing a spurt of molten tears. For a moment she couldn't speak, then she pressed the crumpled napkin to her face, shut-ting herself off from the stranger who'd seen through her faster than anyone she'd met on this trip.

The woman sat silently while Janette struggled to get a grip on her emotions. When she finally looked up, her companion had finished her breakfast and was folding her napkin. Without ceremony she dropped it into the tray that held Janette's uneaten muffin, then she pressed her hands together and looked at Ja-nette, interest gleaming in her brown eyes.

"Go on," she said, her voice soft and far younger than her apparent years. "Tell me everything that's on your heart. We got nothing else to do."

Janette took a slow, deep breath. This woman didn't know anything about her family, and she was probably only trying to be polite. But the fact that she didn't know anything meant Janette could give her the unvarnished story without having to worry about her family's reputation.

Anonymity could be a blessing.

Maybe this lady was put on this train for her, seated next to her for a specific reason. What was the term she'd heard for those haphazard meetings? Divine appointments. Meetings God arranged for your eternal good.

Janette wavered for a moment, then words tumbled out in an avalanche of release. "I love my daughter." She shifted so she could look directly at her seatmate. "I used to adore her, but now I'm at my wits end with her. Sometimes I think she's crazy. Sometimes I think she's going to drive me crazy."

"Young 'uns can do that." The woman tilted her head, encouraging Janette to continue.

"I love her, I raised her, I was the best mother I knew how to be—and nothing about mothering my daughter has been easy. Things were hard at first because as a baby she was so sick—"

"What kind of sick?"

"Um, she had a hole in her heart, a condition serious enough to need surgery. We adopted her at birth, you see, and for two months we couldn't take her home from the hospital because of her congenital deformity. We had to wait until she was big enough to undergo the procedure, and during all those weeks I could only visit and sit beside her in the NICU." Janette's throat tightened at the memory. "I didn't know what to feel. I'd never been a mother, so I didn't know what I was supposed to do. I rarely got a chance to hold her, but I'd sit beside her incubator and put her hand through the opening just so I could touch her.

Sometimes she'd grip my finger—all her fingers could wrap around one of mine—and she'd hang on for dear life . . . at least that's what I imagined she was doing. These days, I don't know how she feels about us. Sometimes I think she hates us. Especially me."

For a moment Janette got lost in the memory, then her companion gently touched her arm. "Did the surgery fix her heart?"

Janette nodded. "It took her a while to catch up, though. She crawled later than most babies, talked later, walked later. She's a smart girl, but she had learning disabilities and she still struggles in several areas. She's never had much self-confidence. She gets frustrated easily, and as a toddler she had temper tantrums that nearly raised the roof. I kept telling myself she'd outgrow them, but she never really did. After ranting like a wild woman, her mood will swing in the opposite direction. Sometimes I find her in her room, sitting and staring into space. It's like she's gone blank. Like she feels nothing at all."

She frowned, realizing that her description made Annalisa sound like a sociopath. "My daughter's not always out of control—sometimes she's as nice a young lady as you'd ever want to meet." Her gaze came up to study the woman who had raised six children, apparently successfully. "You must think only an awful mother would be unable to control her kid's outbursts."

"I don't think that at all." The warmth of the woman's smile echoed in her voice. "A wild kid is sometimes an angry kid, and nobody has self-control when they're ragin'. How's anybody supposed to control a person like that? You can't. You have to wait until they come back into their right mind."

Janette smiled, realizing that this woman probably knew more about child rearing than she ever had. In five minutes she'd made Janette feel better about her situation than any of the counselors she'd visited.

"My problem—" she cleared her clogged throat— "is that though Annalisa's twenty-five, she's still a child in so many ways. She'll go days without taking a shower or washing her hair. She'd wear the same clothes for a week if I didn't nag her to change. Her friends have all moved away, most of them married or in grad school, so she rarely goes anywhere. Sometimes she's a zombie, sometimes she's a maniac, and I never know which to expect. I keep hoping she'll grow out of it, but I don't think she's getting better—I'm afraid she's getting worse." She brought the tips of her fingers to her cheek. "She gave me a black eye the other day."

The woman's brows pulled into an affronted frown. "Honey, that ain't right."

"I know, but what am I supposed to do? Sometimes the least little thing causes her to blow up. The other day her car broke down. She called for a tow truck, had the car towed to a garage, took a taxi home, and then flew into a rage and started breaking things. It's gotten to the point where Harry—my husband—and I have to walk on eggshells in our own house, and I'm tired of it."

The older woman's eyes bored into Janette's. "I can see why you would be."

Janette pressed her hand to her lips and looked out the window, afraid she'd said too much. She knew she was telling this woman more than she wanted to know, but it felt good to release the frustrations she'd bottled up for so long. She glanced at her companion, worried that she was dumping too much on a stranger, but the woman was still listening, her eyes soft with concern.

So Janette took a deep breath and continued. "I thought I'd be done with child-rearing by the time Annalisa turned eighteen. I thought she'd be like me and go off to college, get married, begin a family of her own—you know, become an independent person. But she's still living with us, she's still behaving like a child, and we're still supporting her financially. But the older she gets, the more expensive her mistakes are. Harry and I are supposed to be planning for retirement, but we have to keep bailing

Annalisa out of her problems. Meanwhile, I'm hanging on by the last thread in my rope. The reason I'm on this train is because I decided to run away for a few days. My husband doesn't even know where I am."

Breathless, she looked at her companion, certain that she'd just destroyed every bit of sympathy the woman might have felt for her. Good mothers and loyal wives did not run away. When the going got tough, tough women stepped up to the challenge, they didn't duck and run to the train station.

Janette waited, fully expecting her companion to feign a sudden attack of drowsiness or get up to visit the restroom, but one corner of that lined mouth rose in a wry smile. "There, now. Don't it feel good to get all that off your chest?"

Janette's eyes filled again, forcing her to blink tears away. "It does. But you know . . . I haven't told you the worst part of it."

"What could be worse than all that?"

"Harry . . . my relationship with my husband has suffered. He's a good man, one of the kindest and most tenderhearted people you'd ever want to meet, but sometimes I think his greatest strength is also his greatest weakness. When Annalisa was small, I had to be the one who disciplined her, and he was the one who hugged her and assured her everything was fine. I believe kids need boundaries, but Harry is more of a live-and-let-live kind of guy. I want Annalisa to learn how to cook her own food, do her own grocery shopping, and wash her own clothes, but Harry keeps insisting she'll have time to learn those things when she's on her own."

The older woman flattened her palms against her skirt. "Seems to me it's time to learn those things now."

"That's what I keep telling my husband, but he doesn't want to stress out our daughter. He knows that if we nag her, Annalisa will fly off the handle. If she flies off, I'll get upset. The poor man is constantly torn between the two women in his life."

"Have you talked to him 'bout this?"

"Until I'm blue in the face. I keep telling him he's only post-poning the inevitable, but he doesn't want his little princess to be unhappy. I think he's afraid of Annalisa's tantrums. The girl has already broken a lamp, two potted plants, and six cell phones. She's punched me and she's tried to punch him. I don't think we can afford to replace anything else she breaks—and I don't want to call the police because my daughter assaulted one of us. My heart breaks at the thought of her in jail, but if I have to call for outside help, I will."

The woman studied Janette, her squint tightening. "I hope you're making her pay for the damage she's causin'."

"She does give me money after she's destroyed something . . . but sometimes I think that's too easy. She doesn't understand that some things are worth more than money. She's destroyed photos with sentimental value, and she doesn't understand why I get upset. She doesn't seem to understand anything about Harry or me; everything has to revolve around her. Anytime it doesn't, we brace ourselves because we know there's going to be an eruption."

"How often does this happen?"

"Nearly every night. But if something unusual is going on, she explodes two or three times a day."

The woman clicked her tongue against her teeth. "I don't know how you handle all that."

"I don't handle it well, and that's my problem. We don't have a normal life. We can't do the things normal families do. Birthdays, dinner parties, and celebrations are awful. Harry and I don't go on vacation because we're afraid to leave our daughter alone in the house. We've gotten to the point where we're on pins and needles if we have anyone over for dinner, we rarely go to parties, and I can't play Christmas carols because holidays irritate Annalisa. We try to make our lives as dull as possible be-cause she's already ruined more special occasions than we want to remember."

Janette released a deep sigh and tunneled her fingers through her hair, feeling suddenly drained. Her patient companion watched her, then propped her chin on her hand. "Honey," she said, "you need professional help. Something ain't right with your girl, and you shouldn't let her abuse you."

Janette shook her head. "She's only hit me the one time—"

"I'm talking about emotional abuse. Just 'cause you're a parent doesn't mean you have to stand for that kind of treatment, not even from your own child. If your girl can't get a hold of herself, get her to someone who can help her."

"We've taken her to counselors. They don't seem to help, so after a few sessions she doesn't want to see them any more."

"She's probably not giving them enough time. It takes time to really get to know a person. Are they seein' the girl behind the sweet young face? "

The question hung between them, and Janette didn't know how to answer. She had often wondered what Annalisa and her counselors talked about, but she'd respected her daughter's privacy too much to ask. Since Annalisa was always irritable when she came out of the therapist's office, Harry and Janette tiptoed around their daughter even more carefully on therapy days.

"If she hits you again, you and your husband need to get yourselves to a psychiatrist or somethin'." The woman tapped Janette's arm for emphasis. "Tell them what you've just told me. Tell them about the fighting, the broken things, and the black eye. Tell them you've been assaulted and battered. Tell them everything, and don't leave anything out. Your daughter has to know you're serious about stopping this kind of trouble."

"Maybe I will." Exhausted, Janette faced the front and lowered her head to the seat cushion. "If I decide to go home."

◆

To leave or not to leave . . . the question hovered over her like a burgeoning thundercloud. Should she walk away from the stress—all right, she should call it abuse, since that's what it was—of her home and marriage, or should she go home? Leaving would mean walking away from her husband and her child; not leaving might mean years of more torment and grief.

Her traveling companion detrained at Jesup, Georgia, so Janette rode alone for the next several miles. Since they'd soon be arriving in Jacksonville, she resisted the siren call of sleep and pulled her purse onto her lap. She took out her cell phone and glanced at the list of incoming calls. Since turning off the ringer the night before, she'd received two calls from Harry, ten from Annalisa, and one from a number she didn't immediately recognize.

She listened to three of Annalisa's calls, but her messages were curse-filled rants about how much she hated Janette, how awful life was, and how unfair it was that Dad kept nagging her to take a bath. Life was a waste, she might as well kill herself, the world hated her, and why had she ever been born?

Janette deleted Annalisa's remaining seven messages without bothering to play them. Years ago, this talk of suicide would have alarmed her; now she knew Annalisa made threats only to upset them. One day they might be genuine, but by then Janette would have no more emotions to spare.

Harry's two voicemails were very much alike. He loved her, he missed her, he understood why she had to get away. But his voice cracked near the end of the last message, and Janette's heart broke as she listened. When he said, "I can't do this without you," she clenched her eyelids to trap a sudden rush of tears. "I hope you come home soon," Harry finished. "Whenever you're ready, I'll be here."

She lowered her phone as guilt avalanched over her, pounding her head and bruising her heart. Why was she hurting Harry? Was she being completely selfish to want some breathing space? He needed space, too, and he could have come with her, but he'd never walk out on Annalisa. He was more merciful than she was, or more patient. Or maybe he was just more loving.

But didn't love sometimes require doing the hard thing?

Over the years she had tried to reason with him, strived to convince him that Annalisa needed more help than they could give her. Harry, bless his heart, wanted peace more than anything, so he'd been gentle with Annalisa, listening to her, helping her out, silently bearing her scorn and wrath. He'd been the perfect example of a long-suffering father, yet the result had been anything but good. They lived with an adult daughter who had withdrawn into her own world, who did not date or go out with friends, and who often behaved as though she were living in a drug-induced haze. Janette often wondered if Annalisa was using some illegal substance, but Harry was quick to point out that their daughter rarely left the house except to go to work. "Where would she buy drugs?" he asked. "If she were using, we'd know it."

Janette didn't know what to think anymore. But she knew their daughter needed professional help. But knowing that wasn't enough if your loved ones wouldn't cooperate.

Her gaze shifted to the window, beyond which winter-dead trees pointed accusing fingers at a glowering sky. Did she even have a right to take off, or had she done something unforgivable? She'd been Harry's partner for more than thirty years, and she didn't want to end her marriage because their daughter was driving her crazy. Months ago she had considered giving Harry an ultimatum—someone has to move out, me or Annalisa—to shock him into taking action. But when she thought about some of the problems facing their friends and their adult children, threatening Harry felt like an unreasonable response. It was an unreasonable ultimatum.

She caught her breath as the train rushed over a river, a winding gray ribbon that cut through orange earth and spindly pine trees. Because she couldn't see the trestle beneath them, the view left her feeling as though they were flying through open space. If only she could fly away as easily . . .

The old woman said Janette was being abused . . . and didn't experts counsel women to leave abusive husbands? Didn't organizations establish shelters so these women could go to a refuge? Then why didn't anyone provide abused parents with a safe place to lick their wounds?

A memory brushed her cheek like a low-hanging evergreen. When Annalisa was four or five, she'd gone to children's Sunday school and learned about what would happen when Jesus came again. Later, in the car, Annalisa unbuckled her seat belt and thrust her head into the space between the two front seats.

"Mommy," she asked, her small face twisted into a knot of worry, "when we fly through the air to be with Jesus, will you hold my hand?"

Even then, she'd been afraid to be alone. So how could any compassionate person consider walking away from her?

A tear trickled down Janette's cheek. She wiped it away, willing herself not to cry, not here, not now. She had to think; she couldn't afford to be waylaid by emotion.

So she looked for the positives. Annalisa wasn't lying drunk in a gutter; she wasn't pregnant. As far as Janette knew, her daughter didn't use drugs and she didn't stay out all night. She did hold a job and she was physically healthy.

But her daughter lived life at one extreme or the other — she was either too quiet or too loud, either mute or verbally abusive. She refused to leave home, yet she behaved as though she despised the sound of her parents' voices.

Sometimes Janette was convinced God made a mistake when he brought Annalisa to them . . . or them to her. The girl needed a smarter mother and a more disciplined father. When she and Harry had looked at that helpless baby in the incubator, they had no idea they would be dealing with problems that went far beyond the physical. Maybe the baby's heart condition was meant to be a sign that they should walk away and wait for another child.

Janette had been so naive in those days; she believed infants were blank slates waiting to be inscribed with parental lessons. She had no idea that those little bodies were bursting with genetic codes, inherited temperaments, amazing talents, and the seeds of personality problems just waiting to bud and bloom.

"Jacksonville. Next stop Jacksonville." A conductor strolled down the aisle, reminding passengers to prepare for detraining. Soon Janette would have to leave this coach car . . . and then what?

She hugged her purse to her chest. She knew the world had changed since her young adult days. Like most of her friends, she left home at eighteen, married at twenty-two, and became a mother at twenty-five. By the time she was Annalisa's age, she had a child, a husband, a job, and two mortgages. Yet her daughter wasn't ready to tackle even one of those responsibilities.

What happened? How did the world change so much, so quickly?

Every time Janette convinced herself that boarding this train was the right thing to do, she had to wonder if she was buying into the me-first philosophy that had permeated society. While other women walked away from marriages and went globetrotting to discover inner nirvana, she had honored her vow to love and obey her husband. Mothers didn't take official vows, but when she accepted a child who needed her, she knew she was making a commitment to love and provide for that little girl. Could she walk away because the girl had needed her longer than she expected?

Probably not. But she couldn't stay, either, unless things changed. And if nothing did, what then?

She should run away. She could move to Colorado and live in the mountains, be known as the quiet older woman who kept to herself, attended church regularly, and worked in a department store or maybe an office. When people asked about her past, she'd smile a Mona Lisa smile and leave them to guess about her mysterious background.

Who was she kidding? She wasn't Mona Lisa and there was nothing mysterious about her. She was simply a frustrated wife and a failed mother who was too cowardly to live the life God had handed her.

She had just turned her face toward the window, not wanting her fellow passengers to see her tears, when her purse shuddered beneath her hand. Her phone, of course. She pulled it out and looked at the caller ID. She didn't recognize the number, but it looked familiar . . . because it was the number on her last voicemail, the one she'd ignored.

When the phone stopped ringing, she played the forgotten message: "Hey, Janette, it's Andie Crystal. Just wanted you to know that I'll be meeting the train in Jacksonville, so look for me at the station. Why don't we get our little group together and have lunch in St. Augustine? I have lots to tell you, so I hope to see you soon."

Andie was coming to Jacksonville? Janette glanced back at Matthew, wondering if he'd heard the news, but his eyes were closed and he was still functioning as a pillow for his sleeping kids. He'd probably been asleep since Savannah.

Obeying a hunch, Janette slid out of her seat and walked up to the cafe car. The abandoned USA Today she'd spotted earlier still waited on a table, so she sank onto the bench and opened the paper. She flipped through several pages, then landed on the Life section.

In the lower corner of the front page, she found the news she'd been searching for:

**Mona Huggins Dead at 51**

Mona Huggins, mother and erstwhile star of *Home with the Huggins*, died Friday after a brief struggle with ovarian cancer. She was 51.

Huggins's agent, Oliver Weinstein, says Huggins died Friday at 1:03 p.m.

Diagnosed with ovarian cancer several months ago, Huggins was attended by her family at the time of death.

Huggins, who once told an interviewer that she grew up adoring *The Partridge Family*, pitched her six musically talented children to ETN and suggested that her family would be suitable for a reality television show. The network agreed. The show premiered in 1995 and ran for six seasons.

For a while, the Huggins family members' faces were spotted everywhere—on posters, books, folders, and school lunch boxes. But after a 2001 auto accident resulted in the death of Cole Huggins and a cameraman, ETN cancelled the show and the Huggins children went their separate ways.

Mona Huggins, however, will remain a television icon. Through syndicated reruns, the patient mother whose children entertained millions of American preteens should make music for generations to come.

Janette folded the newspaper and tucked it under her arm, saving it for Matthew. She hadn't told him who Andie used to be, but this would probably be a good time. After that, they could let Andie fill them in on the latest chapter in her life.

Janette would much rather hear Andie's life story than share her own.

# Chapter Fifteen

The Silver Meteor approached the Jacksonville station right on schedule. Janette left the cafe car and grabbed her carry-on bag as she walked past her seat, so she was standing behind Matthew and his family when the train finally stopped. She casually mentioned Mona Huggins's passing as they stood in the aisle, but she didn't tell Matt that Andie planned to join them in Florida. She didn't want to disappoint him if Andie wasn't waiting at the station.

"Mona Huggins?" Matt's forehead creased. "Should I know that name?"

Janette dropped her hand to the top of Emilia's head. "She's the mother on your daughter's favorite TV show, remember? And there's something else you should know—Emilia is one smart cookie. Andie is the former Christy Huggins. She confessed everything in a phone message right after she left us."

Matthew released a brief grunt of surprise, but Emilia gaped up at Janette. "I love Christy Huggins."

"I know you do, sweetie."

They moved down the aisle, following the other detraining passengers.

"So—" Matthew glanced over his shoulder— "do you think Andie's still in Los Angeles?" He passed Emilia's hand to Janette as they walked toward the steps that lead to the platform.

"I don't know where she is, exactly," Janette hedged, watching Matt help Roman down the stairs. "Most families take a few days to plan the funeral and sort through the deceased's personal belongings—"

"What's a deceased?" Roman asked.

Janette pressed her lips together, not sure how she should answer, but Matthew had no qualms about giving his son the raw truth. "Deceased means dead," he said, releasing Roman's hand as he struggled to manage two backpacks and a briefcase. "It's a nicer way of talking about people who have died."

Roman frowned as he watched Janette and Emilia exit the train. "So my mom is a deceased?"

"She is deceased, yes." Janette softened her smile. "You could also say she passed away."

"She died," Emilia said, her voice flat. "She went to heaven while we were at school."

Janette tightened her grip on Emilia's hand and looked around to make sure they had all their carry-ons. "Okay—shall we go inside to get our big suitcases?"

They had walked no more than twenty feet when Janette spotted movement from the parking lot to the left of the platform. Andie was running toward them, her hair flying. She ignored the sidewalk and ran over the dew-drenched grass, slowing only when she reached the surging flood of passengers. Her gaze touched Janette's, she grinned, then she dropped to one knee and held out her arms. "Hey, there!" Joy sparkled in her eyes as she smiled at the children. "Did you miss me?"

"Andie!" Emilia and Roman cut through the grass to greet her. Matt gaped, his eyes widened, then he turned to Janette.

"Could that really be—"

"It is." She extended her hand. "Leave all that stuff with me and go say hello."

Matt dropped the book bags and briefcase at her feet and strode toward Andie, greeting her with a hug—a warm hug, from Janette's perspective, a hug that said more than good to see you, old friend, how ya doin'?

By the time Janette had gathered their belongings and joined them, Matt was holding Andie's shoulders and asking about California. "What happened in Los Angeles? We heard about your mother, so don't you need to be with your family?"

"It's a long story." Andie smiled at Matt as if he had just hung the moon. "And I'd like to tell you all about it, but not here. I've rented a car, so let me drive us down to St. Augustine. We can catch up on the way."

"You rented a car?" Janette grimaced. "I hate for you to go to all that expense if we could take a cab—"

"St. Augustine is more than an hour from here," Andie explained, picking up the kids' book bags. "So a car is the least expensive way to get around, believe it or not. Let me help you get your luggage, then we'll head south. I've checked into a hotel with vacancies, so we can all stay in the same place . . . for tonight, anyway."

In her hesitation Janette heard the thought no one wanted to verbalize: we can stay together until it's time to say goodbye. After St. Augustine, the train tour would officially end. Andie would go back to Rhode Island, Matt would return to Virginia, and she would most likely board a plane or bus bound for Arkansas . . . where she'd have to face the repercussions of running away.

She wasn't looking forward to that journey.

◆

They were driving south on U.S. 1, leaving Jacksonville for St. Augustine, when Janette announced that she wanted to do one thing before her trip ended: "I want to go to the beach."

Roman and Emilia looked up from their new coloring books, but from the front passenger seat Matthew turned to grin at her. "Hard to believe you can't come up with anything better than that."

"Have you ever been to the beach?"

"Of course."

"I haven't. Hard to find a beach in Arkansas, you know."

Andie caught Janette's eye in the rear view mirror. "Don't you have lakes in Arkansas?"

"Those aren't beaches—they're strips of sand along fresh water. I want to see the ocean, I want to pick up sea shells, and I want to see waves—big ones."

"All right, then." Matthew propped his hand on the back of the driver's seat. "Duly noted. We'll try to get to the beach at high tide, whenever that is."

Satisfied, Janette folded her arms.

"Yeah, it'd be a real tragedy for you to come all this way and miss the beach." Andie grinned. "So—what else do you want to do?"

"I want to hear about your trip to California. How'd it go with your family?"

Andie glanced at Matthew, then shifted her weight in her seat. "The trip was good. I did exactly what you suggested, Janette. I went to the hospital, saw my brothers and sisters, and said goodbye to my mother. I even found a video camera hidden in a bunch of flowers, but by that time I couldn't have cared less. I was so happy to be with my brothers and sisters that I would have let almost anyone take my picture."

"And your mother?" Janette pressed gently. "Were you able to talk to her?"

Andie nodded. "She was lucid until the end. I tried to be gentle with her; I told her I loved her and I was sorry for disappearing. And when she died—" Andie's voice cracked, but she swallowed and carried on— "I cried with everyone else, then I hugged the sibs and told them I'd be back soon. I said I wanted to catch up on all their lives, but first I had to spend a day in St. Augustine."

"You're not serious." Janette laughed. "Don't you have responsibilities with your family?"

Andie held Janette's gaze in the mirror for a moment, then she smiled. "Somehow I felt like I had a few responsibilities here, too. The funeral's not until next week, so there's plenty of time for us to tie up loose ends. I had to find out what Emilia and Roman did at their grandmother's house, and I wanted to know how you big people were doing, too."

Andie blushed as she finished her sentence, and Janette couldn't stop a smile. So . . . maybe the friendship between Andie and Matt had potential. Stranger things had happened.

"I'm proud of you," Janette said. "I think you made the right decision with your mother and your family. It's time you got to know your family again."

"I still may be a little camera shy," Andie said. "Unlike my brother Callie, I don't need to be a public spectacle. I'm not that desperate for approval."

"You've never struck me as desperate," Matthew said, pinching her shoulder.

Andie released a short laugh. "I'm as insecure as anyone else, but I'm content with the approval of a few trustworthy friends. It's okay if the world doesn't—or does—know my name."

"I know your name," Emilia said, looking up from her coloring book. "It's Andie."

Andie grinned. "And don't you forget it, Emilia Bodilla."

Janette leaned forward and lowered her voice. "What about the funeral? Do you think it'll be a circus?"

Andie shrugged. "Who knows? The network wants to televise it, so Mom's farewell might end up more like performance art than a memorial service—" a cynical note entered her voice— "but that's what she would have wanted. Ironic, isn't it?"

"Are your brothers and sisters going to sing?" Matt asked. "One of the old songs, maybe?"

"Callie might be the only one who wants to perform, but I'll go along with the majority. Still, I can't think of anything more pathetic than a group of adults trying to look and sound like the teenagers they once were."

"The important thing—" Janette pulled an errant autumn leaf from Emilia's hair— "is that you made peace with your mother. I'm proud of you for going. I'm proud of you for agreeing to go back. You did the right thing all around."

When Andie told them about her visit with Carma's family in Charleston, her voice resonated with a vibrancy and warmth Janette had never noticed before. She had to smile when Matt asked about the disposition of Mona Huggins' estate—clearly, the lawyer in him was curious about the legal details. He had taken an interest in Andie and he was feeling protective . . . and surely that was a good thing.

"The estate has been taken care of, Mr. Lawyer." Andie grinned at him. "And, by the way, I need to thank you for something."

"Me?" Matthew pressed his hand to his chest. "What'd I do?"

"It's not what you did, exactly, it's what you—well, it's what I thought you were going to do. Emilia happened to mention that you'd talked to her about the schools in Savannah . . . and I couldn't see any reason for that unless you intended to let your kids have a prolonged visit at your mom's house."

Janette arched a brow, realizing that Andie was carefully choosing words to avoid alarming the kids.

"I was horrified," Andie went on, "to think you'd even consider such an idea, then I realized I was doing the exact same thing—avoiding my family responsibilities, that is."

Matthew shifted as if he'd suddenly grown uncomfortable. "Yeah. Well." He looked out the window. "Remind me sometime to tell you about my momma."

"But not now." Andie smiled at the side of his head. "Not with little ears about."

He nodded. "You got that right."

"So—" Andie glanced in the rearview mirror, searching for the kids. "What else do we want to do in St. Augustine? There's a trolley, and the country's oldest house, a fort, a wax museum, a lighthouse—"

"The fort!" Roman cocked his hand like a pistol and aimed it at the windshield. "I want to see cannons and guns."

Matthew turned, his brows shooting toward his hairline. "When did you become such a war-monger?"

"Do they have dolphins?" Emilia looked at her father, her lower lip edging forward. "Please, Daddy, can we feed some more dolphins?"

"I'm not sure, honey. Maybe." Matthew caught Andie's gaze. "By the way, you missed a great dolphin ride in Savannah. We took a boat out to Tybee Island and saw dolphins racing right alongside us."

The kids chimed in, and Janette couldn't help smiling when a wistful look crossed Andie's face.

Nestling into the car's leather seat, Janette let the four of them chatter while she leaned back and lowered her eyelids. All she wanted to do was see the Atlantic. Before she had to go home, she wanted to stand on the edge of something far larger, deeper, and broader than all her problems.

She wanted to feel small again, as little and innocent as Emilia.

If she could shrink to insignificance, then her decisions couldn't possibly hurt anyone.

By eleven they had entered St. Augustine, checked into the hotel, and regrouped in the parking lot. Though it was mid-November, the Florida sun was warm on their skin and the kids had put on shorts and T-shirts. Andie had changed into a skirt, a sleeveless top, and sneakers, but Matthew surprised them all. The lawyer look had disappeared, replaced by a Hawaiian shirt and jeans.

Janette gave him a look of wide-eyed appreciation. "I'm surprised you even own a Hawaiian shirt."

"I didn't." He grinned and pointed to the busy street. "But there's a little shop right around the corner."

Dressed in black knit pants and a matching top, Janette was sure she looked dull and matronly. But these friends didn't care what she looked like because they were too excited about seeing the city . . . with each other.

"What do we do first?" Andie asked, her face glowing. When she looked to Matthew for an answer, Janette realized she could easily become a fifth wheel in this band of wayfarers. But that was okay — a friendship ought to develop between those two.

"Why don't we get tickets for the trolley and hop off when we see something interesting?" Matthew suggested. "That approach worked in Savannah."

The kids applauded their approval and Andie quickly agreed. She joined them in the line for tickets, and within a few minutes an orange and green trolley pulled up to the corner.

They joined several straw-hatted tourists already aboard and proceeded to learn about St. Augustine, the oldest city in America. They heard about Henry Flagler, the Spanish conquerors who built the Castillo de San Marcos, and Ponce de Leon's search for the Fountain of Youth. As they passed St. George Street and its crowded pedestrian mall, Andie suggested hopping off to do a little shopping.

So they did. And while her four younger friends headed toward the nation's Oldest Wooden Schoolhouse, Janette excused herself and pointed to a wooden bench under the canopy of a moss-draped live oak. A man sat at one end, an elderly man from the looks of his gnarled hands, but he seemed engrossed in his newspaper.

"I'll wait here," she told Matt and Andie as she turned toward the bench. "I don't think these tight shoes are going to let me do much walking today."

She sat and made herself comfortable. Though her shoes were snug, they were only an excuse to bow out for a while. She wanted to give Matt and Andie a little time to know each other better.

But more than that, she needed time to sort through her feelings about returning home. She'd left home to think, but it'd been easier to shove her problems to the back of her mind than seriously consider them. But time was running out.

If she went back to Little Rock and took a hotel room instead of going home, how could she tell Harry that she could no longer live with their daughter? How could she tell the whole truth without irreparably wounding him? How could she explain that she was drowning in unhappiness and that she had begun to resent her own child? Maybe resent was too lightweight a word—she had experienced moments of sheer loathing. When Annalisa's voice rose to that fevered pitch, when she f-bombed everything in sight, when she cursed at God and Jesus and everything Janette held dear, Janette's stomach churned with bile and her nerves tensed to the snapping point. In those moments, she seriously thought she might be in danger of dying from a stress-related heart attack. In those moments, she hated her daughter.

But how could any mother ever admit to those feelings? How could she think such things about her precious baby girl?

Despite the sun's warmth, a shiver spread over Janette along with the memory of a Sunday morning with her daughter. Annalisa had been to children's church while Harry and Janette attended worship. Afterward, Janette stepped into the ladies' restroom, taking six-year-old Annalisa with her. Janette stood at the sink, adjusting a hank of hair that refused to stay behind her ear, while Annalisa fumed. "Mom," she shouted, ignoring the other women in the room, "I'm ready to go home."

"Just a minute, hon."

"Mom—" Annalisa's face went red— "if you don't come right now, I'm gonna . . . I'm gonna . . ."

Janette watched in the mirror as Annalisa narrowed her eyes, concentrating. "If you don't come now I'm gonna fall down and worship idols!"

Someone in a stall giggled; the woman at the next sink laughed outright. Janette smothered a smile and turned to face her daughter, realizing that the children's Sunday school lesson must have focused on the sin of idol worship.

Annalisa's hysterical irreverence seemed harmless then, even funny. But when the girl made profane comments now, Janette's heart twisted. Her daughter was no longer a child. Annalisa should know better, but she didn't care.

An older couple walked by, hand in hand, their steps small, slow, and even. A stab of bitterness entered Janette's heart as she watched them—in a few years she and Harry ought to be like that pair, happy and settled and perfectly patient with each other. But they would never be that couple as long as Annalisa kept coming between them.

From somewhere deep within her, a hot flash ignited, flushing Janette's face and dampening her skin. She looked at the man next to her, wondering if he'd be willing to part with a page of his newspaper so she could fan herself. Her hands felt like ice, her toes were as cold as popsicles, but she could fry an egg on her chest.

She drew a deep breath and lifted her head, hoping to catch a bit of the sea breeze. This was November, for heaven's sake. Florida ought to be cooler by now. She glanced again at the man next to her, then shifted her gaze when he lowered his paper. She stared off to her right, not wanting to make a stranger uncomfortable, but then he spoke: "I have always loved the scent of honeysuckle perfume."

"It's shampoo," she replied automatically, then she shivered in a moment of déjà vu. Had she seen this man, sat on this bench, before? No. Impossible.

Somehow she managed to smile. "I hope I haven't disturbed you. I'm just waiting on my friends."

He grinned, his teeth gleaming against his ebony skin. "You haven't disturbed me, 'cause I've been waiting on you. The Lord sent me to help you carry the load."

Janette's breath caught in her lungs. What was he talking about? Was he hoping to earn a buck or two helping people carry packages? And of all the benches in St. Augustine, why did she have to choose the one occupied by a senile old man who had Morgan Freeman trapped in his voice box?

She slid sideways, putting a few more inches between her and the confused stranger. "Sorry, but I don't need any help. As you can see, I'm not carrying anything."

Still smiling, the man dropped the folded newspaper at his side. "Aren't you? Weren't you just thinking about the heaviest load you've carried in all your life?"

Janette blinked, then transferred her gaze to the ground. Who was confused here, her or the old man? She had been thinking about Annalisa, and under so much stress that her brain was bound to jump the tracks. In a moment she'd look over and the man would be reading his paper, and she'd feel like one of those old women who mutters to herself on public park benches . . .

Steeling herself to not look at the man, Janette pressed her fingertips to her temple and closed her eyes — the heaviest load she'd carried in all her life. Either she'd misheard him or he was only a figment of her imagination. When she looked over again she might see nothing but dust motes dancing in the sunlight —

But no, there he sat, smiling at her, and now his sunglasses were on top of his head and he was looking at her with eyes of brilliant black, bright and shining and dancing with humor.

"Gentle lady. Child."

That word — *child* — so loaded with love and care and concern, heavy with an invitation to come and rest, to lie down and let someone else carry the load —

A sob rose to her throat as tears stung her eyes. How could this man see inside her heart? Why did he even care?

"Look at this." His long, slender finger tapped the folded newspaper on the bench. "You see this paper? You couldn't see anything on that white surface without dark ink, could you? A sheet of clean newsprint might be pretty, but it wouldn't show you a thing. Even so, the Father uses the valley of shadow to teach you about His sufficiency and goodness. Don't despair, child, while you're walking through it."

Janette stared at the man, her fingers tight across her lips to imprison the sob that threatened to escape. Either someone had slipped something into her coffee or she was having an experience worthy of the *National Enquirer*.

In any case, maybe this trip to crazy would go more smoothly if she cooperated with kindly strangers.

Summoning her courage, she managed a wavering smile. "If the Lord sent you, maybe you can tell what I'm supposed to say when I go home to see my family. Or maybe you've come to warn me that I'm heading for an emotional collapse . . ."

The old man leaned back against the bench, a frown puckering the skin between his brows. "Self-pity isn't going to help."

"I think a little self-pity might be appropriate for a mother who's losing her mind."

"You're not losing anything. Before you drown yourself in a pool of despair you should know you're not the only one suffering from heartache. The people you passed as you walked out this morning — your eyes only grazed the woman whose son is in prison for life, you nearly tripped over the foot of a young mother who just miscarried her baby, and you barely noticed the old man who is so lonely he comes downtown just to be near other people. You didn't see the couple who've recently lost their home, you didn't notice the sad little girl whose uncle has stolen her purity, and you didn't hear the quiet weeping of the father who is so distraught over gambling away his child's college fund that he's considering suicide."

When the man shifted to face Janette, she noticed marks of grief etched into the lines beside his mouth and nose. She recognized those marks because she saw them every time she looked into the mirror. Why hadn't she seen them in the faces of her fellow passengers? Had she been so self-involved that she'd become blind to everyone else?

The man continued, speaking in that slow rumble that was both irresistible and gentle. "You're not the only one who struggles, child."

Guilt clogged her whispered confession: "I know. And I'm sorry—I know I should be more aware."

"Yet your light is brighter than you realize. You've shone the Father's love into the lives of the people you have befriended. They may not yet realize that the Spirit is drawing them to the Father, but they will."

Janette pressed her lips together as her heart welled with gratitude. She might have failed in some important areas, but if she'd been able to do some good . . .

"Remember Jonah." The man smiled as he slipped his glasses over his eyes. "Jonah ran away, too, but his running gave the Father an opportunity to show His power. Remember that, child. Remember."

Still smiling, the old man picked up his newspaper, then stood and walked away, whistling as he melted into the crowd of shoppers.

Janette found herself alone on the bench, surrounded by the

sights and sounds and smells of a tourist town. She felt the sea breeze, she heard the cadences of mingled voices, she saw ruddy faces and pale legs and little girls in hats and frilled sundresses. All her senses seemed to be working, so maybe she wasn't completely crazy.

She had heard about divine encounters, but she didn't think anyone would believe what she had just seen and heard.

# *Chapter Sixteen*

By the time Matt, Andie, and the kids returned, Roman was holding his stomach and complaining of hunger pangs. Matthew pointed to a small restaurant in the pedestrian mall, then looked to Janette and Andie for their approval. "Looks like a burgers-and-fries kind of place, so will that do?"

"Fine with me," Janette said, standing on legs that felt a bit unsteady. "Any place I can get out of the heat would be fine. I think I'm beginning to suffer from heat stroke."

"Really? It's not that hot." Andie looked at Janette with concern in her eyes, but Janette waved her sympathy away. She wasn't sure how to describe her encounter with the old man, and she wasn't sure she wanted to. She had either experienced a bona fide heavenly visitor or her stressed pot had finally cracked.

She followed the others into the restaurant, where they sat at a large picnic table and joked with the waitress before placing their orders. As they waited, Janette looked around, half-expecting to see the Angel Gabriel bussing tables.

The casual restaurant featured plastic tablecloths and standard American fare, but the tables occupied an open patio and bougainvillea dripped magenta blossoms from trellises against the walls. Janette asked Matt and Andie if they found anything interesting on their walk through the mall, and Andie replied that several of the shops offered unique items. "But I don't want to haul a lot of stuff home," she said, her smile fading. "I'd rather take home good memories than a bagful of trinkets."

When she looked away, her chin quivering, Janette suspected that Andie was also dreading the end of this trip. What waited for her back in Providence? From what Janette had been able to gather, Andie would be going home to a lonely apartment and a routine job. But at least she had reconnected with her family. Those siblings were certain to liven up Andie's life.

Their burgers finally arrived. Matt helped his kids prepare theirs, remembering that Roman liked catsup and Emilia didn't like pickles, then he cut both kids' burgers into halves, perfect for small hands. Not until the children were settled did Matthew reach for the catsup and tend to his own meal.

Janette smiled. She didn't know what happened at Momma Scofield's house, but this Matthew was a different man.

She must have been wearing her thoughts on her face, because Matt flushed when he caught her gaze. "What?" He lowered the catsup bottle. "Did I do something? Do I have mustard on my shirt?"

"You're fine." She lifted her sandwich to hide her smile. "You should eat before your food gets cold."

She realized she sounded like a mother, but that was okay. Just because she failed Mothering 101 with her own daughter didn't mean she never learned anything about childrearing.

After lunch their little group walked back to the main road and waited for their transportation.

Emilia tucked Walter under her arm and pointed down the street. A bus sat at a distant red light, an orange and green vehicle affiliated with the trolley company. "Will that bus take us to the beach?"

"That's definitely the right bus." Matt clapped his daughter's shoulder. "Way to watch, kiddo."

Janette folded her arms, her heart humming in anticipation of waves and seashore. The thought of looking for seashells made her like a child again.

"I want to wade in the waves." She smiled at Emilia. "Then I want to sit in the sand and build a toad house."

Roman crinkled his nose. "A what?"

"I saw it in a book. You squat in the sand and cover your foot with dirt. You pack it tight, then you carefully pull your foot back. The sand you packed will stay put, leaving a little toad house."

"Daddy!" Emilia tugged on Matt's shirt. "Will you make toad houses with us?"

Matt grinned. "Sure. And maybe Andie will help."

"Here comes the bus!" Roman was bouncing on tiptoe, tempting Janette to do the same. If she only had only a few more hours of freedom, she would make the best of them. She wanted to build a big castle and drizzle wet sand over the towers. She wanted to look for sand dollars. She wanted to roll up her pants and wade into the water, not caring if she got completely wet. She wanted to feel the sun on her face and the wind in her hair. She wanted to hold Roman's and Emilia's hands and run with them, laughing as they scattered seagulls on the shore. She wanted to stare at the sun-spangled sea and wonder what lay directly on the other side.

For years she had dreamed of doing these things with her grandchildren, but that dream had seemed as distant as the stars . . . until today.

Emilia took Janette's hand and squeezed as a rush of blood warmed Janette's ears. It was probably another hot flash, but she didn't mind. Odd hallucinations aside, this day should turn out to be perfectly glorious.

From somewhere deep inside her purse Janette's phone chimed, distracting her from watching the bus. She had switched off the ringer when they left the hotel, so the three-noted chime meant she'd received a text message. Annalisa rarely sent texts, preferring to vent via voice mail, and Harry would only text in case of an emergency . . .

She was about to ignore a second chime, but Andie turned toward her and Matt, a question in her eyes. "That wasn't my phone — one of yours?"

Matt shrugged. "I left mine back at the hotel."

Janette stifled a sigh. Clearly, hers was the phone that kept begging for attention.

She pulled her purse from her shoulder and dug through it. "Probably a wrong number," she grumbled, though she was secretly afraid Annalisa had graduated to texting her messages.

The beach bus was only a block away when Janette found her phone and glanced at the alert — the text was from Harry, calling on his cell phone. His message was simple: Emergency. Call me ASAP.

A tremor scrambled up the back of her neck. Harry wasn't the type to cry wolf, so she ought to call him right away. Janette glanced at Andie and Matt, but their attention had shifted to the approaching bus.

Her bare arms pebbled with gooseflesh as she pressed the icon for Harry's phone. Her husband answered half a ring later.

"Harry?"

"Thank goodness you called."

Something in his voice sent panic jetting through her bloodstream. "What's wrong?"

"It's Annalisa." His voice was clipped, almost brusque. "There's been an accident; she's in the hospital. Honey — it doesn't look good."

A dull roar filled Janette's ears, drowning out the sounds of traffic, the children's voices, and the growl of the nearby bus.

What didn't look good?

"Harry?" She clapped her hand over her exposed ear to better hear him. "Is she okay?"

"No, she's not." When his voice broke, that sound, more than anything else, revealed the gravity of the situation. Janette's calm, easy-going, peace-making husband was distraught.

"She's not okay—" he steeled his voice— "and this would never have happened if you'd been home where you belong."

Janette turned as the world shifted dizzily around her. Harry was furious, and with her. Because their daughter had had an accident.

As her knees weakened, she reached for a lamppost to keep herself upright. Her lungs were squeezed so tight she could barely draw breath to speak, but she forced words out. "Where was . . . where was she driving?"

"She wasn't driving. She was home, and she tried to kill herself." Harry spat each word into the phone. "If you want to see your daughter alive again, you'd better get here as fast as you can."

If she hadn't run away, her daughter wouldn't be in danger.

If she hadn't been such a coward, her daughter wouldn't be in the hospital.

If she'd been more patient, more forgiving, and more understanding, her daughter would be fine.

Whatever led her to believe she could be a good mother?

Thoughts revolved in Janette's head like a carousel, rising and falling in the narrow space between reason and guilt. Matt and Andie asked what was wrong and somehow she managed to stammer that her daughter was in the hospital and might be dying. Her broken, gasping words were all the motivation her young friends needed to take charge and lead her back to the hotel. If they hadn't been with her, she might have collapsed on the sidewalk.

The next half hour passed in a blur. Emilia cried because they couldn't go to the beach and make toad houses; Andie comforted the girl and promised they'd try to go later. Matthew hailed a cab with firm desperation; he guided Janette into the backseat and herded the others in behind her. They sped back to the hotel. Matt paid the cab driver while Andie walked Janette to her room—the room she hadn't even slept in—and helped put Janette's toiletries case and hanging garments back into her suitcase. Andie was about to zip the suitcase when her gaze fell on the little pocket Bible Janette had placed on the nightstand. "Is that yours?"

Janette nodded.

Andie picked it up and set it on top of the folded clothes, then looked at Janette. "Would you like to keep it handy?"

Janette wasn't sure she'd be able to concentrate well enough to read, but if she was, that's the book she wanted. "I think I would."

Andie put the Bible on the bed. "We'll try to get you a refund from the hotel manager," she said, struggling with the suitcase zipper. "If he'll give you credit for an Amtrak voucher."

Janette picked up her Bible and purse, too numb to say anything.

If she hadn't run away, her daughter wouldn't be in danger.

Andie looked over the room and counted to be sure they had collected purse, suitcase, and carry-on bag. "We don't want you to set this down and forget it," she said, taking the Bible from Janette. She dropped it into Janette's purse, then hooked the carry-on bag to the suitcase. "Let's go."

If she hadn't been such a coward, her daughter wouldn't be in the hospital.

They took the elevator to the lobby and found Andie's rental waiting outside, engine running. Matt stood by the open door, his iPhone in hand and a concentrated look on his face. "A flight to Little Rock leaves in two hours." He looked at Andie. "I think that's our best bet. She'll need time to get through security and check-in."

Janette was about to protest that they didn't need to give up their vacation time for her, she could find her own way home, but Andie wheeled her suitcases to the back of the car. While she and Matt put the luggage in the trunk, Janette slid into the backseat and sat by the far window, staring out at a cityscape that seemed bleached of all color. Roman and Emilia climbed in beside her while Matt drove and Andie sat next to him.

"How far to the airport?" Andie asked.

"Looks like an hour, give or take."

Janette would have sixty long minutes to sit in silence and contemplate her failures. She didn't know what happened in Little Rock and she didn't dare call to ask, but if Harry was blaming her, Annalisa's "accident" was no accident at all—she actually tried to kill herself. She had finally acted on her persistent threats, finally been desperate enough to follow through with one of her plans. Janette doubted that Annalisa would use a gun because they didn't have one in the house, and she didn't think Annalisa would cut her wrists . . . she was too averse to pain. So that left pills. Those they had by the cupful.

If she'd been more patient, more forgiving, and more understanding, her daughter would be fine.

Beside her, Emilia whispered to her much-loved dinosaur, smoothing his tattered fur and straightening his fabric ears. She leaned down and planted a kiss in the center of his worn forehead, a gesture that snagged a memory and brought it swimming up through time.

A snowy morning, Annalisa's seventh Christmas. Beanie Babies had hit the market earlier that year, so Harry and Janette scoured the stores to find all nine of the first series: Legs the Frog, Squealer the Pig, Brownie the Bear, Flash the Dolphin, Splash the Whale, Patti the Platypus, Chocolate the Moose, Spot the Dog, and Pinchers the Lobster. Rather than wrap them, Janette placed all nine in a beribboned basket and left it under the Christmas tree. Annalisa screeched with delight when she came downstairs and found her new treasures; she loved each of them but was especially taken with Squealer, the little pink pig. She carried him around all day, propping him on the table while they ate turkey and dressing, having him wait by the sink while she took a bath.

That night they went next door to visit Mrs. Spencer, an elderly woman whose grandson had dropped by, probably more out of duty than love. He brought gifts—an electric cookie press and a pizza skillet—and his only child, a girl about Annalisa's age. When they arrived the little girl was sitting on the sofa, arms crossed and face puckered in a pout. She might have sulked through the entire visit, except for Annalisa. Noticing that the child had no toys with her, Annalisa smoothed Squealer's fur, kissed his pink nose, and offered him to Mrs. Spencer's great-granddaughter "for keeps."

Watching from the sofa, Janette tried to control herself, but her chin wobbled and her eyes filled in spite of her efforts. Without prompting, her little girl had freely given the thing she loved best to make someone else happy.

Later that night, when she tucked Annalisa into bed and asked why she'd given Squealer away, her daughter looked up and said Squealer wanted to go with Mrs. Spencer's great-granddaughter because she had no one to play with. "I have so many toys," Annalisa said, reaching for the basket that still held eight Beanie babies. "Plus I have you and Daddy."

Janette, Harry, and Annalisa; Harry, Annalisa, and Janette. On that Christmas Day, Janette had felt so proud of her family; she'd been so sure God brought them together.

But now . . . *God, let my little girl live. Please.*

Silence filled the cab, broken only by the hum of the tires and the shush of passing cars. Feeling the pressure of the children's curious glances, Janette lowered her face into her hands. She ought to be crying, surely any good mother would, but the tears wouldn't come. She was a dry well, a hollow cistern that once bubbled with joy but had long been unproductive.

Whatever led her to believe she could be a good mother?

Harry was right—she should have been home. She'd been selfish to walk away from her family. No matter how old Annalisa was, no matter how bizarre her behavior, she would always be Janette's daughter. The lack of a biological tie between them was no more significant than the fact that they didn't share the same hair color. God brought her to them. Janette had promised to love Annalisa on the day they met, and she didn't renege on her promises.

Or she hadn't . . . until she walked out.

No wonder Harry was angry. She had left him alone to cope with Annalisa's tantrums and depression. Even though he seemed better equipped to handle their daughter, Janette had always been his sounding board, his voice of reason, his reminder that Annalisa needed boundaries. When she took off, she left him without a counselor, a confidante, and a friend. Now the worst had happened and he was at the hospital alone.

Janette could count on one hand the number of times Harry had been irritated with her. He had every right to be furious, but the thought of facing his anger made her stomach shrivel. If the tables were turned, if he'd gone off and left her with Annalisa, she'd be so furious that she might not welcome him back.

Yet she had been planning to walk into her home and announce her decision to go or stay. She would have breezed in as though it were nothing unusual for mothers to take two-week vacations from their families; as if every wife occasionally blew off steam by disappearing in the middle of the night and staying away until her money ran out.

If she hadn't run off, her daughter wouldn't be in danger.

Andie turned and looked at her with moisture brimming in her eyes. "Janette, what can we do to help?"

Janette shook her head. "There's no help for it. It's too late."

Matthew looked up at the rear-view mirror, a small smile on his face. "I can promise you lawyer-client confidentiality, if that'll put your mind at ease. You can tell us anything."

She snorted at his dry wit, then lifted her head. As scrubby pines and palmettos glided by her window, in a flat voice she told them how she came to be on the train. About the black eye. About her frustration. About her fractured family and troubled daughter. About Annalisa's horrible attitude and Janette's abysmal failure as a mother. About how thoughts of her family made her feel dead inside because she had come to the end of her rope and let go.

And why she had to hurry home if she wanted to see her daughter again.

She finished, her body quaking as she choked out a dry sob. Then from out of nowhere, a small, cool hand touched her arm. "Miss Janette? Would you like to hug Walter?" Emilia held him out to her, just as Annalisa once held out a little pink pig.

"Oh, Emilia." Janette lowered her hands and accepted the beloved dinosaur, then wrapped him up in her arms. Tears began to flow, but she wasn't weeping—it was more an overflow of feeling, a cascade of love and pain.

As she bowed over well-traveled Walter, Andie reached over the seat to touch Janette's arm.

Praying silently, Janette begged God to save her daughter: friend and foe, delight and trial, gift and burden, sweetness and darkness, love and frustration. Never had a single living being evoked so many different emotions from Janette. Never had she felt so helpless than when faced with her daughter's problems, and never had she felt such frustration with another person.

Annalisa was only twenty-five. Sheltered by their home, she had never taken the opportunity to live her own life. So many avenues were open to her, so many possibilities . . . if she could only accept responsibility and outgrow whatever it is that kept her in such tumult. She had gifts . . . Janette prayed she'd live long enough to use them.

Unbidden, the old man's words flowed into her streaming thoughts: Jonah's running gave the Father an opportunity to show his power. *Remember that, child. Remember.*

Did Jonah hear voices of self-recrimination? Did he remind himself that if not for his disobedience, the ship and all its crew wouldn't be in danger from the storm?

If Janette hadn't been a coward, her daughter wouldn't be in the hospital. If she hadn't been so self-centered . . .

Janette couldn't imagine how running away could possibly be part of God's plan. All she could do was beg Him to forgive her weakness and spare her daughter's life.

At the airport, Matt unloaded Janette's luggage while she stood on the curb like a victim of shell shock. Andie took her elbow and gently guided her to the ticket counter, where Janette showed the agent her driver's license and Andie explained that due to a family emergency Janette needed a seat on the first available plane.

Janette didn't think she'd be able to speak without breaking into gibberish or hysterics, but Andie got her on the 4:30 flight. Janette watched, still numb, as Matt brought in her suitcases and set them on the scale. He was checking her carry-on, but why shouldn't he? In her present condition, Janette would be doing well if she could keep up with her purse and boarding pass.

As she turned toward the security station, Andie took Janette's hand and sandwiched it between both of hers. "Matt and I talked," she said, her voice an intense whisper, "and if you need us to come to Little Rock, we'll come. We'll have to go back to the hotel and make some arrangements, but if you need us—"

"You don't have to do that," Janette said, simultaneously touched and horrified by the younger woman's offer. "It's nice of you to think of me, but you don't need to give up your vacation. I wouldn't expect complete strangers—" She choked on the word, because Matt and Andie weren't strangers any more. They had become friends—good friends—in the time they'd spent together. Bonded by chance and liberated by the assumption that they'd never meet again, they'd been more honest with each other than with most of the people they saw every day.

"I appreciate the offer, I really do." Janette looked up at Matthew, who was approaching with the baggage claim tickets she forgot. "You've both been very kind, and I'll never forget you. Thank you for your help and the pleasure of your company."

Janette knew she was talking like someone in an old movie, but the formal words rolled off her tongue and she couldn't think of anything else to say. She bent and smiled at Roman and Emilia, who looked at her with confusion and a touch of sadness in their eyes.

She was about to tell the children that she had loved meeting them, but a simple "I love you" came out instead. She kissed each of them on the top of the head, then tucked her boarding pass into a pocket of her purse.

Andie grabbed Janette's arms and pinned her in a long, intense scrutiny. "This isn't your fault," she finally said, her lovely eyes blazing. "Some things happen for reasons that have nothing to do with us."

Janette couldn't speak over the boulder in her throat, so she nodded and squeezed Andie's elbow.

"We'd better hurry." Matt glanced around as if he was restless, but Janette suspected he was only uncomfortable with emotional farewells. "You leave through gate A, and security is this way."

Her traveling family escorted her to the security checkpoint, and somehow she managed to put on a brave face as she stepped into the queue. She gave them a wobbly smile, then waved goodbye and turned to face the backs of a dozen other travelers. After a moment she looked over her shoulder and watched her friends walk through the airport doors.

Matt and Andie were holding hands while the children, like matching bookends, walked on opposite sides.

# *Chapter Seventeen*

By the time Janette changed planes in Memphis, landed in Little Rock, claimed her luggage, and took a cab to the hospital, it was nearly 10:30 p.m. Hospital visiting hours had long been over, but the woman at the reception desk took pity on her and gave her Annalisa's room number. Janette took the elevator to the third floor and dragged her suitcases into room 310, where she found her daughter unconscious in a bed and her six-foot-three husband pretzeled in a chair. Despite his uncomfortable position, Harry slept, too.

Leaving her baggage by the door, Janette tiptoed to the side of the bed and looked at her pale daughter. No bandages on her wrists, no obvious cuts or bruises anywhere, but a blood pressure machine beeped at her side and an IV had been taped to the bend at her elbow. The nurses were still monitoring her vitals, but she was alive, and for that Janette was deeply grateful.

She plucked a wayward hank of hair from Annalisa's forehead and combed it into place with her fingertips, smoothing the cowlick she used to subdue with kisses. Annalisa stirred at her touch, but didn't awaken.

"Go ahead and sleep," Janette whispered, tempering her voice with tenderness. "I'll be here when you wake up."

Just like that, she settled her decision. She wasn't walking out on her family, no matter how difficult life became. She had needed time to realize it, but her home was with Harry and Annalisa. What would she be without them?

When she turned, she found Harry staring at her. She braced herself for a confrontation, but she saw no fury in his face, only weariness and grief.

"Honey." She stepped toward him, hoping he would see apology and regret in her eyes. "I'm so sorry I left you alone . . . for this."

With an effort, he untangled his legs and pushed himself out of the chair, then took her in his arms and held her so tightly she could barely breathe. "I'm over being angry. Now I'm mostly relieved . . . and glad to see you."

Janette pulled back. "So she's going to be all right?"

"I think so. She swallowed a bottle of aspirin, but they've been giving her medications and charcoal to clear out her system. The doctor said she probably meant to get our attention . . . which she certainly did."

Janette drew him close and rested her head against his sweater. "How did you know?"

His chest rose as he inhaled a deep breath. "She threw up this morning. And you know how she sometimes jabbers and makes no sense? She was doing that, but making even less sense than usual. Then she started hyperventilating. I thought she was only trying to ruin my morning"—his voice cracked—"until she got up from the table and couldn't walk without stumbling. When she passed out, I called an ambulance."

Despite the warmth of the room, he shivered. "I found an empty aspirin bottle in her bathroom sink, so right away I suspected what she'd done. When the EMTs arrived, I showed them the empty bottle . . . and that, the doctor told me later, is probably what saved her life. They put her on dialysis to remove the drug from her kidneys, and they did something else — gastric lavage, I think they called it. They've put in a catheter and they're keeping a close eye on her. And she's been awake — earlier, she was able to talk to a psychiatrist they sent up to see her. He'll be back, and he'll probably want to talk to us at some point."

Relief rushed over Janette as she realized how fortunate they were. Harry wasn't furious with her, Annalisa would be okay, and she'd be under the care of a psychiatrist so they wouldn't have to carry the burden alone.

She tightened her arms around her husband when he shivered again. "I'm so sorry. I should have been home with you."

"I wasn't mad at you, Jan. When I called, I was mad at myself for not paying attention. I should have noticed something was different this morning."

"But I left without — "

"No one blames you for taking some time to get away. Our home . . . I know it's not an easy place to live. But I've talked to Annalisa. She didn't take the pills because you were gone. She took them because she was terrified."

"Terrified? Of what?"

His Adam's apple bobbed as he swallowed. "Apparently, she's been worried for several months now. She was afraid to talk to us, scared of what we might do."

"Good grief, Harry, why would she be afraid?"

"Because she's been hearing voices . . . when no one's around."

Janette stared at her husband as blood pounded in her ears. Hearing voices was not normal, no matter how angry or rebellious the patient. People who heard voices were mentally ill, as crazy as middle-aged women who talked to strangers and received messages from God.

An icy finger touched the base of her spine, discharging a chill that numbed every nerve.

Since the hospital room had provisions for only one overnight visitor, Janette sat on the edge of Annalisa's bed while Harry went back to the chair. He propped his head on his hand and smiled at her, but after a few minutes his head tipped back and he began to snore.

Not wanting to disturb him, Janette resisted the urge to push a fringe of graying hair from his forehead. The man had to be exhausted. Not only did he have to deal with this emergency, but for the last ten days he'd also been keeping up the house and preparing meals. She was amazed he was still speaking to her.

When Annalisa stirred in her sleep, Janette slid off the bed to give her daughter more room. Annalisa didn't wake, but Janette could imagine how worn out she must be. She'd been exhausted mentally and physically, and she'd been struggling for so long . . . why didn't she talk to them?

Janette swallowed the lump that had risen in her throat and folded her arms across her chest.

Since she wasn't exactly brimming over with energy, she tiptoed out of the room and walked toward the nurse's station. When she asked if the cafeteria was open, the nurse shook her head. "But there are vending machines in the first floor break room," she said, pointing toward the elevator. "Coffee, sandwiches, candy, that sort of thing."

Janette thanked her and took the elevator downstairs, then wandered through the halls, amazed at how much activity existed in a hospital even at such a late hour. Finally she found a room marked "Vending," and through the window she spotted several machines. She pushed the door open and made a beeline for the coffee dispenser.

She dropped quarters into the slot, then listened to the whirr and gurgle of the coffeemaker. She waited until the dark brew drained into the cup, then took it and walked toward a counter loaded with sugar packets and coffee creamers. She was ripping into a pink package of sweetener when Morgan Freeman's voice drowned out the hum of the fluorescent lights: "Glad you found your way home, child."

She startled, splashing coffee onto her sleeve, and turned to see her old friend sitting at a table near the Coke machine. He smiled beneath his dark glasses and rested both hands on the table.

Janette closed her eyes and opened them again, but the apparition remained.

Sighing, she reached for a napkin. "You're not real. You're a figment brought on by my guilty conscience."

Laughter rose from his throat, a rich, full-bodied sound that echoed in the room. "If you only knew," he said, "how many times I've heard that."

She brought her coffee cup to her lips. "My daughter has a psychiatrist now. Maybe I should make an appointment with him."

Another flash of humor crossed the man's face. "You're not ill."

"I wouldn't be so sure about that. For a moment I thought I might have passed a bad gene to my daughter, then I realized that's impossible. We're not genetically related."

His smile broadened. "Your relationship goes deeper than blood and bone. Before the foundation of the world, the Father knew you would have Harry for your husband and Annalisa for your daughter, and that your daughter would have special needs only you and Harry could fill. At the same time, He knew Annalisa would meet needs in both of you."

Janette listened, but his words spun through her head without sinking into her heart. Being a Christian, she supposed it was only natural that her delusions would echo her spiritual beliefs—

"I'm not a delusion, and my words are not an echo." His voice was firmer now, a low rumble that was both powerful and gentle.

Janette barked a laugh. "If you're not a product of my sub-conscious, how can you read my mind?"

"I can't—but I say what the Father tells me to say. He knows what you're feeling about your daughter. So He sent me to show you something."

He reached inside his dark coat and pulled out a small ce-ramic vase. From where Janette stood, it looked like the toothpick holder she kept on the kitchen counter.

"God wants to show me a toothpick?"

His smile flashed in the fluorescent light. "The slips in this bowl represent possibilities that might have occurred if the Fa-ther hadn't matched you and Harry with Annalisa. Take one. See for yourself . . . what might have been if the events of your life depended on chance."

Janette swiveled as something rattled outside the door. Through the square window she saw an orderly walk by pushing a cart. Apparently she was still awake, still hearing and tasting and feeling the warmth of the liquid that spilled on her sleeve . . .

And her odd friend was still sitting by the Coke machine. Okay, then.

She walked toward him and dropped into a nearby chair. He continued to hold out the tiny vase, so she leaned forward and took a slip of paper from the container. The stiff paper, about the size of a fortune cookie insert, was covered with bold black print.

"Annalisa dies," she read. She looked up as her heart lurched within her chest. "This isn't a prophecy, is it?"

"Not a prophecy, a possibility." The ghost of a smile touched the man's lips with ruefulness. "I know you didn't feel like you were connecting with that baby in the incubator, but if you hadn't given her that finger to hold, Annalisa would have died in that hospital. Babies need physical connection, and you gave her what she needed. If you and Harry hadn't been around, she wouldn't have pulled through that first heart surgery."

Janette turned the thought over in her mind. "If you're here to reenact *It's a Wonderful Life*, I've gotta warn you—I'm not nearly as saintly as George Bailey. Besides, if we hadn't adopted Annalisa, someone else would have."

Wordlessly, the man offered the container again.

Janette pulled out another slip and read both sides: "Annalisa adopted by Joan and Roger—Joan dies, Roger abuses Annalisa, who runs away at 16. She has a child that is born addicted to cocaine; baby sent to foster care while Annalisa goes to prison."

She caught her breath. "What is this supposed to be, *Scared Straight*?"

The stranger's brows rose above his dark glasses. "I told you, they are real possibilities. Fortunately, the Father never stops supervising his creations. All the days ordained for you have been written in His book; nothing ever touches you without His permission." He extended the container again. "Want to see another one?"

"What's the point?" She stared at him, her lips pressed together and her chin quivering. Her head felt spongy with repressed tears, and her sinuses were swelling. Soon she wouldn't be able to breathe.

The man shook the container, enticing her. "If you're so convinced you're not the mother for this girl—"

"Okay, I get it. But God couldn't have meant for us to endure these kinds of problems. Annalisa's hearing voices, and that's not an ordinary situation. If she's mentally ill, Harry and I will be way out of our league. We don't have the strength or experience to deal with this kind of thing."

"The Lord gives strength to his people; He blesses his people with peace."

Janette clamped her mouth shut. If he was going to quote Scripture, she might as well keep quiet. This man was obviously better prepared than she was.

Still. She gestured to the pseudo toothpick holder. "Surely there's a possibility in that collection that provides Annalisa with a happier life than the one we've given her. If God is limitless, he must offer limitless possibilities—"

"What God offers—" the man leaned closer— "is a lifetime of joy and refinement into the image of His Son." His face creased into a sudden smile. "Could anything be more precious than that?"

Janette blinked. Of course, he was right. As a Christian, she had committed her life to following Christ, and that meant becoming more like Him and less like her old selfish self every day. But how easy it was to be distracted by serious concerns about family, friends, finances—

"I had forgotten," she whispered, "but of course you're right."

"Your Father knows all your needs," the man said, his voice lower and more gentle. "Trust Him with them. Be filled with His joy in every situation."

Janette swallowed hard and blinked back tears, then she tossed her slips of paper on the table. "This is crazy. When I tell Harry about this, he'll want to check me into the hospital."

"Harry's more open-minded than you realize—and he understands more than you know. Trust him, child. And trust the Father who cares more for your character than for your comfort."

She lowered her head into her hands, wistfully wishing God cared a little less. When she heard the door open, she looked up and saw a young bearded man in surgical scrubs. He nodded, then moved toward the coffee machine.

Like a pebble in a pond, her friend had vanished.

But the printed slips of paper remained on the table.

◆

On the walk back to Annalisa's room, Janette decided not to tell Harry about her encounter in the coffee room. She wasn't worried about him thinking she was crazy—Harry had always believed her, no matter how far-fetched her story. No, she would keep the story to herself because the message was personal, from God to her via a Morgan Freeman sound-alike. As to why God sent an elderly angel to help her out, she could only guess. Maybe she would have been intimidated if the messenger had looked like a haloed Arnold Schwarzenegger.

One thing, however, was clear—though she didn't know why God chose to put her family through this particular trial, she could accept that this valley was part of a divine plan. She didn't know how long they'd live in it, but God had a reason for uniting her, Harry, and Annalisa. They weren't a mistake; they were a family and they loved each other. Believing those things, they could survive.

If she felt the urge to doubt, all she'd have to do was pull those two slips of paper from her wallet and reflect on those possibilities.

At midnight, a pair of orderlies and a nurse came into Annalisa's room and told Janette and Harry that Annalisa was being transferred to the psychiatric ward. "She should have been in that ward long before this," the nurse said, grabbing the end of the bed and pulling it toward the door. "But they were full. Now they have an opening."

Who checked out of a mental ward at midnight? No one, which must have meant . . .

Janette placed the obvious conclusion on a high shelf, safely out of reach. She looked at Harry, wondering if he was thinking the same thing, but his lined face was as expressionless as stone. He gripped her hand. "Will we be able to stay with our daughter?"

The nurse shook her head as the orderlies guided the bed through the door. "That ward permits visitors only from six to seven p.m. You'll have to sign in and out, but you can come back to see her tomorrow night."

Janette brought her hand to her chest, attempting to quell a sudden rise of panic. She wouldn't be allowed to see her daughter whenever she wanted? Her gaze followed Annalisa's sleeping face, her heart sinking at the thought of Annalisa waking alone in an unfamiliar place, but Harry tightened his grip on her hand. "It's going to be okay, Jan. They'll know what to do for her."

Unlike her and Harry, who had never known how to handle their daughter.

The nurse gestured to the closet near the window. "Any personal items in there? If she came to the hospital with a belt, shoelaces, or any drugs, they'll want to take those things and hold them in the office."

"She came in pajama pants and a T-shirt," Harry said. "That's all."

A lump welled in Janette's throat as Annalisa's bed glided away and left them in an achingly empty room. No bed, no daughter, nothing but a small nightstand, a worn chair, and Janette's battered suitcases.

Harry squeezed her hand again, then pushed himself to his feet. The last few hours had drained him, and weariness showed in the sloping droop of his shoulders. "We might as well go home and get some rest."

Janette's nerves were throbbing from exhaustion, but in that moment she wouldn't have traded places with anyone else. Her daughter was alive, she was receiving professional care, and she was going to be continually monitored. She was out of danger, and she didn't need her parents hovering over her. She needed rest, too.

Janette extended one hand to Harry and reached for her suitcase with the other. "Let's go."

Later that night, after brushing her teeth and crawling into bed, Janette lay beside her husband in the warm darkness of their room. She knew Harry wasn't sleeping because she couldn't hear him breathing. He was waiting . . . for what?

Finally, he spoke: "Why, Janette? Why did you go?"

She lay still and sifted through all the answers she'd rehearsed over the past few days. In the light of their daughter's current condition, all her reasons sounded flimsy and self-serving. How could she confess to being fed up with Annalisa's tantrums when she was confined to a psychiatric ward? How could she say she worried about her own safety when Annalisa had tried to kill herself? How could she admit to being mentally drained when she left Harry alone to worry about his wife as well as his daughter?

"Jonah," she finally said, "had to run before he learned his lessons. I guess you could say the same thing about me."

The sheets rustled as Harry turned and drew her into the warmth of his arms. "I'm just glad you're home," he said, his breath brushing her cheek. "Because I'm not complete without you."

# Chapter Eighteen

Two days later, the hospital released Annalisa for transfer to a long-term mental health facility. Janette and Harry offered to drive her to the new place, so now their daughter sat in the backseat of Harry's car, pale and thin in her sweater and jeans. She held her head up in the hard light of the winter sun, and for the first time in a long time Janette realized what a lovely girl her daughter was. She hadn't taken the time to put on makeup, but she had showered and brushed her long, dark hair. Janette counted those as positive signs. Already, she was making progress.

The Bowbridge Mental Health Facility, located just outside Little Rock, was situated on several acres of rolling hills and surrounded by a white wooden fence. "Isn't this beautiful?" Janette glanced at Annalisa as they drove through the gate. "This looks more like a horse farm than a hospital."

Annalisa didn't answer, but neither did she scream and rant. Janette suspected her daughter was still fuzzy from a combination of drugs, but Janette wasn't sure what they gave her in the psychiatric ward.

As they turned into a visitors' parking lot, Annalisa's hand fell on Janette's shoulder. "Thank you," she said, her voice fragile and shaking. "I wanted to tell you what I was feeling, but I didn't think you'd understand."

Janette unbuckled her seat belt and turned to see better, to meet her daughter's eyes. "You can always talk to us, sweetheart."

Annalisa shook her head. "No, I couldn't. The words got all tangled up, and I couldn't. And it left me feeling so terrible, so hateful, so scared and ungrateful. Most of all, I was so terribly lonely . . ."

"Honey—" Janette began.

"No, let me finish. I need to get this out." Annalisa swallowed hard and swiped tears from her cheeks. "I wouldn't wish this problem on my worst enemy. I've felt this way all my life, yet I've never understood why I've felt so . . . defective. I knew there was something wrong with me; so who would ever want someone like me? Nobody. I'm nobody. I couldn't love myself and didn't think anyone could love me. I felt like I needed to hear you say you love me fifty times a day, but even if you told me a hundred times, I still wouldn't believe you. There's nothing in me to love, but I'm desperate to belong . . . to feel close to someone. I know I pushed away the very people who were willing to love me."

Janette reached out and stroked her daughter's cheek, tears burning her fingertips as her heart broke. She'd been so wrapped up in her own frustrations and wounds, she had hardly given any thought to what Annalisa must have been feeling. She assumed her daughter was angry and filled with hate—how could she have been so wrong?

Weeping with Annalisa, Janette succeeded in pushing out the only words she could say: "I'm so sorry, sweetheart. I'm so sorry we didn't see. And we do love you. I love you. I'll say it a hundred times if it'll help."

Somehow Annalisa managed a wavering smile.

They parked the car and walked with Annalisa into a spacious foyer. An attractive woman greeted them, then an orderly appeared to escort Annalisa to her room. Harry reluctantly handed their daughter's suitcase to the orderly, and Janette knew he was hesitant to leave his little girl behind.

While Annalisa settled into her room, Harry and Janette met with her doctor in his office.

Her psychiatrist, Dr. Lee Kraus, told them that their daughter's suicide attempt should not be blamed on any specific incident. "Your daughter has apparently been manifesting symptoms of a mental disorder for some time." He perched on the edge of his desk. "We don't usually settle on a diagnosis right away because we have to rule out other conditions with similar symptoms. I've spoken to your daughter's last counselor, however, and based on his notes and the evaluation she did in the hospital, we feel fairly confident that Annalisa is suffering from paranoid schizophrenia."

Janette sank deeper into her chair, hope draining away like a deflating balloon. She knew next to nothing about mental illness, but the word schizophrenia dredged up images of insane movie characters, homeless people who lived beneath bridges, and presidential assassins.

Harry's face had gone the color of ash. "Isn't that . . . incurable? Will our daughter ever be able to lead a normal life?"

Dr. Kraus gave them an understanding smile. "Fortunately, paranoid schizophrenia involves less functional impairment than other forms and offers the best hope for improvement. We don't speak in terms of curing a patient, but of treating them. Annalisa will require lifelong treatment, but therapy and appropriate medication will help her manage the condition. The most important element in her treatment is her willingness to cooperate. She must sincerely want to get better, but I think we've turned a corner now that we have a handle on the diagnosis. We'll be assembling a team to provide support so all of you will be able to cope with her illness."

A new horde of unwelcome questions attacked Janette's defenses. Hadn't she been a good mother? Did she do or say something to cause this? Was she too demanding or did she not spend enough time with her daughter? Maybe she didn't cuddle her enough as an infant.

Her voice went soft with dread. "What caused this?"

The doctor tilted his head. "No one knows what causes schizophrenia, but most experts believe it originates from a combination of genetics and environmental sources like exposure to viruses or toxins. The condition may even be attributable to malnutrition while in the womb."

Janette caught her breath. "We can't tell you much about that—Annalisa is adopted. We don't know anything about her biological parents, and the records are sealed."

"It wouldn't matter if you did—it's really impossible to pin down a cause. Your daughter has probably been exhibiting symptoms for years without anyone recognizing them."

Harry shifted in his chair. "What kind of symptoms?"

"In women, schizophrenia typically manifests in the twenties or early thirties. We usually see a loss of interest in activities, followed by social withdrawal, a lack of motivation, and neglect of personal hygiene. They may have difficulty paying attention in school or experience problems making sense of information."

Janette winced as guilt pinched the back of her neck. "We saw those things in high school, but we chalked them up to a bad attitude. Her teachers told us she had learning disabilities—"

"Don't blame yourself." Dr. Kraus stroked his beard. "Most patients go several months, even years, before someone suspects something is wrong. But Annalisa's here now, so she's taken that all-important first step. We'll teach her about her condition and explain how she can learn to cope with it. By using a combination of medication and therapy, we'll show her how she can thrive despite it."

Harry looked at Janette, his eyes soft with pain, and reached for her hand. "Thank you, Doctor," he said. "I know this is serious, but for us, this news . . . is a relief. We didn't know what was going on in our daughter's head. For a long time, we chalked it all up to her being an unreasonable adolescent."

Janette was too choked up to talk, but she understood what Harry was feeling. For years she'd blamed the outbursts, the stubbornness, and the defiance on rebellion and a bad attitude. She knew Annalisa had problems, she knew her daughter felt like a loner, but she had never realized that a mental illness could be the cause of so much frustration and pain.

She never realized Annalisa was lonely and afraid.

Janette was about to thank the doctor for his time and help, but Harry's cell phone buzzed and distracted her. She glanced at him, her nervousness swelling into alarm. What if Annalisa was calling to say she'd changed her mind and wouldn't stay? Harry responded to Janette's questioning look with a smile and took the call, whispering his responses to whomever was on the other end of the line.

The call must not have been important.

"Thank you, Dr. Kraus." Janette stood to shake the man's hand. "You don't know how relieved you've made us feel. I've always thought I was a strong woman, but with Annalisa . . . well, I reached my breaking point."

A wry smile flashed in the tangle of the doctor's dark beard. "Mental illness is never easy. The scars inflicted on family members are deep and invisible, but let's not forget that the patient suffers more than we'll ever realize." He waited until Harry finished his call, then he shook Harry's hand, too. "You have my number. Because Annalisa is an adult, I'll be interacting primarily with her, but if you have any questions, please feel free to call me."

They thanked him again, then stepped out of the office, their hearts considerably lighter than they were when they entered. As they walked toward the elevator, Janette gave Harry a sidelong glance. "By the way, who was on the phone?"

His tired eyes twinkled when he answered: "It wasn't our daughter. How's that for a change?"

Harry and Janette drove home mostly in silence, both of them digesting the somber news they'd just received. Schizophrenia. The diagnosis made sense, but Janette never would have imagined that their daughter could suffer from such a disorder. Mental illness was something that happened to alcoholics and war veterans and people who married their cousins. Of all her friends, she didn't know anyone whose child suffered from schizophrenia . . . but she did know families with children who were bi-polar. She knew kids who were ADD. Who had OCD. Who were autistic or had Asperger's or who suffered from eating disorders.

Maybe mental illness wasn't as rare as she thought, but it certainly wasn't the kind of news families trumpeted from the rooftops. They wanted to protect their children, whatever their ages, and they didn't want to send them into the world trailing a string of alphabet letters. They didn't want anything to hamper their opportunities to find happiness and fulfillment.

"So." Janette reached over the automobile console and rubbed Harry's arm. "We're beginning a new chapter, aren't we?"

He shot her a quick glance. "We're going to be fine, Janette. As long as we stay on the same page."

She smiled. Looking out the window and seeing the bare soybean fields reminded her that they would green again in the spring.

She didn't know what the future held for Annalisa, but she was going to educate herself so she could do all she could—all she needed to do—in order to give her daughter the best chance for independent living. Now that they understood the valley they were navigating, she and Harry would do a better job of charting their course.

She also needed to adjust her expectations. She used to envy other mother-daughter pairs, women who shared every secret and spent afternoons shopping at the mall or getting their nails done. Once she hit adolescence, Annalisa had stopped going to Janette with her problems and secrets. They were not like those other mothers and daughters, and perhaps they never would be. But if they could learn to respect each other, if they could treat each other with kindness, maybe they could forge a new relationship.

When they turned into the driveway, Janette noticed an unfamiliar car in front of their house. She looked at Harry, a question on her lips, and he caught her hand before she could ask it. "Honey —" the twinkle was back in his eye— "I have a surprise for you."

She turned to study the vehicle, which looked like a new sedan. "You didn't buy me a new car."

He laughed. "Keep dreaming. No, but the other night when you slipped out of Annalisa's room, your cell phone rang and I answered it. I spoke to a young woman who told me a lot about where you'd been for the last several days, and she asked about Annalisa. So we made some arrangements, and now we have company."

Janette felt the truth like an electric tingle in her fingertips. "Andie? Andie's here?"

"We're coming home to a full house." Harry reached for the doorknob. "I put the guy and his kids in the guest room, and Andie's sleeping on the couch in the den. They're going to stay a few days, I think, maybe through Thanksgiving—"

Janette didn't wait to hear the rest. She let herself out of the car and hurried to the front door, then stepped inside to the delicious aroma of something warm and meaty. She strode into the kitchen and found Roman and Emilia at her kitchen table, each of them hard at work drawing pictures.

"For you!" Emilia waved her paper when she saw Janette. "I drew this one for you!"

Janette accepted the drawing—a stick house, a row of stick people, and one lady standing by herself, marked by a large red heart beneath a pair of stick arms.

"Is that me?" Her throat tightened when Emilia nodded, and she had to blink away a sudden spurt of tears. "It's beautiful." She pressed a kiss to the girl's forehead, then congratulated Roman on his drawing, too. "I'm so glad to see both of you."

"Any of those hugs for us?" a male voice asked. She turned— Andie stood at the stove, stirring a pot of something that smelled like beef stew, and Matthew was chopping carrots and celery next to the sink. She hugged each of them, amazed that they'd travel all the way to Little Rock when they could be spending their vacation days on the beach.

"I can't believe you're here." She sank onto a barstool. "Are you sure you don't want to be with your families on Thanksgiving?"

Matthew smiled at Andie, then shifted his gaze to Janette. "Who says we're not with family?"

Janette covered her mouth with her hand and began to cry in earnest. When she left this kitchen two weeks before, she had been convinced her family had fractured beyond repair. Yet here she was, back in the home she loved with the man she adored, surrounded by friends who knew all about her and hadn't turned away in horror . . .

Harry walked over and slipped his arm around her. Grateful for his support, Janette let her head fall against his chest.

"Thanks for leaving the key under the mat," Matthew told Harry. "We pulled in this morning, probably not long after you left."

"And we have big news." Matthew winked at Janette, then he looked at Andie. "You want to tell her?"

She elbowed him gently in the ribs. "You do it. It's your news."

Matt nonchalantly dropped a handful of chopped carrots into her stewpot. "The kidlings and I are moving to Georgia. I'm going to open a law practice in Savannah so we can have a family life and be close to Momma." He gave Janette an abashed smile. "Washington has more than enough movers and shakers, but my kids only have one dad."

Janette grinned, overjoyed by this bit of news. "Why — that's wonderful. Your mother must be thrilled."

Matt scooped up the rest of the chopped vegetables and added them to the stew. "Roman and Emilia can grow up with Southern accents and learn how to eat crawfish and lobster. Of course, we still have to iron out a few details, but we have time. Momma was thrilled when she heard we were moving."

Janette clasped her hands and smiled at the happy bustle in her kitchen. People needed connection . . . even her daughter yearned for it. If only she'd learned that truth sooner.

"Lunch will be ready in about twenty minutes," Andie said. "Matt, why don't you put some ice in some glasses? Harry, do you have soup bowls somewhere around here?"

"Sure do." Harry went over to the cupboard while Matt moved to the table and helped the kids put away their papers and crayons. Walter had fallen onto the floor beside Emilia's chair, so Janette picked him up and gave him a hug while Matthew sent the kids off to wash their hands.

Janette's gaze drifted to the embroidered sampler hanging next to her kitchen window: *The boundary lines have fallen for me in pleasant places.*

Indeed they had.

# *Epilogue*

The invitation arrived a week or so after the beginning of the new year.

"Since we never made it to the beach," Matthew wrote, "would you and Harry like to join Roman, Emilia, and me in St. Augustine for Memorial Day weekend? I'm inviting Andie, too."

Janette responded to his email with an enthusiastic yes and penciled the date on the calendar.

The remaining weeks of winter passed with glacial slowness. She worked at the thrift center, Harry taught at the high school, and Annalisa remained at the mental health facility. But they visited her every weekend, and every week they noticed subtle signs of improvement.

The biggest change was her demeanor. Having a diagnosis not only provided Janette and Harry with an answer, it helped Annalisa feel more grounded. Before her hospitalization, she'd been terrified by her emotions and mood swings; after her diagnosis she began to accept that they were part of her disorder.

With time, the doctor assured Janette, Annalisa would be much better at handling her symptoms.

As the days grew longer and warmer, Janette made plans for her and Harry to fly to Jacksonville. She reserved a rental car and dreamed of taking a long walk on the beach with her husband. She visited toy stores and looked for gifts Roman and Emilia might like.

May finally arrived. Each morning when the sun spangled the earth, Janette stopped for a moment in her front yard and closed her eyes, imagining herself on a warm Florida beach.

Matthew sent other emails. He and the kids were going to do Disney World before heading over to the coast, so why didn't they plan to meet at the Oceanview Bed and Breakfast on St. Augustine Beach? Janette replied that she and Harry would be happy to meet him anywhere.

After she clicked send, though, she noticed that Matt hadn't mentioned Andie. Had he heard from her? Janette considered emailing Andie and casually mentioning the Memorial Day get-together, but if she couldn't make it, or if she and Matt had had some sort of falling out, Janette didn't want to rub salt in the wound.

Finally Harry and Janette drove to the Little Rock airport and flew to Jacksonville, then rented a car and headed toward St. Augustine. On the way, she dialed Matt's cell number.

After a quick greeting, she said she and Harry should arrive after two o'clock.

"We'll probably be on the beach," he answered. "Just leave your bags with the owner and walk on down. I haven't been able to get the kids away from the water since we arrived."

The Oceanview Bed and Breakfast proved to be a graceful Victorian home, fringed with gingerbread and bordered with wide porches. Harry brought in their luggage while Janette registered at an attractive oak desk.

"Mr. Scofield told us to look after you," the owner said,

handing Janette the key to their room. "He and Miss Crystal took the children down to the beach."

Warmth flooded Janette's cheeks—either another hot flash or a rush of pure pleasure. "Andie's here?"

The woman nodded. "Miss Crystal arrived yesterday, with the Scofields. Apparently they visited Disney World together."

Janette waited until Harry dropped the luggage in an out-of-the-way alcove, then she clutched his arm. "Did you hear that? Andie went with them to Disney World."

"So?"

"So they're still seeing each other. This is good news, Harry, really good news."

Harry placed his hand over hers. "I thought you weren't going to play matchmaker."

"I'm not matching, just observing."

He grinned. "Then let's get down to the beach so you can observe more closely."

They crossed the street, then followed a narrow path through a swath of sea grass that led to a strip of blinding white sand. Beachcombers dotted the sand, but Janette recognized her friends even from a distance. Her heartbeat quickened and she lengthened her stride, practically dragging Harry behind her.

Emilia spotted her first. "Miss Janette!" The girl ran forward, her bare feet flying over the sand, Walter's head thumping against her chest with every step. Janette fell to her knees and wrapped the child in her arms, breathing in the scents of sea, sand, and sunscreen. Emilia hugged her neck, then pulled away and looked up at her husband. "Is that Mr. Harry?"

Janette nodded as Harry helped her up. "Sure is. Remember how he cut you a drumstick at Thanksgiving?"

She nodded. "He's real tall."

"Yes, he is."

The others joined them, so Janette hugged Roman, then Andie, and finally Matthew. Harry shook hands all around, then stood back, his hands in his pockets, as Janette studied the changes in her friends.

"You kids have grown about half a foot, and you all look so good." Her gaze settled on Andie, who was wearing a cute cover-up over her bathing suit. "And you're practically glowing."

"Must be the sun." Andie swiped a smear of sand from the tip of her nose. "I keep forgetting to reapply sun screen."

"I think it's more than that."

Matt grinned, his hands on his hips, then he elbowed Andie. "Are you gonna tell her?"

"Now?"

"Why not?"

Andie's color deepened as she bit her lip. "Matt and I have been emailing since the train trip."

"A lot," Matt added. "Thousands of words."

"Yes—a lot. And last month he asked me to move to Savannah, so I decided to go for it. I handed in my resignation last week."

Janette's jaw dropped. "Just like that?"

Andie smiled at the sandy, bare-chested man who no longer looked anything like a lawyer. "Matt did all the preparation and research. He pulled together a study of the area marketers and compiled a list of the local television stations. The Savannah metropolitan area doesn't have anything like VPN, but it's an open market. Since I helped get VPN off the ground, why couldn't I do the same thing in Georgia?"

Janette shook her head. "You are both amazing."

"That's not all—Carma and her kids are coming down to help me find a place. Carma knows all about historical homes, so she'll be a huge help."

Janette chuckled. "Maybe she'll come on the train."

Matt and Andie shared a smile, secure in their plans and in their obvious affection for each other. Janette reached for Harry's hand, happy to see her friends and to know that Roman and

Emilia would one day welcome Andie into the immediate family. It was only a matter of time.

"And how about you?" Janette looked at Matthew. "How's Savannah? Are the kids adjusting to their new school? Is your mom thrilled to have you around?"

Matt shot her a twisted smile. "Momma's in hog heaven. She picks up the kids every day after school and cooks dinner for us—we usually eat together before she heads home. She even talked me into taking them to Sunday school at her church. I think she likes to brag on them."

Janet sighed in pleasure. "And the law practice?"

"Like Momma said, lots of people in Savannah need help with immigration. I keep plenty busy." He crossed his arms and seemed preoccupied for a moment, as if a random thought had suddenly overshadowed their conversation.

"What's wrong?" Andie asked. "Did you forget something?"

He shook his head as a flush raced over his face. "Just remembered something I wanted to tell Janette."

They waited, and after a minute of awkward silence Janette was tempted to ask if he'd rather speak in private.

"I'm okay." He lifted his head. "One of the things Momma said to me during the train trip was that I never mourned Inga properly. So after we got home, the kids and I went to the cemetery and had our own remembrance ceremony, talking about how we missed her, how much we loved her, and—" he cleared his throat and drew his lips into a tight smile. "Anyway, we took flowers and tossed them into this little creek not far from her grave. That's how we said goodbye. And that's when I knew it'd be okay for us to move to Savannah."

Andie reached across the space between them and placed her hand on Matt's arm. Her expression gentled as she looked at Janette. "How's Annalisa?"

Janette smiled, touched by her thoughtfulness. "She's doing well. She still has a way to go, but she's making progress. She's making friends and learning that she's not alone. The doctor says that in a few more months, she should be ready to move into a supervised housing unit in town. They'll help her get a job, monitor her stress level, and make sure she stays on her meds through the transition process." She squeezed Harry's hand and smiled up at him. "We have great hope for her future."

Matt gestured to a beach umbrella surrounded by towels, lawn chairs, and inflatable toys. "Come make yourself at home. Take off your shoes, pull up a chair, and grab a drink from the cooler. We were thinking about walking down the beach in a little while; there's a good restaurant near the pier. They don't mind if you come in your beach clothes."

Harry moved to a lawn chair in the shade. Janette followed and kicked off her shoes, but before she sat down, she had important things to do.

She wanted to build a big castle and drizzle wet sand over the towers. She wanted to search for sand dollars. She wanted to roll up her pants and wade into the water, not caring if she got completely wet. She wanted to feel the sun on her face and the wind in her hair. She wanted to hold Roman's and Emilia's hands and run, laughing as they scattered seagulls. She wanted to stare at the sun-spangled sea and wonder what lay on the other side.

Before the weekend ended, she wanted to stand on the edge of something far larger, deeper, and broader than all her problems and know that the God who created the enormous sea cared enough to refine her and be her source of joy.

She left the other adults under the umbrella and walked to the water's edge, shading her eyes to stare at the wide horizon. The wind blew harder here, flapping her blouse and sealing her pants to her legs. Roman and Emilia raced to catch up with her, then scampered around her feet like playful puppies.

Janette inhaled the scents of salt and heat and smiled at the shadowed outline of a long barge near the horizon. And then, though she didn't know how it could be possible, she heard the call of a train whistle on the wind.

She glanced behind her, half-expecting to see a railroad track next to the road, but she saw only sand dunes and sea grass. She was hearing things again. Heavenly things. Precious reminders.

She turned back to the sea, crossed her arms, and smiled.

# Acknowledgements

Each novel is a journey unlike any other, and this one required a literal journey from Washington, D.C. to St. Augustine . . . by rail. I owe thanks to my cousin, Ginger Wiggins, who not only went along for the ride, but was great company and a fun companion. We'll have to do it again sometime!

Many thanks to Susan Plett, Kay Day, Ginger Wiggins, and Debbie Young, who served as "test readers" for an early draft. So appreciate your help, my friends!

And as always, thank you to my agent, Danielle Egan-Miller, and a special thanks to my editor, Lissa Halls Johnson, a dainty little woman whose heart is as big as her talent. If the Huggins don't mind me tweaking one of their songs, this book wouldn't be what it is without you.

# Discussion Questions

1.  Each of the main characters in *Passing Strangers* is running away from something. How is the theme of escape reflected in the novel, and why does each character feel the need to escape? Can we ever truly escape from our problems?

2.  Angela Hunt calls *Passing Strangers* a *suite*: a novel composed of three separate but interconnected stories, but with only main character per story. Did you enjoy the unique approach of this book? How was your understanding helped or hindered because you were limited to a particular protagonist in each section?

3.  Have you ever traveled on a train? Did your experience match those of these characters? Is train travel an experience you'd like to repeat again?

4.  How has being a child TV star influenced Andie's life? Do you agree with her decision to change her name and hide even from her family? Do you think she made the right decision regarding her mother? Do you think she made the right choice about dealing with her siblings after her mother's death? How does she change over the course of the story?

5.  Why do you think Andie ate so much in the early stages of her trip? Was she trying to fill her stomach or fill something else?

6.  Matthew seems to assume that his mother will volunteer to take care of his children. Do you think his attitude is common to most men, or is he especially presumptive? Do all children

naturally assume that their mothers are happy to serve them? What is the proper role of boundaries in the relationship between Matt and his mother?

7. What motivates Matthew? What motivated his decision to buy his mother a house? What does this say about Matthew as a person? How does he change over the course of the story?

8. Janette runs away from a difficult situation in her family. Have you personally been involved with someone who suffers from a mental disorder? What are the special challenges of such a situation?

9. At one point Janette tells herself: If I could shrink to insignificance, then my decisions could not possibly hurt anyone else. Is that true, or do our decisions affect other people no matter how "large" or significant we are?

10. What did you think about the mysterious old man who appears to counsel Janette? Why do you think the author chose to use a supernatural visitor instead of another human character to counsel her?

11. How is this novel like others you've read? How is it different?

12. How is each character in the novel a "loner" at the beginning of the story? How do they come to see the value of human connection? Who are some people who have so influenced your life that you wouldn't be the same without them? How does the author emphasize this theme of human interconnection?